Reef Dance

John DeCure

Reef Dance

 ST. MARTIN'S MINOTAUR ☙ NEW YORK

www.minotaurbooks.com

Designed by Lorelle Graffeo

Library of Congress Cataloging-in-Publication Data

DeCure, John.
   Reef dance / John DeCure.—1st ed.
      p.   cm.
   ISBN 0-312-27297-9
      1. Domestic relations courts—Fiction.   2. Custody of children—Fiction.   3. California—Fiction.   I. Title.
   PS3604.E49 R44 2001
   813'.6—dc21

                                                                 2001034898

First Edition: September 2001

10   9   8   7   6   5   4   3   2   1

In memory of Monsignor Thomas Aiken

Acknowledgments

Thanks to editors Steve Hawk (*Surfer*) and Steve Pezman (*The Surfer's Journal*) for their encouragement through the years, and to the readers (and English majors) in my immediate family, including my mother, father, and my sister Suzanne.

I am grateful to Douglas Anne Munson, Paul Levine, Marjorie Leusebrink, Diane Torres, and Natica Greer, for their professional guidance. Special thanks to my editor, Liza Bolitzer, for her patience, judgment, and generosity.

Most of all, I thank my wife, Cynthia, who is my first—and ideal—reader.

In the important decisions of personal life, we should be governed, I think, by the deep inner needs of our nature.

—Sigmund Freud

Who'd like to change the world?
Who wants to shoot the curl?

—*Midnight Oil*

Reef Dance

One

Sigmund Freud didn't surf. Of this I was certain.

Such was the nature of my distraction on this particular morning. I could hardly focus on the Madden case—my last one of the day, thank God. Instead, my mind's eye continuously replayed the splendid barrel I'd tapped into last night at the pier just before dark. I set down the file and sighed, feeling the surge of rolling sea beneath my feet, the breathlessness coming back. Stroking deep and with great purpose, adrenalized, my surfboard's speed matching the rushing peak as I slide to my feet, descending in a low crouch. Banking squarely off the bottom, just ahead of the hissing clatter, the wall ahead forming and gathering itself, dragging muddy green sheets of water off the shallow sandbar, readying to throw. I redirect slightly, set my inside rail in a down-the-line trajectory, weight forward and tucked. The wall hits the bar, the upper third pitching onto the flat in a lazy hook, the wave's ceiling spinning above my head like a beaded veil.

Everything is moving in slow motion. I am locked in, encased in the deepest, purest part of the wave, invisible from shore, entranced by the swirling symmetry. When you're locked, you have little choice but to give yourself over to the wave's dictates. Some barrels you make, some you don't. This one I make.

Somebody spoke, and my surfing reverie ended.

"How about three-D? The Madden minors."

Judge Foley, finishing up a drug-baby case and itching for another, tugged at the collar of his black robe like it was cutting off his air supply. "We ready on this one, people? Talk to me."

No one said a word.

It was Friday, August 30th, 1992. An election year, a time of imminent change. George Herbert Walker Bush was still in the

White House, but the boys from Desert Storm had come home to find a stagnant economy, and lately, a good-ole'-boy named Clinton was dogging Bush in the polls, promising a new beginning.

A new beginning sounded cool to me. I was at work today, in the Los Angeles County Juvenile Dependency Court, browsing the Madden file and, quite honestly, wishing I was somewhere else. Foley was racing through his morning calendar, scarcely glancing up from the stack of manila files to match the names to the faces as he called each case.

Marquez. Jeter. Washington. Lopez. Nguyen. Mornings like this, busted-up families rumble through here like a herd of bug-eyed cows on a cattle drive. Every court day the pace is hectic, but with the weekend glimmering like a distant oasis, Fridays push the tempo harder yet. Friday mornings in Department 302 always remind me of a tune from that old TV show, *Rawhide*: Load 'em up—load 'em up! Move 'em out—move 'em out! Rawhide.

I hummed a few bars of the *Rawhide* theme, watching a heroin addict who resembled a torn-up rag doll stumble out of court after losing her bid to win custody of Shaquilla Bowles, her newborn drug-baby. Then Foley looked up from his pile of grief and fixed on me.

I smiled. "Yes, Your Honor?"

He showed me the face of his watch, a faux Rolex special—so much for county salaries—as if he was about to instruct me on how to tell time. "Ready on Madden, Shepard?" he said. "I'd like to call Madden before noon so we can all go home."

"I'm studying the file as we speak, Your Honor."

He yawned into the sleeve of his robe. "We're waiting, counselor."

Jamming to get the Madden case through before lunch was fine by me. A solid southwest swell was still hitting in Christianitos, my hometown beach, and the water was summertime warm. I could picture the scene, the wondrous, movable stage of blue-green waves tumbling forth, the riders under the pier hooting and scrambling for position, their surfboards banking through the shallows. At water's edge, hungry gulls scavenging for sand crabs in the shorepound. Hot sand littered with college girls in brightly colored bikinis, baking in the midday sun and misting their bronzed skin with plastic squirt bottles while they studied the pages of *Cosmo* and *Mademoiselle* for back-to-school beauty tips and September horoscopes. All of it a million miles outside these institutional-gray walls. Christ, beach days like this were made for surfing.

I scanned the county social worker's emergency detention report on the Madden case. The text was an eyesore, a crude, hastily scrawled hieroglyphic. The county's position, however, was clear: removal of the two Madden minors was essential to their protection and safety.

"Minor #1 indicated his unwillingness to consider viable transitional options." (This meant the kid said no way was he going to any foster home.)

"Minor #2 stated that in the event that removal was unavoidable, she desired placement with her sibling." (I doubted a five-year-old girl would've put that fine a point on her situation.)

Then, the kicker. "Mother" (my client) "exhibits domestic capabilities incompatible with effective parenting." (The woman was a slob.)

But my mind was not on my work, which is why I say that Freud didn't surf. Take his theory on random thought: that a great percentage of our idle thoughts are about sex—random randiness, you could say. I remember how that theory got my entire Psychology 101 class tittering years ago in college. I was a rank freshman, skating on the thinnest intellectual ice imaginable, and I readily bought in too, nervously laughing along with the others while I strained for a peripheral perve on Adina, an Italian beauty just across the aisle. I think where Freud went wrong was not in the theory itself—Christ, I should've received course credit for studying Adina as hard as I did that semester—but in his attempt to apply it across the board. Take me. My mind just doesn't work that way. Adina aside, these days I generally think about riding waves a hell of a lot more than sex.

I picked through the Madden file some more, but before I could absorb anything fresh the court reporter stopped tapping and people rose from the chairs at counsel table. Another shattered family shrank away from Judge Foley, a mother and three small girls weeping in each other's arms while a grave old woman with a permanent scowl kept Father, a handsome young Latino, at a safe distance from her granddaughters. Father was a dapper cat, his black slacks neatly creased, his silk gold shirt snugly buttoned at the top. He slicked his hair as he strolled by, gamely passing me a "How's it?" kind of nod.

Yeah right, guy, I thought. As if getting booted from your own home for making your stepdaughter service you is an everyday occurrence for you, you strutting piece of shit.

I'm not at all keen on people who exploit the innocent. He saw the blankness in my eyes and swallowed his grin on the spot. *Sin verguenza*, brother, have you no shame? My fists were clenched as he drooped by me, my heart thumping to protect a child I would never know. This job still takes my breath away daily.

"Next, twenty-two, Baby Girl Trujillo," Judge Foley droned, squinting at the chalkboard over his clerk's desk that posted the numbers of cases ready to be adjudicated. "Twenty-two was on the board a minute ago—what happened?"

I calmed myself with a little deep breathing and gave the Madden report another go. According to the county, my latest client, Darla Madden, had a home resembling a full-service dump. Spoiled milk in the fridge, a leaning tower of dirty dishes in the sink, and a pile of "moist feces" on display in the living room (I puzzled briefly at how the worker might've field-tested the shit for consistency, but there you have it). A little something for every taste. The Department of Child Protective Services had moved on a tip from a disgusted neighbor, an unlucky renter who'd spent weeks patrolling the complex to pin down the unholy stench that kept wrecking his summer barbecues. I'd read enough and was ready to go find Darla Madden and interview her. Moist feces. Perhaps her aroma would find me first.

The waiting area just outside Foley's courtroom was almost empty—something intense was unfolding a hundred feet down the hallway. A dense cluster of bodies jostled about, making a racket much louder than the standard prime-time din. In the middle of the pack stood a woman in a loud orange blazer, jabbering away as she cornered someone with a microphone. A bearded TV cameraman, his hardware balanced behind one ear, stood next to the reporter, a black wire coiling down his back like a poisonous snake. Nearby, an assistant in a headset held a loop of cable in one hand and steadied a boom mic over the reporter to catch all the jabbering.

TV cameras in this place? So much for the tenet—no, make that the law—that dependency matters are confidential. The jam of on-lookers, a motley crew of the usual hapless-go-lucky dependency participants, crowded in around the reporter for a better look. I studied their faces.

For three years now, I'd boldly ventured into the waiting throng each morning to take on parents too poor to afford a lawyer. At this point in time, they all looked familiar to me.

The thin brown duke in his gray porkpie hat with a black felt band, khaki chinos and an untucked, oversized white-cotton un-dershirt, his forearms defaced by the obligatory set of gang tattoos. The duke's teenaged girlfriend, a graduate of the Tammy Faye School of Mascara Application, crowding in behind the duke as she hoisted a diapered, screeching child above her shoulders. Next to them, a rail-thin black woman with an inverted pyramid of pink curlers on her head adjusted her drooping cut-off shorts with a de-finitive yank, parking the flimsy fabric well up the crack of her ass. Lovely.

Dependency work is a mostly sad affair because of what it does to your perspective. For starters, the sheer volume of cases is absurd. Twenty-four departments on four floors, all of them cranking out thirty-plus hearings a day. Misery, desperation, confusion, ignorance, brutalization, victimization. Interchangeable parts from one pathetic saga to the next. Lawyers referring to their clients not by name, but by the labels "Mother," "Father" or "Minor," not out of insensitiv-ity, but by necessity. With a caseload of three hundred, no one can possibly remember names.

"Mother" is zonked out on crystal meth, convinced that she and the kids have to go totally nude twenty-four-seven because how else will God be able to see their souls? Keep your shirt on ma'am, you say without irony. "Father" was caught inserting hot dogs up his four-year-old's ass while home alone on baby-sitting duty? Don't make any statements to the social worker until your criminal case has concluded, sir, and, by the way, thanks for ruining the next hunger pang I get at Dodger Stadium. "Minor" is hyperactive, asthmatic, three grades behind in school, and likes to pound on other kids. You also read from the worker's report that Mom had a prenatal affinity for cheap wine and diet pills. Oh.

The tools you have to make any kind of assist in these sad lives are so comically insufficient, you know there's really nothing you can say. (What damn good is an apology from your lawyer?)

When every day you ache for changes you can't make, you get tired inside.

"Darla Madden," I called out. No one noticed me. "Darla Madden," I said much louder. Nothing but TV crew ruckus. Few cases rate TV news coverage around here. The most vile child murderers and molesters, whose gruesome deeds occasionally rate media attention based on sheer shock value, invariably enter the building in police custody. Burly officers spirit them through secured, unseen passageways behind the courtrooms. It's usually quite devoid of drama, and as with every dependency case, the public is shut out of the courtroom. But there they were, an entire mobile crew, zeroing in on the misfortune of some anonymous child and managing to create a game-show atmosphere at the same time.

"Darla Madden!" I shouted. Nada. This TV thing was beginning to seriously cramp my morning. I knew Madden was over there, in the midst of the brouhaha, soaking up the spectacle of live TV coverage as if it was all part of a free giveaway. I was still banking on an early exit as soon as I finished with Darla. Still, I wasn't about to enter such a disordered fray just to find her. "Hey!" I shouted at the orange blazer. "Mind your own business!"

The crew people swung around and faced me. I recognized the reporter's hair, a thickly layered, unnaturally brown-blond mane, parted straight down the middle and caroming off her shoulders in a small flip. The color was disturbingly tinny: Miss Clairol with a touch of copper metal-flake. I remembered her name. Holly Dupree, "Channel Six News at Six."

I'd seen the woman's work before. A few years back a popular Olympic athlete was outed by the scoop-whores at Channel Six after someone spotted him being treated at an AIDS clinic. Holly Dupree did the "exclusive" with the athlete's mother the day the story broke, pinning the woman to a parked car and reducing her to a sobbing wreck with the news that her only son was dying (he'd apparently kept his illness a secret). That night, the station replayed the wrenching scene at five, six and ten, accompanied by Holly's inane babbling about "the high price of sex in the nineties," "a real-life tragedy" and assorted other scripted horseshit.

"Are you on the case?" Holly said.

"I'm J. Shepard," I said. "I work here. I'm a lawyer."

She smiled. "I see." Patronizing me. "Thank you." Her crew collectively turned its back on me as if I'd vaporized into thin air.

I contemplated strolling over and engaging Holly in a little spirited wordplay, but the salty scent of the Pacific Ocean still lingered somewhere deep in my bones, and my thoughts returned to warm water currents and late-summer lines of energy peeling evenly over the sandbars beneath the pier. Holly Dupree was not worth the trouble. One more case, over and out.

"Darla Madden? Darla Madden!" Again, nothing. "Surf's up, Darla the default," I said under my breath. I turned to re-enter Department 302.

"Mister?" a boy said as I turned the doorknob. "She's comin'."

The kid was chunky and pale, with a grimy red face and a potbelly protruding from his grease-stained Aquaman T-shirt. Dark, unwashed hair brushed across his forehead in jagged tatters. He was sporting a wide set of whitewalls above the ears and collar from a very recent in-home haircut, but the back and sides of his neck were gritty with dirt. Without a doubt, the boy now tunneling a finger deep into his nostril was little Eric Madden, Son of Slob.

"Mister?" He pinched a crust of snot and smiled.

"Pick a winner," I said.

"Young man, don't you run from me like that!" a throaty voice bellowed. Eric cast his eyes to the floor and stepped aside.

Darla Madden was a rolling mountain of a woman, a startling sight in terms of sheer volume alone. She'd broken from the commotion and lumbered through the low-slung furniture of the waiting area, slowing to avoid the edge of a couch here, the arm of a padded chair there, as if she'd hitched a ride on a shopping cart with a particularly wobbly set of wheels. She wore a billowing yellow dress, the kind of full-length job that looks like a nightgown but thankfully reveals nothing, the bright polyester sloping down her wide shoulders and careening off the front of her huge bust-line like a shade-giving canopy. Her face, round and baby pink like Eric's, was damp with perspiration and fixed with the kind of worn-out expression one often sees in the eyes of the obese. Ringlets of dark curls bounced behind her ears.

I felt the blood rush to my head as she fluttered her false eyelashes and extended her hand.

"Hey, mister sharp suit. You my lawyer?"

"Darla Madden?" I asked, swallowing as her ripe musk lit a fire in my nostrils.

"In the flesh." She slid a meaty forearm over Eric's shoulder and tousled his hair with affection. "Go and sit with your Uncle Pete, young man," she ordered him.

In an instant, Eric was off, sprinting toward a stainless steel water fountain that jutted from the wall two courtrooms down the crowded corridor.

"Right now!" she shouted after him, but Eric was well out of range.

I took her into the windowless interview room located just off the short hallway that leads into the courtroom, and opened the file.

Actually, the allegations against Darla Madden in the county's court petition weren't much: filthy living conditions and the cryptic reference to freshly deposited excrement for added emphasis, but no charges of physical or sexual abuse, the two top drawing cards in dependency court. And yet, the emergency social worker had still seen fit to pull Eric, who was twelve, and his sister Stacy, five, out of the home and give temporary custody to their paternal uncle, Pete. The case was a bit of a rarity: a "dirty house" detention.

"I'm J. Shepard." I handed her a card, which she held away from her body and inspected.

"Dependency Court Legal Project . . . what's that?"

"A law firm. The county pays me to represent people who can't afford a lawyer, which is just about everybody in the place."

She raised her right hand as if to solemnly swear. "You got that right, Mister Shepard. I'm as poor as a church mouse."

"Well, don't worry, I won't be sending you a bill. That's one thing about this wonderful experience you can actually bank on. They can charge you for removing your trash, but not your kids."

I regretted my words as quickly as I'd spoken them. Darla's eyes swam in a glaze of tears, her chest heaving in a hiccup as she fought to compose herself. But it was too late. I handed her a tissue and closed my eyes as she began to weep in earnest.

A dirty house detention. In the grand scheme of government-regulated child welfare, Darla Madden's shortcomings as a homemaker were of almost laughable concern to the county. But there was nothing funny about her current state of abject humiliation.

"I'm sorry, Ms. Madden," I said. "I know it's hard having your kids taken away from you. Trust me, I do."

She straightened. "That man!" she said. "Bastard!"

"What man?"

"That . . . stupid social worker, the one who took my Eric and Stacy. They're my pride and joy. He hates me, I know it!"

I flipped through the social worker's incident report attached to the petition. "Ms. Madden, if you don't mind, I think I should tell you a few things about this court and these proceedings. When I'm done, you can tell me about your case."

She smiled, wiping the tears with the back of her thick hand. "You're all right. I can tell you care about me."

"It's my job," I said.

I suspected that Darla didn't quite believe me. "Well thanks for the hanky, anyway."

We weren't getting anywhere. "Okay," I said, "California's got laws about how a kid can be treated. County social workers go out to do an investigation when the Department of Child Welfare gets a report that a child has been abused or neglected, or abandoned, and—"

"How about sold?"

"Sold? What are you talking about?"

"You heard me. What if somebody tries to sell their kid?"

"Ms. Madden," I said, "if you'd just let me get through the basics with you without interruption."

She bowed her head. "Sorry. But, can I ask ya just one little baby-sellin' question?"

"No, you can't. Look, Ms. Madden, a minute ago you were crying about your kids being removed, remember?" She nodded. "Well what do you say we stick to your case and how we're going to get those kids home today, all right?"

"Oh." She smiled. "I get it. So you're the only one in here doesn't care, huh?"

"I thought you just told me I *did* care."

"I don't mean about me. Nah, I mean about the baby-seller case."

She ignored my impatient sigh. "All right," I said, "let's hear it."

"Well," she said, her voice dipping, "word is, this young girl had a get-rich-quick scheme that backfired. She gets herself pregnant 'n' finds about five different rich couples to adopt her baby. Guess when a girl's both white 'n' pretty good lookin' everyone wants the fruit of her loins, if you get my meaning."

"Don't worry, I get you," I said. "What else?"

"Well, so they're all givin' her money and clothes and expensive things, jewelry, sky's the limit! But here's the catch: they all think they're the only ones gonna get the baby, 'cause none of 'em know about the other couples! But wait! That ain't even the worst of it!"

"Don't tell me," I said wearily, "she wants to keep the kid."

It stood to reason. Why else would the case land in here if custody of the baby wasn't the key issue? In dependency, custody is that which defines winning and losing, the ultimate prize.

Darla looked deflated. "How'd ya know?"

How could I not have known?

"Now, if the county thinks a kid's been abused or neglected—"

"We talkin' about my case again?"

My face went stony. "They can remove the kids temporarily," I continued, "but they've got to get a judge to agree with them that the abuse or neglect happened. If the judge agrees, he can decide where the kids will live and who can visit them, what schools they go to, medical procedures—a whole host of things."

She sighed and shook her head. "It don't seem fair."

"Today, the judge will decide whether your kids come home right away or not."

Darla suddenly looked scared. "You will get 'em home to me today, won't you?"

At last I had her full attention. "That's why I'm trying to stick to your case here, Ms. Madden. We have to figure out what to do to get them back."

She smiled. "You look like a lifeguard. How'd you get such a good tan?"

The tiny room felt like a jail cell. "Okay, Ms. Madden, what do you say we not waste each other's time? You want these kids back today or not?"

The coy pucker vanished from her plump cheeks. "That man from the Child Services hates me, I'm telling you." Her eyes narrowed. "He just plain hates me!"

"Don't take it personally," I said.

"You know, I'll bet you think I'm a real dumbfuck." She eyed me head-on. "Bet you wish you could tell me to shut up, but you can't, can you? Judge would have your little fanny in the fryin' pan, wouldn't he?"

"Don't push it," I said. "I don't want to make you cry again."

"Yeah, I'll bet."

My client and I were at rock bottom, precisely the level on which I like to operate. "This is really just a dirty house case," I said, perusing the file. "What a dump. You're just going to have to commit to giving it a major going over."

"It's an apartment, not a house, and it ain't no dump. Read me what the bastard wrote."

I went through the report, paraphrasing as I turned the pages, pausing briefly at the motorcycle rebuild currently being conducted in the rear bathroom's tub, a curious detail I'd missed before.

"That's a 'fifty-eight Harley, flat-pan, suicide shift," she said.

"Right." I paused on the report's final page. "Moist feces on entryway floor. Nice."

"My mistake on that. The rest is done—all done!" she shouted. "I had the damn place cleaned up before he even started writing that pack o' lies! I told you, he hates me, he hates my kids, and he hates Max! Now how about gettin' me my kids back? Eric's got a leaky faucet, at times. If he wets his bed in a foster home, the other kids'll laugh at him, maybe even beat him up. And Uncle Pete's a long-haul driver, and he's leavin' for the East Coast in the morning.

He can't take care of 'em past today." She rolled her head balefully, her fists knotted in her lap.

I scanned the names listed on the petition. Only one word had been committed to the task of summarizing the story of the childrens' father, Lyle Madden: "deceased." No mention of anyone named Max.

"I don't know about the social worker not liking you, but this case should be simple. Do a major cleanup. Kick start the Harley." Darla's face was a blank. "I mean, get it out of the tub."

"The Harley? What for?"

"Look, if you don't know enough, I mean, if you aren't even willing . . ." I shut the file, my energy gone. "Just do what I tell you. I know. You'll get your kids back."

She shook her head. "Nuh-uh. He's got it in for me."

What about this Max? Couldn't Darla have a boyfriend, a lover? Perhaps Max was the road rebel rebuilding the Harley in the tub. Weren't bikers known to have eccentric tastes in women? If Max was any match for Darla Madden, perhaps the two of them combined were more than any social worker could handle in one brief visit. It took no great stretch of the imagination to picture the scene in Darla's grubby pad last night—the dishes, the shit on the floor, the bathroom porcelain black with cup grease, an ugly standoff. The whole little sweaty tableau. The social worker shifting stiffly in the living room, reciting the usual chapter and verse from the Welfare and Institutions Code for her, baffling her but good with his substantial-risk-of-harm shuck. Maybe even making her cry, which she seemed to do pretty easily. Big Max, coming down the hall with a socket wrench in hand, looking to even the playing field a bit.

"You mentioned the social worker hated Max," I said. She nodded. "Did Max try to intervene with him?"

"Oh yeah, he intervened all right. Max goes nuts if anyone touches those kids."

"He lives with you?"

"Been with us since I got the place. Let me tell you, Max let that man know his kind wasn't welcome."

"How's that?"

"Damn near tore his head off, lemme tell ya. If I didn't tell him to back off, he would've killed the guy. That's my Maxie."

"The department wants the judge to order the kids to keep staying with Pete after today, or go to a foster home if Pete can't handle them." My eyes met hers. "Are you sure your apartment's clean?"

She swore to me that it was spic 'n' span. "Ya know," she said, "I like that you're taking me so serious, I like that. I thought for sure you were gonna make some smart-ass remark about Max having to get his shit together, or you're in deep shit, lady, hardy-har-har. But you didn't."

"What are you talking about?"

She blushed. "The shit in the report, there. It was Max's shit. You gotta understand, when Max went after him, the guy slipped on it trying to make for the door." She snorted. "Took half of it down the hallway with him on the bottom of his shoe."

Darla Madden must have seen the confusion streaking across my face. "Well duh! You didn't know Max was our dog?"

I backtracked through the pages, still puzzling. "No, just, the report . . . didn't say."

"He's not just any dog, Mister. Champion breed Rottweiler, F-Y-I. Biggest pup we could find, and we checked a lotta different litters. Best dog in his class when he graduated last month."

"Graduated?"

"Fulton Attack-Dog School. Right over there on Atlantic, off the freeway near the soap factory? They got classes there every—"

"Okay, that's it!" I held up my hand to halt her next words. This damned interview was sliding through my fingers like—oh, hell, like so much moist feces. "Let me make this really easy for you," I said. "It's either Max or the kids, but you can't have both." Her eyes welled with tears again. "So Max is gone. Find a relative who will take him, or give him away, I don't care, but he's gone. It's that simple."

Darla's lower lip protruded into a major pout. "Couldn't I keep him on the balcony? What if I lock him out there when the social worker comes over?"

"A dog that big? It's inhumane. You're in a two-bedroom

apartment. Might as well give him the kids' room if you keep him, because no social worker is going to write a positive report after being chased to the door by Max the killer Rottweiler. Besides, it sounds like a two-bedroom litter box. Don't you think the kids deserve a little better?"

"All right, all right, I hear ya," she said. "Say amen, already. Jeeze lu-weeze, Mr. Shepard, ya don't have to get so worked up about it."

"Seems like the best way to get your attention."

The surf beckoned. I flipped to a clean sheet of legal pad and started to write. "All right then, let's talk about what we're going to tell the judge."

With a brief rattle, the doorknob turned and the door cracked open. A woman popped her head in and peeked at us. "Excuse me," she said, "I'm Sue Ellen Randall. I'm looking for an attorney named J. Shepard."

She was tall and slender, almost gaunt, and her hazel eyes jumped about as she fought to regain her breath. She couldn't have been much older than nineteen or twenty. Her skin was a soft, polished white, but as she inhaled deeply her cheeks filled with heat. She had a small mouth and nose, a delicate face. I had detected a southern twang in her reticent self-introduction. Another dependency bottom-feeder? I couldn't tell yet. As I stood to intercept her, she slid inside the door and dug the heels of her white sandals into the carpet in an attempt to barricade herself.

"Miss, I'm sorry, but I'm with a client," I said.

"That's right, honey, he's all mine," said Darla. She cocked her head slightly and eyeballed the woman's outfit—tight-fitting jeans and a matching denim vest over a long-sleeved white blouse—with amusement. Darla nodded approvingly at me before facing the girl. "You'll get your chance with him, honey," she told her, "but not just yet."

"We're having a private conversation," I said, words that sounded a mite ridiculous as they left my mouth. "Would you please wait outside?"

The woman named Sue Ellen Randall lowered her eyes to the floor, her chestnut hair falling over her slight shoulders. "I can't. Those TV people won't leave me alone," she moaned, her voice quavering. The doorknob rattled and she dug in deeper, spreading her arms across the door.

"I need you to help me get my baby boy back, Mr. Shepard. The lady inside said you're going to be my lawyer."

So that was it: They'd assigned me another case when I wasn't looking. "They made a mistake," I said. "I have other obligations this afternoon." I didn't want another case, didn't want this woman's particular custody headache.

"Miss Randall?" a perky female voice called over the rap of knuckles on the door. "I'd just like to talk with you, that's all, maybe have a cup of coffee downstairs. What do you say?"

I motioned for Sue Ellen Randall to step aside and whisked open the door. Holly Dupree nearly fell into my arms, but she caught her balance and instantly recovered with a cheery, prime-time smile. Behind her, the door to the waiting area cracked open and a crewman slipped in wielding a silver boom mic extension like he was about to gaff a large sporting fish. "Zeke's ready, Hol," he said as the cameraman popped his head in and focused his lens on Holly and me.

"Who's representing the mother, sir?" Holly asked.

I moved in close on them. "Here's a news flash. You've got no place in here. These cases are confidential."

"So you're taking the case?" she said without flinching.

"No, Ms. Dupree, you're taking a stroll out that door right now or I'll have the bailiff come and throw you out." The microphone hovered beneath my chin, and I caught hold of it just as Holly's crewman read my intentions and tried to jerk it back. I held the mic firmly, studying the black cone as if I might decide to dine on it.

"Give . . . ahh . . . give it back," the crewman complained, but I held on. The veins bulged in his skinny neck and arms as he squirmed at the other end of the chrome extension.

"Give it up, killer," I said. Finally he let go. I turned to Holly. "Are you leaving now?"

"We'll try again," Zeke appealed to Holly, his camera off his shoulder. She dragged her fingers through her hair, regarded the standoff this had come to, and reluctantly signaled her agreement. Her sound man did his best to act deeply injured as I handed him the mic.

"Gee thanks, counselor," he said without looking at me.

"Tell your buddy Zeke he'd better keep that lens out of my face," I said. "I hate people who point."

When I went back inside, Darla was standing behind the door as if she'd been trying to eavesdrop on my exchange with Holly. "It's her!" Pointing a finger at Sue Ellen Randall. "You're the one who sold your baby!"

Sue Ellen shook her head and sighed. I could tell she'd been on the receiving end of this kind of finger-pointing too many times to count already. She seemed very much alone as she stood up to go. Giving in to some mysterious impulse, I privately said oh, what the hell, she needs help.

"No, wait. Please, stay," I told her. "We were pretty much finished here, anyway."

"Oh, thank you, sir," Sue Ellen said. "Thank you so very much."

Damn. Recognizing that my gesture had probably cost me the afternoon, I sat back and closed my eyes for a brief respite. I don't want your problems, dear, I thought, or your thanks for that matter. I was tired. I didn't want to be needed any more today.

Darla sat back as if ready for a new diversion. My selfish desires for a midday surf were obviously headed out with the afternoon tide. But if I had to be stuck here anyway, the travails of Sue Ellen Randall might be more intriguing than Darla's dirty dishes and dog shit.

The young mother sniffled into her sleeve like a scared child, and I wondered whether Darla Madden had heard the truth about the charges down the hall. Young, alone, out of sorts, Sue Ellen Randall didn't look like much of a con to me. But then, I'd been scammed by clients too many times to count. Father swearing he never diddled the kid, persuading you until you notice the woody he's nursing just from sitting amongst children in the waiting area. Mother swearing she's clean, her hand shaking perceptibly, then uncontrollably as she takes the business card you hand her. People always swearing this and that on a stack of Bibles as they lie to your face. I learned a long time ago it's better not to probe too deeply for the truth. You might not like what you find.

Looking at this jumpy, nerve-wracked hayseed named Sue Ellen Randall, I decided I didn't really care to know whether she'd sold her baby as Darla had claimed. Even assuming the worst, matters were probably not so bleak for the infant child born to Sue Ellen. The adoptive parents obviously wanted him. And now—God knows why now—so did Sue Ellen. Two sets of parents looking to love the boy as their own. In this place, those were heady numbers.

County hospitals harbor too many shivering drug babies no one will ever want. Even so, you pray the birth parents will walk away and keep going, wreaking no further havoc on their childrens' already-cursed lives. But this baby boy was lucky. One child's good fortune—*that* should have been Holly Dupree's scoop.

In truth, a lot of these kids are blessed because more often than not, their parents—my clients—are willing to fight for them. This I can't easily comprehend. Most of my clients are poorly educated, lower income, perpetually unemployed hard luck stories, society's true bottom-feeders. For them, losing is an intransigent fact of life, almost their sole birthright. And yet, against great odds and entrenched histories of seriously fucked-up thinking, they consistently defy their social workers' dire predictions of imminent failure and somehow locate enough dignity and inner strength to kick booze and longtime drug habits, break away from abusive spouses, and face down molesting relatives. They see shrinks they can't afford, tolerate repeated jibes from invasive civil servants, endure lengthy separations. They do whatever the court tells them to do, often at great peril and tremendous personal cost, because they want so very much to stand beside their children. I don't know what drives them to do what they do, but I am deeply, secretly envious of them.

I was certain Sue Ellen Randall had her reasons for giving up her baby boy, then for trying to take him back. Confronted with a stack of Bibles, she'd surely swear on them. I was just as sure that I didn't want her case.

My own mother left me when I was sixteen. My father had died ten years earlier, so when Mom bailed, I became an orphan. All that was a long time ago, but not long enough to ever forget what it felt like.

Darla grinned as she studied Sue Ellen Randall. "Young lady—"

"Stay off her back," I said. "Her problems are none of your damn business."

Darla erupted with laughter, and as she tried to catch her breath, her gelatinous rings of fat teetered like an unsteady pile of inner tubes beneath her pumpkin-round head. "Easy, Mr. Shepard. I wasn't gonna lay into her, though I probly ought to. I was just gonna make a friendly suggestion."

"What are you going to do," I said, "pitch her on the new Wonder Scrubber from Kleenco, takes care of those tough tranny fluid stains in the bottom of your bathtub in a jiffy?"

Darla laughed. "Good one! You can be pretty funny, Mr. Shepard. I like it. Nice break from your tight-ass approach. Nah, I just wanna say one thing, and it ain't nothing bad. Listen, dear," she said to Sue Ellen, "this man's gonna take care to listen to your problems. I know, 'cause he's the first one yet to listen to old Darla's tales of woe, so don't you worry. Just don't make it hard for him."

"Make what hard for him?" Sue Ellen asked.

Darla cocked an eyebrow. "Just give it to him straight, honey. Like, if there's any shit in that report they write on you, you just tell him right up front who that shit belongs to. Trust me, girl, he'll know what to do from there."

With that ringing endorsement, Sue Ellen Randall became my newest client.

Two

Willow Reece, the head of the Legal Project and my boss, is an administrator, which means she rarely makes it into court for reasons other than problems with personnel. The last time I saw her face in this department one of our more burned-out attorneys had royally pissed off Foley by rather loudly advising a client not to fear the "old goat in the black robe who thinks he's God."

Not much ruffles Willow, but now, when I saw her in the hall, I felt an unpleasant shock of fear. Willow probably read the trepidation on my face.

"What's the matter, you forget I work here?" she said. Every lawyer in the Legal Project carries a crushing case load, and Willow has taken her share of backbiting for sticking purely to the non-legal tasks involved with running the office. Not that I cared; she'd hired me a year out of law school at a time when a hundred new lawyers like me were scrapping for every job opening. I owed her.

"I've got a few files that can get you right back into the swing if you want," I said.

Even in her sleek black silk and gold pumps, Willow was a foot shorter than I. Her brown hair was naturally streaked with red, and her face was aglow with the tan she'd brought back from her stay on Maui a week before. Her husband was an entertainment lawyer who did music deals for several big-time rock 'n' roll acts, and the rumor among our staff was that Willow didn't really need to work. But I viewed that kind of talk as rather cheap, because the Willow I'd known was always serious about the job and cared about her people.

I wanted to know what she was doing here, but didn't want to sound pushy. "What's new?" I asked.

Willow took me into the interview room and closed the door without a word. "I need to talk to you about a case."

My first thought was that I'd blown somebody's representation without knowing it, and now they'd taken their beef to the top. "Sure," I said, "anything. Anytime a client's not happy, I want to know about it."

We both sat down. "No J.," she explained, "that's not it. I want to talk about this new one you've got, the adoption case."

"Sue Ellen Randall." The case I'd decided to withdraw from as soon as I could talk to the judge. My palms began to itch. How could Willow have known what I was about to do? "I want off the Randall case," I said. "I'm sorry."

"Off? No, you . . ." She looked peeved, but she got herself together again quickly. "J., you don't mean that."

"I do," I said. "I've never turned down a case before, but I'm doing it this time."

"May I ask why?"

I never spoke of my mother. That part of my life had been closed to the public for thirteen years now. "Sue Ellen Randall reminds me of someone I once knew. I don't know whether to lend her my hand or smack her in the face."

Willow didn't react. "I see."

"She needs an advocate, not someone who's going to judge her. I'll let Foley know."

We sat in silence, and for an instant I thought our little talk had ended. "I need you to do something for me, J.," Willow said, her eyes wide. "For the Legal Project."

"Sure."

"Stay on the case."

"I don't want it. Personal reasons." I looked away.

She sighed. "There's something you need to be aware of, J. Our budget's up and the board of supes hasn't agreed to a new deal yet. And you know how the panel feels about us."

Ah, the panel. Several years ago a panel of private lawyers exclusively represented the parents and most children in dependency and billed the county a pre-set hourly rate. With an endless supply of new cases rolling in every week it was a lucrative enough gig, but a few on the panel couldn't resist the temptation to get rich in a hurry and gleefully overbilled the crap out of their cases. When a county audit revealed the abuses, the Legal Project was created as a county-funded counterweight to the panel. Because Legal Project attorneys like me are paid salaries and don't bill for their services, the county's overall cost of providing lawyers in dependency has gone down. But so have the livelihoods of every lawyer on the panel, and for this, many of them despise us and want the Legal Project gone.

"We'll get a new budget," I said. "You said so in our last staff meeting."

"I said it looked reasonably promising," she said.

I could feel myself getting sucked in. "What is it about me and this case?"

"The adoptive mother's got everyone's attention, including the media. The supes will notice it."

"You mean, they'll judge us by what I do?"

"They will. They're getting pressure from the panel not to renew our deal."

"I'm still in my twenties."

"You'll be thirty before this case is over."

"We've got lawyers with five times my experience. Why not sub in one of our veterans?"

"They're all swamped. Besides, you're good. You care. And you're the only new lawyer I ever hired who knew dependency walking in the door."

"I was just a law clerk before."

"For Nelson Gilbride, one of the best-known family specialists in the state," she said.

"He didn't even know my name."

Willow smoothly folded her arms as if she were shifting gears. We'd had our colleague-to-colleague chat, but now I knew she'd lay down the law as my superior. "I need you to do this for me, J. Do your best, that's all I ask."

I told her I didn't know whether we'd prevail, or whether Sue Ellen Randall was even telling the truth about why she'd broken up an adoption in the eleventh hour. I said nothing of Marielena Shepard, the old feelings of desertion and betrayal re-awakened in me. But no matter, for I could tell Willow didn't really want to hear any details.

"I'm glad we talked," she said. "Try not to worry about the hoopla. In the end, it's just another case. You'll get it handled."

I stared at the gray wall, silently counting back the years. Willow was standing at the door when I heard her say "J., are you okay? You look like you're somewhere else."

"I'm fine," I said, waving her off. "I'm fine."

The summer of '79, my senior year in high school just over the horizon. The day began, fittingly enough, as fragments. Pieces of an unfinished dream.

Water, wind in my face, gliding. Free. Beneath the surface shimmer, a large red starfish is watching me. He smiles as he eats a hamburger and I flash on how a TV commercial is appropriating my dream. But the big starfish stays—he's stopped eating the burger—and winks at me as I speed by. I know now that a wave is powering this dream—and me—onward. Head and fingertips tingle with the hum of forward thrust. The hum grows louder, more punctuated. The phone is ringing on my dresser across the room.

The room is dark. Shit, the phone will wake my mother. I leap out of bed to catch it before the next blast.

"Hey J., it's Mikey. What's goin' on?"

"What time is it?"

"Time for a dawn patrol, dude. Rise and shine, already. How's South-side? You check it yet?"

Mikey Venegas, a local pier crew friend, lives in one of the housing tracts on the inland side of Pacific Coast Highway. Mikey hasn't had driving privileges since the night he got hammered on Southern Comfort and warm Coke and gunned his father's brand new Chevy Caprice across his driveway, over a low hedge and into the next-door neighbor's pool.

"Venegas, it's not even light outside," I said. "Just borrow your sister's Schwinn and go for a pedal." Earlier this summer—sometime after his parents lifted the house arrest but before he got his license back—a few of us caught Mikey slinking down Main just after dark on a girl's hot-pink two-wheeler. White banana seat, sissy bar, neon flower-power stickers, the full feminine complement. He was pedaling no-hands and balancing on his lap a twelve-pack he'd scored for himself and a few other grommets at

Pier Liquor. Scoring brew on a girl's bike—talk about lack of pride. Mikey had understandably died on the spot.

"That is a low blow, J. Ancient history. I'm not on pedal power anymore, you know that."

"Then why don't you drive down to the pier and take a look for yourself, Mike? I'm a little short on Zs."

"I'm still barred from using the old man's ride, you know that. C'mon, just take a peek off the balcony. Tell me if you see any whitewater."

I'd made the innocent mistake of showing Mikey the view from the second-story balcony on the ocean-facing side of my house one windy fall afternoon a few years back. If you stand upright on the redwood railings and steady yourself using the chimney bricks as a handhold, you can see a wide swath of wave zone down at the end of Porpoise Way. When the waves are sizable enough for good surfing, the shoreline glows an ethereal pre-dawn white.

I couldn't see the clock on my desk. "What time is it anyway?"

"Five forty-five."

The day promised to be the biggest commercial Saturday of the summer in this town, the first day of the September Labor Day weekend crush. Every inch of street curb would be fender-to-fender by 9 A.M. But for now, Porpoise Way was serene, the house enveloped in a peaceful blue light. I didn't want to wake my mother. She'd been up late last night, staring at a fat new moon from the antique rocker on her balcony, unable to sleep for the fourth time in as many nights. I listened for a sound. I'd have to slide through her bedroom and out onto the balcony for a gander at the surf.

Marielena Shepard was a light sleeper, no thanks to my many late nights out recently on the local derelict party circuit. There was the night I came home so buzzed on Thai and Schlitz malt liquor that I missed our house entirely, strolling into a neighbor's living room and passing out with a dive over their coffee table. The night I got picked up during a raid at the Marmaduke with a draft beer and a shooter in each hand and a fake ID in my pants pocket. The Bowie concert in San Diego, topped off by a midnight sampling of Tijuana nightlife—and a three-day stay in a Mexican jail. I'd put her through plenty silliness of late but she never complained, never condescended when she laid down the law. I knew she caught glimpses of my father in my rebellious behavior, my passion for the ocean, a likeness that probably left her heartsick from the memory of her dead surfer husband. But somehow, she sensed that I was growing tired of the excess even before I felt the change coming over me. My mother knew me better than I knew myself, and that made me love her even more.

"You got a lot of sack to be bugging me at this hour, Venegas," I said.

"Dude, you know I just wanna surf," he said, taking his shot at sincerity.

"The tide's too high. Go back to bed."

"A three-point-four at five A.M. is not that high, J. It's already headed out. C'mon."

"I don't want to wake her up," I said.

"Aww fu—dgesicles," he said, catching himself. Patience is not one of Mikey's virtues, particularly when he's lusting for a surf. "Bud, your mom is the coolest and you know it. She never wigs."

"Have a nice day. I'm hanging up."

"You do, I'll just call back. Then she'll really be awake."

Truth was, now that I was up I wanted to surf, too. I set the receiver on its side and pulled on a T-shirt. Then I went into the hall. The house was completely silent. My mother's bedroom door was cracked open. I knocked lightly. "Hey, Mom, morning," I whispered, peering inside.

Her bed was already made. The white lace borders of the handmade quilt dangled straight-edged above the floor. A note lay on her pillow: "Son, say three prayers for me today. Love you, Mom."

The closet door was open. Something was missing from last night, her overnight bag, my birthday gift to her last year for her trip to San Francisco with the Saint Ann's choir. The bag I'd seen resting at the foot of her bed when I said good night seven hours ago. I slid the closet door sideways and its rollers gave a great moan. She'd left it open to keep from waking me. Or maybe she'd been in a hurry.

I went out onto the balcony and propped myself against the chimney long enough to catch a chill. When I came inside again Venegas was still on the line.

"What took so long? Big lull?" He waited for a response that didn't come. "You woke her up and she busted you, didn't she?"

"No. I didn't. She didn't." I didn't know what was going on, or what I was saying. Marielena Shepard was very consistent at being Marielena Shepard. But this was not like her.

"So how's it lookin', boss? Like, compare it to our session at Northside yesterday afternoon. Head high? Bigger than yesterday?"

A sense of dread slowly overtook me. "Go back to bed, Mikey," I managed to say.

"C'mon J., what's the word?"

"You want the word? Flatness. Pancake city. No surf, Mike."

"No way," he whined. "You didn't wait for a set, did ya? Check it again. C'mon, J., just—"

I hung up on him.

That day was the beginning of a prolonged flat spell, the bane of every serious surfer's existence. It was not until the second week of October that the first major winter storm in the Aleutians sent swell lines stacking across the Pacific toward Southern California and the sandbars off Christianitos Beach that my phone began to ring again early in the morning. But the balcony surf checks were not a problem. My mother was gone and had yet to return.

⬡⬡⬡ ⬡⬡⬡ ⬡⬡⬡

Sue Ellen Randall's case was the last to be heard in Department 302 that afternoon, closing out a depressingly routine parade of crack-addicted babies, belt-wielding disciplinarians and teenage welfare moms with kids named after comic strip animals or pop icons, past and present. Snoopy, Garfield, Hammer, Ice Cube, Sonny and Cher. Whoever coined the phrase "Elvis lives" wasn't shitting, because a new king graced Department 302's calendar about twice a month. The last pint-sized Elvis I represented had a sister named Priscilla, and mom was pregnant—with the Colonel, I presumed.

Darla Madden was first up when court resumed after lunch. She stalked through the swinging partitions like a twitchy gunfighter, hiked up her drooping ankle-hose and started right in on Judge Foley, griping that the county had no right to discriminate against a good family with an inadequately housebroken pet and a washer and dryer in serious need of several parts that—"Swear to God on a stack a Bibles, Your Honor!"—had been back-ordered since the time Eric was still in diapers.

Of course, Foley's decision to release Eric and Stacy to Darla's custody didn't hinge entirely on Darla's impassioned diatribe. In my opening remarks, I informed the Judge that I'd made arrangements for the imminent departure of Max. But I was not about to deny the woman her moment of glory.

My influence in the outcome of the proceedings passed unnoticed. Darla did not so much as glance my way when her hearing concluded. Instead, she thanked Judge Foley a dozen times, God-blessed him a few more, and squeezed through the exit, Eric and Stacy clutching her waist on both sides like angels propping a sinner.

Foley surveyed the courtroom. The long black second hand on the industrial clock buzzed in a slow circle on the side wall. Two-eighteen.

I sat at the long, crescent-shaped counsel table, hands folded, waiting. Shelly Chilcott, the Child Services court liaison who'd stuck me with the Randall case just before lunch, worked the phones from a desk buried in paper near the opposite end of counsel table. Behind me, the bailiff creaked in his swivel chair as he shot a rubber band at Shelly's potted cactus.

The entire rotation of 302 regulars was hanging around, lounging on three rows of spectator benches. A low dividing wall ran the width of the courtroom, broken in the center by partitions separating the gallery from the legal arena. Gerry Humbert, a rumpled, private panel attorney in a jacket that in another bygone era probably resembled tweed, sat in the first bench with a *Daily Journal* in his lap, play-acting at actually reading it. Gerry never reads anything. Hasn't perused a legal opinion since law school, but argues the latest case law regardless. "What's the citation for that one, Gerry?" I love to say whenever I catch him citing bullshit precedent. This rankles him to no end. Gerry's always on hand if there's a chance I might get my ears boxed by Foley. Sue Ellen Randall's case must have struck him as a choice opportunity to see me pull a major belly flop.

Ken Jorgensen, another attorney from the panel, sat a few feet away from Gerry, wiping the strands of gray across his sweating dome as he loosed a silver western-style belt buckle from beneath his beach-ball gut. He was still recovering from his lunch at the Burrito Shack, a local dive on the Health Department's top-ten list where Fridays are always celebrated as Macho Chimichanga Day. Like Gerry, Ken has an ongoing love affair with the sound of his own voice, and resents my lack of reverence for the unholy union of excess verbiage and soft-headed sentiment that results when he argues a point by the seat of his pants. Ken hates everyone who works for the Legal Project. He once told me I'm the reason he drives an old Honda with two hundred thousand on the odometer.

Patty Irving, another attorney from my firm, was working on a crossword puzzle as she checked her lip gloss in a compact mirror. Two or three other lawyers whose cases had wrapped up well before lunch sat behind Patty, their eyes on me.

My insides fluttered. Last case of the day, the week, and really, the summer. The courtroom should've been near-empty on a Friday afternoon with the day's calendar behind us. But everyone here seemed to want a piece of this case, and whether those pieces would be carved out of me or Sue Ellen Randall seemed insignificant.

Patty got up and came over to me. "Hey, J.," she whispered, leaning over the partition, "how much?"

"What?" I whispered back.

"You know, for the kid. How much did she try to sell—"

"People, might I suggest you get a life?" Foley frowned at the lawyers in the spectator gallery. The seal of the State of California hovered on the wall behind him like a magnificent brass gong. He opened the file in front of him.

"Just a minute, Judge." Arthur Rivas, the court clerk, was on the phone, standing up at his desk just left of Foley's slightly elevated perch (in an effort to create a "child friendly" atmosphere, none of the courtroom furniture was built to rise above belt-level). Arthur held the receiver to his breast and leaned over to whisper something. Foley nodded in agreement.

"Sorry folks," said Foley, "emergency call. Ten minute recess. Don't anybody wander away," he warned, "because I'm going to call this case the minute I get back."

A few more minutes might help me prepare. I bolted to the interview room where Sue Ellen was still holed up from our lunch-hour meeting.

I'd tried hard to keep the tone unemotional when Sue Ellen and

I had first gone over the details of what went wrong, to stick mainly to the file and the county's allegations. But the social worker's report was a scathing rap. To the department, my client was a crass, money-grubbing flesh-peddler. I could scarcely find a sentence in the report that wasn't high-handed, a factual detail that didn't rankle or offend. The young woman flinched as I recited her alleged sins.

"They didn't even interview you or your husband?" I'd asked her during my first read-through. They hadn't, she said. So far, Sue Ellen was not exactly a font of information. Her responses had a curious lack of focus. Not the usual pack of lies desperate parents throw at me, but still, some big pieces were missing. She seemed to lack fire and had none of the righteous indignation I would've expected from a woman wrongly accused of selling her baby. "No, no, it wasn't like that," she kept saying. "They don't understand." And they wouldn't at this rate.

I closed the door behind me. Sue Ellen smiled weakly as I sat down, the sandwich I'd bought for her downstairs in the cafeteria still untouched and wrapped in cellophane. "Okay," I said, "we've got a few more minutes before the hearing. Give it to me again."

"We have no home," she began.

A morbid economy in Kentucky, and nothing but a couple of high school diplomas between Ty and Sue Ellen Randall. Ty pulling down a shabby eight bucks an hour driving a public school bus, Sue Ellen making preserves and pies she'd sell to a handful of local restaurants in town, watching *Oprah* on a tiny black-and-white from the kitchen table. Marveling at how women with not much more than the right attitude could seemingly change their lives for the better. A long drive cross country in an old pickup. Wheat harvest in Kansas, a few dollars in their pockets. A fuel pump shot in East Texas. Waiting outside while Ty pawned his coin collection and the black-and-white in Yuma, Arizona, to pay for a master cylinder job. Living off twenty-nine-cent burgers from McDonald's. Limping into sunny Southern California looking like the Beverly Hillbillies. High rents, no steady work for Ty, an unplanned pregnancy. The ugly realization that the right attitude alone would see no one but a damn fool through life's troubles.

I liked the way she looked right at me when she told me that last part.

Sue Ellen and Ty had been evicted without notice the night before when their landlord saw their booking photos in a TV news report about the case on Channel Six. When Sue Ellen returned alone to the darkened Silverlake bungalow after three nights in the county jail and tried the front door, the locks had been changed and the porch was littered with clothes—a pink blouse on the front step, a wool sock on the mat, Ty's Wildcats Football athletic shirt, his favorite, rumpled into a twisted ball beneath the creaky porch swing— as if a hurricane had blown through the place. The side windows were all locked shut, the hidden key swept up from under the mat. She poked around a bit and found some of their things in a dumpster behind the property. With the neighborhood dogs howling now and porch lights flipping on in unison, she scrambled to stuff a curling iron, a box of stationery, the toaster Ty's Aunt Pauleen had given them as a wedding present, and some more clothes, smelling of rotting garbage, into a dirty trash-can liner.

The pavement was strewn with splintered debris, and as she was leaving, she slipped and turned her ankle on a shard of beveled wood. Sue Ellen cried when she recognized the piece as a rail from the crib Ty picked up at a yard sale a few days ago, after they'd decided they wanted Nathan back. She held the piece of crib, staring at it as the tears ran down her cheeks and into her mouth. Ty had found the crib just in time—the day before Nathan was supposed to come home. It had seemed a good omen, but omen or no omen, they'd been arrested when they went to the Danforth's house to pick the baby up. She dropped the chunk of railing and ran to her car, a trash bag full of worthless possessions bouncing off her hip.

"Never been hated like this," she said. "It feels bad, real bad."

I have trouble tolerating bandwagon-jumping ignorance. "They don't know shit . . . I mean, they don't know anything about you," I said.

She swore to me again that they never took anything that wasn't given to them by either adoptive couple. The first ones, the Pontrellis, said they'd agree to an "open adoption" in which Sue Ellen and Ty could still see the baby from time to time as hazily defined "relatives." But as the weeks passed, the Pontrellis seemed to lose interest in the arrangement. Then Mr. P stopped by to fix the garbage disposal one night when Sue Ellen was home alone and put a sweaty hand down her top. That ended the first adoption arrangement.

The second couple, the Danforths, seemed nicer at first, but once Nathan was born, they slowly stopped taking Sue Ellen's calls and returned the clothes and gifts she'd bought for Nathan still in their wrapping paper. They, too, had agreed that the adoption would be "open," had worked out some specifics about visits and photographs, got the baby, then made it clear they wanted nothing to do with the Randalls. When Sue Ellen stopped by unannounced to see Nathan for the first time since the hospital—a promised first visit that should have happened weeks earlier—they blocked her at the doorway and had their gardener run her off. She was so upset she flooded Ty's old truck, cursing herself for being such a complete fool. When the truck started she found a phone booth, called the Danforths' lawyer and told him she wouldn't be signing the consent papers. The Danforths would have to have Nathan ready by tomorrow afternoon. Ty had a job interview at a shoe factory in Vernon so he needed the truck. After that, she'd come right over.

The department's emergency worker's report had a markedly different take on the events of the past eight months: Ty and Sue Ellen Randall conned one couple, Joe and Margaret Pontrelli, and then a second, Corwin and Kitty Danforth, into giving the Randalls money—nine grand and sixteen grand, respectively—in return for their soon-to-be newborn. The Pontrellis were first in line for the baby and for a few months at least, all was well, but when they began objecting to Sue Ellen and Ty's ever-increasing demands for money, the Randalls dumped them and left no forwarding address.

Enter the Danforths and more cash and nice perks flowing the Randalls' way. Then, on May the sixth, a healthy, six-pound-ten-ounce Nathan was born, and went home as scheduled from the hospital with his loving new parents, the Danforths.

"Yeah, and the promise that Aunt Sue Ellen could come see him as soon as he got settled," Sue Ellen said.

That would have been the end of the story, but last week, having milked the Danforths dry, Sue Ellen had refused to give final consent to the adoption and demanded Nathan back. The Danforths, certain they'd been defrauded, called their adoption lawyer, who in turn called the police.

"Tell me again, what did you do with the money?" I asked Sue Ellen.

"What money? They were supporting us, not handing us stacks of bills. No one never gave us any cash. You kidding?"

"Sorry, that wasn't clear in the report."

"That report of yours is hogwash, Mr. Shepard, pure hogwash!"

The door opened. It was Belinda McWhirter, a gung ho young charger who'd come to County Counsel at the beginning of summer. Before that, she'd been an associate at Burke and Lyman, a downtown insurance defense firm, where she'd earned a reputation for taking a particularly bloodless approach to settlement negotiations with overreaching policy holders. By my estimation her modus operandi hadn't changed much from those days.

"You wanted to talk to me, J.?" she said.

"Be right there, Belinda." I closed the door again. "I'll be back," I told Sue Ellen. "I'm going to talk to the county's attorney about your case."

Belinda and I stood in the small anteroom between the courtroom and the outer lobby. "Who's representing the baby?" I asked.

"Lily Elmore." Belinda didn't bother to hide her pleasure with this revelation.

Great. Lily Elmore, a chain-smoker from the private panel with a quick temper, a spotty memory—"Which case is this?" is a favorite starting point for her when her turn comes to argue—and zero trial skills. Whenever she's the minor's lawyer, she always blithely sides with the county "Just to be on the safe side." Protecting a kid's interests usually takes the least lawyering, a fact that weak attorneys like Lily bank on. I could expect no support from her in these proceedings.

"You want to talk, then make it quick, J.," Belinda said.

Belinda was her usual priggish self. Flat cheekbones and a turned-up nose, a mildly pretty face, but a joyless countenance that always keeps you at a safe distance. Plain-wrap brown hair, short bangs in front. A tailored charcoal business suit, expensive, a remnant from her high-salaried days at Burke and Lyman.

I looked at my notes. "Mother is staying with a friend right now, and Father's in jail. She's not ready to take the baby home today, so we won't be arguing detention." No need to duke it out with her.

"Not ready! Are you serious, J.?" She shook her head. "You're not a parent yourself, so I guess I can understand why you'd even think that that criminal has a chance of getting her hands on that child again."

Aah, Belinda. I wave a white flag, and she responds by judging both me and my new client in one shot.

"Oh, I forgot, you're raising a litter of Hitler Youth these days out on the farm in Thousand Oaks. Guess that makes you a more sensitive human being."

"You're a jerk, Shepard!" she snapped, retreating into the courtroom.

"*Sieg heil*, Belinda!" I called out as the door drifted shut behind her.

I led Sue Ellen into the courtroom. All conversation stalled, then began again. "Looks like white trash," I heard someone whisper as we reached counsel table.

Sue Ellen raised her head gamely and met Judge Foley's eyes head-on as I opened the partition and guided her into a seat. She was calm, refusing to dignify the onlookers with even the slightest glance. We sat very close together at counsel table.

"And where is Father, Ms. McWhirter?" Foley said.

"Well, Your Honor, Father has been arrested for felony fraud and grand theft," Belinda answered, a small smile curling on her lips.

Foley froze. "Ms. McWhirter, this is an *arraignment* and detention hearing. Arraignment of the father, Mr. Ty Alvin Randall, cannot proceed—I can't arraign someone that isn't here now, can I?"

Belinda shifted her weight from one leg to the other. "Uh, the worker should've filled out transfer papers to get him out of Central downtown, but—"

"Well, then, the department is wasting this court's time today. I'm putting Father's arraignment over until next Thursday, September five, at eight-thirty A.M.," the judge went on. He looked at Sue

Ellen, who stood now at my right elbow. "Mr. Shepard, arraignment of Mother. How does she plead to the petition?"

"Denied," I said.

"We can discuss detention now."

"Perhaps I might wait until Father is arraigned," I said.

Foley pondered my strategy. "I see. Next Thursday, Ms. Mc-Whirter. The department will make Father available to us by next Thursday, I'm sure."

Belinda exchanged whispers with Shelly Chilcott, then faced Foley. "Yes, Your Honor."

"Thursday's fine, then, Your Honor," I said. "We'd rather argue detention Thursday instead of today." A chorus of moans went up from the gallery. "My client needs to get a settled living arrangement first," I added, trying to bolster Sue Ellen's respectability. "I'm sure the court can appreciate that."

"Know any good freeway underpasses?" Ken Jorgensen muttered. A few low chuckles followed.

"Very well." Foley lowered his gaze on Sue Ellen. "Ms. Randall, you are ordered to return to Department three-oh-two next Thursday morning, September fifth. Calendar-call is at eight-thirty, so don't be late. If your husband is out of jail by then, be sure to bring him with you to court. Any chance he'll make bail?"

Sue Ellen stiffened in her chair.

I nodded. "Go ahead."

She stood up. "Well, sir, I don't have the money for bail, and his family's back in Kentucky, and they don't have much. Ty's momma had a stroke in March of this year."

"What about your family?" Foley asked.

"My daddy wired bail for me, but not for Ty." She paused. "I don't think he'll be posting Ty's bail for him. They don't really get on so hot."

Foley leaned forward on his left elbow and ran his thick fingers over his bald pate, holding his hand like a visor above his graying eyebrows as he studied the court file. A ring on his finger flickered under the glare of the fluorescent ceiling lights as he turned the pages. The stone was a deep red garnet. His class ring from the University of Southern California, the proud symbol of Duane

Foley's passage, twenty-plus years ago, from the snow-dusted sticks of Fiedler, Minnesota, to the heart of the California Dream.

"All right then," the judge said, "Minor is to remain as placed with the foster parents, the Danforth family. The matter is continued until Thursday, September five. The department is to transfer Father to court on that day, and Mother has been ordered to return to court as well."

Foley closed the file. Belinda and Lily Elmore started packing up. The peanut gallery rumbled a bit and began clearing out.

"Mr. Shepard," Sue Ellen whispered, "I haven't seen Nathan in going on four months."

Christ. I'd completely forgotten to ask about visitation. "Your Honor, one thing briefly," I said. "Mother would like to have visitation with the minor before the next hearing."

"Yes, yes. The court orders monitored visitation for the mother," Foley said.

"But Mr. Shepard," Sue Ellen whispered again, "how's that gonna work? Kitty Danforth said on the news she'd do anything to keep me from ever seeing Nathan again. She isn't gonna let me see him in her home."

Excellent point. "Your Honor, visitation might be a problem," I said.

"Pardon me for interrupting," a dapper, older gentleman declared from the back of the courtroom. He stepped to the partitions and stood behind them. "But I couldn't agree more with what that young man just said." He kept his eyes on Foley. Gerry Humbert and Ken Jorgensen eased back into place to watch.

"I apologize for being late, Your Honor, but I was downtown in a deposition all morning—I'm an expert witness in a precedent-setting custody matter." The man smiled at everyone. Belinda beamed as if the guy were her ace in the hole. "My clients—"

"And who are you?" Foley said.

"Yes, yes of course." The man seemed amused that Foley didn't recognize him.

I knew him first from *Bundle of Joy—A Practical Guide to Child Custody Matters in California*. 1978 edition. More hair, and darker, in that old photo, but the same face, the same confident twinkle in his blue-gray eyes.

I'd also done a six-month internship as a clerk with his law firm during my third year of law school, a low-paying stint that caught Willow Reese's eye and got me hired by the Legal Project.

"Permit me to introduce myself. If it pleases the court, Nelson Gilbride, attorney and legal expert in adoption matters, representing Corwin and Kitty Danforth, the poor parents who have suffered so greatly through this terrible ordeal."

One look at Nelson Gilbride and you knew the Danforths were anything but poor. He wore a wide-pinstripe, three-piece suit that looked like Brooks Brothers, a dangling gold watch-chain and gold cuff links adding a flash of gilt. His silver hair was slicked neatly behind his pink ears. He could not stop smiling.

Foley frowned. "I've made my orders already, Mr. Gilbride."

"Yes, Your Honor, and I'd ask only that the court consider making one small change." Gilbride zeroed in on Sue Ellen and raised his eyebrows slightly as if he was about to inform on her. "This young woman"—pointing a finger—"has caused enough grief to the Danforth family already, and untold damage to little Corwin Junior."

"Not Corwin, Nathan!" Sue Ellen shouted. "We agreed on Nathan. You were our lawyer too, mister!"

"That's enough!" Foley said. "Mr. Shepard, control your client."

"It's okay," I said, touching a hand on her forearm. "We'll get our turn."

"Thank you kindly, Your Honor." Gilbride smiled and bowed slightly, savoring the spotlight. I was certain he didn't recognize me. "Now, Your Honor," he said, instructing the court, "my clients opened up their hearts as well as their pocketbooks to the Randall woman . . ."

"He the same guy who handled the adoption?" I whispered.

"That's him. They said he was the best in the business. So did he, even if you didn't ask him." She was still fuming.

Fascinating, I thought, how a single attorney could represent both couples in such a sensitive transaction. Talk about your potential conflict of interest.

". . . such a cruel hoax," Gilbride was saying, "a vicious fraud worked upon them, but still, Kip and Kitty Danforth . . ."

"Kip and Kitty?" I muttered. Oh boy. Weren't we getting familiar in a hurry. Sue Ellen craned for a better look at Gilbride.

". . . thinking only of the welfare of their child," Gilbride went on. "And they are both deeply concerned about Miss Randall having any contact at all with their baby. If she gets her hands on the poor infant, who knows what she'll do? Actually,"—he paused to make sure the whole courtroom was hanging on every word—"we believe she's plotting to sell him again to yet another unsuspecting couple."

A large buzz went up around the courtroom. Gilbride cracked a delicious grin. When I was clerking for his firm I'd never seen him in action, but I'd heard he was quite the showman.

Sue Ellen was on her feet, shaking a fist at Gilbride. "You're the one who said it would be an open adoption! Monthly visits, remember that part Mr. Gilbride?"

Foley's eyes bugged. "Miss Randall, this is your last warning!"

But my client was beyond anyone's control. "How about Aunt Sue Ellen and Uncle Ty? Forgot about that one, didn't you, Mr. Gilbride!"

"We are against any visitation, Judge," Gilbride said.

"Your point is well taken," Foley said.

"Wait, Your Honor," I said, "this man has no right to come in here and try to argue visitation when his clients aren't even the child's natural parents. They have no standing in this matter, Judge."

Gilbride nodded at me as if my presence was merely intended to lend support to his bravura performance. "I'm sure you've all heard of de facto parent status," he said. "Here we are"—pulling a blue-backed document from his black leather attaché and handing it to the clerk—"my motion for de facto status."

He split the partitions and handed me a copy while Foley read silently. "This one's for you, son," he said as if he were handing me a popsicle.

"Gee, thanks," I whispered, pinning the motion under one arm. "I'll give it a read when I get back to the tree house."

I tried Foley again. "May I be heard, Your Honor? My client has every right—"

"Mr. Shepard, I think I've heard enough for today," he said. "No visitation for now. We'll sort out this motion next week. You can argue visitation when you argue detention next Thursday. People, we are adjourned."

No visits for at least a week. I'd let Nelson Gilbride, a total newcomer to Foley's court whose clients hadn't even bothered to appear, talk right over me as if I wasn't there. Not that Foley had been much help. I slapped my case file shut. Sue Ellen sat perfectly still, staring at the green carpet as I sat down.

Within three minutes the courtroom was empty. The bailiff finished clearing away the newspapers and paper cups left behind on the spectator benches and turned off the tiny fan above his desk. Then he carefully folded the latest issue of *Guns and Ammo* and slipped it into his back pocket, pulled on his green Sheriff's windbreaker, and motioned to me that he was ready.

"The bailiff is going to take you out the back way, so you can avoid those people from the TV station if they're still here," I explained to my client.

Her face was serene, as if she'd become used to accepting defeat. "Thank you."

"That was pretty bad. I blew it when I didn't—"

"It's all right," she said. "Could we please not talk about it now?"

I was happy to oblige. "I'll see you next Thursday. Try to get a place as soon as you can, and call the worker when you do so she can check it out. We need to give them something favorable to report on. We'll get 'em Thursday."

"God bless you, sir," she said, which made me blush, considering the pointed boot up the ass I'd just received. She went with the bailiff past the gold seal and Foley's empty chair, then curved away, down the walkway reserved for the most hideous tormentors of children.

Nelson Gilbride was waiting for me when I reached the elevators.

"A moment of your time?" he said, offering me a handshake. His hand was like a soft, pink pillow. I could have sworn there were no bones in his fingers.

"You know," he said, "I like that judge. Serious. Fair-minded. I'll have to be on my toes with him."

I checked my watch. "I'd love to chat, but I can't."

"Right, right." He smiled, rolling with me. "It's just been a few years since I've tried a case. I hope you can keep me on the right track."

Tried a case? The man was probably dicking with me. "And what makes you think you're going to be trying a case in here?" I said. "Your clients are *caretakers*. They don't even have standing as parents. The only reason you even got to participate today was because the judge was tired and wanted to get his weekend underway. If this thing goes to trial, all you'll do is silently observe, Mr. Gilbride."

He chuckled, calm as ever. "We'll see about that."

I pushed the down button and stepped back to get a full view of the three elevator doors before me.

"Now please, don't go yet," he said. "Please, we haven't really talked about what's important."

I was tired of talking with him. "Sir," I said, "your clients and my client want the same thing, custody of that baby boy. Beyond that, not much else is important."

"Aah, that is where you are wrong, my friend. Think about it. Why did our two clients even meet, but for the very different needs they both have. I've never seen a couple want a child of their own as much as Kip and Kitty do, but God didn't bless them with the ability to have one on their own. They want a child so badly, need to love him so badly, their hearts are just breaking." He shook his head.

A large Hispanic family shuffled past us and into an open elevator. A small girl in a ruffled white dress and scuffed Sunday shoes dawdled near me as the others crammed in. *"Mira!"* an old woman barked, jerking the girl's arm. The doors closed and we were alone again.

"Now take your client," he went on. "Young, inexperienced in life, wondering if her marriage was a bad mistake. Family thousands of miles away, no support system. She needed care, food, rent, money. Kip and Kitty"—the sing-song alliteration stopped him cold, this time—"the Danforths, that is, they gave Miss Randall all that." He leaned closer as if to appeal to my good sense. Making his pitch. "They can still help her."

He hadn't said they'd be willing to buy her off, but he certainly came close. "But Mr. Gilbride, the problem is, Sue Ellen wants her baby," I said.

"She thinks she does, but she really doesn't know what she wants. Just think about it, for now." He handed me a business card.

I wanted to counter him. For starters, what about the hypocrisy of his clients calling Sue Ellen a baby seller when they were so blatant about the buying end of the bargain? But he held up his hand in an appeal for me to let him finish. "Might I inquire as to what it is you're doing in this place?"

"Obviously, I'm in it for the money and prestige," I said without smiling.

He seemed slow to pick up my sarcasm. "Yes, right, very good, very good. But really, let's stop playing games, shall we? They say you're the best lawyer in the rotation."

I flashed on Gerry Humbert and a molestation trial a few weeks back, Gerry's vehement objection to an expert's use of an anatomically correct doll because the doll's pubic hair looked like shag carpeting instead of real hair, a discrepancy Gerry truly believed might "throw off the witness." And I remember wishing for someone, anyone, to come along and throw Gerry off the top of a very high building.

Some compliment. "Wow, Mr. Gilbride," I said.

"Nelson."

"Wow, Nelson. The best in that stellar rotation. That's really saying something."

His face showed fatherly concern. "No, I really mean it. Why are you here? You're obviously dissatisfied."

Was Nelson Gilbride, a man who didn't even know I'd once worked for him, genuinely interested in me? I didn't know or trust him, but in those six months I spent part-time in his offices I'd seen a lot of satisfied-looking clients walking the hallways. The man got results. I was certain there was more in store, and I wanted to hear it. "The D.A. had a hiring freeze when I finished law school. I haven't bothered to reapply in a while."

"Tell me, what do you like most about criminal law?"

"I don't know—distance I guess," I said, unsure of my footing. "I'd be representing the State of California, not some needy client who's right there, pulling at my sleeve every second I'm in the courtroom."

"It must be very tiring, a drain. You are tired, aren't you?" Showing concern.

I stared back, my jaw set. This whole conversation was a pretense. Nelson Gilbride may have been a famous lawyer and expert, but he didn't know me in five minutes time. I wasn't going to answer his question. Never mind that he was dead-bang right.

"Submit another application," he said.

"Pardon me?"

Gilbride showed no impatience. "Just do it."

"Why should I?"

"I know some people. I can help you. We can help each other."

"How?" I wanted him to say it.

"I've heard you can be very persuasive. To the benefit of your clients, of course."

"Of course."

"Just keep an open mind, that's all I ask."

"You flatter me, Mr. Gilbride," I said, "making this case out to be all about me. The problem is, my client wants the kid, not my happiness."

"Perhaps. But in a case like this emotions run high."

"Emotions run high in this court every day of the week."

"Not what I mean. A case like this, publicized this way, it can attract strange people."

"Look around you next time you come to this court. This place is full of those, too."

He winced a little. "You're not following me."

"Feel free to clarify."

"Things could happen. To Miss Randall, or to you."

I frowned. "Are you threatening me?"

"Absolutely not! Wouldn't dream of it. A little friendly warning is all. Cases like this stand for different things to different people."

He was right about that much. "Thanks for the tip," I said.

"But I think there's something else you should consider," he went on, "something more important than the needs of both our clients. We're dealing with the life of a wonderful little boy." He glanced about as if he'd just been tipped off that an insidious virus hung in the air. "That may not always be a matter of great consideration in this place, but it should be. After all, the best interest of the child—"

"Is ultimately the best interest of society," I said, completing his sentence.

"That's right, Mr. Shepard! So, you've obviously read my book—marvelous!"

"I did, but don't get excited about any royalties," I said, stepping alone into an empty elevator. "I checked it out at the library."

The doors closed before he could speak again.

Three

I followed Ocean Avenue off Pacific Coast Highway and down to the sea. Ropes of swell rolled in the hard sunlight, but the tide was at a minus low and a strong westerly wind had churned the surf into choppy, unrideable slop. I walked onto the pier. Seagulls adjusted to my presence with each creak of my wingtips. A few small boys were riding tiny lines of foam on boogie boards in the Southside shallows. A young woman paced expectantly on shore not thirty feet away, a pair of beach towels wrapped around her like a shawl to break the chill westerly. The boys surged forward on a wave, and I saw the woman freeze in her tracks to watch. Their ride completed, they scrambled across the inside bar for another without hesitation. The woman waved, but to the boys, she was not there.

I'd looked forward to this moment with sweet anticipation all day, but the ocean was indifferent to my schedule. My hopes plummeted further with the crash of each shapeless dumper. It's an unhealthy practice I've fallen into, allowing the sea to dictate my mood, relying on surfing to redefine my sense of self. Like a needy lover, my desire is beyond reason. I want more than the act of surfing a wave can deliver. I want to commit to something greater than the sum of my feeble humanness, to glean life from a crisp bottom-turn, find meaning in a heartless underwater drubbing. I suppose my passion has gone beyond the bounds of standard surf-stoke. I want more than to ride a wave with style and skill. I want to belong.

I saw the two boys again, caught them in a flash of movement through the railings, weaving below like coasting birds. Their mother on shore watched them with me. I stood a while longer and wondered how old I'd been when I mastered the art of tuning out adults.

My house is a few blocks from Main and the pier on a narrow

street that runs up from the ocean about a quarter-mile until it hits Pacific Coast Highway. Parking on Porpoise Way is limited on weekdays and near-impossible on weekends when tourists roll out of the inland suburbs in droves to hit the beaches south of L.A. I always park in my garage, which faces into a narrow alley behind the property, but this afternoon, some clown in a white Ford delivery van was double-parked in front of the garage door and I didn't feel like waiting. So I tooled the Jeep wagon around the block and onto Porpoise and lucked into a beautiful spot a few doors down. On my way through the front gate I stooped to pick up the *Nautilus*, the local freebie newspaper. Just then, looking up from the short brick walk to my front porch, I thought I saw a figure moving through the back of the living room, toward the kitchen.

In the twenty-nine years I've lived in this modest two-story— my entire life—at 115 Porpoise, my parents and I had never been ripped off, but plenty of the big three-story glass palaces down on the sand had been burgled at one time or another. I stayed in a crouch and crabbed across the postage-stamp lawn to the big window. The living room was empty now. I thought about calling the police, but the Christianitos police force operates on a modest budget and cruisers are pretty scarce on sunny weekdays in late August.

I stayed low, remembering now the white van double-parked in the alley. Thinking about some of the burglaries reported over the years in the *Nautilus* "Crime Blotter" section. Nonviolent crimes— wasn't stealth the key? I hoped so. Say, Cary Grant in black tights and turtleneck on a rooftop in Monte Carlo, that would do. I could foil the heist by coughing, run him off with a squeaky heel on the hardwood. My thighs were coiled and burning. I readied the front-door key in one hand and dropped my briefcase near a plot of neglected rose bushes. When I turned the knob I thought of Cary, skipping from chimney to chimney down Porpoise. The blood pounded in my ears.

No one leapt at me from behind the furniture—thank you Jesus. I eased the door shut. The living room and hall were empty, the dining room cool and shaded by drawn curtains and blinds. I couldn't yet get my feet moving forward. I know this house very well, can feel its emptiness pressing in on me when I come through the door every night. Something felt different.

As a man of action I was failing badly. I needed a plan, but all that was forthcoming was a bellyful of fear and the urge to take a whiz. A cabinet clicked in the kitchen before I could think of anything. He was in there.

I looked for a weapon and found one in the form of a mahogany plaque—a "secret Santa" Christmas gift to me from Foley's clerk a few years back—upon which were mounted three brass weather gauges that measured temperature, humidity and barometric pressure. When I hoisted it off the wall my spirits sank at how light the thing was, for the mahogany was nothing more than particle board with a dark coat of stain. But the edges were trimmed with shiny brass fittings. It would have to do.

Another minute ticked by in total silence. I slid along the dining room wall toward the kitchen, my palms greasy with sweat as I death-gripped the cheap little plaque. I was two feet from the kitchen doorframe, close enough to reach out and touch the white wall-phone when it rang with an awesome clatter.

Two rings, and not another sound in the kitchen. A shame-filled dialogue was unfolding in my head—man of action, my ass, you chickenshit . . . that sort of thing. It was time.

I whirled past the phone to face my opponent. Nothing—that is, nothing but the usual scene: shining white tiles, a frying pan I'd left on the stove this morning in a rush to get out the door on time, chrome appliances crowding the countertops. A third ring echoed off the walls as I noticed the door to a utility closet cracked open, about six inches. The click I'd heard from the dining room was a match. He was hiding inside, among the mops and brooms and spare light bulbs. I raised the plaque to strike a swift downward blow and jerked the door open, and as I did, I saw a bolt of something black rush at my thigh and felt my flesh being punctured in a dozen places.

Wincing, I swung blindly where I thought his head might be, but the blow merely clattered across a mop handle and clanged off the water heater, splintering the particle board in my hand and sending a shattering vibration up and down my arm. I looked down and saw the cat, a big, fat long-haired old Siamese named Smoky who lived a few doors down, its claws still buried in my leg. My cat burglar. I dropped the clock, and as I did, the phone continued to blast. The kitchen door that opens on the back patio was open just enough for Smoky to have slipped in. I'd left for work ten minutes late this morning, maybe in too much of a hurry to have locked up.

As I picked up the receiver I heard a car engine starting in the alleyway. "J.? Oh good, you're home." It was my girlfriend, Phoebe Davenport.

I was thinking about the white delivery van blocking the garage, the flash of a figure I'd seen through the front window, bigger than a fluffy Siamese by any measure. Big enough to drive a van, and maybe smart enough to work a door-lock open.

"Pheebs, where are you? Can I call you right back? I gotta—"

"L.A.X. I know, I'm home early, and no you can't call me back, I have something to say that can't wait."

I could hear the van's tranny clicking into gear, the tires on loose gravel behind my house. "Pheebs, if you could just hold the phone a minute."

"No, I cannot hold the phone!" she said.

Christ, I thought, if I can break loose for ten seconds I'll at least get a license plate number. "Pheebs, please, just—"

"I'm *breaking up* with you, J.," she said. The van pulled out, its engine revving down the alleyway as I stood dumbly holding the phone, staring at Smoky's luxuriant tail. A long silence followed. "J., are you there?"

I felt my insides tightening and wished I possessed the sack to be a true man of action and just hang up before she read the laundry list of reasons we would never make it as a couple: my emotional unavailability, a certain secretiveness about my past, the void of family history that was downplayed at every turn but apparent just the same. Here it comes again. The tiresome part was that I'd heard the same list recited enough times by former girlfriends, I could have done the talking for Phoebe.

"I'm here," I said, leaning on the counter. "I'm here."

By the time I got off the phone the van was long gone, and Phoebe was on her way out. But I still clung to the hope that I had a sliver of a chance with her, and that chance was tonight. She had dumped me about six hours ahead of schedule, for tonight I was to be her date at a dinner in honor of her father, William Davenport, for his fundraising efforts on behalf of a children's hospital. I'd rented the tux, I reminded her—which was a total lie—and besides, she'd need a date and I had no hard feelings, really. The least she could do was say good-bye to me properly, in person. Yes, she said. Phoebe agreed that she owed me that much and thanked me for taking the news so well. I'd see her at seven.

I tried to picture Phoebe's father attending a social event, sipping a drink, happily unwinding with friends. The images didn't come. I saw William Davenport as a shark who never stops swimming, a snake with no eyelids. Unwinding was not in his repertoire. I knew the man disliked me for some unspoken reason, as well. I checked the time: 4:55. In a mere two hours Daddy Davenport and I would be exchanging false pleasantries over paté and crackers, smiling through clenched teeth as I did my damnedest to change Phoebe's mind, the scene sliding from the merely hopeless to the macabre. But I was going, and I needed some fortification—and a tuxedo—to bring this one off.

I spent about three minutes in the tux shop being fitted with a jacket that felt like an open parachute on my back and taking the pants on faith. What a blunder. When I got them home, the pants fit as if they'd been tailored for a rodeo clown. My first impression with the well-heeled Davenport crowd was sure to be memorable.

I blinked and visualized the polished dance floor, the chandeliers, the glittering swirl of Beautiful People waltzing with austere grace. Off in a dark corner, yes, that's me, hunched over and cursing my sagging drawers, hiking a fist full of ill-fitting fabric up my ass with the same bold yank I'd seen the pink-curler gawker use at court this morning. I remembered the sage words once spoken to me by a well-meaning law school professor: a good lawyer learns something from every client. I suspected the seat-of-the-pants ass-grab was not what he had in mind.

A few hours later I eased off the northbound 101, took a left on Fourth Street, and sailed over the bridge toward the glass high-rises of downtown L.A. The sun was the color of ripe peaches as it sank into a dusty, smog-tinged haze. A cloudless sky arced high above the tallest buildings, reflecting the heavens in a flawless, Hollywood-backdrop dome of airbrushed electric blue. I was seriously late.

I motored past dank Skid Row beer joints and blocks of sooty, urine-stained buildings with storefronts boasting names like Mac's Mega Burger, Try Us! Discount Stereo, and La Bonita Fashion. Darkness was gaining, and the sidewalks on some of the side streets were already cluttered with cardboard shelters. A scant few blocks ahead lay another world, the Biltmore Hotel looming over Pershing Square like a stately antique, its patterned brick soaring above a phalanx of graceful arches and columns in an eloquent tribute to old money and faded West Coast elegance.

The Biltmore lobby was nearly empty but for a trio of Asian businessmen in silk suits. Near the front desk stood a statuesque bellman, his brow rumpled in an expression of supreme boredom.

I unfolded my invitation and skimmed the gold-lettered print for details. "Which way is the Tiffany Room?" I asked the bellman.

He saw the invitation, then grinned as if he knew in advance how many interminably dull speeches were on tap tonight. "On your right, all the way down the hall, then left."

There would be speeches, all right, glowing tributes, good-natured jibes, witty asides, charming anecdotes galore. Patron William P. Davenport. You can't help but love a guy with so much money he needs to give it away to feel good about himself, even when he's a controlling prick. But I didn't care. I wanted one more shot with his only child, Phoebe.

I found the Tiffany Room at just after eight. With any luck, the cocktail session was just breaking up by now, the guests were ferrying their vodka martinis and flutes of Chardonnay over to their assigned tables, and my entry would go unnoticed. I inhaled deeply, opened the ballroom door, and sauntered in.

"Sir, please!" A firm hand clamped down on my shoulder. A

swarthy waiter fought for balance beneath a colossal tray of rolls and tossed salads. In my effort to radiate maximum aplomb I'd strolled headlong into the man's path without looking.

"Sorry, friend," I said. It felt like the hundredth time today that a person shot me the stink-eye when the waiter took his turn.

I surveyed the long, rectangular room. Every last guest was seated at one of thirty or so round banquet tables, half of them presently studying this new arrival in the floppy tux.

Phoebe stood at the head table until she had my attention. She wore a sleek black halter dress, silk with a criss-crossed pattern of crystal beading; the dress clung to her svelte shape like a mermaid's tail. Her bare shoulders peeked out teasingly from beneath the dense, honey-blond waves of hair flowing down her back.

"A tuxedo, J.?" Phoebe said when she saw me. "You were serious."

"Only the best for the beloved honoree," I said. "You don't like it?" I privately kicked myself for asking such a set-up of a question.

"It doesn't matter. I'm glad you came." Her eyes traced the lumpy line of my jacket.

I could feel her disappointment. "Okay, I know. Don't even say it."

She shook me off. "You're even good-looking in a generic tux, J."

Kind words, but good-looking is not how I would choose to describe myself. I'm tall—about six-two—and on the solid side. Like most surfers, my legs appear to be a touch skinny beneath a top-heavy chest and arms built up from years of paddling a surfboard through advancing lines of soup. My olive skin and brown eyes I took from my mother, and my almond, sun-streaked hair from my dad. My nose is straight, but thick in the middle, like a street fighter's (I broke it a few years back when I took a fallen rider's loose board square in the face on a crowded day at the pier).

"You nearly missed dinner," she said.

I felt ill at ease. Perhaps a touch of levity would loosen things up. I opened my jacket and tugged at my cummerbund until the heads of three large safety pins protruded from the front of my pants. "The guy who rented me these pajamas told me don't worry, the waist is adjustable. Don't let me doze off tonight, Pheebs. I could slip beneath the belt-line and suffocate."

She laughed for half a second, then said, "A man should have his own formal wear."

It was the kind of subtle put-down I'd heard many times before from Phoebe, a reminder that we were from different worlds. And yet, because I had nothing to lose I felt I could afford to let it slide.

My social indifference had become a source of strange wonder to Phoebe. She seemed to marvel at my lack of enthusiasm for the accouterments of the yuppie class, my uncanny ability to wear the wrong clothes at the wrong time, my well-tempered disdain for authority. I suppose I'd supplied a certain entertainment value to her life just by being myself.

"Loan me a few bobby pins," I said, "and we'll dance later."

This time she truly laughed. I suspected the baggy-ass fit was just fine with Phoebe.

My eyes passed over the other guests at our table: distinguished older couples picking through their salads like cautious birds, the women dripping in diamonds and gold jewelry, the men in monogrammed shirts and seamless black jackets. No tuxedos.

Phoebe recognized my dismay. "What's wrong?"

"Nothing," I lied. Just then a waiter in a tux very similar to my rental—but better fitting by a mile—squeezed behind us with a pitcher of ice water. I watched him circulate as he poured, wondering whether I should just go and help out in the kitchen.

The ballroom seemed to shrink around me. I was bombing with a girl who'd dumped me a few hours earlier. I was out of my depth with her, and moments like this only proved the point more emphatically. "Pheebs," I said, "how about a quick one at the bar? I need a real drink."

But Phoebe didn't hear me. She had turned to greet a society matron seated at the next table, a woman who was suddenly laughing her ass off at something. A coincidence, I hoped.

The salad before me held no appeal. My appetite had disappeared. Soon I was playing with my silver, drawing figure-eights with my knife as I studied the guest of honor from across the table. William Paul Davenport, attorney at law, senior partner at Davenport, Hobbs & Frank, one of L.A.'s most prestigious firms. Major Republican party booster, president of the California Lawyer Reform Commit-

tee (don't ask), and, if the tax benefits are aligned like a major con-
stellation across his accountant's desk blotter, philanthropist to boot.
His iron jaw was working a sirloin-kabob appetizer with the zest a
starving Doberman might have brought to the task. A fat priest with
a tan had leaned over behind his chair and was apparently telling a
riotously funny story. As they laughed together, Big Bill looked up
and saw me. I smiled and raised my hand to wave, but he turned
to the priest before I could complete the gesture.

I thought of the little get-acquainted outing Phoebe had instigated
last month, our fateful rendezvous on the golf links at Bill's club for
a round of eighteen. We were supposed to be a foursome, but the
other two guys—lawyers from his firm—were called away by last-
minute business, leaving the two of us alone and, for the most part,
deathly silent. I remembered the way Davenport had looked right
through me at the green on ten, not even a trace of good humor
on that granite face when I regaled him with a tale about my dad
and his best friend, Grog Baker, and a Tijuana bullfight they'd once
interrupted. His was a face that, in its own restrained, establishment
way, still managed to say "you're just a punk," with enviable clarity.
I surmised that he didn't recognize what I did for a living as "real
law," and that he thought I was joking when I told him how much
I derived from surfing and a life spent in contemplation of the
ocean's moods. He never came out and told me I wasn't worthy of
Phoebe, but it was there on his face, a smugness that had left me
speechless, twisting the grip of my three iron until my palms burned
a florid pink.

A jazz combo was set up in the far corner of the room. The
leader, a tall black man in dark shades and a suit the color of scrambled eggs, stepped forward and began a smoky run on his saxophone.

"I don't know, Pheebs," I said. "I don't think your father appre-
ciates my being here."

Phoebe paused to consider my charge. "He just thinks you're not
my type, which isn't as bad as it sounds. To him, no man is good
enough for me."

Her hair fell over her eyes, and she threw her head back lightly
to clear her vision. I wanted to stroke away her silken tresses with
my finger and kiss her gently on the nose, but we were still

technically broken up, and with the Big Man at point blank range, I thought better of it.

"He also thinks you've got one thing on your mind," she said.

Davenport had a lot of sack to say that, considering that Pheebs and I have never slept together. We'd met at the wedding of a dependency court judge I'd worked for before Foley, Arthur Hodges. By an uncommon stroke of luck that day, my name was left off the seating assignment, and since I'd come alone, the wedding organizer quickly placed me in the only single seat remaining, next to Phoebe and her father. She wore a velvety, blue floral dress with a broad-brimmed hat and delicate white gloves, and I was immediately stricken by her quiet charm and refinement, her shy beauty. We spoke tentatively through dinner. I was nervous and strained in my attempts at conversation, not my usual self, and although she'd agreed to dance with me twice, I could feel my presence with her fading. A long, awkward silence fell upon our table like an invisible plague, and I resolved to save myself any further embarrassment by bailing out as soon as the cake-cutting ceremony was done.

But then, by a second intervention of blind luck, I suppose, Phoebe asked about my family. Breaking my usual silence, I allowed her the small discovery that I, too, was an only child. She spoke of losing her mother to a swift and sudden cancer the month before, and was touched by my understanding of her sense of loss. Of course, I knew all about losing a loved one suddenly, but didn't let on—didn't have to, as Phoebe was so wrapped up in her mother's story that day. The reception ended, but the two of us segued to the hotel bar and carried on over coffee. I drove her home near midnight.

Four months of sporadic dating and long-distance calls followed. Phoebe's commercial acting and modeling schedule kept her away a lot, and we seemed an ill fit at times, disagreeing about everything from pop music to politics, uneasy with our disparate backgrounds and reluctant to announce ourselves as a couple to our respective friends. But she continued to grieve her mother's passing and I became her confidante. In truth, the support I gave her was little more than the assurance one drunk offers another when sharing a bottle: better to be miserable together than alone. But we never shared a bed together; between Phoebe's long patches of sadness, her constant travel and her residence in the Davenport manse, with old Iron Jaw right across the hall from her bedroom, the opportunity had never really arisen.

Yet here I was, tagged by a protective father as a lad just primed to get primal. But Bill Davenport didn't know me or my problems. I'd been alone too long to know what to do with myself. To make matters worse, I'd fallen into a pattern of chasing women who were either just out of reach or were so needy themselves that they didn't mind the distance I kept. Phoebe fit neatly into the former category, and she had a point about my emotional unavailability. She really didn't know anything about what went on inside my head.

The jazzmen heated up with a driving Latin number. "I want you to talk to Daddy," Phoebe told me before floating away from our table to circulate. She moved with a slenderness and grace so sweet to behold that I felt pained to watch, and a hollow ache arose in my throat.

Perhaps this was a final invitation from Phoebe. If I was going to make it with her I had to try again with Daddy. Five minutes later, when the fat priest moved on, I slid into the empty chair next to Bill Davenport. We said our hellos and chit-chatted for one brief, effortless moment. Then somehow, the conversation turned ugly.

"Pheobe's a big hit in the Far East," I said, complimenting the proud dad on how well his daughter was doing with her modeling (her print ads were an apparent smash in the Asian motorcycle market). I was half-expecting a brief, commiserate "Yup," followed by another long, awkward silence, but Bill Davenport surprised me.

"A calculated hit," he replied. "If there's one thing I know, it's how to call in a favor."

"A favor?"

"I know every man on their board of directors by his first name."

We regarded each other unsmilingly. "You're saying it was you who got her the Suzuki work?" I asked.

"My firm's won five huge product liability cases involving Samurai jeeps in the last year. That certainly hasn't hurt her career."

"Oh, so it's you and the firm."

"That's the reality. But we can be kind about it."

There was something terribly unfatherly about the way he told me this. I didn't believe him, either. He was on some kind of power trip, showing off his control over his daughter, pointing out my own insignificance, by comparison. When he grinned, I could see specks of black pepper lodged in his teeth.

"You know," I said, "I think you're overestimating whatever string-pulling you've done. Phoebe's really a bit of a sensation in Asia."

He was not used to impertinence. "Suzuki makes a stellar product. Those jeeps sell themselves in Japan."

"Well, Mr. Davenport, I really think it goes beyond brand recognition. Don't tell me," I said, "you're not taking credit for her calendar deal too, are you?"

"She hasn't done any calendar."

"Not yet, but she will, and I for one can't wait to see it. Twelve months of no one but Phoebe, twelve different swimsuits. Can't wait to see the Korean Coke commercial that's coming up." I'd gotten his full attention now. "Did she forget to tell you about the Coke ad?"

He glared at me as if I was peddling pornographic glossies of his mother. "I started her modeling with the Suzuki ad," he said. "It got her out of that . . . funk."

"You mean her mother's death."

"That's all there is to this new modeling thing."

I looked toward the jamming musicians and tapped my fingers in time on the table. "Maybe," I said as calmly as I could manage, "but in that part of the world, most women tend to be dark-haired and diminutive. A blond Amazon like your daughter, she's the Asian everyman's erotic fantasy, and fantasy sells product."

No doubt, Bill Davenport was not pleased by the notion that he himself had put his little girl's sexuality into play with a million unseen male consumers. "Why are you here?" he asked me.

I summoned the courage to shoot him a small, phony smile. "I'm your daughter's date."

Soft jazz floated in the air. Phoebe sliced a string bean but left it on her plate. "I missed you while you were in Japan, Pheebs," I said. "What are you doing tomorrow? Keen on hitting the beach with me?"

Across from us, her father hacked into his baked potato as if he bore a personal grudge against it. "We're broken up, remember? And what just happened between you and Daddy?" she said.

"Nothing. But I've been doing a lot of thinking about what you said, you know, about me not being as accessible as I should have been."

She put down her fork and folded her arms. "Really."

"Really. For starters, you've never even seen me surf." She nodded. "Why don't you stay at my place tonight so we can get an early start? You know, give me a chance to slide a few peaks before the wind starts howling."

"Dawn patrolling, eh dude?"

We both laughed. "Where did you pick that up?" I said.

"They have surfers in Japan. You should know that." She paused. "There needs to be more to this than just going surfing."

"There is. Just give me a chance. And promise me you won't say 'dude' again. It's cheesy."

"All right. I don't mind if you want to be up early," she went on. "Just wake me gently."

After four months of chivalry and respectful distance—too much distance on my part—there it was. We were still alive. My hand shook as I reached for the last dinner roll on the table.

Dessert was served. Phoebe was coming home with me later tonight. Life was beautiful. I was sitting in my own warm little bubble when a wrinkle-free maven seated with her husband at the table turned her full attention toward Phoebe and me. She introduced herself as Betty Forrester, "of the First Savings and Loan Forresters." I was tempted to announce myself as J. Shepard of the Student Loan Shepards.

Both Mrs. Forrester and her husband, Neil, were instantly charmed by Phoebe. Naturally, they wanted to know more about me.

"I'm a lawyer," I told them, noticing that Bill Davenport was listening now.

"And what type of law do you practice?" Betty Forrester said.

Oh, boy, here we go. I launched into my standard spiel on

dependency, making myself sound more like a social worker interested in safeguarding the institution of family than helping deficient parents regain custody of their damaged offspring. Nelson Gilbride would have been proud of my rhetoric.

Phoebe wasn't falling for it. I know she finds my line of work distasteful, a waste of some hidden talent I have yet to even identify myself.

"What kind of 'issues' do you mean?" Mrs. Forrester said, cocking her head like a lovely china doll.

"Physical abuse," I said. "Emotional abuse."

"Sexual abuse," Phoebe added, her eyes on her empty plate.

Betty Forrester gulped. "Oh, my."

"You know," Neil Forrester said, "I saw the damnedest story on the six-o'clock news tonight, just before we came down here. There was a woman in there today—I think it was the dependency court—who'd sold her baby." The others gasped. He then did a decent job relating the basic thrust of Holly Dupree's one-sided report to the whole table. "Sold the child to the highest bidder, then stole him back when she got the money."

"That's not true," I said without thinking. All eyes were on me.

"Why not?" Phoebe said. "He heard it on the news. Holly Dupree did the story."

I held up a hand in protest. "Holly Dupree. The woman did a piercing segment on talking orangutans last month." Mrs. Forrester laughed nervously.

Phoebe looked offended. "I suppose you know better, J."

"I believe I do," I said. "That woman—the baby seller—is my client." Painful silence.

"It must be hard representing people like that," Betty said. "I mean, people so . . . confused. How did you get into this line of work?"

When someone inquires about my life to this extent I instinctively fall into an evasion mode, but I knew that if I was going to keep Phoebe, I had to show her I was willing to peel back a few layers. "Student loans," I said, "and I needed to pay my property taxes. It was the best job I could find at the time. I thought it would be a way to get some trial experience." Phoebe was trying to act cool, but I could tell she was hanging on every word.

"What are your future plans, as a lawyer?" Neil asked. As if no one could imagine doing dependency work on more than a temporary basis. Actually, he wasn't that far off base.

My conversation with Nelson Gilbride came back to me. "I'm considering working for the District Attorney's office," I said.

"Deputy D.A., huh?" Bill Davenport said. "That's a sought-after position these days, isn't it?" Was he subtly taunting me?

"I suppose."

"May help if you know someone who could give you a leg up on the competition," Davenport said. Everyone knew he was Mister Connected. If you needed help wiping your ass, Bill Davenport could arrange it. But no offer of assistance from Big Bill followed.

I smiled at all of them. "You're quite right," I said, "and as a matter of fact, I do know someone." I studied the centerpiece of gold and ruby-red poppies.

Phoebe slid her arm beneath mine. She looked relieved. "That's wonderful, J. Why didn't you tell me before?"

I thought of what I might do, what words I'd have to say to convince Sue Ellen Randall to give her baby back to the Danforths. I started to speak, but Phoebe leaned in and kissed me on the cheek, her eyes the freshest green, like wild, shivering grass. Suddenly we seemed closer than ever. Perhaps she would stay with me, after all. Perhaps tonight, at my place . . .

Four

Ahead of me, Phoebe's white BMW whipped through the empty streets past rows of darkened mansions fronted by sloping lawns and mature trees carefully pruned into horticultural works of art. I followed in my Jeep wagon, struggling to keep her taillights in view, relieved when I glimpsed a freeway overpass slicing through the treetops.

We blew down the fast lane along the wall of eastern foothills that so effectively hem the city's smog in on stifling summer days, then headed south through the vast strip-mining holes of Irwindale, where huge piles of discarded car tires glowed in the moonlight at the bottom of tapped-out pits. The drive quickly became dull and lonely. I regretted having let Phoebe take her own car.

I'd wanted her to ride with me, but she convinced me she needed to get home Saturday afternoon for a hair appointment. No point making me backtrack to San Marino the very next day. I'd conceded, but not without noting that Phoebe Davenport had never, on even a single occasion, allowed me to drive her anywhere.

Twenty-five monotonous freeway miles later we reached Christianitos. We followed Pacific Coast Highway down to Main, where I honked and pulled up alongside Phoebe's car.

"Follow me into the alley. We can put your Beemer in the garage."

I had to swerve to miss a foaming beer can as we rounded the end of my street and started up the alley. My side window was still down, and I could hear music with a deep-bass, tribal thump coming from the direction of my house. One of my neighbors was apparently hosting a little weekend rage.

We double-parked across my garage door in time to hear Bob Marley's distinctive Jamaican phrasing drowned out beneath a chorus of intoxicated wails: "Let's get to-ge-ther and feel all right!"

Christ. The reggae was playing on the stereo in my living room. My chance to be alone with Phoebe had just been blown by someone who knew where I hid my spare key. The state of affairs between Pheebs and me was tenuous enough already. I didn't need any pals crashing on the couch, plying me for a surf at an uncomfortably early hour, manufacturing small talk at the breakfast table while I whipped up an *omelet especial* for my special guest.

The gate rattled open and two tow-headed blond kids who surf Northside every day before and after school staggered out into the alley. "Hey, J.," one of them said, "crankin' party, man."

"You little chuckleheads are drunk," I said, which made them laugh sheepishly. "It's way past your bedtime, boys, so run along or I'll get your mommies on the phone." Conceding, they nodded as if all was cool, hopped on their skateboards and kick-turned down the unlit alleyway.

Phoebe shook her head. "I thought you said we'd be alone."

I sighed. "Trust me, this wasn't part of the master plan."

"Shouldn't you call the police?"

"No. They're probably just friends . . . I mean, some people I know."

Phoebe's stare was pure confusion. "What difference does that make? They're in your house, J."

"I know a lot of people in town on a pretty casual basis," I said, which was true.

My answer seemed to disappoint her. "I see. So this is how you do things at the beach, let your friends wreck your house while you're gone? No wonder you've never said anything good about home."

I took Phoebe's hand and led her through the gate and along the narrow path, past the garage and into the small backyard. The porch light was off and the kitchen door was ajar. A shaft of yellow light angled through the screen door, illuminating the brick steps like a sci-fi entrance into another dimension. Across the dark yard I could see several figures outlined against the white brick wall in the far corner, under an overgrown pepper tree. One slender, silhouetted male dangled his thumbs in his front pockets in a casual slouch I immediately recognized.

"Britt," I called out.

"J., what's the haps?" Britt Baker stepped clear of the others and met us with his usual air of exuberance, his straight white teeth and lively eyes glowing beneath a thick mat of brown hair tipped with sun-bleached red. He was dressed in old blue jeans torn at the knees and a Mexican serape woven from deep cords of blue-and-white rough cotton, a pair of green thongs—the kind you buy at Thrifty Drug for three bucks—on his nicked-up feet. Britt despises shoes. "I called earlier but got your recorder," he said. "My truck's having mixture trouble again. Shop teacher, Mr. Flagly—remember, faggy Flagly—he thinks my carb's shot."

"The man knows his carburetors," I concurred.

"Well, hello," Phoebe said. I'd waited too long to introduce her.

"Right. Britt, this is Phoebe," I said. "Pheebs, meet Britt Baker."

Britt held out his hand in a shy gesture of chivalry. His lack of confidence seemed to expand Phoebe's sense of her own presence. She cocked her wrist delicately and laid a knee-knocking smile on him.

"Nice to meet you, Phoebe," he said, his voice cracking. "That's a pretty name."

"Thank you. I believe you're the first friend of J.'s I've ever had the pleasure of meeting," Phoebe murmured. "You're in high school?"

"I've known Pam and Grog—Britt's mom and dad—since he was in diapers," I said, not wanting her to corner him about his age. Grog Baker had been there when my father died. He and Pam had spared me from foster care in the months following my mother's disappearance, taking me in until I turned eighteen and became a legal adult. The Bakers were the closest people to family I had.

The languid scent of reefer wafted over. "Something's burning," Phoebe said.

"Don't worry about it," I said.

"They're smoking marijuana in your yard?" Phoebe's tone was grave.

"No problem," I assured her. "They'll be heading home in a minute."

She sniffed the air. "I've never used illegal drugs."

"Listen, Britt," I said, "I don't mind you having a few friends by once in a while, but you should have cleared this with me. As you can see, I have company." The shattering of breaking glass resounded high above the branches of the pepper tree. A noisy pack of revelers was on the upstairs balcony that ran along the side of the house and faced west, toward the sea.

"Who, them?" Britt said, nodding at the house. "This? Oh, no, this wasn't my idea. Didn't you know? Jackie's back. He called my mom, asked her if she could pick him up at the airport this afternoon. She told him to get a cab—and stay away from me."

No, I thought, not Jackie Pace. Not now. Tonight's party suddenly made sense. Jackie was the one man I knew who could spark an offhand happening in no time. It hardly mattered that I hadn't heard from him in six months. He's the only friend I have who always seems to slide back into my life through a side window.

"Who brought him here?" I said to Britt.

"Said he met some African dudes at the baggage carousel. They were headed somewhere else, but he conned 'em into giving him a ride. When they got down here, they stopped in for happy hour at the Captain's Galley and the Africans flipped out on all the free food. It was a scene!"

A group of girls in sleeveless, Hawaiian-print dresses pushed open the screen door and stepped onto the porch. They peered into the darkness at us but quickly lost interest. One of them was barefoot and waved a white sandal in her hand at her friends. "No, we can't leave!" Drunk. "My . . . foot, is . . . naked!" Her companions burst into breathless, high-pitched gasps of laughter.

"How did this thing get started?" I said.

Britt grinned. "We all got tossed. Jackie kept dreaming up these Olympic events. One of the Africans lost his lunch right after the chicken wing marathon."

"So you all just popped over."

"Nobody really thought about it. Didn't know you gave Jack a key to the house."

"I forgot I loaned him a spare, that time he came back from Peru with food poisoning," I said. "He bailed for the Islands before I could ask for it back."

"Maybe this is your chance," Phoebe said.

I gave her a small hug with one arm. "I thought you said you wanted to see some of the beach life."

Her face was tense. "I was thinking more along the lines of palm trees and cool ocean breezes."

I turned to Britt. "Help me get them all out of here."

Britt began dispatching those outside while Phoebe and I went indoors. The small living room looked mostly intact. No one was sitting down. The room was packed with tanned young faces, some that I knew, most of them at least familiar. The guys wore mostly jeans and T-shirts adorned with airbrushed surf scenes or manufacturer logos. A few nodded and said "Hey" to me as we pushed by. A smaller contingent of girls were sprinkled here and there, enjoying the males' undivided attention. Bob Marley had given way to the Sex Pistols, and people standing next to each other had to shout over Johnny Rotten screeching "Pretty Vacant." No sign of Jackie.

Phoebe's entrance seemed to change the temperature in the room. Guys stopped talking and turned to look, which at least got her smiling again. She threaded her way through the pack of bodies, her lips tart and pouty, her delicate swirls of amber hair glowing in the room's soft lamplight.

"Look, it's Barbie," a tall girl with white braids and a peeling red nose said.

"Yeah," said her friend. "Must be looking for Ken."

I reached the front door and squatted to straighten an Indian throw rug that lay rumpled in the entryway. "Ahh . . . J.?" Phoebe called out behind me. A short, hard-muscled party boy had stepped into her path and was cornering her against the wall, his tattooed forearm locked like a steel bar behind her ear. He had a small gold nostril ring and a thick goatee that gave his face the look of a barnyard animal.

"Get with it, Miss America!" he shouted over the grinding rhythm guitar. "It's my birthday so you gotta kiss me!"

I reached him just as he put his hands on her shoulders. "Take your paws off her," I said, tearing his forearm away.

He turned and confronted me, his face flaring red. "Who the fuck are you, pal? You got no right! I'm gonna kick your ass for that." Phoebe stepped clear as he began to remove his wristwatch.

I was exhausted, emotionally beaten-up from court and the Randall case, from Phoebe's breakup and the high-wire display I'd pulled a few hours ago at Bill Davenport's dinner. Definitely not in the mood for a melee in my own house. I stepped into him without hesitation, drove him into the wall and pinned his chest with my left forearm. He yelped breathlessly as I took his nostril ring between my thumb and forefinger and tugged down on it.

"Hey birthday boy, you may not know this, but you're in my house, in my living room. That means I've got all the rights, understand?"

"Yeah, man, yeah."

"The lady you just accosted is my guest. In fact, she's the only person who was invited here tonight." I kept all my weight against him. "Two things. First, you apologize to her, then you split, got it?"

Beads of sweat curled off his forehead and streaked his temples and jaw. "Got it. I'm cool, I swear. Lemme go."

I took a step back. He faced the wall, rubbing his face and nose, and turned to Phoebe. "Sorry."

Phoebe barely looked at him. "All right," she said.

He glared at me for an instant, and I saw a combustible mix of hatred and humiliation brewing behind his beady eyes, but he'd lost his nerve. "Later," I said, holding the front door open.

Phoebe brushed the hair off her forehead and tucked in the front flap of her shirt.

"Punk," I said. "The kind of guy that experiences a major testosterone surge with his second beer."

She eyed me as if wary of something new. "You looked like you were having a surge of your own. I didn't know you were so readily prone to violence."

"Readily prone? Pheebs, you've got it all wrong."

"No, no, I'm impressed," she said. "A little shaky, but impressed." I put an arm around her shoulder. She was quivering. "You're full of surprises tonight," Phoebe said.

I didn't know whether to draw encouragement or despair from her last remark, but I knew our intimate evening was beginning to resemble many former, typically doomed romantic campaigns. "I'll have this under control in five minutes," I said.

A burst of raucous laughter rained down from the second floor. We stood at the foot of the staircase, which rose in fourteen straight steps along the house's center-dividing wall to a small landing above the living room.

"We've got to find Jackie," I said.

"Really," Phoebe said. "I'm not so sure I want to meet him."

"He'll help wind this thing down in a hurry," I said. I led Phoebe to the upstairs hallway and my bedroom, which, to my relief, was empty save for two girls in their late teens. They sat on the edge of the bed, quietly leafing through a surf magazine together.

"It's getting late, ladies," I said through the doorway. "Time to go." They put down the magazine and left without protest.

The heavy action was going on across the hall, in my mother's old room. "One, two, three!" The cheer came from the outside balcony. I stopped at the bedroom door and drew a heavy breath.

"Come on, aren't we going in?" Phoebe said.

It's not as if I dress up in my mom's clothes or have long chats with empty chairs when I'm in her room, which is seldom. I'd just never been able to pack up all her things and convert the space to another purpose. To me, this was still her old room. A long time ago, when at eighteen I was safe to move back home on my own, I tried to erase her presence by boxing up her belongings and storing them in the attic. But I hadn't the resolve to finish the job. I kept picturing her returning, gazing at an empty room, a good life prematurely dismantled by a son who'd given up on her. Or perhaps it was she who'd given up on her son, a boy who, as he grew into a man, reminded her daily of her dead husband. A sad reminder, so sad that eventually the boy's company became simply too much for her to bear.

"Was this your mother's bedroom?" Phoebe asked.

"It's a spare."

She took in the armoire, the antique dresser, the vanity along the far wall. "Oh. Looks like the master bedroom to me. J., how long ago did you say your mother—"

"Look—he's out on the balcony," I said, anxious to end Phoebe's line of questioning.

Through the open sliding glass door, I could see a huddle of young surfers outside, some wearing nothing more than shorts, tees and open Pendeltons against the late-night chill. Together, they formed a tight circle, and their backs rose and dipped in unison. The smiling face of a bald black man in a white dress shirt and loose necktie rose above them, dropped, then rose again, bouncing like a ball in the center of the circle.

Jackie Pace, the master of ceremonies, commanded the balcony at the place where the railings formed a V, his legs splayed like a rodeo rider straddling a bull-chute as he presided over the festivities. His face was that of a wild-child, a feckless explorer intoxicated with the freedom of the moment yet, at the same time, tempered by a fierce bent to move on to the next conquest. At forty-two, it was still a face of considerable youth and formidable intelligence.

Jackie was dressed in his usual straight-legged black jeans and faded black alligator-skin cowboy boots. A white V-neck tee stretched flat across his chest as if it was concealing two steel plates, the rolled sleeves resting high on his sinewy arms. His wavy, medium-blond hair curled between the widow's peak on his tanned forehead, hooked neatly behind his ears and grazed the square of his shoulders. As usual, his eyes were hidden behind a pair of black wraparound shades, but I knew them to be a startling, impudent blue. A dark, carefully trimmed mustache curled down to his chin like a claw. Combined with the small tuft of beard just beneath his lower lip, the mustache gave his face a mildly menacing slant.

"What's that on his head?" Phoebe said.

With a final touch of the outrageous rather typical of the man, he'd fitted on his dome a black paper pirate's hat fashioned from a folded Captain's Galley kiddy menu.

"This ship is mine!" he roared in a thick pirate's brogue. "Make no mistake, lads: them that sails with me shall do my bidding!" A chorus of whoops went up beneath his feet.

They were using a blanket to toss the man into the air by snapping it tight, then slackening it to catch him. To my horror, I realized the blanket was not one of the extras stacked in the hall closet but the quilt from my mother's bed, a lacy, hand-stitched beauty her great aunt Miluca had toiled over for months before proudly presenting it to her as a wedding present. This was too much. I pushed out onto the balcony just as they gathered themselves to send the man airborne another time. "One!" they counted, dipping and rising together. "Two!"

"Put down the quilt!" I shouted. "It belongs to Marielena Shepard!"

Why I blurted my mother's name to a bunch of kids who were probably still drooling toddlers when she was last seen, I will never know.

"Marielena Shepard?" Jackie said.

"Put it down," I said.

"Aye, mates," Jackie said, "ya flipped enough cakes to feed the crew fer a week! Fine work, lads, but yer dooties be done fer now."

Jackie's suntanned buccaneers loosened their grip on the quilt and gently released the African man onto the decking just outside the sliding glass doors. He rolled himself over a few times until he was at our feet, face down in a drunken heap.

"Show's over, Long John," I said over my shoulder to Jackie.

"Aye, maties," he said with mild resignation, "Master Shepard's returned to reclaim the ship, and with a fine lass in tow I might add. We best be making port 'fore a tempest starts a brewing." The crew disbanded and the onlookers slowly dispersed. Jackie leapt from the railings and landed before us both. "Aye, mate!" He got me in a headlock and hugged me. Phoebe stood by, the passive observer. "How about an intro, Master J.," he said, smiling at Phoebe.

Before I could oblige, a blast of whining machinery and hooting came from the kitchen below. "Come on!" I shouted to Jackie. We tore downstairs, leaving Phoebe behind.

"Look at me, I'm locked in the barrel!" A sloe-eyed surf punk known as Stone Me Stevie crouched on the dishwashing machine's open door as it sagged nearly to the floor beneath his weight. He was shirtless and stripped down to a pair of shorts and slip-on tennies. His wiry frame was compressed into a tube-riding surfing stance as the glass-holder carousel spun madly, shooting jets of water over his head and across the room.

"Shut it off!" I yelled at a half-soaked cohort of Stevie's who was stationed next to the machine, laughing uncontrollably. He didn't budge, so I stepped closer and took a shot of water across the face and chest. "Now!"

Stevie's pal reached into the machine and jiggled something inside, and the motor shut off. At the same instant, the door's hinges moaned and broke, sending Stevie to the floor in a splash of steaming water.

The kitchen door burst open and Britt stormed in, blowing by us to collar Stevie and the other kid. "You little kooks are dead!" he shouted into their startled faces.

I wiped the water from my eyes with my shirtsleeve. "Just take them home," I said.

Britt kept his hands clamped on both their necks. "Don't worry, ladies," he said, "I'll be taking this out on you in the water. Any wave you paddle for is mine. You kooks will get no quarter at the pier." He shoved them through the kitchen door and followed them into the night.

The hinges jutted from the dishwasher like a pair of badly broken fingers. "That is just too out of hand, man," Jackie offered after a prolonged silence.

Phoebe walked into the kitchen and leaned against the far counter, looking like she'd had about enough of this little surprise get-together.

"Who's the major talent, brah?" Jackie whispered, taking in a full view of her curves. "You must've done some heavy spadework. She's a fucking goddess."

"Gee, thanks," I whispered back. "And to think, this was going to be our first night alone together. That is, until you and your three-ring circus blew into town."

"No worries," he said, his eyes lighting with a new scheme. "Jackie will fix all."

"Jack, no, don't!" I stuttered, but I wasn't quick enough, and he straightened up to meet Phoebe's eyes with a boldness that only fools or unreasonably handsome men like himself can muster when addressing a beautiful woman.

Jackie bowed gently, extending his hand to Phoebe. "Permit me to introduce myself properly, my sweet," he said. "John Hampton

Pace, the Third—not that anyone's counting," he added, "but I'd like it if you'd call me Jackie."

Phoebe was keeping her distance and seemed flustered by the grandeur of Jackie's self-introduction. "Nice to meet you," she said, tilting on her heels.

"My sincerest apologies to you for interrupting your special night with J."

"Special night?" Phoebe glared at me. "What did J. tell you?"

"Why, only that the two of you had a quiet evening alone in store, and, forgive me for being so bold, but I can see that an exclusive rendezvous with someone as fetching as yourself would be special indeed. I do apologize for this most unfortunate intrusion on your plans."

"Intrusion? I think it's called breaking and entering," Phoebe said. She retreated a step and cast a full-length glance at Jackie, her hands on her hips and chin raised imperiously. Facing off toe-to-toe, the two of them were of equal height.

"Well, now," he said, "I won't quibble about the legalities of the situation, but I should point out that this little gathering was totally spontaneous, and these good-natured young ruffians will clear out in no time flat if I give them the signal."

"Give it to them, Jack," I said.

Phoebe sighed. "I feel tired. I'm going home."

From the moment she and I arrived I had feared it would come to this. "Pheebs," I pleaded.

"Oh no, no, you can't go!" Jackie insisted. "Please, my dear." He eased her from the door. "You must stay a little longer, really, I mean it. You see, I've just returned from an extended sojourn abroad, and I've brought my old friend J. a gift tonight, a very precious gift, so fine it simply has to be shared among a select few friends. And who better for us to share it with than you."

Phoebe glanced at me as if for guidance, but I had no idea where this was going and merely shrugged.

"All right," he said, as if we'd just sweated a closely guarded secret out of him, "it's an extremely rare and valuable bottle of sherry, given to me by an itinerant bureaucrat from the British government. We met during a rather nasty sandstorm not far from the Skeleton

Coast. His Land Rover was in a ditch, night was falling and a rather sizable pack of hyenas was loitering in the dunes nearby, eyeing the poor chap's sunburned limbs like so many choice cuts hanging in a meat-market window." He raised an eyebrow at Phoebe. "Brazen little beasts. Noisy as hell, too. Anyway, you could say the old dog was forever grateful to me for the bit of winch wizardry I performed to pull him out and deliver him from harm's way."

"It's late," Phoebe said, trying to look bored, but I knew a part of her was digging Jackie's attention.

"So it is," said Jackie, "so it is. You know, I think it's time I leveled with you."

"Jack, please," I said, "enough." I'd never known Jackie Pace to lay bare his true feelings, so naturally I was highly skeptical.

"No, J., I must," he said.

"Let him say his piece, J.," Phoebe insisted. "I want to hear it."

"My dear," he said, "there's a woman upstairs, her name is Fiona, and while she may not be a jaw-dropping betty like you, she does know the words to a song or two about a man like me and—how can I say this?—she knows about the music that can make a man like old Jack crazy. And that's a good thing, no doubt about it."

"A good thing, right," I said. "Maybe Phoebe and I should—"

"Oh yeah, Fiona wants to make me sing tonight," Jackie said as if I wasn't there. "And myself? Well, suffice it to say, time passes mighty slowly in West Africa when it's just you and a coyote crooning a lonely ditty at the moon. A man begins to see the world through a different prism, a window of intense longing, of skewed desire. Your mind begins to warp. Strange thoughts take hold, strange . . . possibilities, if you will. In time, even the wild animals start to look good. You find yourself—"

"Hell of a story!" I said, stepping between them before he could spool out any more wisdom on the topic of unbridled lust. But Jackie wasn't finished.

"Out of my way, J.," Phoebe said, her eyes on Jackie.

"Just picture it!" he exhorted her. "You and J. and Fiona and me, reclining comfortably and toasting away, our glasses brimming with those brilliant libations. Van Morrison commanding the stereo, revealing the romance of the soul to us. Forgive me, but"—he seared me with a look of unbridled enthusiasm—"I can feel it in the air, and you can too, J., I know it! My sweet, this is going to be a slam-fest to remember!"

Phoebe's jaw went slack. "Good night, J.," she said at last, hiking her overnight bag on her shoulder. As she reached the door, she turned as if to say something to Jackie, whom I guessed was still savoring the thought of an impromptu orgy behind those dark shades and a lunatic grin. But apparently she thought better of it and instead stalked through the kitchen door.

I ran out behind her, catching her at the back gate. "Pheebs, wait!"

"I'm going home now, J.," she said. "Let me go."

"Babe, wait. Jackie's a bit of a wild man, but he's—"

"It's all right. I don't care about him."

"Then stay," I pleaded. "He's leaving, right now. They all are."

She dropped her bag, car keys still in hand. "It's not just the party. It's everything." Checking her leather boots instead of my eyes. "It's you."

This sounded familiar—and very bad. "Tell me," I said. "Please."

She dug her hands into her jeans pockets and traced an invisible line on the brick walkway with her toe. "I don't really know much about you, do I?"

"What do you need to know?" I said. "I'll tell you now. You name it."

She shook her head and flipped a wave of amber hair off her shoulder. "It doesn't work that way, J. You know that."

I felt my defenses kicking in. "This is about your father, isn't it? He told you I popped off on him. I can explain that."

"No," she said. "He doesn't like any of the men I date. I told you that months ago. Daddy is just . . . Daddy."

"I was going to tell you about the D.A. job sooner, when it was a done deal. When I finish this baby-selling case, I'm through with dependency."

"I care about you, I do. You're a nice guy, J."

Her last words signified that the situation was hopeless. "Wait," I said, waving her off. "If you don't mind, I don't think I deserve the 'nice guy' speech."

My hopes of a miraculous save with this girl were deflating. I felt drained. "Sorry about Jackie and all this," I said.

"Don't apologize for him. At least he's not shy about saying what's on his mind."

A car backfired out on Porpoise Way. We watched a white rabbit leap from a bush near the kitchen door and dart across the yard. Some neighbor's pet, on the loose. Just then I felt tired of the close proximity of these beach lots to one another and wished I lived alone, on some windswept mesa out in the desert. I dreaded the thought of going to work again Monday, swimming into that stream of humanity, breathing through a straw in my teeth. I wanted to turn inward quietly, be left to myself, in need of no one. But I felt that tug in my chest for Phoebe beyond all reason. I wasn't going anywhere.

"I like your way," she went on. "You've been good to me, understanding. But my mother's gone and I'm over it."

"Come on," I said, "that's not all I have to offer."

Phoebe opened the gate and we both stepped through it, the latch clattering behind us. "I won't argue with you about that," she said. "But it's what you do best. Look at these friends of yours. You're the same with them."

I was not prepared to let her drive away without some signal about where we stood. "So then, what do you want to do?"

She kissed me lightly on the lips. "Good-bye, J."

Jackie was slumped against the Formica counter next to the dishwasher when I came back inside. I held up my hands. "A slam-fest to remember? Nice touch, slick."

"A minor miscalculation, I admit, Master J.," he said.

"Jesus, cut me some slack. No more Pirates of the Caribbean tonight."

"The scabbard is stowed."

I tried to smile. "The cartoon never ends. Tell me, how long have you been locked into this comic book persona of yours?"

"Cartoon?" He shook his head. "Nugatory, my friend. I like to think of myself as possessing a fresh perspective on a world that's lost its capacity to be fresh." He tipped his shades and shot me a rascally wink.

"Hey, Meesta Jackaay mon!" a drunken African voice wailed from the breakfast room. "Need more beer, mon. More da hot wings, and da tacos, too!"

"I want them out of my house—now," I said.

"You got it, brother," he said. "We will leave you in peace."

I knew he was playing me but I was too tired to offer up resistance. "You know I don't mean you."

"Ho, thank you, man. You don't know how much it means—"

"Save it," I said, bending to pick up the badly tweaked dishwasher door, then handing it to him. "Here's the deal. You're welcome to stay with me until you head off on your next adventure, but this time, you're gonna pay your way around here."

He shrugged as if I was asking for a miracle. "You know I'm operating on extremely limited fundage, boss."

"Then you'll work it off."

Jackie tapped his fingers on the dishwasher's control buttons. "Sorry, man, but fixing appliances isn't my gig."

I smiled at the misguided nature of his gambit. "Oh, no. No way are you getting off that easily," I said.

"Then what do you want me to do?"

"I don't know yet," I said, pausing to consider the kitchen in its present chaos. My new client, Sue Ellen Randall, instantly came to mind. Her tangled little mess, an ugly scene for all involved. One child, four would-be, wannabe parents, the irony of such a situation in a court system bursting with discarded minors. No easy resolution in sight, no matter what the great Nelson Gilbride promised on the side, the little snake. If we went to trial he'd be smart and relentless. I would have to do a lot of legwork—not all of it behind a desk—to have a chance. I would need help, maybe from Jackie.

"Hey, where'd ya go, chief?" Jackie said. "You're spacing."

I snapped back into focus. "Don't worry," I told him, "I'll think of something." I folded my arms like a parent. "You owe me."

I thought he was going to laugh me off, and his head rolled back the way it does just before he flings a comeback at you, but he let it pass. "No shit."

That night, long after we put the Africans in a cab to their hotel, I lay in bed and stared wide-eyed at the ceiling, counting empty beer cans in a futile attempt to unwind. Thinking about that last conversation with my friend, thinking . . . Jackie owing me—what a concept.

Jackie Pace was arguably the greatest and most influential modern surfer California has ever seen. He was certainly the only celebrity that Christianitos, our hometown, has ever produced.

In the sixties, the long, sliding point break stage at Malibu was the performance epicenter of the West Coast. Longboarders on nine-sixes perched and posed-on-the-nose and arched their backs deep into the Cove like the shiny, winged hood ornaments you see on classic cars. Casual flow was the standard of excellence.

Jackie bought into none of it. Like my father (and later, me), he'd learned to surf in local beach break that jacked and dumped far more violently than the elegant lines fanning the point at Malibu. Here, the rides were short, steep and intense, requiring a series of quick, hard turns. Maneuverability was essential in a beach break board. At fifteen, Jackie was easily the hottest young rider at the pier, with a forceful, slashing style and uncanny wave judgment, but he was frustrated with the stiffness and excess bulk of the modern longboard. Malibu offered no alternatives—too crowded already, and too tough a hierarchy for an unknown, down-souther kid to crack. Besides, style-conscious cruising was of no interest to Jackie. So he decided on a different approach, a superior approach that would demand a superior wave-riding vehicle.

Jackie turned to a local shaper, Chas Lingus, to build the equipment he envisioned. Chas, a former navy pilot who shaped out of an old airplane hangar a few miles inland, was a true eccentric, a guy who thought nothing of strapping himself to the wing of a friend's aircraft to test one of his theories on aerodynamic flow. Another time Chas had sailed a tiny skiff across the Pacific to chart the migration of Southern Hemisphere–bound whales—alone. Though he had a small, hardcore following of customers around town, Chas's reputation wasn't such that a collaborative effort with a young upstart like Jackie would harm his credibility, and like Jackie, he loved to try new things.

The two worked in relative secrecy for months, Jackie test-riding alone at first light while Chas squatted in the sand with an old Nikon 35 slung around his neck, drawing light sketches in a tiny notepad. The first few boards were about seven-six—radically short for the times—with narrower, scaled-down nose and tail areas that departed greatly from the standard longboard outline. Jackie was thrilled with the reduction in length, but the boards paddled poorly and pearled (nosed under) a lot, and when, on the first morning of a big summer south he snapped both boards in an hour following back-to-back wipeouts, he was resigned to starting over entirely.

But Chas continued to take notes. A few days later, he answered with a board with more rocker (bottom curve) in the nose and tail to counter the pearling effect, and a raked-back skeg that resembled a dolphin's dorsal fin—the result of a long-time side project—to provide better acceleration out of turns. Jackie took to the new design immediately and on the next sizable swell, beneath a mob of spectators on the pier, he was drawing radical lines that had been as yet unimaginable.

He surfed with a vengeance on the boards Chas shaped, his deep-carving style virtually redefining the limits of stand-up wave riding. Where before, the best surfers had been content to draw mostly horizontal lines across unbroken faces, Jackie attacked vertically, screeching off the bottom and blasting straight up into the breaking lip, then redirecting with huge power-hooks of frightening force. He was arguably the first surfer ever to attempt to impose his will over a wave, and with his catlike agility and phenomenal sense of balance, more often than not he brought it off.

Jackie was a competitive machine as well back then. He won the World Amateur Contest in France in 'sixty-six and took the U.S. Surfing Championships at Huntington pier the next two years. Nearly every other lesser event he entered he simply won going away. Every new surf movie devoted at least one meaty segment to Jackie's prodigious riding, and surfers in darkened auditoriums up and down the coast hooted in unison at his astounding moves in California beach breaks and big Hawaiian conditions alike. Orders for "Pace potato chips" poured in, forcing the big-name surfboard manufacturers to embrace the breakthrough technology developed by Chas and Jackie almost overnight. (Rather typically, Chas had developed a newfound passion for mountain climbing by then and wasn't around to cash in.) By his eighteenth birthday, Jackie was the most widely imitated surfer in the world. "Live to surf" was his unabashed credo. No obstacles, he believed, should ever stand in the way of the quest for good waves.

The ideal itself was nothing new, at least not in California. In the decades following the Second World War, a lot of disconnected young men cruised the coast, sleeping in old station wagons and panel vans and even on the sand so they could rise early to greet the surf. My own father and his friends spent years chasing waves with few concerns beyond when the next swell might arrive and what the wind and tide would be like when it did. But Jackie carried the quest farther than anyone else, it seemed, never wavering from his stance as the rest inevitably did when adult responsibility came calling. To this day he has consciously foregone any trappings of a conventional life—wife, kids, career, mortgage—to pursue his passion.

How a man now backing his way into middle age can continue, as he has, to travel the world in search of clean, unspoiled surf, is one of the sport's enduring topics of debate. Some say Jackie is nothing more than a glorified con man and horrendous moocher. Others mutter about trust-fund dollars (Jackie never speaks of his family, but it's rumored that they're moneyed folk). A few who claim to know him believe he gets by as a welcome guest to a legion of well-placed friends who are charmed by his quick wit, his ever-inventive comic verbiage and his status as a bonafide surfing legend. My guess is all of the above, though I know little about his family ties. But to quibble over details is to miss the point, because with Jackie, the stance is the thing.

One of his early schemes illustrates this truth nicely. In 'sixty-nine, his letter from the draft board came, and with a single, random lottery pick, all the chicks and parties and contests and good times were poised to disappear overnight. But Jack was unfazed; he plotted. A few days later he blew into a packed induction center passing out tiny American flags and saluting everyone in sight. He also sported a pair of black-framed glasses with Coke-bottle thick lenses (on loan from a nearsighted, elderly pier wino) and orthopedic shoes that looked like Frankenstein's. In his front shirt pocket he carried an inhaler, which he sucked on like a pacifier every minute or so to ward off asthma attacks. His long blond hair was mostly hidden, piled up beneath a chin-strapped vintage leather football helmet on his head. Jackie kept his eyes crossed through two physicals, and wept convincingly when the examining M.D. broke the news that a sight-impaired lad with an eggshell skull would best do his duty by fighting the war on the home front. Despite his dizzying surfing fame, Jackie was certain no one on the army staff would recognize him, and he was right. "Told you Uncle Sam didn't surf," he reportedly cracked to an astonished pier crew the next morning as he stroked past them and into a building peak.

What is not debatable is that I owe him. Major.

Almost thirteen years ago, Jackie Pace plucked me from a torrential sweep of whitewater as I gasped for breath and clawed at a spinning gray sky. I was alone on a big-wave reef half a mile from shore and had lost my board in a heavy rip. My shoulders ached and my arms hung from them like dead weight. My calves were cramping with vicelike compression from the persistent cold. In all likelihood I was dying when Jackie appeared seemingly out of nowhere.

Since that day we've become odd friends, stalwart in our alliance to each other yet at the same time wary of forming the kind of deep ties that might lead to disappointment and loss. We circle each other cannily, respecting the distance that lies between our disparate existences and content not to press closer. In spite of all the banter, a good deal is left unspoken.

What more could I have expected from such a famously unrepentant hedonist as Jackie Pace? He's a loner. But he is my oldest friend, consistent in his loyalty, and through the string of empty years following my mother's departure, all the birthdays come and gone and holidays passed on without celebration, this has counted for plenty.

The faint sound of a TV sports report drifted upstairs. Rubbing my tired eyes, I blinked, and in the dark shapes across the ceiling I saw the scene out on the balcony again, Jackie perched on the railings, barking orders, my mother's quilt pulled taut by twenty grabbing hands and the weight of a happy inebriate. I closed my eyes, ready for sleep, and felt that certain restlessness of the soul that always accompanies my oldest friend's presence.

Five

Holly Dupree's three-part report on the Randall case began Monday night, following a weekend of Channel Six promos hyping the controversy. There was cuddly little Nathan, writhing like an earthworm on a gorgeous Oriental rug in the Danforth home while some announcer's voice-over spun off an alliterative gem about bouncing baby boys on the black market. Cut to the horrid birth mother, rushing past the camera in a parking lot somewhere, shielding her face like a newly indicted Mafioso. Now back to Nathan's chubby smile, a drop of drool on his chin, and ponder how his parents could have ever willingly parted with him. Holly would tell all at six and eleven. I was hooked.

Just watching the little cherub squirm and coo made me feel disloyal to my client, Sue Ellen Randall, the woman who'd relinquished an angel. I felt glad Nathan was too young to comprehend what Sue Ellen had done, the trade-offs she'd made. But there was no give-and-take about Holly Dupree's dissection of my client. Indian giver, manipulator, baby seller, fraud. Anything but mother. Monday night I sat on the edge of my bed, the walls pulsating with an icy TV glow, and I pasted a few typical Dupree labels on Marielena Shepard for size. Deserter, victimizer, weakling, coward. Anything but mother. My anger left me staring at the ceiling in bed well past 2 A.M. I knew the Matter of Nathan Randall, a Minor, would be my most important case to date.

Most of my cases are outright losers, so I advocate hard but always keep something in reserve, as if I'm working a trapeze routine with one eye on a safety net below. My clients are usually too confused and distracted by their own fucked-up situations to notice if I should grab for a ring and miss. But in this case everyone would be watching—Holly Dupree, Nelson Gilbride, Willow Reece, old Bill

Davenport, Phoebe and Jackie—and I was mildly paralyzed by a newfound fear of heights.

By Tuesday I had no choice but to sit still and crank out an opposition to Gilbride's motion for de facto parent status for the Danforths. Court was unusually slow. I'd picked up only two new clients, a waiflike teen mom with a runny nose and a nasty crack habit and a dour Filipino father whose "tough love" methods of corporal punishment had a distinctly medieval flavor. Both detention hearings were decided quickly, Foley ignoring my doomed arguments with equal dispatch. I was back in the Legal Project offices well before noon, determined to blaze into the tiny law library at the end of the hall, clear the mess of unshelved law books and discarded coffee cups from the wooden conference table and conjure a brilliant response to Gilbride's opening salvo. So ingenious, so spirited would be my motion that it would tilt the balance of the Nathan Randall proceedings in our favor for all time. I was upbeat, even buoyant. No distractions could sway me from my purpose.

Until I passed the door to my crammed, file-box-laden office and saw the red message button on my phone blinking like a motel sign on a lonely highway.

Had Phoebe called?

Fragile, beautiful Phoebe. I'd been ringing her since Saturday with no response, catching only her recorded message—the friendly greeting and banal suggestion that just for today I give miles of smiles. The memory of Friday's grand fiasco still smarted like hell. Pheebs would be flying to Hong Kong in a few days and I wanted to talk to her so badly I was certain my life depended on it. I felt like the guy in the old cartoon poster, the dude with his head up his arse and the wry caption, "Your problem is obvious." Lonely for a woman who said she didn't want me. Unwilling to let go of a hopeless situation. Yearning to tell her I loved her yet unsure if I really did. My problem was obvious.

There was one message on the tape. "Mr. Shepard, h-hey . . . m-man." A young man's voice, skittish and probably boosted by an amphetamine high. "It's me, man. Gotta talk to you about my case, ya know, the program, visitation. Oh, gotta talk about some other shit that came up. Call me."

That was it. No case name, no return phone number. Another no-name client who thought my job revolved around his shit that came up.

Nelson Gilbride knew his motion was shaky. "Equity and the pursuit of justice," his argument concluded, "dictate that the Danforths, as de facto parents, be allowed to participate in all stages of the proceedings, especially at trial, so that they may readily assist the Court in its fact-finding mission." Equity is an attorney's last refuge for argument not supported by law. I'd learned this lesson years ago, clerking for Gilbride's firm. At times I was tasked with preparing baseless motions with just enough substance to provide a launching pad for the man's considerable oratory gifts. Equity came in very handy.

I wrote my response in half an hour, the law on my side. Gilbride's motion would fail, but he was fighting for something else, which was to keep Nathan Randall with the Danforths for as long as possible. My real battle with Gilbride would be over the slippery concept of "bonding."

Young children naturally take to—and depend upon—whoever consistently cares for them. The problem for my typical client is that if her child is removed from her custody, the child will immediately begin to bond with the new caretaker. Some experts believe that as time passes and a strong new child/caretaker bond has formed, removal of the child for return to the parent can be devastating for the child because that new bond is shattered. In cases in which a new bond has formed over an extended period of time, the county has actually argued that the child should not be returned to the parent at all. Because the "best interest of the child" is paramount, judges sometimes listen.

I pondered the bonding question from my own experience. I'd felt the pain of a severed bond as a first grader when my father died suddenly. That day, I was painstakingly hand-sanding the rail of a vintage surfboard he was restoring, hoping to finish the job that weekend and collect my five-dollar fee. The fiver was going to buy me two cans of red metal-flake paint to paint my bike, a secondhand Schwinn Stingray coated with beach-town rust. He was going to help strip the metal, show me how to mask off the chrome parts that didn't need paint. I never so much as looked at that piece of shit bike again.

My mother's disappearing act was more nebulous. I was older and had lived through some disappointments by then, but that was only half of it. All these years later I still didn't know what to make of Marielena Shepard and what she did to me; I never learned what really happened, or why. The whole subject was as disorienting as pea-soup coastal fog in June.

Somewhere down the hall Willow Reece was picking up a conversation with another attorney about a drug program that catered to minors. Jesus Christ, I thought, what kind of world. Fighting nausea, I closed the door and gulped a few deep breaths. Then I shoved my mother out of my mind for the ten-thousandth time and picked up the Randall file.

Unlike me, Nathan Randall was barely four months old now, so young he'd probably be capable of bonding with his mother one week, the Danforths the next, and a pack of wolves the week after that. A completely dependent little infant wouldn't know any better. Nathan couldn't differentiate between a bed in a homeless shelter and the leather seats in a twelve-cylinder Jaguar coupe, he just needed to cling to another for sustenance. But for now he'd spent every day of his short life bonding with the Danforths, and Nelson Gilbride would soon have the finest expert money could buy instructing Foley that in terms of bonding, Nathan Randall had already passed the point of no return. My objective was to see Nathan delivered back into Sue Ellen Randall's waiting arms as quickly as possible.

I got to court early Thursday morning, hoping to slide past the Channel Six cameras with a minimum of friction, yet ready with a few well-rehearsed jabs of my own just in case. It was a little before 8 A.M. and Holly was not in the building. Neither was Sue Ellen, who I'd hoped would show up early to meet me. Like Phoebe, Sue Ellen hadn't called me back. There was much to discuss, such as whether she'd found a place to live. Whether her husband, Ty, was out of jail. Whether she'd made preparations to receive Nathan today if Foley was inclined to award custody to her. I'd read the petition again and again. The county's case was all hype and hyperbole. If Sue Ellen made a strong showing this time, Foley just might return Nathan to her before sorting out the allegations.

After last week's debacle, I was ready to deliver some good news, too, the very real likelihood that Gilbride would be sidelined if we went to trial. I was pleased with my opposition to his motion. Sue Ellen needed my encouragement. If we were going to win Nathan back, we'd have to work fast, and as a team.

There was also the matter of Gilbride's offer. We should hear him out, I'd advise her, consider every option. Perhaps the adoption could be salvaged, the criminal charges dropped, the dependency matter dismissed without engaging in heavy warfare. I would make Sue Ellen listen.

Foley finished his 8:30 calendar-call in ten short minutes. Only Belinda McWhirter was present for the Randall case. I shuffled out with the rest of the daily horde to look for Sue Ellen again. Instead, I found Darla Madden.

"Good to see you, sharp suit!" she said. She was wearing another big, billowing gown, a pink and orange Hawaiian print that made her look like a walking flowerbed.

I frowned. "You're not on today's calendar. What are you doing here?"

Darla looked miffed. "Man, thanks for the warm reception. Having another bad day Mr. Shepard?"

"Look," I said, "I'm very busy. You can't just show up like this."

She folded her arms. "I'm your client."

I stared back at her. "I've got a lot of clients." She didn't budge. "Okay, what do you need?"

She paused long enough to give herself away. "Thought maybe we could talk about my domestic arrangements."

I didn't believe her. "Guess what, I have a phone."

"Ya never pick up."

"Leave a message." I was still looking for Holly Dupree and her crew, and Sue Ellen.

"They're outside," Darla said. Obviously, she was tuned in to the Randall case, too.

I stood there and just stared at her, disgusted. "I knew it. Listen, you can't be a spectator. These cases are confidential. Besides, it's none of your—"

"That news lady asked me if I knew you!" she said. "You seen her face close up? Boy, howdy! Never noticed those wrinkles around her eyes before when I seen her on TV. Those crow's feet are a bitch. Bet she's a smoker. I use Oil of Olay morning and night. Crucial step in my daily beautification and maintenance."

"What did the news lady want to know?" I said.

"Don't worry, she didn't hear nothin' from me! But some old geezer in a fancy suit showed up out of nowhere and the camera guy ran to him like he was hypnotized."

"Nelson Gilbride," I said. "I'd better get down there."

"The lawyer, he mentioned you," she said before I could break away.

"What did he say?"

"Oh, some stuff about justice, respect for the law. Said you couldn't keep him out of some case because the truth needed to be told—yeah, he was going to see that the truth be told. And he was talking about the gal who sold her baby being brought to justice. You ever heard of somebody selling their own baby?" She glanced about again before looking me straight in the eye.

"Yeah," I said. "We've covered this territory before."

"Mr. Shepard?" A familiar female voice called out behind me. I turned and saw Sue Ellen standing by the door to Foley's courtroom, looking pretty tuned up for this time of day. Slowly she made her way over to Darla and me.

Darla didn't notice Sue Ellen. "What kinda' mother is that, would sell her own child?" she raved. "That is sick! I hope they lock up the little bitch 'n' throw away the key!"

Sue Ellen stopped cold five feet away from us, quivered at Darla's remark, then burst into tears. Her eyes said "How could you?" to me. Then she turned and fled.

"Way to go," I said to Darla.

"Sick, sick, sick. Just throw away the key, I tell ya!"

It was so simple to feel that way about the case, about any woman who would abandon her own. Too simple.

"You're wrong," I said. "Things aren't always what they seem." I looked away, searching the congested hallway for any sign of Sue Ellen. I should have met her early and brought her in through the back entrance. Holly Dupree and crew were more than Sue Ellen could manage alone. They'd probably already knocked her down before Darla piled on.

Darla looked down her nose at me, her mascara-ringed eyes widening as if she'd just made an important connection. "Oh."

I exhaled and didn't suck another breath, my lungs slowly heating to a burn. "Gee, Darla, sick is a pretty strong word, don't you think? Some people might think making two kids live in a pigsty like that apartment of yours is sick, too. But hey, who am I to pass judgment? Tell me, Mom, you shovel all the dog turds off the carpet before you left this morning?"

The tears came immediately. "I, I'm sorry. I'm n . . . not a bad mom. I love my kids."

She was suddenly like a child who'd been scolded by Daddy. But Darla could not be faulted too severely for feeling the way she did about the Randall mess. She carried her guilt like an anchor, as my own mother must have done after she'd ditched me. The notion of Darla Madden and my mother having a significant shared experience darkened my mood.

My vision blurred momentarily. Marielena, Sue Ellen, Darla scooping poop after breakfast, heavy parental guilt. Not even 9 A.M. yet, and I felt dead on my feet. I blinked hard. This job had become a matinee horror show. My clients didn't listen, but neither did I. I'd become a robot, stuck in an endless routine of empty gestures.

"Of course you love your kids," I told Darla. "That old geezer you saw downstairs was giving the cameras a watered-down version of the truth. The lady isn't sick, and she didn't sell her baby. She gave him up for adoption, but changed her mind about it. Now she wants him back. That's it."

Then, rather inexplicably, I found myself rehearsing a few bits and pieces of the argument I'd planned for the Randall hearing today. Nelson Gilbride was very, very good. I'd heard the stories when I clerked at his law firm, seen the view from the forty-fifth floor of his beautifully appointed offices. Heaven help me, I thought, I'm out of my depth.

My knees wobbled. "We're going to win," I said, pissing into the wind. "Excuse me, Darla, but I have to go find my client."

"She went to the ladies room," Darla said. "I saw her go in. Been watching the hall down there. She hasn't come back."

"Okay," I said. "I've got a minute. Want to talk about your current progress?"

"Not really."

"Me neither." My mind was on Sue Ellen and Gilbride, Phoebe, the D.A.'s office—anything but Darla's problems. "But you're here. We should anyway."

We talked briefly about Uncle Pete, Eric and Stacy, the apartment and Max the Rottweiler. "Go home," I told her when we were finished. "I don't want to see you in here again until your case is back on calendar. Good luck. Now leave."

"But, can't ya get me in to the hearing? I gotta know how it turns out."

The situation was hopeless. "Sorry Darla," I said. "The box office is totally sold out."

The Sheriff's Department had processed Ty Randall's transport papers correctly this time, and he was led into a small holding cell behind Foley's courtroom some time after 10 A.M. When Shelly Chilcott, the court liaison, heard Ty had arrived, she quickly made up another file and motioned to Boris Kousnetsov to come pick it up.

"For me?" Kousnetsov leaned over with a crooked smile, his teeth a tobacco-stained, canine yellow.

"You've got Father," Shelly told Boris, handing him the file. "He's in lock-up. Oh, and talk to J. 'cause he's got Mother."

Boris shuffled back to the small gallery and sat down again on the bench in front of mine, a cloud of cherry cough syrup and Old Spice settling back in with him. He straightened his black suit coat and swiveled to see me. "Did you hear, Mr. Shepard? We are working together. We will discuss our strategies, as lawyers must do." He nodded eagerly.

"Absolutely," I said. When he turned away, I shot Shelly the dirtiest look I could muster.

As I came and went from the courtroom over the next half hour, busy with other cases, Boris pored over the Nathan Randall file like a jeweler studying a mound of glittering stones. I guess he could afford the luxury of time since his triple bypass surgery last January had gutted his caseload so deeply. Boris was not renowned for his courtroom mettle and his seventy-four-year-old body was falling apart, his eyes failing, his knees and elbows crimped with arthritis. Yet he still possessed a spark and managed to hobble into court each day to handle a case or two, do some crosswords, and read from the books he carried with him in his otherwise empty briefcase. Though he never spoke of his family, I imagined Boris was rather adrift since the death of his wife two summers ago. More and more he seemed to crave human contact, if only with the few clients he still represented.

"What a case! In a moment we will confer," he said to me, his face already haggard.

I tapped my watch. "Okay, but let's do it sooner than later."

I liked Boris as a man, but as a lawyer he would be a liability on the Randall matter if I didn't keep him on track. As he reread the file, I spied the book he'd been leafing through just before Shelly Chilcott gave him the case. It was a hefty hardbound number in the *Time-Life* mode with a bright jacket consisting of three horizontal strips of photographic action: a forest fire burning orange and wild, an ominous black tornado, and a horrific side view of a pancaked high-rise building. *A World of Disaster*, the cover fairly screamed at me.

"What's the idea?" I whispered to Shelly Chilcott when I was out of Boris's earshot.

"He hasn't had a new case in three days. I had to give him something."

"Thanks, Shell."

"Think about it, J." She pulled on the sleeves of her pale blue sweater and straightened a pile of papers on her desk. "Your client's the one who's on the hot seat, not Father. Boris will be glad to let you run the show. Besides, I didn't think you'd want Jorgensen to get Father, and he's the only other panel lawyer picking up today."

Against the far wall and directly beneath the clock, Ken Jorgensen slouched in a plastic chair, working a sausage-like index finger into the gaps in his teeth, picking leftovers from his breakfast. I cringed. "Judas Priest."

Shelly's nose crinkled. "Ugh. Reminds me of Little Jack Horner."

"Yeah," I said, "if you're on acid. Guess we should be grateful his hemorrhoids aren't bothering him today. You're right, I'd rather make do with Boris."

I trust Shelly Chilcott's judgment, even though she works for the county agency that, in the usual game of keep-away between county and parents, generally functions as my arch adversary. She's a longtime social worker who'd gone into civil service straight out of college twenty years ago armed only with an undergraduate degree in psychology and a folk singer's passion for helping the less fortunate. She'd taken her current position a mere week before my own fumbling debut in Foley's court and had shown a good deal of patience in the face of my numerous missteps. Today Shelly lives a paper-pushing existence, doling out new files to overworked attorneys, scribbling orders on sheets of paper to hand to chastened parents as they back away from Foley's probing gaze, and phoning field workers none too pleased to be informed that their reports and recommendations are being questioned in court.

But Shell doesn't complain. I suppose the reason lies beneath her thick, kinetically frizzy brown hair, which these days she gathers behind her shoulders with a hand-painted, rainbow-colored clasp some distressed kid made for her in a crafts class at MacLaren Hall. Two dull purple scars curl up Shelly's neck like tiny fingers just above her right collarbone. Some time ago an ice pick slashed her to the floor during a fairly routine stop-in on what was to be her final field visit as a county social worker. The boy who'd stabbed her was only ten, but he was big for his age and knew what an ice pick could do, for he'd seen his mother wield the same point of rusty metal many times before in the faces of neighborhood hypes wanting to strong-arm her stash. Shelly bore no hard feelings toward the child who put her behind a desk. He had only confirmed what she already knew: somewhere down the line she'd lost the idealism that drew her to child welfare in the first place, and with it, her nerve.

Shelly smiled big. "Jack Horner on acid? You were a baby in the sixties, J., what do you know about acid?" Across the room, Ken Jorgensen belched like a sated bullfrog and shut his eyes.

Boris turned once more to the first page of his file and began to read the file all over again. "That's it," I said. "Time for a kick-start."

I had the bailiff lead Boris back behind the courtroom to Ty Randall's holding cell. Belinda McWhirter and Foley were just fin-ishing a hearing when they both stopped and looked at me as if my jacket were on fire. Shelly was dialing a number at her desk a few feet away, but she broke off and set the receiver back in its cradle. I turned around just as Sue Ellen Randall reached out and touched my left shoulder.

My quick turnabout had startled her. "Oh! I'm sorry," she said, withdrawing her hand. We were face-to-face and she seemed flus-tered by our close proximity.

"Where have you been?" I said, acutely aware now that the usual courtroom chatter had dried up instantly.

"Sorry about that out there." She made a hangdog face. "I shouldn't a run away."

"Listen," I said, "you can't let what people say—"

"I know, Mr. Shepard, I know. Can we talk? I got some things to tell you."

"Hang on a minute," I cautioned her. "This way." I led her into the interview room.

Today she wore a short-sleeved yellow and white checked dress with lace borders that made her look very young, like a girl I might have enjoyed flirting with at Sunday mass not so long ago. I thought I saw a trace of terror in her eyes.

I tried a warm smile. "I can't help you if you hang out in the ladies room all day."

"Sorry, I know I should've come back sooner," she said.

I went into my file and pulled out a legal pad with a series of questions I'd written out the night before, questions about some of the details in the social worker's report that hadn't yet been satisfactorily explained by Sue Ellen. But instead of traveling down my query list, I spent five minutes crowing about my sparkling opposition to Gilbride's motion.

"Your husband is here," I told her. "His lawyer is interviewing him. Have you made any headway toward bailing him out yet?"

She gave pause before responding. "His folks came out from Kentucky last weekend," she said. Her eyes were red and irritated from crying. "Mr. Shepard, there are some things we need to talk about."

Boris Kousnetsov knocked and poked his head into the room.

"I am so sorry, J., and forgive me to interrupt, madam," he said, sounding very Russian and bowing formally. "The judge is ready for us now."

I was caught by surprise. "What? Tell him to forget it. We're not ready yet," I said.

"The case has been called and the parties are coming in now, my friend J.," he said. I heard Nelson Gilbride's voice in the outer hallway directing someone to put away his cellular telephone.

"Like hell," I said, going for the door. "I'll tell Foley myself."

"Is okay," Kousnetsov said. "You will see. The child is already safe."

Boris was making no sense at all. Nathan Randall was still in the Danforth's custody, and they surely were not giving in. I was equally shocked and angered to think that Boris was leading on this, my most important case ever.

"Bailiff, find Mr. Shepard and get him in here now," I heard Foley demand from inside the courtroom.

Boris led Sue Ellen through the partitions and up to the far right end of the counsel table, past Gilbride and, on Gilbride's left, a stone-faced Belinda McWhirter. On Gilbride's right and standing straight and proud was an exceedingly well-coifed couple that had to be the Danforths. Corwin Danforth's eyes were vaguely unsettled, but his ice-green, double-breasted silk suit was a beauty. Kitty was cooler and seemingly privately tickled about something. She was marvelously put together in a conservative but stylish knee-length dress, camel with black trim and gold buttons. Both were in their middle to late forties, obvious proponents of gracious living—in a word, smart. I didn't like them.

Ken Jorgensen had been evicted from his plastic chair, which the bailiff had pulled forward to seat a shackled Ty Randall. Sue Ellen looked at Ty without smiling, and he stared back sullenly, tugging at his handcuffs. Everything about Ty was plain. Average height and build, red cheeks and a weak, stubbled chin. His long hair was dark and dirty, covering his ears and the blue collar of his county jumpsuit. Though he'd just been brought in, he slouched in his chair, as if at any moment he might melt into a puddle. I looked away, less than thrilled that my client's husband had the look of a common criminal.

"All right now, let's begin with our appearances," Foley said, peering over the edge of his file. "Miss McWhirter for the county, Mr. Gilbride with his clients—"

"Yes, good morning. Your Honor," Gilbride said, "if I might—"

"Not yet, Mr. Gilbride, not yet," Foley said. "You'll have your turn."

"Amen," I said through closed teeth.

Foley glared at me. "What was that?"

"Just a cough, Your Honor."

"I'll bet," he said without looking at me. Foley's mood had been downbeat and irritated all morning and showed no signs of improvement. "Miss Elmore?"

Lily Elmore, the lawyer for Nathan, peeked out from her chair just behind Belinda's place at counsel table. "Right here, Your Honor," she said with a wave of her hand.

"And Mr. Kousnetsov, whom I am now appointing to represent Father. All parties to the petition are present." He surveyed the jam of bodies in the courtroom. "Mr. Shepard, in all the excitement last week, I can't recall if I arraigned Mother."

"I believe you did, but no matter," I said. "We deny the allegations, Your Honor." Then Foley arraigned Ty Randall, Kousnetsov denying the petition as well.

"Two things to discuss today," Foley continued, "Mr. Gilbride's motion. Also, this is Father's first appearance, so he has not yet had a chance to argue detention. Of course, I'll allow argument from all of you on the issue of detention, but let's start with the motion made by Mr. Gilbride."

Gilbride argued first, making the same points he'd covered in his motion and puffing on and on about the Danforths as if they were the greatest parents in the history of mankind.

"Thank you, Mr. Gilbride." Foley massaged his right temple, his eyes slitted from the throb of a tension headache. "Mr. Shepard, proceed."

My response was simple, stressing the Code's unequivocal charge that no de facto parent status could be granted until trial has been concluded and the court has taken jurisdiction over the child. "There's no place for the Danforths until after trial," I concluded.

"I agree," Foley said.

"Your Honor!" Gilbride had leapt from his seat. "There are any number of significant equitable considerations to be made in a case like this. Now my clients, these wonderful, willing parents"—Gilbride gestured at the Danforths as if they were the glittering prize behind Door Number Three—"have been with this child since Day One. They are the only Mommy and Daddy he knows. Justice dictates that they must be allowed to participate."

At the last hearing I'd been a mere spectator, but this time, I was determined to break Gilbride's stride. "Your Honor, Mr. Gilbride speaks of equity and justice because he knows the law is clear."

"Mr. Gilbride, I've made a ruling," Foley said.

I wasn't through slamming Gilbride. "What troubles me is that he speaks of equity and justice, yet every time I turn around, there he is, in front of the TV cameras, revealing confidential information about this case. Perhaps the Court can remind the esteemed Mr. Gilbride that if he wants to squawk about fairness, he should consider the absolute unfairness to this child, my client and even the Court for his shameless grandstanding. He's transforming a confidential case into a public witch hunt."

"This is America!" Gilbride shouted. "I've got a First Amendment right to free speech."

"Perhaps the flag Mr. Gilbride has wrapped himself in is blocking his view," I said, "but—"

"Silence!" Foley demanded. "Mr. Shepard is right, Counsel," he said. "Mr. Gilbride, you should know better than to discuss this case with the press. The confidentiality rule is in place solely for the protection of the children involved."

Gilbride's cheeks were flushed. "Your Honor, if I may be ever so brief," he said. "Mr. Shepard should not be casting the first stone here. Why, not thirty minutes ago one of his clients—Dolly Madden, she called herself—went before the cameras and related several confidential facts about this case, facts she said she heard from Mr. Shepard."

Christ, what had I been thinking? I felt the moral high ground I'd been treading until now shifting beneath my feet like a great tectonic plate.

"Is that right, Counsel?" Foley said, glaring directly at me. "An outsider"—Foley nodded at Gilbride—"I can understand, but you're in here every day, Mr. Shepard. You should know better. I don't like this."

I fought off a hot rush of embarrassment and groped for a little composure. If Foley booted me now I'd be letting down a lot of people. "Your Honor, I believe that what Mr. Gilbride is—"

"Oh, don't deny it!" Gilbride said. "I can get the newswoman, bring her here for you, Judge. Why don't we look at her footage in your chambers, let you decide."

With that, Gilbride unwittingly let me off the hook. Foley scowled as if offended by the nightmare vision of Belinda, Lily Elmore, Boris, Gilbride and me cramming into his private office to view a salacious TV interview with a slovenly dependency mom while he massaged a big-time headache. "Enough, Mr. Gilbride, enough already!" he barked. "I'm ordering both of you, all of you"—his eyes swept the courtroom—"not to discuss this case with the press or anyone else for that matter. If you choose to disregard my order, sanctions will be calculated at five hundred dollars per comment. Now, as to the matter at hand, once again, I'm denying Mr. Gilbride's motion."

Sue Ellen breathed a tiny sigh and touched the top of my right hand with the tip of her pinkie. I took her gesture as a thank you and felt a wave of relief. I'd been beyond stupid to talk to Darla Madden that way. In the far right corner of my vision, I could see Ty Randall shifting uncomfortably as his wife retracted her hand from mine.

Gilbride and Belinda McWhirter simultaneously objected to Foley's ruling against Gilbride's motion, and a silence followed as they deferred to each other to speak next. But Foley was too quick for them. "Enough about the motion, I've made my ruling," he said. "Let's move on, people.

"Excuse me, Your Honor," I said, glancing in Gilbride's direction, "but shouldn't the Danforths and their counsel wait outside now that his motion has been denied?" I wanted him the hell out of this case. It was time to get Nathan back to his real mother.

"These people are the child's caretakers and true parents," Gilbride said. "I can see no harm in letting us sit in."

"The harm is apparent every time counsel opens his mouth to jump in," I said. "His love of country is inspirational, but it is not his constitutional right to loiter in these proceedings."

The watchers in the gallery murmured behind me, a few repressed laughs escaping.

"Your Honor, this is an outrage!" Gilbride shrieked.

"That will do, Mr. Shepard," Foley said. "Calm down, Mr. Gilbride. You and the Danforths may sit in the gallery."

Gilbride huffed, then followed the Danforths through the partitions. The gallery held only three pews, large enough for about six people each, and the rear seats were already filled to capacity with attorneys and social workers from this and other departments—a host of Channel Six watchers, I reckoned. My boss, Willow Reece, had slipped in and was leaning against the back wall, arms folded across her black silk blouse, quietly keeping tabs. Ken Jorgensen was a one-man crowd, his sweaty rolls and a whopping thigh sprawled across three normal spaces next to Gerry Humbert. Ken looked perturbed when he realized he was about to get squeezed. The gallery went quiet when Kitty Danforth took a breath, tucked in her elbows and sat down next to Ken like she was guiding herself onto a filthy toilet seat.

"Just tell me your living arrangement is settled," I whispered to Sue Ellen as Belinda McWhirter argued for Nathan to remain detained with the Danforths. "I can feel it—I can get him home to you right now. Are you ready?"

Her eyes were wild with hope. "God, do ya think so? I'm staying with friends from our new church, First Baptist up in Eagle Rock. He'll have his own room."

"Perfect." I glanced at her scraggly-ass husband. "Why is Ty still in jail?"

"Long story," she said.

Lily Elmore argued next, echoing Belinda's main points and adding that if Nathan were released to Sue Ellen, "she might just sell him again. And I'm sure," Lily said, wagging her finger like a schoolmarm, "that's something none of us would want to have to live with."

Lily had gone too far. "State your case, Miss Elmore," Foley said, "but let's leave out the moral guidance, hmm?"

I argued that this was not a case of baby selling, but was instead no more than an adoption that imploded for understandable reasons. The allegations of fraud had only surfaced after Sue Ellen realized the "open" part of this open adoption was a pipe dream and the Danforths had no intention of letting Sue Ellen and Ty become part of Nathan's life. The Danforths reneged before Sue Ellen legally consented to the adoption. Regardless of the way one might personally feel about a young woman relinquishing her child, Nathan was Sue Ellen's boy, and she had a legal right to keep him. I implored Foley to release Nathan to Sue Ellen, so that mother and son might immediately begin the important process of bonding.

"Mr. Kousnetsov," Foley said when I'd finished, "I take it you concur with Mr. Shepard's recommendation that the minor be released to Mother?" I was pleased to see Foley assume Boris would follow my lead.

This time I patted Sue Ellen's hand. For the first time since she'd stumbled into my life, this case was under my control. Never mind the kooky allegations of emotional abuse in the petition; we could deal with a minimal finding by the judge on some cooked-up charge as long as my client had custody. I was in my element, and it took a good deal of self-restraint not to turn and find my old employer Gilbride in the gallery and flash him the classic shit-eater. This kid was coming home.

Then the prop came off the flying machine.

Boris rose slowly and hacked and rattled to clear his throat. "Yes, but I have something to add, Your Honor." He glanced at Sue Ellen and me as if to say Boy, will you two be grateful to me for this. I was too late, I realized. Boris's strange remark about Nathan already being safe was about to be explained to everyone in the courtroom.

"Your Honor, may I have a moment to confer with Mr. Kousnetsov?" I asked.

"No," Foley said. "Mr. Kousnetsov, you have the floor."

"I say, what is the point?" Boris shrugged.

"Come again?" Foley said.

"Your Honor, what is the point, all of us arguing over where this boy should be, with these people"—gesturing toward the Danforths on my left—"bringing a lawyer here to fight for them, and the boy's father, still in jail, in handcuffs." He looked at Ty. "Maybe we even have a trial to decide this case, waste more of the court's time."

Foley glared at Boris. "Waste of time? I'm not following you, Counselor."

Boris bent over to whisper into Ty's ear. "We must tell him," I heard him say. Ty's face flashed with panic. "You sure?" he whispered as Boris privately quieted him, their backs to the rest of us. Then Ty shrugged at Boris as if to silently give his consent.

"The child is no longer here in California," Boris said, facing Foley again.

A collective gasp went up from the gallery. Christ, I thought, what have they done? I stared at the side of Sue Ellen's face, but she kept her eyes straight ahead.

"His grandparents come and take him few days ago," Boris continued, "back to Kentucky to live with them. It is the best idea. The adoption is over. We are all sorry it did not work. The parents, they are struggling, struggling to find a home, a new place to live. Mr. Randall is fighting to have the criminal case against him dropped, and . . ."

No, Boris, I thought. What more could go wrong now? But how, how could they have wrested Nathan from the Danforth's? I was lost.

So was Foley, and he was on fire. "What do you mean, the boy is in Kentucky?"

An awful thought gripped me. I had written the words "preschool" on my list of questions to ask Sue Ellen before the hearing today. In the social worker's report, Kitty Danforth's statement included a lengthy harangue about the many expenses the Danforths had covered for the Randalls as part of the adoption agreement: partial rent, food bills, gas, electric, prenatal care, preschool. Last night, when I was re-reading the report, I'd stopped at preschool, wondering if it was an error, a misprint, words too quickly run together late at night by a mentally fried county worker.

"I missed it," I said to no one but myself.

The Randalls had a second child.

"I tried to tell you," Sue Ellen whispered to me. Shelly Chilcott was already dialing her phone to try to find out how the social worker had missed it as well.

"You didn't try hard enough," I said. "We're hosed."

"Your Honor?" Gilbride had seized an opening, bounding out of the gallery and planting himself just behind the partitions. "I think I know what Mr . . . uh," he looked at Boris.

"Kousnetsov," Boris said, bowing.

"Uh yes, Mr. Koosentop." Gilbride bowed in kind. "What he's talking about is the Randall's eldest child, I believe his name is Ronny."

"That so?" Foley said. "Ronny." He fixed on Sue Ellen. "How old is this child?"

"Three, I believe," Gilbride said. "From what I've gathered—"

"Counsel," Foley said, rolling his eyes, "I was asking the mother."

I was determined to stay on Gilbride's back. "I thought Mr. Gilbride was relegated to the gallery because he doesn't even represent a party with standing in this case," I said. "He's muscling in all over again, Your Honor."

"Well I'd just like to find out what happened here, Mr. Shepard, so calm down," Foley said. He gazed at Sue Ellen again.

She stood to address the Court. "Ronny just turned four two weeks ago come Sunday," Sue Ellen said. "We took him to the beach to have a pony ride, but the beaches here aren't like the ones we been to in South Carolina. They don't rent ponies on the beach in Santa Monica." A fat tear rolled off her cheek and spattered the front of her dress.

God, she was a depressing sight, and married to the glowering roughneck in the county jumpsuit, at that. This woman could never win against the likes of Gilbride and the Danforths.

"Miss Chilcott, why wasn't Ronny referred to in the report?" Foley said to Shelly. "Why isn't he part of the petition?"

Shelly tilted her head to cradle her phone on her shoulder as she tore through the social worker's report. "I'm sorry, but I don't know yet, Your Honor. I'm trying to reach the worker's supervisor right now, but I'm on hold."

"No, no, I don't have time for that now," Foley said. "The boy is already out of state, from what Mr. Kousnetsov tells us. I don't like this, not at all. How can the county assess this child's situation if he's out of state, and why didn't they do so in the first place? And you, sir"—he glared at Ty—"had no business sending the boy off with your parents. You know I can bring him back here if I want, don't you?"

Ty Randall wisely said nothing.

"Your Honor, may I be heard?" I said. Foley nodded. I shifted my weight and coughed, stalling. I needed to string together an explanation, words that wouldn't make Sue Ellen sound like a total sneak for shuttling Nathan's older brother out of Foley's immediate jurisdiction. I'd blown it by wasting time telling Sue

Ellen about my fabulous opposition to Gilbride's motion. Had I cut the small talk we might've gotten to my question about pre-school in time, talked about Ronny, fashioned some damage control. I should never have walked in here without making Boris tell me what he meant about the child being safe. Like me, Boris had seen only one minor on the petition. Later, when Ty broke the news of Ronny's flight to him, Boris confused Nathan with Ronny, believing the case was all but over with the child no longer present. A huge mistake, but the kind Boris was prone to committing due to his advanced years. But what of Sue Ellen's responsibility? Was her failure to tell me she had another child an honest oversight—like Foley forgetting whether he'd arraigned her last week—or a lie?

"Any time now, Counselor," Foley said. "Today would be preferable."

"Thank you," I said. "Let me first say I'm sorry, Your Honor, for not bringing this up with you last week. Like everyone else, I read the petition and the social worker's report, with Mr. and Mrs. Danforths' statements attached. Because there was absolutely no reference to Ronny in any of the files, and because Ms. McWhirter made no mention of Ronny when we spoke about the case"—I regarded Belinda—"I assumed the department had no issues regarding Ronny, nor did you, Your Honor. I can see now that my assumption was incorrect, and I was remiss in not mentioning Ronny. But I would suggest, Your Honor, that although the Randalls were certainly premature in making arrangements for Ronny to stay with his grandparents without the court's permission, it was an understandable mistake."

"To say the least," Foley said.

"Everyone here has been focusing on Nathan because this petition is about an adoption gone bad," I said. "It's not your typical sexual or physical abuse case where every kid in the house is at risk as long as the offending parent is around. No one was concerned about Ronny, except his mother, who sought to protect him by removing him from the public eye. But the real case, Your Honor, isn't about Ronny, it only concerns Nathan's adoption."

"How do we know they won't try to sell the other child, too, Your Honor?" Gilbride said.

I was not about to give Gilbride an inch. "If the Danforths were concerned about the welfare of Ronny they certainly had a unique way of showing it," I answered, holding up my file. "There's page after page of information here, most of it provided by the Danforths, and not a word about Ronny. It's everyone's fault, Your Honor, but then again, it's nobody's fault." I paused to glance at Gilbride's clients. "The Danforths only want Nathan."

"I still don't like what your clients did," Foley said. His eyes were right on Sue Ellen. "But the department paved the way. I don't like being in the dark like this, Miss McWhirter. Shoddy work." He slapped down the court file.

"Your Honor," Belinda said, "Mr. Shepard should've told me last week—"

"Told you what, Counsel?" Foley said. "That you should look into seeking jurisdiction over another one of his client's kids? He's a *defense* lawyer in this matter, in case you haven't noticed. Don't expect him to do your job for you." Foley fixed on me. "And you, you could have made this easier for me, Mr. Shepard, but you didn't speak up last week. I don't like to be deceived."

"That was not my intention, Your Honor," I said.

"Your Honor," Belinda said, "if you might grant us leave to amend the petition, perhaps—"

"I will do no such thing!" Foley shouted, slamming his hand on his desktop.

"Your Honor," Lily Elmore said, standing shoulder-to-shoulder with Belinda, "I would like to at least have the opportunity to interview the other child."

"Miss Elmore, you don't even represent the other child," Foley said. "Haven't you been listening here? Find the page and get with the program, will you? The boy is in banjo country, two thousand miles away, and I'm not using taxpayer money to bring him back here just so you and Miss McWhirter can decide what you might want to do." He looked at all of us. "The petition will not be amended to include Ronny Randall."

"Excellent," I whispered to Sue Ellen as she stared at the judge.

"Uh, Judge," Nelson Gilbride said, "might I interject—"

"You may not," Foley said. "Here are my orders. The minor Nathan Randall is to be detained with the Danforths . . ."

"Oh no!" Sue Ellen said, the tears starting.

"Hang on," I whispered to her. "Foley figures we're going to trial. He doesn't want to ping-pong Nathan back and forth between you and the Danforths depending on what happens in the case." But that was only part of it, I knew. Because of Ronny, Foley now believed he could not trust Sue Ellen.

At my insistence, Foley ordered that Sue Ellen be allowed twice-weekly visits with Nathan at the department's offices.

Foley looked up at me, then toward Belinda. "Any chance this case might be settled without a trial?" he asked us.

"I'm always open to settlement discussions, Your Honor," I said, trying my best to sound affable as I opened my weekly calendar. "But if you're not inclined to release Nathan to his mother, I'll have to request that you set this matter for a no-time-waiver trial."

If a child is not returned to the parents at the detention hearing, the parents have a statutory right to a trial within ten court days. Asking for a no-time-waiver is a gamble, since two weeks is not much time to prepare for trial, but it's a risk worth taking if the department's case appears jumbled or fatally flawed, for you can force a bad hand and regain custody of a minor in short order. I didn't want the Danforths to automatically keep Nathan for two to three more months, which is the standard wait for a trial. They would gain too great an advantage as the bonded caretakers. A no-time-waiver would put the pressure on everyone to be ready. Or settle this thing, which was to be my next objective.

"Mr. Shepard can't ask for a no-time-waiver now," Belinda said. "He had to ask for it last week, at his client's first appearance."

"That's right," Foley said.

"Begging your pardon, Your Honor," I said, "but you arraigned my client today. I didn't argue the issue of detention last week."

"Uh, Your Honor," Gilbride said, back on his feet and roaming the space behind the partitions, "if I might be heard on this?"

Foley smiled at his clerk and shook his head. "Good Lord, this case never quits," he said.

"Just a minute, Your Honor," I said. I quickly stepped around Sue Ellen and whispered some short directions to Boris.

"Your Honor," Boris said, his voice still rattling with the remnants of a chest cold, "on behalf of Father, I request a no-time-waiver trial." Because this was Ty Randall's first appearance, there could be no controversy in his asking for a no-time-waiver.

"Very smooth, Counselor," Foley said to me. "Let's calendar this thing."

Sue Ellen had not even seen Nathan since the day he was born. On the bonding front, every day she spent apart from her son meant more ground lost to Gilbride and the department. A no-time-waiver trial would get Nathan home to Sue Ellen quickly. That is, if we prevailed.

"Monday, September sixteen, and every day thereafter until we're done," Foley said, studying his personal calendar. His clerk nodded in assent.

"We'll be here, at this table, ready to go," Gilbride said, waving a hand at the counsel table six feet in front of him.

"Excuse me, Your Honor," I said, "but the Danforths' counsel lost his motion for de facto parent status. He should not be at this table." I mimicked Gilbride's sweep of the hand.

"Don't push it," Foley said to me. "This issue was already decided. Mr. Gilbride and his clients may sit in the gallery, but you, sir," he said to Gilbride, "will not participate during trial."

Belinda and Gilbride exchanged secretive nods in a way that made me think I'd missed something. She was a competent trial lawyer, but perhaps not so confident in her skills to turn down the infamous Nelson Gilbride if he offered to be at her service. One day last summer I saw Belinda reading a copy of Gilbride's book, *Bundle of Joy*, as she sat in the gallery waiting for her cases to be called. I figured that same copy would be autographed by the author himself before Foley decided the Nathan Randall petition.

We scribbled on our legal pads until the judge finished making his orders. Trial was in two weeks, and I didn't know a damn thing about what really happened between Sue Ellen and the Danforths.

The death grip I used to clutch my pen brought on a savage hand cramp, but I kept up with my notes as Foley made his orders.

"Your Honor?" three attorneys said at once.

Foley closed the court file. "Good-bye, people," he said without looking up. "Go in peace."

Six

We had two options now: settlement and trial. I asked the others on the case to stick around until after I had a chance to confer with Sue Ellen. Perhaps she'd have another change of heart about her son.

Sue Ellen shook her head. "That was brutal." The courtroom had cleared for noon recess.

"Get used to it," I told her. "Those people want your baby." I looked away.

"You're upset I didn't tell you about Ronny, aren't you?"

I didn't bother to respond.

"I shouldn't have listened to Ty," she said.

I was sick of clients not heeding my advice. "I had to lie for you to keep you from looking like the liar in there. What else haven't you told me? Did you really take those people for a ride?"

"Of course not!" Sue Ellen took a tissue from a box on the table and dabbed her eyes. "Don't ya believe me?"

"Your credibility is shot. We're lucky Foley listened to me. Let's get something straight right now, okay? We won't get far this way, especially at trial. You want your kid back, you have to tell me everything, no surprises. No holding back."

She continued to sob. "I tried to tell you before the hearing. I just didn't get a chance."

"Oh, come on." I recalled our conversation of a half hour ago. She had tried to spit something out before Boris Kousnetsov burst in on us, scuttling the interview. Sue Ellen's turn to speak had never really come.

"I tried, Mr. Shepard."

"Okay. But you still went about it wrong," I said. "You blew any chance of getting Nathan back today." I remembered my list and the question about preschool I failed to ask in time. I'd blown it, too.

She gritted her teeth, her eyes fierce. "No holding back, huh? Well what about you? You didn't even try to get Nathan back to me last week, you said we'd get him back this week. Now look at us."

"Listen, you didn't tell me about Ronny. You also had no place to live."

"I want my Nathan!"

"Then start paying closer attention to what I tell you," I said. "What's your husband been cooking up that sounds so much better than your own attorney's specific advice? And why didn't his parents bail him out? He looked like a . . ."

Sue Ellen looked at her white Keds. "What, a criminal?"

"Never mind," I said.

"His folks couldn't raise enough money. His daddy wants us to enter pleas with the D.A., take a misdemeanor and probation."

"Well gosh, don't you think you should talk to your public defender about that? There's no way the D.A. can prove felony fraud against either of you. The money you received was all support as part of the adoption agreements. You sent Kitty Danforth home from the hospital with Nathan." My client seemed incapable of seeing this case as I did. I felt utterly exasperated. "I told you all this last week, in detail. Their burden of proof is very high, and there are too many facts that count in your favor. Haven't you talked to Ty about this?"

"I told him everything you said."

"No response?"

"He said you don't know what you're talkin' about 'cause you're just a kiddie lawyer." She hesitated. "Even worse than his public defender."

"Is that so?" It was wrong, I knew, to get so hot over a loser client, to bet heavily on myself when I alone couldn't win the case. But Ty's remark had nicked my pride. "Well, fuck him if he can't take a joke."

My remark apparently offended her. "Oh, I get it," she said. "So he's right after all?"

In that moment I glimpsed what I had become: a watered-down advocate, a gracious loser. With recognition came anger.

"He's right all right," I said. "Your man's quite the arch strategist, real Phi Beta Kappa thinker, isn't he? Tell you what, next time you see big Ty, you tell him—"

"Stop it!" She cupped her hands over her ears. I checked my watch, insensitive to her pain. "He won't listen to me," she cried. "Can't ya see? He's still upset at me 'cause my folks wouldn't bail him out. My daddy called him a luckless fool."

My client's daddy probably had plenty of evidence to back up his claim. I felt my anger draining away. Ty Randall's opinion of me didn't matter. "Sorry," I said. "Let's just get through this, okay?"

Sue Ellen had recovered somewhat. "Guess Ty's stock didn't go up any this week, did it?" She waited for my response, but none came. "I'm thinking about leaving him," she added.

"Tell me," I said, "was the adoption his idea?"

"It was mostly mine. I didn't want an abortion, but Ty didn't want another mouth to feed." She told me that Ty had worked security at a frozen food warehouse but lost his job a few weeks after she found out she was pregnant. "It was my idea to come to L.A., too. My girlfriend Rayanne, she moved here last year and got a job cleaning cruise ships while they were between cruises? Said she could get Ty a job in maintenance, but when we got here, the position was filled. We told Rayanne we'd stay on a week or two, just until Ty found something else, but he couldn't find anything that suited him and three weeks turned into three months. Then she found out Ty turned down a sanitation job with the cruise company, got mad and gave us the boot." Sue Ellen shrugged. "Can't really blame her. Didn't have no room for us in the first place."

"Have you ever worked?"

"Not since I married Ty. He won't let me."

"Great. Unemployed, but he has his pride."

"He's not such a bad fella, Mr. Shepard."

"How are you going to make it if you leave him?" I said.

"I'll go home to my folks for a while, maybe go back to school, junior college. My Aunt Maddy's got a hair salon. I could probably work for her." She ran her fingertips together as if she was about to pray.

"Kentucky?" I asked.

She nodded. "Gotta go back to get Ronny now, anyhow."

We both stayed silent for a time. "Stay with him," I said.

"Who?"

"Your husband. Think about it. What could be worse than a baby seller? A baby seller who's a single mother."

"I did not sell my child," she said.

"I know. I just think your chances of getting Nathan back from this judge are better if your situation looks as stable as possible."

"Even if it's a shambles?" she said.

"Yes. We need every advantage."

Sue Ellen had a thought. "That first couple, the Pontrellis? That report makes it sound like we ditched them."

"The worker says you terminated the adoption without even giving them notice."

"Not so! Go talk to the landlord at the apartment the Pontrellis were helping us rent," she said. "We gave him notice, a letter. The landlord's Mr. Pontrelli's cousin."

"Have you got a copy?"

"Most of our stuff got thrown in the trash over at Los Feliz."

"Great," I said. My faith in Sue Ellen's honesty was on the wane; it seemed too conveniently impossible to verify any part of her story. "I'll check out the landlord. What else?"

"Corwin Danforth even paid for the moving van when we quit with the Pontrellis. Now they're tryin' to make it sound like we're frauds because we skipped out on the Pontrellis, even though the Danforths knew all about it."

"It doesn't matter. The Danforths will deny knowing anything about your arrangement with the Pontrellis." I took out a legal pad. "What else?"

She told me about the recent visit a private investigator made to the Los Feliz neighborhood. He'd apparently stood on every porch in the neighborhood, a coat hanger in hand, asking if anyone had seen Sue Ellen beating Ronny with it.

"Who told you this?" I asked.

"Arturo. I don't know his last name. Lives at the end of the street in a house with a fence around it and a big dog in the yard. Arturo's old, but he takes a walk every day around noontime. Used to stop and talk about anything, his rose bushes, the street gangs on Sunset. You'll find him easy enough."

We talked about Lois Nettleson, the adoption counselor—or baby broker, as Holly Dupree's reports had tagged her—who'd connected the Randalls first with the Pontrellis, then with Gilbride and the Danforths. Lois Nettleson was the person Sue Ellen had contacted to demand Nathan's return when she realized the "open" part of the adoption was never going to happen. The good counselor Lois had done everything she could to talk Sue Ellen out of reclaiming Nathan. So far the case report contained no information about Lois Nettleson; the social worker said she tried to reach her before completing her investigation but never connected. But the Danforths' statements referred to Lois as if she were a key witness to the Randalls' fraud.

"I have to talk to Lois Nettleson," I said. "The department will probably call her to testify."

"She's one of the D.A. witnesses; that's what my public defender says," Sue Ellen explained.

"Any idea why Lois Nettleson is against you?"

"No sir. Maybe she doesn't get paid if the adoption falls apart."

"Good point," I said. Sue Ellen smiled cautiously. "We'll find out how she got paid."

I took down the name and number of Sue Ellen's public defender. Lois Nettleson's address and phone number were not in the report. "Is Lois Nettleson in the phone book?" I asked.

"Santa Barbara. When we read her adoption ad in the yellow pages, we were at a motel out in the desert on our way to L.A. We thought she lived in the desert, too. I didn't know it then, but she had this local phone number that switched you over to Santa Barbara. Went up there once. Other two times she came down to L.A."

"You signed a contract with her?"

Sue Ellen nodded. "I think so."

"I need a copy of it."

She sighed. "Gone, along with our other stuff."

"Right." Another important document conveniently missing. We were making little headway. "What about Gilbride?" I said. "What was your arrangement with him? Did you sign anything, like a retainer agreement, when you first met him?"

"I don't think so. I could be wrong."

"Try to remember," I said, "and call me if you think of anything. I'd like to know more about how he came to represent both you and the Danforths, especially after the baby was born."

Sue Ellen fairly jumped. "Oh! The obstetrician who delivered Nathan! Talk to that guy. Big jerk. Name's Weinstein, Doctor Harley Weinstein. Ask him about May sixth." She was crying all over again.

I wrote down the name and date. "What about May sixth?"

"My due date—that is, the one I calculated—was the fourteenth," she said bitterly. "Doctor Weinstein was sure I was wrong, said the baby was due almost two weeks earlier. As if I wouldn't know! God, I was so stupid." Her voice broke and her shoulders quaked a little. "He was supposed to be my doctor, but he just did what Kitty Danforth told him to, I know it."

"You think he caused you to have Nathan early?"

"I know he did. Induced labor. There were . . . some complications." She looked away.

"What kind?"

"Try unbelievable pain—unbelievable! Thought I was gonna die right there on that table. I begged him for an anaesthetic, but he wouldn't give me one." She stopped to straighten the pleats above her knees. "You find out why they put me through so much pain to have that baby on May sixth, Mr. Shepard."

"I will. What else?"

"Nothing I can think of right now, but I'll keep tryin'," she said.

I made the last of my notes in silence and gathered up my things. "Call me by early next week with the addresses and phone numbers I asked you for," I told her. "Visit Nathan every opportunity you get under the visitation order, and call me if they pull any funny business with your visits. The social worker's going to be watching how often you see Nathan and how you interact with him, so be careful."

She looked at me as if confused. "Why would she do that?"

"To gauge your intentions toward your child. If your interest level isn't appropriate, we'll read about it in the report the worker submits before trial. Don't let the worker interview you. You're going to testify, so I don't want you giving any statements. They'll just twist what you say."

"Lord almighty," Sue Ellen said. She looked queasy, ready to fall apart. "This is insane."

"They're going to try to show you're a fraud," I said, "and it's going to be close. All they need to do at trial is beat our case by a preponderance, their fifty-one percent to our forty-nine."

She managed a timid smile. "I will help you."

"Think about what I said about Ty."

Sue Ellen Randall's face was as poised and still as a toy doll's, but her stare was piercing, as if she was observing me at a carefully measured distance which she did not wish to shorten. "You're different from last week," she said.

"What do you mean?"

"You don't believe me, do you?"

I tried, but I couldn't make eye contact. "It shouldn't matter what I think as long as I do my part."

She wasn't sold on my matter-of-fact assessment. "Well, it matters to me."

"What do you want to do?" I asked her.

"They're still here, Gilbride and the others?" she said. I nodded that they were. "Do they still want to talk?"

"I think so. Probably as much as you do."

The tears were rolling again. "Talk to them for me."

"They want Nathan," I told her. "You know that."

"I know. You think I should give him back. You think I did wrong."

She looked sad and utterly lost, and much to my private shame, all I could think of at the moment was doing jury trials with the D.A. and the surprise in Phoebe's voice when I announced that I was out of this sinkhole for good. With shocking ease I found myself feeling no allegiance to Sue Ellen Randall, and I despised myself, but not enough to change course now.

"In a situation like this, there are no easy choices," I said, a voice inside telling me no shit, Sherlock. I was selling her out and I knew it. "But it can't hurt to look at all your options. Maybe raising two boys is more than you're ready to take on."

"They'll let Ty out of jail?"

"I'm pretty sure they'll drop the criminal charges. This case will probably be dismissed, too. I think the Danforths will still be willing to give you those privileges you were supposed to get in the first place."

"Don't be silly, Mr. Shepard," she said. "I'm not that stupid. They don't want nothin' to do with me and Ty and you know it."

"I know, but I think the court can order visitation, depending on what your previous agreement covered. And I can probably get them to pay, I mean, to help get you back to Kentucky. That is, if that's what you want."

She glared at the floor, her arms folded. "It's not about money. Never was."

I was on the verge of losing her. "Of course. I'm sorry, Sue Ellen."

"Go talk to them for me," she said. "See what you can do." She put her head in her hands. "This has been such a nightmare, I can't even think anymore."

In one of my more despicably transparent moments ever as a legal advocate, I gave the woman a comforting pat on the shoulder. "Are you willing to give him up?"

"I don't know yet, Mr. Shepard, but I gotta set this right. I can't take it anymore."

I turned toward the door. "Wait here."

Sue Ellen stood when I reached for the doorknob. "Mr. Shepard, can I ask just one thing?"

"Sure."

She paused as if she were too shy to continue. "With everything that's happened, I know I probly shouldn't be asking, but it ain't right."

"What's that?"

"Thirty-nine dollars. For the shoes I bought Ty."

"Sue Ellen, considering the money this whole adoption must have cost the Danforths, I'm not so sure we should be—"

"I don't want it from them!" she shouted. She blushed as if surprised by her outburst. "Sorry, Mr. Shepard, I meant Mr. Gilbride. He's the one who should pay me back the thirty-nine dollars. For the shoes I bought for Ty. It ain't right."

I eased away from the door and we both sat down again. "What isn't?"

"About a month before Nathan was born, me and Ty were really stretchin' to make ends meet. The Danforths knew it. Ty couldn't get hired on anywhere. Mr. Danforth talked to him about his attitude, improving his outlook, but I don't know, it's hard to have a positive outlook when no one wants to hire you. Seems like everybody's been down on Ty ever since we got to California."

"What about the shoes?" I said.

"I can see it all so clearly, now," she said, sniffling into a ball of blue tissue. "Gilbride musta talked to the Danforths, got nervous that we might just up and leave, head back home before Nathan was born, what with Ty's employment situation. So he told him he knew a super on a maintenance team, City of Glendale, could get Ty a job with benefits, good pay, the whole thing. Ty said what do I do, and Gilbride told him to just apply first at City Hall, he'd take care of the rest. Told him he should have work boots, show up like he was ready to work, 'cause the super likes a go-getter. I found a pair Ty's size at a discount store, couldn't believe my luck. They were marked down from seventy-eight dollars, half off. Irregular." She smiled. "Couldn't find a thing wrong with 'em."

"He never got the job," I said.

"Never even got an interview. That was our grocery money for the rest of the week. Ty waited almost two months for a call that never came. Course, by then they had the baby."

"I'll see what I can do," I said. "I don't foresee any problems."

"You know there wasn't no super," she told me. "We checked with the city."

Gilbride had suckered them. "I know." I handed her a fresh tissue but she waved me off. Sue Ellen Randall was finished crying.

Gilbride and the other lawyers on the Randall case were waiting outside Foley's courtroom, milling about as if they knew my intentions. Ty Randall was still in the holding cell behind the court. Boris told me he could secure Ty's consent to a fair agreement if it meant a free pass from jail. Belinda readily agreed to seek a dismissal when she heard my pitch. Lily Elmore was out on the mezzanine balcony having a Pall Mall, but no one was too concerned about her position since she followed Belinda's lead every time.

Gilbride and I discussed the terms of the adoption. He fed me a long string of assurances, but as I listened I kept seeing Ty's new steel-toe boots, and a sense of dread welled up inside me. My personal escape plan was to ride Gilbride's D.A. connection right out of this place, but if all I had to go on was the man's word, I was in trouble. I needed confirmation; a simple assurance would do. So I walked him down the hall for a moment, alone and away from the others, and surprised him.

"I want the name," I said.

His face was all innocence. "What name is that?"

"Your contact in the D.A.'s office. The person you're going to talk to on my behalf."

"Oh, yes, yes of course." He showed me his dirty secret smile. "Well, if you don't mind, I'd like to handle this in my own way."

"Oh, absolutely," I agreed. "I don't intend to step on any toes. Just tell me who he is. I know this is silly, but I'd feel better if I knew his name."

He considered my request. "Oh, all right. The name is Clarence Milton."

I'd never heard of the man, but in an office of a thousand lawyers, this meant nothing.

"Director of Personnel," Gilbride added.

My eyebrows shot up. "Impressive."

"Very busy too, so don't you bother him. I'll handle it for you. I'll take care of everything." He startled me by shaking my hand.

"Well, okay," I said. "So, you two are pretty tight?"

"Very."

"Go back a ways?"

"Quite a ways."

I did my best to appear satisfied. "Excellent. Well, thank you, Mr. Gilbride. I guess you'll make the call to Mr. Milton when you're ready."

He grinned like a disciple of the power of positive thinking. "It's as good as done. Anything else?" he said.

I studied his perpetual smile but found nothing behind it. "No. Thank you again." We strolled back to the group and I told him and the others I needed to run everything by Sue Ellen and would be right back. But I was operating on a purely selfish level; my client could wait. I went back into 302 and over to Shelly Chilcott's empty desk, picked up her phone, and punched in the county code for an outside line.

"Mr. Milton's office," a secretary answered.

"Hello, is Clarence in?" I said, imitating Gilbride's affected speech.

"Who's calling, please?"

"This is Nelson Gilbride. It's a personal matter. Will you tell Clarence I'm holding, please?"

"Yes, sir, one moment."

A muffler ad rattled away while I held. "Uh, sir? Mr. Milton is unavailable to take your call just now. Perhaps you could leave a message."

I'd gotten the standard blow-off. This wasn't working. "Ma'am," I said as reasonably as I could, "I just want to ask you one thing. Did you give Mr. Milton my name?"

"Sir, you'll have to leave a message, I'm afraid."

"Please, just tell me if you gave him my name, Nelson Gilbride."

There was a long pause. "Yes, Mr. Gilbride, I gave it to him."

I had to know. "I'm really sorry to bother you, I am, but—"

"Who is this?" she demanded.

My Gilbride imitation had slipped badly. "Just one more question, I promise. Please."

I heard her sigh. "All right."

My head ached and my palms were clammy. The big clock buzzed like a live prison fence across the deserted courtroom. I was afraid of what I was about to hear.

"What did Mr. Milton say when you told him Nelson Gilbride was on the line?" I asked.

She paused. "You won't be offended?"

"I promise, I won't."

The woman sighed as if she knew my predicament. "He said 'take a message.' He'd never heard of you before."

I thanked her and hung up, gut-shot. Not about losing Phoebe, for she was already history, I knew. But for what I'd done to Sue Ellen Randall, the way I'd thrown in with Gilbride, put my selfish needs ahead of my client's wishes. Just as Sue Ellen was strung along for months with financial incentives and visitation promises to keep a doomed adoption alive, I'd been sized up as a righteous burnout desperate for an escape route from the dependency grind. In our own ways, my client and I had both become corruptible.

Sue Ellen listened patiently and accepted my apology, but her face tightened when I told her I needed to withdraw for personal reasons from representing her. I counted out thirty-nine dollars from my wallet and handed it to her.

"Don't do this to me, not now," she said. "Help me."

"I'm no damn good for you," I explained. "I'm no good for this case. I have a few problems of my own about what you're accused of having done."

"I'm not a bad person," she said.

"I know that."

She forced a smile through her disappointment. "I made a mistake. At some time or another, people are just gonna have to accept that and let me go on with my life."

"I admire your courage," I said.

She dabbed her nose with a tissue. "Courage? No. I just love my son. Mr. Shepard, can I be straight with you? I still want you as my lawyer."

She needed to know. "Let me be straight with you, Sue Ellen," I said. "My own mother left me when I was still technically a kid. It hurt." I looked away. "A lot."

Sue Ellen reflected for a moment. "I'm very sorry about that," she said, "truly I am. But you're my lawyer."

I knew what she wanted of me, and there was only one way I could deliver. "Don't ask me again if I believe you. It shouldn't matter."

She nodded. "Fair enough. So what now?"

My whole body tensed in anticipation. "If you want your boy back, we're going to trial."

The other attorneys descended on me the instant that I walked Sue Ellen out of 302 and started down the hallway. "Wait! Where are you going?" Belinda said. I didn't feel compelled to answer her.

Gilbride had been seated on a wide couch with the Danforths, but he rushed in behind Belinda as if he sensed something was awry. "J., have we got a deal?" he said. It was the first time he'd ever used my first name.

"We do not," I said. I kept powering down the hall alongside Sue Ellen, but he and Belinda stayed with us step for step, Lily Elmore tagging behind.

"J., wait a minute," Gilbride said. "Let's all of us talk this thing out."

"I've discussed your offer with my client," I told them. "I apologize for making you wait. See you in two weeks."

Belinda was instantly hot. "You're making a big mistake, Shepard," she said.

Knowing I could not deny her charge, I walked on.

I talked the sheriff's-office receptionist into letting Sue Ellen and me exit the building through their back entrance. Holly Dupree would have to make do with a sound bite from Nelson Gilbride for tonight's telecast. We rode the elevator up to the third level of the parking structure in silence, as if an untimely word might bring an entire news crew running. I stepped out with Sue Ellen and surveyed the floor. About a third of the parking spaces were now empty; those whose cases were heard before the noon recess had cleared out. Lucky bastards, I thought.

Sue Ellen spotted the truck. "I'm over here," she said. She seemed wiped out as I walked her through the shadows of concrete and steel. A sluggish midday breeze filled in behind us.

I helped her into the cab and we said our good-byes. By the time I'd walked back to the elevators she'd tried the starter four times without success. I turned around and went back.

The truck was a tired-looking Ford F-250, faded red with Kentucky plates and coated with a glaze of highway soot. The cab's rear window was so filthy I could've written "wash me" across the glass with my index finger. I didn't relish the prospect of poking around under the hood in the diminished light.

"Maybe you flooded it again," I told Sue Ellen, remembering her story about stalling the truck in Los Feliz the night she was thrown out of her place.

A middle-aged guy in jeans and a black cotton short-sleeve shirt was standing five feet away from me near the truck's rear bumper. He was wearing outdated mirror shades and looked like he'd forgotten to shave this morning. I hadn't even seen him walk over. "Sounds about right," he said.

I nodded, trying to ignore the guy, but he just stood there, hands on hips, as if he wanted to help. At my direction, Sue Ellen slid the truck into neutral and I pushed it backwards and out of the parking spot. Without my asking, the man in the black shirt ran around to the passenger side opposite me and helped me push.

"Think a push start'll work?" he said.

"We'll see," I told him.

Something about the man was wrong.

The parking structure was laid out in a typical ascending spiral design. Sue Ellen pointed the truck downhill and let it roll about twenty feet before popping the clutch. With a blast of white smoke out the tailpipe, the engine shook and shimmied to life. She was idling, warming it up a little, when I got to her window.

"Good thinkin'," she told me. "Thanks for walking me out. I was wondering, you know, about that visitation order?"

The man in the black shirt was three feet behind me now.

"Take off," I said quietly to Sue Ellen. "We'll talk later."

"Guess that did the trick," the man said. "Listen—"

In a city this size, this guy was far too eager. "Thanks for the assist," I said.

"Mr. Shepard," Sue Ellen went on, "like I was saying, do you think—"

"Go," I told her. "Now." She looked bewildered, but I didn't care to explain. I could feel an attack coming.

"This thing's really a sorry piece of shit, isn't it?" the man said. "I mean, how can someone who can't even afford a decent car think they can afford to raise a baby?"

There it was. I slapped my hand flat against the door. "Go!" I yelled at Sue Ellen, who finally got the message and gunned it down the aisle and out of view. When I turned to face him he was already squaring off for action.

"You're a sorry piece of shit too, aren't you partner?" he said. He was holding a metal object that looked like an unopened knife in his right hand.

In an instant I saw his eyes registering my dimensions as if he was calculating odds. I was easily his size—maybe thirty pounds heavier—and at least ten years his junior. A flicker of doubt was all the invitation I needed to begin talking my way out of a fight.

"Don't do it," I said, stifling my fear just enough to force a smile. "I get hold of you, I'm gonna drag you over to that parking block and break your legs over it. You ready for that reality?" I settled into a solid stance.

He eyeballed the leg-breaking device I'd just pointed out. "The woman's bad news," he said. "You better stay the fuck away from her." He hadn't budged.

We faced each other tensely, pacing and shifting for half a minute without speaking. I didn't want to fight here at my place of work if I didn't absolutely have to, didn't want to find out how much it hurt to get cut by a blade, if that's what he was holding. Just my shitty luck, I'd worn the light gray, glen-plaid suit today; a roll on this oil-spotted cement would ruin it. I couldn't afford to replace the glen-plaid, couldn't even afford to fix the broken dishwasher in my kitchen. The thought of being further impoverished by this phony Good Samaritan pissed me off, and I struggled to turn my anger into something approximating courage.

"You did what you came here to do," I said. "Walk away."

Just then Sue Ellen's truck rounded into view from below. In the cab with her was a parking attendant, the Hispanic guy who worked the toll booth downstairs.

"Lookie here, it's the cavalry," my opponent said. Without another word he turned and sprinted toward the stairwell and disappeared.

Sue Ellen jumped out of the cab and ran to me. "What was that all about?"

My heart was thumping, but the last thing I wanted to do was freak Sue Ellen. She needed to keep her composure over the next few weeks, long enough to have some nice get-acquainted visits with Nathan and help me tighten up our defense for trial. But the guy was after her; I was just the unwitting chaperone who got in the way. She had a right to know about any potential danger she'd be facing. I had to tell her, but I also had to choose my words with the utmost precision.

"I'm not sure who that was," I said, "but he doesn't want you reunited with Nathan. Probably just a bozo who believes whatever he hears on TV just because it's on TV."

"Oh my god! Did he try to hurt you?" she asked.

I did my best to appear nonplussed. "Does it look like it?"

Sue Ellen flipped her hair back and relaxed a little. "You don't scare very easy, do you Mr. Shepard?"

Right, I thought, my heart still thudding inside my chest. "Listen, I don't want you getting hassled by any kooks like that, so if you're going out, take your husband or a friend. Don't go out alone."

"I won't," she said. She held her gaze on me. "Thank you. You make me feel safe. I really appreciate it." Her eyes never blinked.

I'd seen the look many times before, the universal sign of longing, part of that ancient, unspoken dialogue between the sexes. Fuck me, I thought, don't do this, Sue Ellen, not now.

"I've got to get back," I told her, my voice cracking like a nervous schoolboy's. As I walked away I heard her giggle just before the roar of the old Ford swept her away.

My briefcase was still parked in the interview room off of Foley's courtroom, but the bailiff had locked up for the noon recess. I had no cases left on the calendar for the day, but I was stuck and had to wait out the long noon recess reading the *Times* and eating a peanut butter and jelly on wheat from the cafeteria.

After lunch, Shelly Chilcott took immediate advantage of my surprise reappearance by assigning me a physical abuse detention. The case involved a large Salvadoran family with Mother, Father Number One, Father Number Two, and three girls who told three distinctly different stories to the emergency worker about how their arms had gotten freckled with cigarette burns. Every available pick-up attorney in 302 was already on this one, Shelly explained as she handed me a fresh file. My client, Father Number Two, was the model citizen with the chrome lighter outlined in his jeans pocket when he straightened up to shake my hand. The man was ready to fight, but he spoke only the most rudimentary English; as such, his opening tirade was all but lost on me, and I could only nod along dumbly as he vented. After ten vein-popping minutes, he flat ran out of things to say and I slipped back inside.

A fresh headache throbbed behind my eyes. The Randall case had tapped most of my energy and I wanted to go home, and soon. But this one would take time to get all the lawyers in sync. The others would need to know whether my client the pyromaniac would agree to temporarily move out so the kids could avoid a stay in foster care. Of course, since my client and I hadn't actually spoken, I couldn't say. Our language barrier was bogging down the whole damned effort.

I searched the halls for Alfonso, the Spanish interpreter that usually worked 302, but had no luck. Then I tried the office upstairs by phone, but no one picked up. I headed for the elevators.

The door to the interpreters' office on the fifth floor was locked. I knocked but heard nothing. I tried to envision the rest of my day outside this place. A dip in the ocean, a brisk swim out around the pier and back followed by a stop-off at the Captain's Galley. Happy-hour shrimp and finger tacos washed down by a liquid dinner, enough alcohol to numb the brain and cleanse the lingering aftertaste of dependency from my gills. I knocked again.

Only two courtrooms operate on floor five handling overflow cases from downstairs. But they must have recessed for the day; the waiting area was empty, and beyond the wide windows in the distance, low cement buildings and warehouses shone in faded yellows and tans above a snarl of treetops, marking the sun's slow retreat.

"Hello?" I called through the door. At the far end of the corridor, a lone janitor methodically stroked a dust mop over a long, rectangular strip of linoleum as if he were mowing a lawn.

Another door was open twenty feet away, so I headed over and poked my head inside. A young woman who looked to be in her mid-twenties was seated at a single desk, twisting a phone cord in her long fingers as she recited a series of highway directions into the receiver. When I heard the coordinates, I knew she was talking about MacLaren Hall. "Right with you," she whispered as she motioned me to come in.

I set down my briefcase and settled into one of the two chairs opposite the desk. The chair was small and hard, a stiff little armless job that instantly reminded me of my time served in Catholic school. The desk was crammed with low piles of files and papers, a computer terminal dominating the corner nearest the door. To my right, against the far wall, a bookcase was stacked with rows of ring binders labelled with names like "West Covina Pilot," "E. L.A. Lifeline" and "Downtown Outreach." Another shelf held a block of thick hardbounds on parenting and child development. The social worker's tools.

"Why don't you read that back to me so we'll be sure you'll get there in time to have a visit today?" she said, sharing a small smile of understanding with me.

I surreptitiously studied her. She didn't resemble any social worker I'd ever seen. Much, much prettier. A kind, lovely face, straight nose, cocoa-brown eyes. She laughed at something, and as she did her fine black hair swished lightly across the front of her sleeveless beige dress. I was certain I'd never laid eyes on her before in this building; this was a face I would have committed to memory.

She put down the receiver. Feeling like I'd intruded, I stood up quickly. "Hi, I'm J. Shepard. I work in the building."

"Sit down." She waited. "Was that you knocking just down the hall?"

I nodded. "Nobody there. You wouldn't happen to know where I could find a Spanish interpreter, Ms. . . ." I wanted to know her name.

"Carmen—Carmen Manriquez." I thought she would offer her hand but she stayed behind her desk.

"I work in three-oh-two, Judge Foley's court. My client doesn't speak English. Our usual interpreter must've bailed early. I'm kind of stuck."

"*You're* stuck?" she said. "Think how your client feels."

"Yeah, well, it's my . . . our last case on calendar today," I said. I looked around. "I've never been up here. The interpreters usually leave this early?"

"I don't know. Let me call them," she said, flipping through a master phone list that dangled from a thumbtack on a bulletin board behind the desk. We waited as she rang. "No one there."

"Great. Why does my last client of the day always seem to speak Spanish?" I smiled, turning to go.

She seemed mildly taken aback. "Let me see. About sixty percent of L.A. County is Hispanic. That could possibly have something to do with it."

"So what's the answer?" I said. "We all learn Spanish?"

"Why not? Lots of Europeans speak the languages of their neighboring countries. Look at the map."

"I know. This used to be Mexico."

"My point exactly."

"I know some Spanish," I said, not wanting to appear too completely out of touch.

She folded her arms like an inquisitor. "High school?"

I nodded, and when I did, I could tell she thought she had me. "But I learned some at home, too," I told her. "From my mother."

"Oh, she's a Latina?"

"She was—she is. From Chile."

"I see." She sighed as if mildly disappointed, then dialed the interpreters' office.

"What do you mean, you see?" I said.

"Nothing." She put back the phone.

I was intrigued. "Don't say nothing. Tell me."

She eyed a stack of papers on her desk. "Well," she said, "you really have no excuse."

"No excuse?" I said, fearing an imminent attack. A good many social workers despise attorneys; some workers even have trouble distinguishing counsel from the perpetrators they represent. "I didn't know I needed an excuse." I liked the way she could hold my gaze, even in a budding argument.

"The language. It's part of your mother's heritage."

"My mother's heritage is a bit more complicated than that," I said. "Listen, you're right, learning Spanish is a good thing, and I shouldn't bitch about needing an interpreter. But what difference does it make as to *why* I learn another language?"

Carmen Manriquez looked bemused. "You may want to ask your mother about that."

My next sparkling witticism was a long way down the tracks. We both endured a patch of silence. "I knew you were a lawyer," she said.

"Boy. You don't quit."

She nodded. "No, no. Your briefcase."

I'd lugged the thing upstairs as a sort of penance for leaving it behind before lunch, an oversight that had cost me the afternoon. "One of these days I'll give it a decent burial."

My briefcase opened across the top, with zipping side pouches that stay out of the way of a file-toting cavern through the middle. I'd paid for it with funds from my first Legal Project paycheck, choosing it solely for its ability to hold more paper than any other case I could find, and it had done the job. But by now, after years of daily poundings, it was scuffed beyond belief, the top zippers frozen in place. Inside, a leather crease was studded with paper clips and a few cheap ball-point pens, the Sports section from yesterday's *Times* wedged between the Randall file and a never-used commuter train schedule. Embarrassing.

I did my best to appear breezy. "I suppose my briefcase is a microcosm of my legal career here," I said. "A bit of a mess."

She laughed. "So why do you do it?"

"Do what?"

"Why do a job you don't like?"

It was the same question Phoebe had put to me at her father's award reception, and I remembered my overly defensive reaction that night. But Carmen Manriquez had a different way about her, a directness that probably made her a very good social worker. This was no rich little daddy's girl handing down judgment.

My face felt flushed as I tried to compose an answer that wouldn't sound too hard-bitten. I hardly knew Carmen but I wanted to make a decent impression. "It's not all bad," I said. "Just having an off day."

"I hope that one day you find what you really want to do," she said. She'd mildly hassled me about the Spanish, but she had an appealing gentleness about her now. I imagined what it might be like to kiss her full on the lips. "And good luck with your adoption case," she added.

I realized she knew me from the Channel Six TV reports, but I didn't want that spectacle to invade our conversation. "What do you do?" I asked.

"You've heard of Las Palomas? This is our office. You just can't see the sign when the door's propped open."

"Good plan—hide the sign," I observed. "Keep those friendly stop-ins at a minimum."

"You're awful."

"Las Palomas," I said. "I send my clients to your programs all the time. Wow, did I ever have a prime candidate for your in-home skills course last week."

"Why didn't you send her up?"

"I did. Darla Madden?" Carmen didn't react. "Let's just say you'd know her if you saw her." I nodded at the door. "Darla would cut a rather dramatic swath through a space this size."

"I remember her," she said. "Really raring to go. Told me her lawyer would—what was it? Have her 'fanny in a frying pan' if she didn't enroll right away, that's it."

"That's my Darla."

"You sound like quite the motivator."

"Why, thank you."

I settled back into my rock-hard little chair, content to stay put for the time being. Carmen picked up the phone and began calling other court departments, asking for someone who could help build a bridge between Father Number Two and me.

Seven

I was easing the Jeep into my garage when Jackie bolted through the back door and rapped on my window.

"What now?" I said. It was 9:15. My ass was dragging after a few slack hours of wrap-up at the office and a freeway trek at bumper-car speeds. I had just enough energy left to shower and dive into bed.

"We got a visitor. Looks like a freakin' gargoyle from hell. Scared the crap outta me, boss." Jackie pointed across the dark backyard. A guttural snarl emanated from the spot Jackie had singled out. "Must be on some kind of a chain, or it'd be feasting on filet of Pace right now," he said, panting.

I crept through the back door and peered into the dark. "I think it's hurt," I whispered. "Listen, it's wheezing."

We tiptoed another twenty feet along the side yard and sidled up the back porch. When I rattled my keys the unseen animal let off an unnerving, malevolent bark that made Jackie and me leap back, but the beast didn't advance. "He's tied to the tree," I said. I opened the door and flipped on the porch light.

"Judas Priest, what a specimen!" Jackie cried. "The biggest, mackingest Doberman I've ever seen!"

"He's a Rottweiler," I said, and he truly was a creature of majestic proportions.

A folded note rested in the screen door. It said:

> *Mr. Shepard, Darla says tell you she did tried, but no one would take him on this short of notice. He is a good dog—no, really the best, likes a lg. can of Alpo with his dry, morn and nite. (Drinks lots of water, of coarse) THANKS for been our last resort, we owe you one, Pete. P.S. The kids would like to visit.*

"Look at him!" Jackie called to me. He'd moved in close enough to pet the toothy monster on the head.

I circled the thick trunk of the pepper tree, my eyes following the counter-clockwise loops of chain. "Let's get him untangled. Lift his paw."

Left alone and disoriented, the dog had run circles around the tree and lashed himself fast against the trunk. When I freed his front paws he raised his huge, rock-like head and licked me across the chin.

"Good boy! He likes you, J.! What's his tag say?"

"His name is Max," I said without looking.

Jackie was puzzled. "So whose dog, man?"

"Mine, I guess, at least for tonight. He belonged to a client."

"They dropped it off?" He stared at me incredulously. "They know where you live? You're fuckin' kidding me."

"I know, I shouldn't have given them my address. But this lady, if you could see her, she's pretty witless."

Jackie shot me a quick stink-eye. "Excuse me, man, but you've told me enough about those dipshit derelicts you represent to know you don't ever want 'em dropping by the humble abode."

His words were dead-on. A few years back an L.A. dependency lawyer was murdered by one of his clients. The shooter was a distraught father who'd lost his job, his family and his marriage when his daughter testified that he'd made her jerk him off when Mommy wasn't home. Of course, Father said he didn't do it and sat back as if that was enough to win at trial. It wasn't. The lawyer had been foolish enough to give Father his home address before the hearing so that Father could deliver a last-minute psych evaluation to him. A few days after the judge made her orders, Father was waiting at the foot of his lawyer's driveway next to the Sunday paper, a loaded .38 in hand.

We untangled the dog together.

"He's purebred—aren't you, killer?" Jackie cooed at Max. "You ask me, J., your client's *mondo estupido*. What fuckin' fool wouldn't want this big hero?"

"This fuckin' fool," I said. "Careful man, he's supposed to have a mean streak," I added just as Max rolled onto his back to let Jackie

and me stroke his muscular chest. Christ, even the dog was playing me.

"Why'd you have to take him?" Jackie asked.

"The house was a dump and the social worker on the case was
considering sticking the kids he lived with in a foster home. Old
Max here almost bit the dude in half."

Jackie delighted in this tidbit of information. "That is fresh. You
da man, Max! Nobody rattles your cage."

"This yard's way too small for a dog this size," I said.

"Then we'll just have to walk him every day, that's all."

I cocked an eyebrow. "We? Pardon me, Jack, but last time I
checked you weren't too enthusiastic about domestic chores."

"Bygones, my man. You're lookin' at the new me."

"Fine," I said, "but it's the old you that worries me. Remember
me? I'm the guy who spent a week picking Cracker Jacks out of
the living room carpet after your little Vegas night marathon got out
of hand."

"What can I say, we ran out of chips," he said. "I was up huge.
Had to keep the game going somehow."

"It's all a game. Like with those bikini models you finger-painted
on the front lawn that time."

Jackie shrugged. "Didn't know the paint was oil-based."

I rubbed Max's forehead gently between his eyes, which set his
big pink tongue wagging. "You could've read the cans. That little
cleanup party killed half the grass."

"Oh, that little strawberry blond, what was her name? Chloe,
Joey? The one with the freckles . . ."

"Since when have you been so hot on having a dog?"

Jackie shook the dog's club-like front paws and made goo-goo
sounds as if he was wooing an infant. "Since I was a kid. I wanted
a dog bad, real bad, practically begged my old man to get one, but
he wouldn't let me. Dichondra. Di-fucking-chondra."

"I don't know," I said. "Grog told me your old man used to live
in the Back Bay, big-ass two-story sitting in the dunes, lots of glass
windows. I didn't hear anything about dichondra."

Jackie brushed Max's jet-black mane. "I didn't live there when I
was a kid, Einstein. But whatever."

"Your old man must be loaded. How else could he afford the Back Bay mega-pad? He probably could've bought you ten dogs."

"He's not loaded, dim sum," Jackie said. "The land the house is built on is unsuitable for building, a fucking quagmire if you must know. That's why he got it cheap. Foundation's so shaky—huh . . ." He chuckled through tight lips. "One day the earth's gonna open up and just swallow the fucker whole."

In the dozen odd years I've known Jackie, I'd never heard him venture even this much information about anyone in his family. I was instantly curious. "How come you told the magazines both your parents were dead?"

"That was a long time ago," he said. "In the sixties, parents were a hindrance, man. Mine were definitely uncool."

Max continued to lap up the attention Jackie and I were lavishing on him. He rolled onto his back, his tongue sliding sideways over a very serious row of teeth. "I don't know, Jack," I said. "Everybody goes through that phase sometime around junior high, their parents embarrassing them. So what? I heard you always did whatever you wanted."

"Yeah, and what did any of my accomplishments have to do with them?"

I looked up from Max. "I heard they bankrolled your act."

Jackie sat up, his jaw rigid. "That's a lie!"

I stood up, still holding Max's chain. "A lie, like what you told the mags about them being dead?"

"Hey, fuck you!" he said, standing and circling as if to orient himself. I'd really tapped a vein. "My mother died in 'seventy-four," he said. "Haven't spoken to the old man in almost that long. If he's so rich, then how come I been living in the lap of luxury like this ever since you've known me?"

"Most people work for a living, Jack."

"Shepard, you're being a dick right now."

"You talk about lies," I said as he stared at the ground. "I don't know. Sometimes I think you pretty much say whatever you want, even to your friends."

"I'm always straight with you, man," he said, conjuring a scrap of dignity again.

I can't explain it, why I trust some people and not others, but somewhere, in some unconscious corner of my mind, I take a pulse on the truth, and something—a thought, a feeling, a voice, a memory—informs me. And in that instant I know. At least, that's the illusion. A priest I once described the feeling to told me it was a kind of grace. I didn't argue with his assessment; whatever the source, I'll take all the help I can get.

"I think you stroke me all the time, like the tale of your old man's dichondra. Only most of the time I let you slide."

He held up his hands like a preacher beseeching the Lord. "Okay, okay. I want the damn dog. Nothing deep, nothing Oedipal. No stroke job, no dichondra. Happy?"

"I don't need a dog," I said. "Especially one that might dine on the next bonehead who stumbles into the yard to read my gas meter."

Jackie started to speak, but conceded. "That's fine, boss," he said, his shoulders drooping. He bent down and stroked Max's chest forlornly. "No dog."

Nice touch, Jackie, I thought as he soothed Max. He thinks he's got me, doing his Little Orphan Annie.

The curtains were drawn across the upstairs windows so that the glass reflected the black night sky. The place was as cold and still as a dollhouse, like some child's abandoned toy.

"I'll be back in a few," I said as I headed for the garage.

"Where you going?" Jackie called out behind me.

"To get some food for him. Couple of big metal bowls. He'll need some rawhide toys so he doesn't chew the siding off the house. Get the wetsuits off the garage floor before he eats them."

"Epic call, J.!" he shouted. He hung an arm around Max's head. "We're keeping you, buddy! I am so stoked! Hey, Maxie boy, are you stoked?"

Exhausted, I climbed back into the Jeep.

"Hey J.—J." Jackie's voice sang out from the backyard, echoing off the ancient Shepard big wave guns that hung in the rafters and along the walls. "Max says he's stoked!"

I heard Max bark happily from the yard as I hit the ignition. Good Max, I said to myself, Jackie will entertain you for now. But make no mistake about this. I will be your master.

Jackie and Max were gone when I got home from work the next evening, a Friday. A bold, late summer westerly rustled the high palms and blew dead leaves down from rain gutters. There would be no surfing in onshores like this, and I didn't bother to check the conditions.

The swells this morning had been chest-high and infrequent at the pier. I'd surfed for an hour at dawn with Jackie and Britt, riding paper-thin peaks that the rising sun showered with molten red then drops of brilliant gold. We'd spoken little during the lulls between sets, each of us staking out our own little corners of sandbar twenty yards apart, scanning the ocean surface for the next advancing lump and hoping that the dropping tide wouldn't further dilute the surf's power. Had I checked the waves alone I would not have gone out in such delicate swell conditions, but Jackie had insisted—it was always good to get wet, he'd said. I counted back in my mind through the recent spate of waves and tides and ocean moods come and gone. In the week since Jackie had returned I'd surfed six times, about twice my average. The man may have been a bullshitter supreme, but his stoke was powerful, and contagious.

I slipped into a T-shirt and shorts and laced up my running shoes. On the way out the front gate I stopped to stretch, then dropped onto the cool grass for some sit-ups, keeping up until a cramp stabbed me below the ribs and stole my breath.

The Southside beach was dry and blustery, sandblasted by a stiff wind that crabbed millions of scars onto the ocean surface and quickly chilled the sweat on my skin. The sunbathers had been driven away hours ago, and a swirl of blowing granules bit my shins as I crossed the pink sand. I dropped down to the hard pack at water's edge and jogged toward the pier until I was beneath the wet pilings. The boisterous conversation of two fishermen above me came and went as they watched me slip from their view. Reemerging on the wider, flatter Northside shore, I ran hard against the onshore breeze until I reached the jetty marking the north end of town, where warm water from the Edison plant flowed down a long man-made channel and into the sea. A man in a sleeveless undershirt and cutoffs was studying the rocks, stooping to snatch up the small crabs that thrive there in the artificially balmy water. A boy and girl raked long-tailed dragon kites against the sky, darting sideways in the wet sand as they reeled on their spools in a duel for superior position.

I jogged back to the pier and onto the Southside beach, then sprinted the last hundred-fifty yards down to the long south jetty, where I stopped and did forty push-ups against a huge flat rock, then rested and did forty more. My breath was nearly gone and stars burst before my eyes above the jetty rocks, but the physical exertion felt right in some fundamental way.

I stared into the face of a curling shorebreak dumper and mind-surfed my way through the tube before the wave disintegrated into whitewash. I could feel the Randall case pushing its way into my thoughts, a slew of loose details pressing in on my temples, but I consciously resisted. It was Friday; I needed a break.

The surf continued to bang against the jetty, the white foam fizzing and popping as it slanted back into the sea. I sat on the rock with my legs pulled into my chest and my arms locked across my knees to deflect the wind. Once more, the matter of Nathan Randall invaded the moment.

Every time I prepare for trial, the facts of the case consume me for weeks on end. I've begun to resent the intrusion. After all, I'm court-appointed counsel. I'm paid to be sure that those who can't afford a lawyer get one, not to work legal miracles. Perhaps Phoebe was right to have asked what in hell I was doing in dependency. Coddling sadists and pedophiles, dope addicts and dropouts, dull-eyed children for whom "Daddy" is the government check Mommy cashes every month, that's what. Obsessing over trials I often have little chance of winning.

I get too wound up, and for no good purpose. I can't fix my clients' problems quickly enough from one progress report to the next, and the repairs I perform are superficial quick-fixes anyway—a pep talk here, a counseling referral there, but nothing truly lasting. I'm also not above playing the savior. J. the Magnanimous, the kind and wise lawyer whose ability to give refuge to Rottweilers can be the difference in a tough dirty house case. Sometimes, in some cases, I manage to check out entirely, inured to the chaos around me. My clients can talk and beg and lie and cry and stamp their feet and feel sorry for themselves all they want, and I see to it that every one of them has his say. But I remain fundamentally unmoved. Their needy wishes cannot compete with the endless spinning waves I swoop through in that perfect lineup in my mind.

The Randall case was a mess I should have settled without hesitation. With Sue Ellen and Ty as my witnesses, the trial would play like a car crash in slow motion. What was I thinking? We were going down in spectacular fashion.

For the first time in years I realized how much I missed my father, and I regretted the fact that my memories of him were so timeworn and incomplete. I longed to seek his counsel, to draw from his reserve of low-key confidence. Consumed again by my doubts about the Randall matter, I engaged in a round of self-pity, wondering if Robert Shepard would have equated losing with not giving a shit.

A kiddie lawyer, Sue Ellen had said. Some rapport. There seemed to be no point any more in attempting to ingratiate myself with my clients; by now they knew I was putting them on. Results were all they wanted—children returned, the county off their backs. No grand, benevolent gestures. No heroics. Just results. I decided I could live with that.

A gull cried overhead. I watched its flight as it sailed beyond the surf and out along the jetty for two hundred yards or more until it fell in with a flock that was arching against the wind. Beneath the cloud of birds stood a lone figure on the rocks, a quarter mile out from where I rested. He was casting into the deep water inside the long jetty, whipping a thin fishing rod above his ear. It was Jackie, I knew, as this was our favorite spot to fish for halibut during the warm currents of summer. Max's head bobbed in and out of the rocks not far from Jackie, no doubt terrifying the small crustaceans hiding among the crevices. The gulls circled patiently, watching Jackie make his casts.

Ten years ago I'd shown Jackie how to fish for halibut here, how to snare live minnows that swim among the rocks with a long-handled net, bait the hook with the minnows still alive, and toss a delicately weighted line toward the reef that lies below in the deep water just off the jetty. That first time had been magic. We'd landed five or six big ones just before dark, which is the best time for catching halibut. Jackie was amazed at my proficiency. Ironic, he'd observed, that I could master the reef at Holy Rollers with a fishing pole, when this same reef had nearly pounded the life out of me the first time I'd ridden a wave across its jagged spine.

The sweat on my body was dry and a chill rippled through my shoulders. Time to go. I turned and saw Max poised atop the jetty, barking and wagging his stubby tail. Jackie looked up and waved, then yelled something I couldn't hear. I waved back and gestured toward home, then jogged up the berm and across the empty sand. A week of washing dishes by hand had made fixing the broken dishwasher a priority, and I wanted to be home before sundown. It would be no pleasant task to climb up into the attic and look for the dishwasher's service manual in darkness.

I stood on a chair in the upstairs hallway and pushed aside the panel of wood that covered the hatch in the ceiling. Then I slowly lifted myself, flashlight in hand, into the attic space. Stacks of cardboard boxes lined the unfinished wood-frame walls. A string attached to a bare bulb dangled from the ceiling. I tugged and heard a click, then boom!—a flash of light gave shape to the hulking shadows for an instant. Then darkness.

I flipped on the flashlight and sucked in the stale smell of sea salt and damp lumber. Forget going back down for a fresh bulb—this attic was not a place I enjoyed entering twice on the same day.

I hadn't passed through this hatch in a dozen years, since the day I'd set out to dismantle my mother's bedroom. Wouldn't it be funny, I remember thinking back then, to pack her things off to this dank space only to have her rattle through the front gate the very next day, demanding in agitated Spanish that it all be put back just as it was, *inmediatamente*. But there had been no surprise return, no small-scale tantrum to weather.

The flashlight's beam illuminated an array of objects stacked against the walls. Above me, the pitched ceiling was covered with rows of aged insulation that looked like pink cotton candy affixed to tar paper, probably oozing asbestos. Great—another costly fix-it job to tackle during a future flat spell. Behind me, a tennis racket with broken strings and a rusted speargun once owned by my father leaned against each other. To their right, a cluster of cardboard storage boxes were nestled like mortarless bricks in a wall. I scanned the felt-pen lettering on each box: X-MAS, KEY DOCS, 57 BEL AIR, CUSTOM ORDERS/RECEIPTS, STATE FARM, and so on. Fourteen boxes of long-forgotten junk.

A spell of sadness descended on me, and I wondered what I was really doing up here. Christ, I could buy a new dishwasher at Sears and pay it off in monthly installments. But that wasn't the thing. I was searching for something that had been missing from me for too many years. I'd forgotten the bass note in my father's voice when he called me in from the street at dinnertime, the effortless tumble of his laugh, the way he braced a screaming planer in his hands as he plowed it over a fresh surfboard blank in the garage. He died early enough to miss most of my youth, never coaching my Little League team or making it to parent-teacher night at Saint Ann's. Never glimpsing the person I was to become.

My mother was as gone to me now as my father, but in my mind she still wasn't dead. I remembered much more of her. She was the one who'd raised me, especially when it was just us. She'd been there through measles and chicken pox and flu seasons and times I lay in bed all day immobilized only by the permanence of my father's absence from my world. Those first years after he died, my mother and I functioned best side-by-side. Saturday household chores, grocery shopping, homework, ice-cream runs at Grandma's across from the pier—it didn't matter. We grieved my father's passing but honored his memory by relying on each other to make a good life together as his remaining heirs. But of course, I had to grow up, and like a typical teen I did so with all the grace and subtlety of a runaway bull. Experimenting with enough foreign substances to know why Kerouac had trouble finishing his sentences. Falling in love with a thirty-year-old woman who happened to be married at the time. Surfing up and down the coast, staying away a little longer with every trip. By the time my mother left me, I was every bit the surly, headstrong kid you see staring at you from the senior photos in any high school yearbook. I never accepted that she could have simply bailed. For her I'd kept a long-standing vigil, blinking at the shadows on the front walk at night for so many years that by now, Marielena Shepard had become a ghost, loitering somewhere between my dreams and waking prayers.

I'd never really admitted that for my mother and me, the end had come and gone. I had yet to mourn her passage. If I had learned anything from the work I did in dependency, it was that the world was a place of abject indifference to personal suffering and loss. Nobody cared.

Nervous breakdowns probably start like this. I'd lost it in front of Jackie and Phoebe at the party. "Marielena Shepard!" I'd shouted, as if she mattered to anyone but me. And Carmen Manriquez, she hardly knew me, but she seemed to sense an uneasy disconnection. I took in my immediate surroundings: remnants, no real heritage to speak of anymore, only an attic full of junk. I had stopped looking for Marielena Shepard many years ago when I never should have desisted, and just now, I despised myself for my failure.

I turned my self-hatred on my mother, how she could leave me like she did. I closed my eyes and prayed for a sign that she was dead, dead and gone for what she'd done to me. But I couldn't wish her out of my mind, not for a single, self-pitying minute. I wanted to cry, but the tears wouldn't come.

I was fucked.

I lacked the courage to go forward, but hadn't a reason in the world to turn back. There was nothing more to do but find out what had become of Marielena Shepard.

I swept the flashlight from left to right and settled on an old metal file cabinet my mother had once used to keep her accounting records. I remembered removing the drawers so that I could shove the cabinet up the hatch without breaking my back under the weight of it. It was beige and frosted with dust, a gold key protruding from the top drawer. I'd laid some of my mother's personal things in that top drawer and turned the key back in December of '79, a few short days after the infamous Jackie Pace found me on the reef at Holy Rollers.

The key clicked over easily, but the rollers groaned as I jerked the drawer open and poked the flashlight in. The drawer was filled with an assortment of items: a folded shawl, a few silk scarves, a black ring binder stuffed with loose papers, some thin manila folders in hanging files. I took my time, removing the contents one at a time and placing them on the floor next to me.

Many of the objects were religious. A tiny, gilt-edged black pocket Bible, the one she used to bring to mass. A larger, hardbound King James version. A stack of holy cards bound by a single rubberband, some in Spanish; one commemorating my first communion, another the death of my father. Two display candles, the kind that burn their way down a large, colored-glass cylinder. The kind you use for prayer vigils. Both candles were adorned with decals showing the benevolent face of Christ, eyes raised slightly, a gold halo behind his tilted head. Inside his chest his ruby heart was ringed by a wreath of thorns and glowed at the edges with spears of yellow light. Beneath his robe was a scroll bearing the words *Sagrado Corazon de Jesus*, Sacred Heart of Jesus. Three sets of black rosary beads, one white. A withered string of bleached white garlic bulbs—my mother's method of warding off demons. Marielena Shepard could not have been a prude to have married a free spirit like my father, but she was spiritually grounded in a way that, through practice and ritual, probably made her life feel safer and more predictable.

She was also very superstitious. Devoted to God but fearing Satan with equal intensity, my mother believed the two were in constant combat over her soul. Her nature was low-key and peaceful, but in times of adversity she would strain to see signs in ordinary occurrences, signs that she hoped might signify that the Lord was indeed winning the battle. The signs she saw were not always encouraging. One omen she never bothered to explain kept us off a rather important bridge in the L.A. Harbor for two years—until, that is, a sizeable earthquake caused enough structural damage to close it for two more years for repairs.

Another bad sign had led her to distrust doctors. My dad's old friend Grog Baker told me of the omen my mother thought she received the day my father's heart gave out on him. Grog and my father had been surfing more or less together that day but were lining up two or three sandbars apart to wait for the swells. Grog was the first one there to see my father go down, and he acted fast, dragging him from the water and administering CPR while he listened for a heartbeat. But nothing worked. A lifeguard-paramedic appeared a few minutes later and took charge in a blur of motion, shouting directions at Grog while he alternately pumped my father's chest and blew air deep into his lungs. According to Grog, the paramedic had that gunfighter's cockiness some doctors seem born with and really believed he was going to save my father. But his jump-starts failed. The guy took it hard, pacing and cursing and taking the Lord's name in vain several times. Later, at the hospital, Grog was still reeling from the ordeal and unthinkingly told my mother everything, even the part about the paramedic's frustrated rant. Those blasphemous words probably assured my father's death, my mother told Grog. Not so Marielena, Grog pleaded, the doc did everything he could to save a life. But her mind was made up. It was a sign.

The last object I removed from the trunk was a brown leather portfolio with a sleek gold buckle and the letters MS engraved above the clasp and finished with gold paint. Marielena Shepard. It looked expensive and of fine quality, an extravagant accessory I could not picture my mother purchasing for herself, the engraving adding a special touch. This was a gift.

There wasn't much inside, just a gold pen and pencil set tucked into their leather holders and two rubberband-bound bundles of papers. I flipped through the first bundle, a dozen air-mail envelopes, all addressed to my mother, all previously opened and bearing a return address of Ritoque, Chile—my mother's hometown—along with the name "M. Elizalde." These were letters from my mother's revered great aunt, Miluca Elizalde.

Aunt Miluca had been the central adult figure in my mother's life, raising her, sponsoring her education, and eventually paying her way to the United States with an entree to an accounting position at a Long Beach import-export company that traded in fine Chilean wines and produce. My mother's father was one of many Chileans to die in the government-owned silver mines high in the Central Andes. Her mother was killed a few months later in a freak accident, returning from the central market in Puerto Montt in a public bus.

The bus driver swerved to avoid a man lying in the road but lost control, the bus flipping over and rolling into the sea. The man in the road was drunk and attempting suicide, but when he saw the bus roll into the sea he ran away. My mother was orphaned at four. She relied solely on God's grace to get through, she once told me, but at that age, she could not have comprehended much. Her Aunt Miluca took her in and raised her as her own. To my mother, Aunt Miluca was *Luz Guidora*, her guiding light.

A few letters were brittle and yellow with postmarks from the mid-sixties, but the rest bore seventies postmarks, three with 1979 stamps. One was postmarked August 16, 1979, which meant my mother had read this letter a mere three weeks before she'd disappeared. I unfolded it and pored over the first few lines, but the text was in Spanish, stopping me cold. I'd have to find a translator— someone at the courthouse first thing Monday.

The second bundle was a stack of faded fold-out brochures, the paper crackling at my touch. A sales brochure, some kind of real estate come-on for a place called Sea Pointe.

A half dozen or so developments had been carved out of the low bluffs and sandy lots around Christianitos over the last twenty years. Puerto Mar, Maison de Rose, Sea Ridge, Christianitos del Mar, The Bluffs. A few more neighborhoods had corny seaside names that temporarily escaped me, but I was certain none were called Sea Pointe.

I studied the artist's rendering of a large, spacious home over-looking an inlet of water and rugged, unscathed bluffs. A fold-out page contained a map divided into grids and marked with tiny reference numbers. The brochure touted the "unparalleled ocean and city views" and "favorable zoning" that apparently made these parcels such a steal for building that dream home. I read on. "Priceless solitude," they boasted. Priceless my ass. Another rich developer— "Provencal Ltd." was the name above the call-for-info number— getting richer by carving up the last few open spaces along an already overpopulated stretch of coastline.

I could think of no immediate connection between Provencal Limited and my mother. She could not afford a big lot or the price tag to build a custom home, to pay such an inflated ransom for a piece of priceless solitude. Besides, she loved this house and her roses, the short walk—two blocks—to choir practice and Sunday mass at Saint Ann's. She loved our close proximity to the shore, where she would stroll in the late afternoon, dropping rose petals into the foaming water down at the end of Twelfth Street, the place where my father had taken his last breath. As far as I knew she'd been perfectly content living here on Porpoise Way.

She could have done some accounting work for the developer, Provencal. Once the Chilean import-export business folded (the market for Chilean wines grew smaller as the California vineyards came into their own), my mother had decided to go it alone. She picked up odd assignments here and there through a local business-networking group sponsored by the chamber of commerce. An ad she placed in the Saint Ann's Sunday bulletin also brought assignments. If Provencal had needed help maintaining their books, they might have used her.

I closed up the file cabinet, dropped the letters and brochures into the lighted hallway below, and eased back down the hole until I felt the top step of the ladder. Thinking about the expensive portfolio, Sea Pointe, whether my mother had a lover. The letters might explain a lot of things. I shut the hatch, remembering that I was still without a working dishwasher. What the hell—things like dishwashers you can replace.

Jackie and Max were back from their fishing expedition. Max was soaking wet and covered with sand, barking his head off. Jackie crooned "Light My Fire" as he fed the flames in the backyard barbecue pit with a long squirt from a can of lighter fluid. "Yo, J.-man the sha-man, I am *starving*," he said. He eyed the bundles I'd brought down from the attic. "Whatcha got, some old love letters that need torching?"

"Stuff for work," I said. But Jackie seemed uninterested.

"You're working too hard," he said. "Take a break for a few hours, boss."

Jackie would not be hearing about my discovery in the attic or my decision to look for some answers after all this time. Not tonight, at least. I knew I was breaking a very old promise to him and that sooner or later he'd catch on; when he did he'd be pissed and demand an explanation. I'd hear his "shit happens" speech, the timeworn platitudes about moving on. The guy meant well, but his counsel would do nothing but erode my tentative resolve.

I went in through the open kitchen door and stuffed the bundle of letters into a side pouch of my briefcase, which was already overstuffed with files. The Sea Pointe brochures wouldn't fit. I nearly jumped to see Jackie standing in the doorway behind me.

"It's Friday, says I," he said. He raised the lighter fluid and pointed the spout at me as if I was next to be incinerated. "Party or die, says I, party or die."

A wicker basket full of the week's discarded newspapers lay next to my briefcase on the floor. I casually dropped the brochures atop Wednesday's front page. "Okay," I told him, "you win. It'll be twenty minutes at least before those coals get hot enough," I said. "Let's see what you caught, Ahab. I'll do up a little tartar sauce and marinade." To my relief, he didn't seem to have noticed the drop I'd made. Or at least he hadn't seen fit to comment.

"Prepare to view the catch, mate," Jackie said. We walked to the picnic table, where he hoisted two flat-faced halibut the size of serving platters. "You're lookin' at two of the best fish I've ever caught on a line, and get this, I snagged 'em on back-to-back casts."

"At dusk?"

"Right after Max saw you. You were our good luck charm."

"I'd better get on the phone," I said. "We'll need Britt and a few of his delinquent buddies to help us out. There's no way we'll even eat half of it ourselves."

"In the bag, mate," he said, waving me off. "I've already made a few arrangements. Hope you don't mind," he added when he saw the stress lines rise on my forehead. "Mondo good times in store for tonight. I give you the Pace guarantee."

I said nothing, not wishing to spoil his triumphant mood. I was wasted from court, tired of making argument for the day. Though the house had barely recovered from the last happening he'd commandeered, I didn't much feel like playing the heavy.

A short while later the back gate began to clatter open and shut. Max played the *maitre d'* by ambling over to simultaneously greet and scare the holy crap out of each arriving guest. An unusual mix of people came to dine with us. Britt was in attendance, of course, with three surf-team pals who chowed down until towels had to be applied to their sweating foreheads. But Britt's fourth guest was a quiet, exceedingly polite girl from the ladies squad with long, sun-streaked brown locks and unusual poise for a seventeen-year-old. Her name was Shannon, and her presence had a visible effect on Britt. When she arrived she quickly offered me an assist in the kitchen, dicing vegetables and tossing a salad while I scrubbed potatoes and cleaned the fish. We talked about surfing and school, her plans for college and a future surf trip to Costa Rica. Britt kept popping his head inside to see what was up, but we didn't need his help. Yet each time Shannon sent him away, she did so ever so gently. The girl knew exactly what was up.

A couple of Jackie's Hawaiian friends—two brothers, both built like professional wrestlers, with long, wild black hair and necks as thick as tree stumps—drove up from Huntington Beach. A hush fell over the group when they pushed through the back gate looking like the party crashers from hell as they balanced cases of beer, pineapples, a guitar and a ukulele on their shoulders. Max didn't hesitate to mob them with affection. It was as if Max, an awesome physical specimen himself, knew that he'd found two kindred spirits, and he stayed at their feet the rest of the night.

Percy Wrightman, a local fisherman and boat-builder who still surfed whenever he could find time, brought wine, a half gallon of ice cream and two apple pies. Jackie phoned him primarily to boast about his catch, so Percy also had a camera and tape to record Jackie's feat. When I told Percy I'd already filleted both fish without even weighing them, he rolled his eyes and chuckled, openly accusing Jackie of landing his big catch at the fish market.

"J., get Percy a cold one," Jackie groused as Percy dabbed tears from his eyes, the others roaring, "and don't forget to spit in it first."

Our most unexpected guest was Marion Blume, a fiftyish widow from across the alley who had came over to ask the owner of the black panel van—the Hawaiians—to please move it, as it was block-ing her "egress and ingress." Her voice trembled but her tone re-mained firm, as if she expected a confrontation. She didn't get one.

Jackie charmed my lonely neighbor while the van was moved, engaging her in a spirited chat about horticulture and landscape de-sign, two subjects of which he knows not a thing. I brought her a plate of food while they talked, Jackie nodding intently as she listed the virtues of homemade mulch. Though she was the first to go—just after nine—Marion took the time to shake hands with every guest before she ducked out. Ten minutes later she reappeared with a bunch of fresh-picked roses for my kitchen and a soup bone for Max. Jackie found the perfect gesture, as he is often wont to do, bowing to kiss Marion's hand as the rest of us hooted.

The night air warmed as a thick overcast floated in from the sea. I removed the grill from the barbecue pit and threw some logs on the smoldering embers. We sat in a close circle on lounge chairs turned sideways, eating pie and ice cream and clinking beers as the invigorated flames climbed higher. Britt and Shannon floated marsh-mallows out over the pit on the ends of trembling coat hangers, feeding them into our mouths as if we were baby birds. The Ha-waiians broke out their instruments and began to play, prefacing each tune with brief explanations of the history involved, the hope and heartbreak betrayed by the soft strains of Island melody. We listened in rapt attention as they harmonized, their meaty fingers coaxing impossibly delicate sounds from the twinkling strings.

Jackie smiled at me as if to say, not bad for back-to-back casts, eh? I was happy to share the vibe going around this circle and shot Jackie a grin in return. But the Island music was pulling me in another direction, gnawing at a forgotten parcel of memory.

They sang a traditional tune about the rape of the land, the tram-pling of Hawaiian culture by white missionaries, their peoples' will to persevere. Mako, the older Hawaiian, laid down his guitar and described the jolt he'd taken on his last trip home when he four-wheeled out of town to surf a semi-remote secret spot and found a shopping center blocking his path to the beach. Jackie quickly com-miserated, decrying the congestion that has all but throttled so many of the world's most pristine coastlines. "Same old story everywhere,"

Jackie said. "I've seen this place go from a quiet little town to a pimple on the ass of greater L.A."

"If we didn't have Save the Back Bay," Britt said, "it'd be a parking lot by now."

Britt's remark reminded me of the brochures I'd found earlier in the attic, the ones I'd slipped onto the pile of old papers in the kitchen. Now would be a good time to slide them out of view. Like a good host, I took a few drink orders before slipping inside.

The Wednesday front page stared up from the top of the pile. No brochures. I scanned the dining table and surrounding countertops, rifled through the trash basket near the door, then poked around under the sink and in the cupboards. The Sea Pointe brochures were gone. Quietly I checked my bedroom, the upstairs bath, the living room, the entry hall table, every conceivable place where they could have been mislaid. But I knew I hadn't mislaid the brochures. Someone here had taken them.

I handed out a few beers and sat down before the fire. The brochures were my mother's, stashed in a private, forgotten place all this time. Why would anyone here even care? Hell, none of the faces sitting beside me had even known Marielena Shepard, not even my friends. Britt was a small boy when she disappeared, and Jackie and I didn't first meet until three months after the fact. Jackie said he'd never known her before he saved me on the reef at Holy Rollers; I'd never questioned him on that. After all, what could a quiet, well-modulated single parent have shared in common with a surf star who openly cited Mick Jagger and P. T. Barnum as role models? Just one odd thing: years ago when he saved my life, I made a promise to him that I would end my search for my mother.

"Hey Jack," I called out across the flames, "ever hear of a development around here called Sea Pointe?"

He kept his eyes on the fire. "Sea Pointe? Can't say that I have, Master J.," he replied with no visible discomfort or emotion. He seemed to be telling the truth—or he could have been playing it cool to the hilt. Sometimes you needed a road map to follow his line of jive.

No one else had heard of Sea Pointe either.

The Hawaiians played on and the last of the logs popped and

split. I grew transfixed by the pulsating flames. This evening had been a truly fine time until someone had to go and lift those brochures. The visit to the attic weighed heavily on my mind. The letters, the portfolio, Sea Pointe—tracing my mother's footsteps. Moving ahead after thirteen years of inertia.

Minutes passed. When I looked up again, my eyes immediately met Jackie's, and I had the distinct feeling that he'd been watching me all along, tapping my thoughts. His gaze was intense, and yet I did not resent the intrusion, but rather welcomed it. I was apt to benefit from Jackie's watchful presence.

December, 1979

Holy Rollers looked big to my eyes, even from the pier, a solid quarter mile from the reef. Booming, violent. I felt more like a roped-off tourist watching the detonation and collapse of large buildings than a lone rider checking out a surfable wave. A mysto spot, all right. For anyone with the audacity to even think of paddling out on days like this, the anxiety hangs in the air like a gypsy curse. Nerves of steel turn to quivering jelly. Old sports injuries mysteriously act up. Long-forgotten side projects suddenly require urgent attention; wives and girlfriends, special treatment. Maybe another day. I knew the deal. Holy Rollers would always be msyto, I decided, because surfers wanted it that way.

Today it was my turn to be cursed.

Never mind the curse, you're ready, I told myself. After all, I surfed nearly every day, played water polo for the high school team, and could handle myself reasonably well in overhead beachbreak conditions. My big-wave-riding genes were unparalleled.

I secretly harbored a few grand aspirations, too. One day I would travel to the Islands, the North Shore of Oahu, and hunt the big stuff as my father had done. Holys was a natural stepping stone toward that goal, a full-tilt big wave training ground right in my own backyard. I'd observed my share of rumbling, white-knuckle days out there the previous winter, leaning against the bait shack wall at the end of the pier and squinting through binoculars as thick lips poured onto the outer reef in what seemed like slow motion. Occasionally a few surfers from Huntington would show up and paddle out, guys with Island experience and a lot of big days at H. B. Pier under their belts. But more often than not, the lineup I studied was empty. In our town, only Jackie Pace had the skill and experience to regularly handle a complex, dangerous big wave spot like Holys. But I didn't know Jackie Pace—he'd rocketed to stardom when I was still a child—and he hadn't been seen around these parts much in recent years. The playing field was wide open, yet eerily deserted.

I silently reviewed the rules of the game. A low tide rising to medium is usually optimal, because on higher tides the volume of water pulling up the face is too great to make that drop over the ledge—and the last thing you want to do at a spot like Holys is get hung up at the top and pitched over the falls. At Holys, you surf the right, which is not self-evident since the peak breaks cleanly both ways. But only the right dumps you into a deep paddling channel at the end, ensuring a reasonably safe trip back outside. The best swell direction is a strong west with some north in it, anything over ten feet. Swell direction is important. The peak stands up and dumps on the outer reef, then lines up into a long right wall that goes hollow near the end in an inside bowl section known as the Tabernacle. On a straight west, the inside bowl produces a wild and beautiful barrel, but it tends to shut down too soon, swatting the rider before he can escape cleanly. A touch of north, however, angles the swells in a tad wider and holds open the Tabernacle's door, as they say, making tube riding less dicey.

Wipeouts are usually cold, deep and violent. Size-wise, no one knows how huge a swell Holys can handle before closing out, but the bigger the better seems to be the rule. In the epic winter of '69, the outer peak hit twenty-five feet plus several times and still held rideable shape.

A trio of tortured souls huddled nearby on the pier, alternately watching, pacing, and crapping their pants at the spectacle of big Holys. We exchanged nervous nods.

A gargantuan deep-water wall exploded, sending a slight but bone-chilling tremor quivering through the wooden planks beneath our feet. The inside reef was boiling white now, like an underwater nuclear bombsite. I was hoping the other surfers would stick around and paddle out with me, but when I turned my back on Holys, they were shuffling off the pier toward Main and drinking in a commonplace, yet now oddly wonderful, view of advancing terra firma. A giant tube yawned and slammed shut the Tabernacle door, and I hooted, but no one heard me. The boys were already lost in debate over which restaurant offered the best breakfast special.

The sky was a soft, misted gray, the kind that closely follows a rain, and the air was cold and clean. In the wet sand below the pier, the children's playground was half underwater, giant puddles hemming in the jungle gym like a moat around a castle.

I'd been staying with my father's old friends, Pam and Grog Baker, for three months now since my mom had left or disappeared—or whatever. Like my dad, Grog had been a big wave rider in his time. He'd kill me if he knew I was doing this, I thought. Well, he wouldn't know. No one was on the pier when I trotted down the metal gangway to the boat landing, stretched my legs a bit, and jumped in.

I paddled slowly but at a steady clip, reminding myself to reserve enough energy for the long paddle back in. Two other older surfers from Long Beach had shown up a half hour earlier, just after the under-gunned trio had begged off and headed to breakfast, but they were nowhere to be seen. We'd hooted at a big set, chatting without eye contact. One of the Long Beach guys knew all about my father and spoke reverently of his contributions to the evolution of the big-wave gun. I told him I'd let him ride Honey Child—the board my dad had shaped for me when I was just a baby—once I'd had my fill.

At least, I hoped that Robert Shepard had made Honey Child with me in mind. He died before I ever got the chance to ask him. I'd found the board in the rafters a few months ago and shown it to Grog. My father was always tossing off nicknames, Grog said, and I was a very blond baby, so . . . well, you never know.

The board made me feel safer, somehow, as if my father was with me now in spirit. That was the idea behind this first-ever session at Holys: to strengthen my ties with him by putting Honey Child to its intended use—and to help put my deserter of a mother behind me for good. But as I approached, the outer peak was lonely and menacing in its desolation. Behind me, cold swells rolled unscathed toward shore, no other paddlers in sight. I removed a chunk of wax I'd tucked under the wrist of my wetsuit and rubbed it into the middle of my deck, then worked on the tail area a bit. Ten minutes of tense anticipation passed. When the first set lifted in front of me, I felt very much alone.

Paddling over those first few swells was almost surreal, so much more mountainous were they than any waves I'd ever attempted. The fifth and last wave was the biggest in the set, and as I scratched to escape over the top, I hesitated for an instant to look back. Ten feet to my right, an improbably thick lip was already pitching way, way out onto the flat some twenty-five feet below. I pushed over the back before the lip broke the surface, but the explosion was deafening. Behind me, the wall humped over as it wound down the reef, huge bursts of spray squirting out the back as it peeled away. Something shifted deep in my stomach and I felt like puking.

By the time the second set arrived, I'd all but forgotten the hype I'd been feeding myself about riding Honey Child for my father. My focus was now on survival, and I set about reviewing everything I'd ever heard about surfing Holys at size.

The first two waves were clean, but I let them pass, not wanting to have to contend with the rest of the set if I were to blow the takeoff and get stuck in the impact zone. The third was a fat, good-looking one, and I turned and dug for shore with all my strength as the trough sucked out far below me and a wet mist whistled up the face, blowing back my hair. I was scared, but I wanted this wave.

"When you think you've got it, paddle hard twice more before you go!" a voice in my head shouted in last-minute instruction. It was one of my father's rules, and I dutifully followed it, but when I stood, the wall jacked so steeply beneath me that for an instant I felt betrayed, like a trusting soul driving off a cliff, road map in hand. Fuck me, this spot wasn't surfable after all.

The next few seconds I was falling, weightless, and I braced for the horrid wipe that was surely in store, but a third of the way down I felt my inside rail slice cleanly into the rushing bottom-suck and somehow found my balance as the wall hooked over behind me. My bottom-turn was weak but sufficient to project me around the peak, and I climbed slowly back up the thrice-overhead wall as it stretched out before me like a tilting, blue-green meadow of heavy water. I was not really turning, but merely trimming across the open face on this handsome bullet train of a surfboard my father had made just for this wave. Aah, Honey Child! The speed was intoxicating, so much so that I forgot about the bowl section yet to come and failed to link together any solid, momentum building turns.

I was flying, yet falling behind, for the wall was still gathering speed as it hit the Tabernacle section and began to warp into an almond eye. All I could do was feebly tuck in as high and tight as I could and watch the silvery daylight funnel away.

I imagine I was riding inside the tube untouched for only a few seconds, but at the time, it felt like an extended stay. Then everything got dark and foamy and I found myself bailing off the front of my board as it tracked up the face and over the falls. I tried to penetrate the surface but landed awkwardly, with a skip and splatter. An awful suction drew me high up inside the wave as if I was caught on a conveyor belt. For an instant, my head popped free of the tumult, and I glimpsed a faraway patch of white cumulus and pale blue winter blue sky before plunging into utter darkness.

A deep, roaring thunder engulfed me. I was being bounced and scuttled across the inside reef, the turbulence tearing at my arms and legs until I instinctively rolled into a fetal ball. My shoulder slammed flat onto the bottom and I loosened up, an icy blast of water coursing through the new tear in my wetsuit. Then, just when I thought the pounding had let up, I was ripped down over a ledge into even deeper, colder water, and pummeled again.

Another wave had hit the inside reef. The tiny breath I'd stolen just before bailing out was gone. My lungs were on fire. If I didn't break the surface before the next wave, I was sure I'd drown.

I opened my eyes and squinted through the brine, swimming hard, fighting to find light. The first thing I saw when I burst to the surface was a row of beachfront houses way inshore. I'd barely gulped a quick breath of air before another sickening crash exploded a few feet behind my head. The next wave took me deep again, flushing me through the full rinse cycle, then rejecting me as if it was spitting up an unwanted seed. When I broke the surface again, my head was ringing from lack of oxygen and my shoulder throbbed. Honey Child was gone. I treaded water for a few minutes and tried to plot my next move. Then I threw up.

Five minutes later, I was caught in the rip and headed straight out to sea. My choices were few. I could let the rip take me and hope to keep afloat until a passing boat might spot me before I drowned, or I could hack back over to the outer peak and try to get washed in by a set. I chose the latter. It took fifteen minutes of hard swimming to get back to the outer peak, but I made it. My plan was to wait for a set, dash in over the reef and get washed in by a smaller, hopefully less psychotic wave, then swim for the jetty for all I was worth. But the surf seemed to be picking up by the minute with the rising tide.

Three more sets hammered the reef. When I made my break for it, the double-thick inside wall that rolled me was no smaller than the sets I'd passed on earlier, when I was still riding my board, and no less violent. By the time I surfaced, my arms had rubberized and my wetsuit felt like a coat of armor on my back. Shivering and utterly exhausted, I drifted into the seaward rip yet again.

My life was slipping away, and I felt a fool, ashamed of the end I'd met. To dishonor my father with such an ill-conceived plan to surf his favorite reef. My first time out, and alone—blind audacity. And all to spite my mother, who'd never, in her entire life, done a thing to hurt me.

"Climb on!" someone shouted.

I felt a strong arm reach under my aching shoulder. He was on a bright red big wave stiletto, a dark blond whose deeply tanned face I vaguely recognized from a time and place I could not quite recall. He pulled me across the deck of his board and let me rest for a few seconds, then directed me to get on his back and clutch his waist as he began to paddle.

"We're outta here!" he cried as a hulking wall clattered a hundred feet behind us on the outer reef. "Keep your weight centered and don't let go!"

My rescuer dug straight for shore until the whitewater engulfed us, bucking and buffeting the surfboard like a twig in a rushing torrent. But we held on. Seconds later, the nose of his sleek red gun shot ahead of the turbulence and we were planing again over smooth water.

I crawled up the sand and sat back on my elbows, the earth still listing beneath me. "Thank you," I said when I regained enough strength to speak. He looked away. I studied his profile. "You're Jackie Pace." He didn't answer in a way that told me I was right. "I'm J. Shepard."

"I know who you are," he said.

"You saved me. What you did out there for me . . . Christ, you're a hero."

He gazed at the roaring ocean. "Save the flattery, kid. Your old man was one of the best shapers in the world."

"What do you mean?"

Jackie Pace's eyes stayed fixed on the reef. "Bailing you out was the last thing on my mind. I was going for your board."

I laughed weakly, but he didn't sound like he was joking. At the moment I felt too giddily grateful at being back on dry land to care. A few rays of sun broke through the cloud cover and shone like a spotlight on a metallic slick of water out past the pier.

"I want you to have it," I said.

He regarded me with instant suspicion. "What are you talking about?"

"The board. You said—"

"I know what I said. Suppose I was being ironic."

"Oh . . . right, I knew that."

He looked at me and almost laughed. "I didn't say I was. By the way, what the hell were you doing out there anyway?"

I told him about Honey Child, my father, and my mother. He listened to all of it without speaking.

"That board isn't mine," I said. "It deserves to be ridden by a surfer like you. Take it. It's what you wanted."

He sniffed at my gesture. "What I wanted." A rush of foamy soup splashed at our feet, then slithered back into the sea. "Look, man," he said, "you know what, don't worry about what I want."

"But you saved—"

"So what?" he shot back. "People do what they, do, okay? We all have our motivations. Why are you so bent on rooting them out?"

Jackie Pace was not exactly digging my company. I was mortified. "Okay, sorry." The turmoil of the past three months welled up behind my eyes. "I've been kind of . . . upset."

"Tell you what. Your stick's probably out to sea in the rip anyway, but if I find it, I'll take it on one condition."

"You got it, absolutely." Shit—I'd used a little more enthusiasm than was called for.

He regarded me with caution. "Right. Go home. Pack up your mother's things, sell 'em, throw 'em out, whatever. Pull yourself together, man. And don't trouble yourself about why she split. People do what they do. The less you worry yourself about why, the better. You'll be a lot less miserable in life if you can remember that."

"Thanks," I said. I started to offer him a handshake, but he looked away.

"Still surfable," he said after a time. A series of steel-blue mountains rose and fell out on the reef. "Later." He trotted to the water's edge, waited a minute for a lull in the surf, then sprinted into the heaving shorepound and was gone.

Jackie Pace left for Tahiti, Sumatra, and parts unknown a few days later, but before he caught a cab for the airport, he called me at Pam and Grog's house, described the upcoming trip, and asked me to watch the lineup at Holys for him while he was away.

I promised him that I would.

Eight

I was planted before the kitchen sink, hand-washing silverware and lamenting the automatic dishwasher's passage into Appliance Heaven, when the phone rang. Jackie was on it as if he knew the call was for him. "*Chez* Shepard," he said, his back turned. Making a lady-friend connection, I assumed.

Britt and Shannon were flirting and snapping dishtowels at each other as they dried for me. "So J., about tomorrow, you're cool with Oceanside?" Britt asked me as I handed him a dripping salad bowl. I nodded yes. He had a contest down south and his truck still wasn't running right, so I was driving.

"No, no, I said *Chez* Shepard, as in this is the man's pad," Jackie said into the phone. "Slow down Joe, I'm not going anywhere, I'm not him."

"Take a break," I said to Jackie, motioning for the receiver.

"An asswipe by the name of Nelson Gilbride for you Mr. Shepard?" Sounding like a dutiful secretary.

Ten o'clock on a Friday night. I took the phone and exchanged a curt greeting with Gilbride. "This had better be an emergency," I told him.

Wonderful news, Gilbride said. He was at the Danforth place, and can you imagine! His clients had invited Sue Ellen and Ty Randall into their home for the first court-ordered visit with Nathan. The visit went well—very well. They talked, they laughed, they cried. It was a miracle of sorts, an understanding, a healing.

"Let me speak to my client," I said. I knew where this was headed. "Right now."

Why, that was the purpose of this call, Gilbride explained. The parties had agreed to the adoption after all, but Sue Ellen wanted to clear it with her attorney. He signed off with a counterfeit little editorial on the best interest of the child.

Sue Ellen sounded like hell, all broken up and afraid, just like the day I'd first met her. Muttering something about not wanting to let everyone down, not wanting to let me down. Christ, as if what I thought of her should even figure in to her decision to relinquish her baby for all time. She was in no condition to make this kind of decision. I told her to stay put, got some highway directions from Gilbride, and hung up.

"We still going to the contest tomorrow?" Britt asked.

I assured him I'd be back in a few hours.

Jackie sucked a final hit off a beer, his tanned triceps flexing under a black T-shirt as he tilted the bottle over his head. "Another client with a serious pet problem?" he said.

"Don't lecture me," I said, rinsing my hands. "This was totally unexpected."

Jackie flicked his fingernails across the side of his empty bottle like a guitarist tuning up. "Then how'd they get your home number?"

I couldn't think. Sue Ellen had my office line only, as did the other attorneys. My home phone was perpetually unlisted. "I don't know, Jack," I said. "I'll ask the asswipe when I see him." I dried my hands and left the sink.

The Danforth home looked something like a big, two-story country English through the night shadows and heavy foliage. I parked on the street and walked up a long driveway that curved left toward a three-car garage. A brick walkway sprinkled with tiny white petals led me past a flower garden and under a vine-laden archway to the front door.

Corwin Danforth answered the doorbell. I followed him down a long entry hall toward the back of the house, where Gilbride and Mrs. Danforth were seated in a huge living room cluttered with unmatched furniture and fine objects in the classic British manner. Sue Ellen was at the far end of the room, standing near a grand piano as if it were a museum piece she was afraid to touch.

I said a few very brief hellos to Gilbride and his clients. Mr. Danforth asked me if I wanted a drink. God, I was tempted to order a shit-face special like a double Dewars on the rocks just to see his mindblown expression, but I politely said no. Cigar? No thanks. These ones were Cuban. No thanks, I said again. Both of the Danforths looked terrific as usual, he in tassled Italian loafers, pleated gray slacks and a navy polo shirt buttoned to the top, she in a white cotton dress embroidered with creeping flowers. Gilbride could have come straight from court in his Brooks Brothers three-piece. The guy probably had no life. Then I remembered that I, too, was here in Pasadena, at 11 P.M. on a Friday night.

Sue Ellen and I stood alone near the piano while she recounted her first visit with Nathan since she'd relinquished him at the hospital. The Danforths had phoned earlier in the day with a kind offer to let the first visit take place in their home as opposed to the Family and Children's Services offices. Tonight was convenient. Sue Ellen was thrilled to get a visit so quickly—she thought the social worker told her early next week would be the soonest. Ty had made bail that morning. They could go together.

I caught a flicker of movement outside, through the broad glass windows that faced onto the backyard porch. Ty Randall was out there in a dirty yellow windbreaker, alone with a fat cigar, puffing into the darkness with one hand in his jeans pocket.

Over my left shoulder, Gilbride and the Danforths were staying put on a kidney-red leather sofa and matching chair, giving me enough space to confer with my client. "Don't tell me," I said quietly to Sue Ellen, "you and Ty are impressed by all this."

"How can't we be?" she said, wide-eyed. She described the baby's room in full detail—the musical mobiles floating like glittering clouds, the motorized fire engine, the gingerbread-man motif. An electric train layout full of switches, tunnels and bridges. Anna—Nathan's nanny—baking cookies and folding colorful baby clothes. Nathan looking disoriented when Sue Ellen held him in her arms for the first time in four long months. Nathan crying first, then Sue Ellen.

"So now you want to give him up again," I said. "I suppose you feel inadequate as a mother."

Sue Ellen seemed surprised that I'd tapped her dilemma so quickly. "Well, yeah, kinda."

"Don't be a fool," I said. "The whole thing's a setup." I glanced over at Gilbride, who just happened to be watching me at the same instant, and he smiled ingratiatingly and waved. I didn't bother to wave back.

"I'm sorry to drag you out here," she said. She looked like a teenager in her jeans and a sleeveless white blouse. "I figured you'd say that."

We both stared at her husband's forlorn silhouette, the roughneck given an expensive cigar and sent packing when he tried to light it. I recognized then what was going on here. "That's fine, but you promised you wouldn't bullshit me, Sue Ellen," I said. "If you do, I'm walking straight out of here and you can get yourself another lawyer." She probably knew I was serious because she didn't flinch. "Tell me the rest."

She started to protest but reconsidered. "Forty-five thousand, no questions asked."

"Oh, I see." I sighed long and hard enough to let her know how happy I was to be her court-appointed lawyer at this particular moment. "How'd you settle on forty-five?"

Sue Ellen peered over my shoulder to make sure the others were sufficiently out of earshot. "Gilbride came up with it. On account of my pain and suffering during the pregnancy. Five thousand a month all the way to term."

"I thought you said this wasn't about the money."

"It wasn't," she said.

"It is now. You want my advice—is that why you dragged me all the way out here on a Friday night?"

Her eyes were filming over with tears. "Ty wants the money, Mr. Shepard, not me."

"Right, you're just the one who feels she's a bad mother," I said.

Her shoulders were beginning to shake. "You told me to stay with him, so I did. You think this is easy? And don't forget, they put me through hell having that baby early."

She had a point. Gilbride knew a down-and-outer like Ty would bite at the prospect of quick cash even if Sue Ellen wouldn't, but he had couched the payoff in human terms, making the buyoff sound like restitution. It was a damned brilliant idea, and suddenly I felt better about driving all the way over here to run interference.

"Listen," I said, "staying with Ty doesn't mean letting him do the thinking for the both of you. Not to mention, this shit is totally illegal, don't you know that?" I fished a fresh handkerchief out of my khakis and gave it to her.

"He said there are ways to get around that."

I rolled my eyes. "Please."

She wiped her nose. "Course I know. Guess I had to hear it from you, though. That's why I had 'em call you."

"Good. You were smart." I waited for her to pull herself together some more. "You'd better go talk to your husband," I told her. "Set this straight."

She pursed her lips and gave me the nod. "I will." She walked to the sliding glass door. "Mr. Shepard," she whispered. The others were still a mere thirty feet away. "You think we can win this—I mean, in court?"

It was the easiest question I'd been asked all week. This woman was weak and unpredictable at times, yet she was a pillar of might compared to her husband. But I wasn't inclined to give her the blue-sky routine. We were both stuck in this thing until its conclusion. "We've got a chance at trial," I whispered back, "if we stick to-gether."

Gilbride walked over to me as Sue Ellen met Ty on the patio. "Good of you to come on such short notice," he said, taking a moment to whiff an unlit cigar.

I glared right past his joviality. "How did you get my home phone number?"

He patted his thick and forced another smile on me. "I asked around. Imagine my surprise when I found a file on you in my own office."

"I'm still trying to live that episode down," I said.

"They said you were good."

"I needed the money."

"You were good." He paused to let me bask in his little compli-ment. "I was a fool to let you slip away," he added as if he was swimming in regret.

I stepped back a foot so I could eye him more fully, this grinning, beardless Santa who apparently never grew tired of working an angle.

"Thanks for the kind words," I said, "but you must be joking. You didn't even know I was working for you back then."

He pointed his stogie into the air to let me know a big thought was coming. "No joke. Rest assured, you've got my undivided attention now, J."

Corwin and Kitty Danforth were standing now, watching Ty and Sue Ellen through the glass. Kitty caught her breath as if she'd seen an apparition, but it was merely the same old bitter disagreement being played out yet again. Relinquishing a child—what a flipping minefield. I wondered, for an instant, whether my mother had argued this way over leaving me. But then, my father had been dead for ten years by then. Suddenly, I regretted not having ordered that double Dewars.

The room felt still as a museum as Corwin slid an arm around Kitty's shoulder to steady her. I could see my reflection, the skeleton eyes ringed with black; beside mine, Gilbride's gumdrop outline was full of twitching energy, the shining forehead and white hair. Outside, Sue Ellen was gesturing as if she was pleading now, Ty shaking his head to ward off her points, shifting from side to side.

"I think it could be very good, you and me working together," Gilbride said.

"That's why I'm here," I answered, my eyes on the budding argument outside.

He chuckled. "No, no, J. I mean work together every day, you and me. I want you to come back to my firm. I'll pay you well, very well in fact. We can talk about salary as soon as—"

"You're serious," I said. After everything I'd slung at him in court. And after I'd uncovered his phony D.A. connection—which he probably figured out by now, since I'd stopped asking him about it. I was baffled beyond words.

His face was aglow. "I can think of a hundred good reasons for you to work with me."

More heat through the glass—a real standoff now. Gilbride shut up and turned his concentration to the back patio. Ty was calling his woman out, and I saw Sue Ellen's lips spit out a defiant, last-stand "No!" Ty absorbed the shot wordlessly. He was shaken and seemed to shrink in stature, his whole body drooping. Then he threw down his cigar and stomped off into the dark.

"I can think of about forty-five thousand reasons not to," I told Gilbride.

"That's not . . . now J., really, I think your client might've misunderstood . . ." he muttered, but he was stuck without a ready explanation.

It was time to bail. "No deal," I said as I slid past him to go.

"I know all about you, J.," Gilbride said before I'd gotten across the Oriental throw rug I'd seen on Holly Dupree's TV spot.

I slowed up. Knew all about me, my ass. Nelson Gilbride seemed to have a real knack for pushing one too many buttons with me. "From what, that little file of yours?" I said over my shoulder. "Don't make me laugh, *Nelson*." I passed the Danforths on my way to the front door. Kitty was clinging to her husband for strength. Whatever bravado I'd just milked out of my exchange with Gilbride evaporated when I saw their despair. "I'm very sorry it didn't work out," I told them. "Good night."

"No parents—mother ran out on you at seventeen," Gilbride spouted from across the room. "That's right, I know all about—"

My face felt hot. Suddenly I needed air. I blew through the front door and down the long driveway, not looking back until I was inside my car.

Windows up, cold leather, black street, the engine still ticking under the hood. I tried to rub the sting out of my eyes, then clung to the steering wheel the way I'd seen Kitty Danforth grip her husband. Gilbride couldn't know this was dogging me now, or was I that obvious? Christ, I hoped not. Marielena Shepard had gone her way and I'd grown up anyway, got educated, become a professional. So what if she'd run out—was that what the Santa man said? I knew it was. I tried to put the key in the ignition, but I couldn't work my hand up to the keyhole. Gilbride's parting words had spun my head like too much cheap wine.

Cracking the window a few inches, I pushed my chin up and chugged the night air. The keys rattled onto the floor—fuck it, I thought. My face looked pale and drawn in the side-view mirror.

I remembered the plush green carpet in Gilbride's offices—the color of money, I used to think. A clipboard and a standard job application several pages long. A routine interview, Gilbride's associate impressed with my scope of knowledge. The usual pack of lies I relied on to get myself hired. Nothing said about Marielena Shepard. Not a chance.

A mother who ran out on me—he'd used those words. I wanted to drive, hit the speed lane, windows down, crank some rock 'n' roll on the stereo until my ears bled. See if I could outrun the ugly little truth Nelson Gilbride had spoken. But his words had delivered me right back to that time and place yet again, and I wasn't going anywhere anytime soon.

November, 1979

Senior year. Shakespeare, World History, Calculus. Each day passing slowly and uneventfully, without a word from Marielena Shepard.

Cooking for one. Tending her roses. Lying to the neighbors, certain that sooner or later, some local busybody would call the authorities.

Unplugging the Frigidaire and blowing out the pilot in the stove. Dragging a suitcase down the block to the home of Pam and Grog Baker, two of my father's old friends who, by necessity, would now conveniently become blood relatives. A temporary stay, just until she came home.

Finding the board my father called Honey Child one night in the garage. Begging Grog to take me out at Holys—absolutely not, too dangerous.

Grog asking how he might score some county financial aid for putting me up. Accessing Bundle of Joy, *a remarkable how-to manual I'd found behind the reference counter at the Christianitos Public Library, to answer Grog's questions. Studying that book every day after school, until I'd mastered the legalities of my current situation. Empowered by knowledge.*

Accepting the reality that she wasn't coming back. No longer feeling empowered about much of anything.

There was a rap at my side window. I lifted my head and saw Sue Ellen Randall standing beside my car. I briefly considered opening the door, but my legs felt like they might fall off my body, so I reached over and rolled down the window.

"Mr. Shepard, you all right?" She was huffing lightly and her dark hair looked wild and windblown. I could smell her breath on me: white wine from earlier this evening, bittersweet.

"I'm fine," I said.

She glanced behind the car, back toward the house. Nothing stirred. "I been standin' right here a minute or two. Thought you were dead or something."

"Just resting. It's been a long day."

"Your face looks wet," she said.

I pressed my palms over my eyes and wiped my cheeks. "What can I do for you?"

Her eyes were full of concern, and I saw in them a softness that threatened to pull me into another place, somewhere warm and very private. Then I felt a pleasant but unwelcome twitch in my loins.

"Ty's still pretty upset, won't shut up about it. He's scary behind the wheel when he's mad." She flicked back her hair, showing me her long, white neck. "Guess I could use a ride home." She rested her forearm across the door and waited for an answer.

Oh, how easy it would have been, to click open that door and just free-fall with my feelings. And oh, how hard the landing.

I reached down onto the floor mat and patted it until I found my keys. "Don't run away," I told her. "Take it from me, that approach doesn't work. I want you to go back there and talk to him, and listen to him, too. Even if he's a royal pain in the backside, just do it. If you're going to get through this, you'll have to be stronger." She couldn't hide her disappointment and didn't try. "Do it for your little boy, Sue Ellen," I said.

The Pasadena Freeway snaked along like an abandoned Grand Prix racetrack toward downtown. I took it easy, floating through fields of floodlit yellow, my front tires chasing the curling white lines. My driver's-side window was still lowered from my talk with Sue Ellen. But she was gone.

I pulled the Jeep into the parking lot just south of the Oceanside pier an hour before Britt's surf contest was to begin. A few other cars were parked nearby, but the rest of the lot was deserted. A pair of brown sparrows pecked at a discarded fast food wrapper and regarded our arrival with disinterested caution. Behind us the edge of town inched onto an unsteady dirt bluff overlooking the shore.

Britt stirred from his sleep. A row of straight-edged swells was advancing from the south, inky and thin, each line chased by a muted band of whitewash. "Classic setup, J.," he said. "I'm amped."

The day promised to be a long one. Britt was surfing in the amateur trials, competing in four-man heats where only the top two point-getters would advance. If he rode well enough to advance to the quarterfinals, which were scheduled for Sunday, he'd have to surf three times in a five-hour stretch.

Jackie was stretched across the back seat snoozing happily, half-hidden beneath a blanket. Britt sat across from me up front, timing the set waves. The early sun was blunted by a thick marine layer, the sea reflecting a bland, gun-metal gray sky.

"Thanks for the lift, J.," Britt said. "I know it was pretty last-minute of me to ask." He slapped the dash. "Can't believe my dad, man. He was gonna pick me up at eleven last night, then he calls at nine-thirty and bails. Another fucking emergency."

Grog Baker had been notoriously inconsistent this year, ever since he started pouring all his time and money into his latest commercial venture, some sort of "must have" golf accessory.

We stared at another set through the windshield. A thin kid with a serious face and a high-performance surfboard tattooed with industry logos stalked across the sand and began an elaborate stretching ritual at the water's edge. At this hour, just watching his workman-like limbering routine made my bones ache.

"I'm thinking fish," Britt said. The fish was his loosest, most versatile small-wave board.

"Those lefts will get fatter with the incoming tide," I said. "Use the fish."

Jackie was awake now. He leaned forward and gazed with us at the makeshift tower in the sand, the advertising banners plastered across the back of the judges' platform and VIP tent like bright stamps pasted into an album.

Jackie draped his forearms around both our necks. "Tell me, boys, what do radial tires, alkaline batteries and a Euro beer that tastes like the brewmeister took a leak in it have to do with amateur surfing?"

"Read the banner on top," I said. "Windjammer Pro-Am."

"Well, 'Pro-Am' it is," he said. "Not just your schoolboys today, but right here with them, the lucrative pro surfing scene, where the purses are so generous you gotta take the whole event just to cover your costs."

I'd heard all the stories about the early years of what amounted to pro surfing's infancy, the years during which Jackie had regularly blown minds. In those days, someone's girlfriend sewed together the colored jerseys the night before the contest, the judges brought their own pads and pencils to keep score, and the top prize ranged from a thousand dollars or so—if the check didn't bounce—on down to a new wetsuit which the winner could only hope was his size. But Jackie was the one guy who'd seemingly breezed—he'd won nearly every big event, traveled to all the exotic locales when they were still unspoiled, rather publicly had a hell of a good time, and somehow cultivated the belief in others that just maybe this pro surfing thing had a future. Then he walked away from the whole show.

I swiveled to face Jackie. "Where do you get off being bitter about the pro scene? You were one of the first and only guys who went places." And, literally, he did. Australia, France, Brazil, the Islands every winter, that first-ever contest in Puerto Rico. "Whatever you had, they wanted it. Seems to me you did pretty well before you bailed."

"You don't do pro contests for the prize winnings anyway today," Britt said. "You want sponsors. They pay."

Jackie smirked at Britt. "Don't delude yourself, laddie. If money's what you're after, you'd be better off playing slots and keno with the polyester-pantsuit crew in Vegas."

"Things have changed since you were on the contest trail, Jack,"

I said. "Britt's right. Surf-wear is a big-time business. The top guys are making six figures on endorsements alone."

Jackie rubbed his eyes. "You're not following me here." He scratched at his moustache. "Surfing for me has never been about the green, not even the contests. There has to be something more."

I frowned. "Don't start with that business about the search for the perfect wave. It's tired. And what about *Be-boppin' Beach Bash* and *Hot Bikini Heaven*?" I said. "Don't tell me you went Hollywood out of a deep desire to communicate the beach aesthetic to the landlocked masses. That was all about the green."

Jackie sighed. "Some minor stunt work was all I did, *no mas*. I never traded off my image."

"You'll grovel at the trough just like the rest when you need money," I said.

"That was a long time ago."

"My dad says you'd do anything for a buck," Britt blurted as he stared through the windshield.

Jackie looked surprised by Britt's challenge. "Your dad," he told Britt, "is a world class expert in how *not* to make a buck." He nestled his wraparound shades onto his face.

"You don't know Grog," I said. "Where do you get off saying that?"

"We know each other. From way back." Jackie cracked a tiny smile. "I know what I'm talking about."

"What, you give him the Pace Guarantee on something that didn't pan out quite like you promised?" I asked.

An oily-smooth left lifted up and made a fifty-yard dash toward the pilings.

Jackie straightened his back, grimacing. "I was the first serious pro out of California, man, and I'm not ashamed of it. But my comic sidekick here"—he pointed a thumb at me—"misses the point. No small wonder. When I was establishing my rep on the international scene he was sticking playing cards in his bicycle spokes for kicks."

"Point that thumb at me again, Mister Surf Legend," I told him, "and you'll be using it tonight up at the freeway onramp."

"All right, man, be cool," Jackie said. He turned to Britt. "Listen, I've learned a few things about competition. I know you don't try

to win contests just for the money. You're an amateur anyway, at
least for now. But what I'm saying is, if you want to make your
mark, you gotta set your sights on something bigger."

Britt was enthralled. "Like what?"

Jackie leaned close to Britt's ear. "You gotta have something to
prove."

The car was silent. A wiry kid in a turquoise spring suit hustled
by us on his way to the water. "Don't you prove something just by
winning?" Britt said.

Jackie rubbed his chin. "You're getting the chicken and the egg
confused here. First, how do you win? You see, when I started out,
all the judges cared about was nose-riding, that was it. Didn't matter
if I rode a wave perfectly—late drop, cranking bottom turns, cut-
backs, off-the-tops. If some other guy got a wave half the size, stumbled to the nose and hung his toes over the tip for three or four
seconds, the judges would cream their shorts."

"But they're the judges—don't you have to give them what they
want?" Britt asked.

"No, no, you can't do that! Not if your way is better. Mine was.
So I made it a mission, like me against the world."

"Your way," said Britt. "So, it's like you have to have the right
motivation."

"It's key, man," Jackie said, "absolutely key. A higher purpose."

"I'm not sure I'm following this," I said. "You were the most
famous surfer in the world at one time, a contest whiz, founder of
the shortboard power school. Where do you get off playing the
underdog?"

Jackie glared at me. "J. here's still without a clue," he said to
Britt. "Do you really want to win?"

Britt nodded. "Yes, I do."

Jackie's eyes narrowed. "Good. Then you find someone to prove
yourself to, and you show them. You prove 'em wrong, in your
contests and on land. You approach each challenge like you were
born to win it, like you're the most righteous son of a bitch on
earth and no one can deny it. And *then*," he said, the lesson complete, "you will go places, my friend."

Britt stared out to sea in silent reflection. A decrepit lime green station wagon with a pile of surfboards strapped to its roof creaked and shimmied into the space next to ours, its pistons clattering loudly as the motor died. Britt opened the front passenger door.

"Where you headed?" I asked. But Britt didn't hear me, and he cut in front of the Jeep and strolled down to the shore without looking back, his eyes fixed on the silky peaks that pulsated over the outer sandbar.

"Do me a favor," I said, eyeing Jackie in the rear-view mirror. "Consider a few things about Britt before you pop off with another big lesson. He's going through a difficult spell. His parents just split and he feels like the earth's moving beneath his feet. Thinks it may be his fault. And don't sweat it, he's already a competitive little shit in the water."

"Your point being?"

"He'll probably go to college next year, not on the tour. Don't fuck with his head, Jack."

"That how you see it?"

"He's pissed at his dad, and what do you do? You call Grog a loser."

Jackie shook his head. "I didn't say that."

"You didn't have to. Hey now, I wonder who Britt's gonna find to prove himself to. To prove him wrong."

"Well, spank my chimp. Try to help a kid better himself and what do I get for my trouble."

"We can't all be world beaters like you."

"You mean, we can't all be winners." He nodded like he had something on me. "I guess with you, I can understand this."

"Understand what?"

He gazed at the pier without expression. "Nah. You're my friend."

I knew he was toying with me. "Say it."

Jackie sighed and sat back, stretching his limbs like a cat. "Let it go."

An elderly man in baggy sweats and a U.S. Marines baseball cap waddled by on the sidewalk in front of the Jeep, wrestling with a gangly black dog on a leash as the dog tugged hard to sniff at the gum-stained cement. He caught my eye and waved. I didn't return the gesture.

I faced Jackie. "You think I'm holding Britt back?" He didn't answer. "Well, hey, if it means helping him set himself up for a decent life, one where he might get some education so he can take care of himself without leeching off everyone around him, then—"

Jackie bolted upright. "You calling me a leech?"

"I didn't say that."

He glared at me. "You didn't have to. But I wish you had the sack to just say it."

"What difference would it make? Wouldn't change anything."

"Say it."

"All right then. Sometimes, you can be . . . a leech."

"All right then," he said, mimicking me perfectly. "I appreciate the honest assessment."

"Don't mention it."

I stacked some loose tapes into the slots in a cassette holder. Jackie sat tight—he wasn't through with me. "Now I'll take my shot at a little honest assessment, brother," he said. "You didn't get what I was telling the kid, 'cause you lack it too. It's how you've always been, long as I've known you."

"Come again?"

"I mean, you're smart. You know what's what, but it's like, you're just going through the motions, not really digging your scene."

I looked for a breaking wave, a surfer whose moves I could follow. But no one was up. A half mile past the end of the pier, a sailboat chugged along on motor power.

"You saying I don't know how to win?" I said.

He paused. "Your problem is you don't know what you've got."

The observation seemed well intended, but felt backhanded just the same. "I've gotten on with my life," I said. "But thanks for the pop analysis. You should have your own talk show."

He smiled with the mistaken belief that I'd just complimented him. "*No problemo.*"

Seagulls glided out beyond the surf line, circling and diving to snatch tiny fish in their beaks. Britt squatted to pick up a shell, skimming it across a shallow pool of reflected gray near shore. The sky cast a leaden gloom, as if the hidden sun had altogether passed on making its appearance for the day.

Loser. Jackie hadn't used the word because, as he'd pointed out before, I was his friend. And because consciously, I hadn't pushed him that far, which I almost regretted now as we resumed our silent perusal of the morning's waves. I thought of Sue Ellen Randall, the reviled baby seller or would-be mother, but my client nonetheless, a woman for whom I'd barely secured monitored visits with her child. So far I'd been nothing more than an also-ran to Nelson Gilbride in the great Nathan Randall Child Custody Derby. Not a loser yet, but give it time.

The biggest set of the morning rose up and crashed on the outer bar with a series of brief explosions. Two surfers who'd just paddled out were caught inside and pounded by the lines of whitewash until they were knocked off their boards. Disoriented, they ducked beneath the last advancing soup, towing their boards on their ankle-leashes like anchors.

My father used to dig conditions like these: the swells fast and critical and verging on unrideable. Robert Shepard had a reputation for charging big, unruly waves, skittering down impossible walls with no more than a few feet of inside rail providing the demarcation between an insane ride and a horrifying hold-down. He would have toyed with a few little beachbreak surprises on a morning like this.

At that moment, I had a vision of my father squeezing Nelson Gilbride's puffy pink hand and smiling as he permanently tagged Gilbride with the name Baby Face Nelson. The vision gave me a certain confidence, and an energy I hadn't felt in years.

"Something's about to happen," I said to Jackie. "To me. To my life."

"Is that right?" he said with no apparent interest.

My mind seemed to quicken. "You know how sometimes you're waiting for a wave," I said, "you haven't had a good one in a while, and you can't really see anything coming, but you feel it? You don't even know what's making you believe, but you know it's coming. So you paddle to a certain spot, like you're caught in a magnetic field. And then you see it, biggest wave of the day, bearing down right on you. And all you have to do is turn and go."

"Totally dialed in."

"I mean it." I wasn't sure he was with me. I tapped my hands on the steering wheel and sighed.

"You seem a little bummed," Jackie observed.

"Unsure is more like it."

The Randall case, losing a big, high-profile trial. Searching for my mother—and maybe finding her living somewhere else, a new and happier life built up around her like a wall from her past.

"I don't know if it's gonna be really good, or really bad, but something's gonna pop. It's strange. I can feel it."

"One request, lad," he said. "If you're gonna spin out big-time, just give old Jack a little warning." He strained a laugh.

I shifted in my seat to face him. "I feel like you'll be involved, either way," I said.

It was not the time to tell him about my mother. Not yet.

He reached behind him, fished a sweatshirt out of a pile of wet-suits and open bags, pulled it over his head and leapt out of the car. "Check ya later," he said through the passenger window. "I'm gonna go catch up with the young gun, help him tune up."

Spotting Britt, Jackie whistled, then trotted down the beach in the wet sand to meet him. I watched them study the horizon to-gether, Jackie gesticulating like a fervent preacher as the waves rolled through. I could almost hear his voice leaping forth with another fire and brimstone sermon on the psychology of winning.

Grog missed Britt's first two heats, which Britt survived with a win and a second place. The sun broke through the haze at noon and the throng on the beach mushroomed.

"I feel like sliding a few, boss," Jackie said to me as Britt toweled off and slipped on a pair of shades. The final heat of the day had just ended. "Let's go for a paddle on the Northside."

"I'm gonna take it easy," Britt said.

"Good idea, you're dad's probably looking for you," I said.

Britt lay sideways on a striped beach towel and scanned the crowd up above. "Thought I heard him hoot at me from the pier when I got that long one to the beach. You seen him yet, J?"

I hadn't. "He's around," I said, hedging.

Jackie was onto me. "Yeah, right," he said.

I quickly shot Jackie a look that said Shut Your Mouth.

"We'd better hit it now," I said. "Feels like the wind's going to kick up soon."

I waited for Jackie to pipe up with his assessment of the conditions, but he avoided my gaze and pulled on his wetsuit in silence.

Thirty surfers—mostly locals, I figured, by the way they hung together—were crammed into a takeoff zone no bigger than a dance floor, and they looked fired up, tearing into every surfable section as if in a state of frenzy. The presence of a large crowd on both sides of the pier, cheering and jeering the action in the water, added a circus-like element to the ongoing session.

Jackie was chatting on the beach with a Hawaiian who'd recognized him and run over to say hello. I'd told Jackie I wanted to avoid the Northside crush by jogging up the beach a ways before paddling out, but he wouldn't hear of it. "Take what's yours, man," he'd said. "It's your birthright."

And so, I paddled out not to have fun—which to me is the whole point—but to prove to Jackie that I wouldn't back down.

The trouble started immediately. On my first wave I was unceremoniously shoulder-hopped (in surfing etiquette, the rider farthest back gets priority) by a scowling punk whose purposely delayed bottom-turn sent me careening ass-first into the soup. I paddled farther out into deeper water, figuring I'd be better off waiting for the odd larger wave than fighting the pack. To my surprise I was instantly rewarded with a well-formed outer peak. I sprouted to my feet and took the drop, which was steep but routine, then readied to bury my rail into a swift bottom turn. But two surfers were caught inside, splashing through my path of trajectory and scrambling to submerge the noses of their boards for a duck-dive through the back. I took my eye off my turn for an instant to avoid them, just long enough to catch my outside rail and go down with a back-flopping splat. When I surfaced I was greeted with a smattering of groans and catcalls.

"Give it up, tourist," a kid half my age said under his breath twenty feet away.

I climbed back onto my board, adjusted the ankle strap on my leash, and dragged myself over the top of a frothy inside left as two young hotties streaked by below my tailblock, banging rails with each other.

What a miserable session.

"You look like the invisible man out here, J!" Jackie shouted as he burst over the back of an inside closeout. He was paddling hard, head down and in perfect form, his strokes deep and clean, every movement swift and assured. The others took instant notice of him, as if his presence had charged the air with millions of ions. Several riders backed away to a more respectful distance as he clawed by me and took up a position ten feet beyond the edge of the pack.

A sizeable peak loomed outside. "Yahaa!" Jackie cried as he paddled closer to the pier and into position. His cry had let the others know he'd marked his prey, and none of them dared make a move to challenge him. He stroked twice, found his feet beneath him, and swooped into the steepest section of the wave. His inside rail flashed with swordlike flourishes along the mirrored crest, fanning sheets of water far out the back of the bowling left wall. Loud, raucous whoops sang out from the gallery on the pier as the wave went hollow and Jackie's form compressed into a tube stance. Another big cheer rained down as he burst free of the collapsing hook with speed to burn, buried a final, flying cutback just short of two frozen paddlers on the shoulder, then drifted casually over the back to begin paddling again.

Another wave rolled through, but no one made a move and it peeled by unridden. The other surfers seemed temporarily paralyzed, as if a man-eating shark were basking in their midst.

"You're amping too much, Master J.," Jackie said.

"It's a zoo out here," I said. "I'm ready to paddle up the beach."

"No way," he said. "Fun stuff. Just be cool, my man. One of the things I didn't cover in our little chat about winning is that you can't always do it all by your very own."

A clean left lifted in front of us.

"So take advantage," he said over his shoulder as we dropped to our decks and began to paddle.

A guy in a red wetsuit vest who'd been hogging a lot of waves shot into view and dug hard in front of the building swell, but Jackie cut directly in front of him and sat up, blocking his path. "Go, J.!" he said loud enough for the entire pack to hear.

The red-vested surfer sat up and splayed his legs out to keep from colliding with Jackie. "Hey, hey, hey!" he yelled, but he was already out of the action.

I spun around, unchallenged by the others, and slid down the rushing peak. Banking back up the face, I climbed and dropped, my back tight and cupped against the wall, my rails connecting a series of momentum-building turns with the familiar rhythm of a favorite dance step as the falling sections ran down the sandbar and away from the pier. The wave held up beautifully, losing none of its shape as it raced to shore. When it finally reared and dumped in the shore-pound, I floated on its back and plunged over with the falling curtain as the whitewash bounced in a foot of water. Outside, Jackie powered into a head-high right and gouged his way toward the pier, scattering paddlers as he went.

I dug hard through the rolling swells, greedy for another peak. The brilliance of the midday surface sheen temporarily blotted my vision. For the first time in many days, my mind unclenched. I had a sudden inspiration.

"I've been thinking about what you said earlier, in the car," I told him when he reached the sandbar and sat upright on his board beside me.

"You have," he said. "I see. Well hey, listen, I didn't mean to piss you off by—"

"No, it's okay, man," I said. "I'm all right with it. In fact, I agree with you Jack. I've gotten too used to losing."

He didn't seem ready for this revelation. "You have."

I brushed the wet hair out of my eyes. "I need your help. I want you to work this case with me. The baby selling case. The one the TV people are interested in."

He smiled. "The big one?"

"You owe me from the party," I reminded him. I needed a commitment.

"Yeah, but—"

"No buts," I said. "No big discussion. Enough said."

He nodded as if he was too tired to disagree. "Amen."

"I want to win this case, and, bizarro as it sounds, you're gonna help me. Come Monday, you're my chief investigator."

This time he didn't argue.

A low-flying pelican glided by us, air-surfing the updraft from a rising line of swell.

Jackie turned and began to dig for the wave at the same instant that I did, but we both pulled up short, thinking the other would go. Too late—the wave passed beneath us unridden. It was the only tentative move Jackie had made all day.

"Teamwork," he muttered.

Nine

The waitress brought Grog over to our booth and cleared away a clutch of empty beer bottles as he sat down across from me.

"Moondoggie," he said. Grog likes using corny surf-monikers from the fifties and sixties.

"Kahuna," I said. "How's it hangin'?"

"With authority."

He was dressed in blue jeans and a red T-shirt with horizontal blue and white stripes that made his midsection look as solid as a battering ram. His coarse gray hair was pulled back into a short ponytail.

"*¿Quieren mas cervezas?*" the waitress asked. She was slight, with straight black hair and a glint of silver in her mouth when she smiled. She looked a lot like a mother I'd represented last year, a woman whose husband had beaten their infant to death with a rolling pin. The baby had colic and cried too much.

"*Dos botellas de Carta Blanca, por favor,*" I said. "*Y si puede, mas tortillas.*"

"*Esta bien.*"

The kitchen was closed, so the waitress didn't offer Grog a menu. She added the beer orders to her little white pad and left.

"Dusting off the *español*, eh?" Grog said with a grin. "Very nice."

I thought of the darkly lovely Las Palomas social worker, Carmen Manriquez, and wished she could have seen me now. "Making an effort."

Grog and I sat alone at opposite ends of an immense table strewn with rumpled napkins and red-stained dishes left over from dinner. Across the dining room at a dimly lit corner bar, Jackie held court with his back to us in a crowd of contest-goers. He'd defected from our table halfway through our meal when a semi-famous rock 'n' roll band who'd stopped in for drinks spotted him. They sent over a pitcher of margaritas and a bottle of mescal, gratis, with a message that it would be an honor to have a drink with the great Jackie Pace. The Legend had quickly obliged.

The waitress brought on the reinforcements. Grog inhaled a half dozen chips and slugged at his beer, lifting two fingers at the waitress before she split. "Haven't seen you since Vic and I opened the new warehouse in Costa Mesa," he said.

"How's that going?" I asked, which took some courage. Just last month, the phone in Grog's new apartment had been disconnected because his account was past due.

"All right, man, quite all right," he said as if to convince himself as well as me. "Now that we got the manufacturing part wired, all we need is orders. But we're going for it, man. Got a booth at the golf products convention next month. That's when we unveil the 'Kovr-Kleaner.' "

"Outstanding," I said.

His face lit up. "Fits any size club head, vinyl or real leather on the outside, specially treated chamois on the inside that shines while it protects. We're gonna sell a million! Comes in black, white, red, navy, cocoa brown . . ."—he paused as if to hear himself—"sorry, J. You don't need the full-on pitch."

"Sounded solid, Grog."

"Thanks for the loan last week." He picked up a fat red candle from the middle of our table and used it to light a cigarette.

"Consider it an investment," I said. "You can put it toward the shares I'm going to buy when you guys get organized."

We watched Britt leaning on a pinball machine near the bar, body-torquing the flipper buttons as a few other amateurs from the Christianitos High surf team looked on.

"Your boy surfed well today," I said.

Grog smiled. "Did he? Right on, it's in the genes." We tipped our bottles. "Hey, J., thanks for bringin' him down this morning. Vic and I visited several stations of hell yesterday. Our manufacturer in Mex missed his shipment of materials. Twelve people standin' there with nothin' to sew."

I sighed. "Nightmare."

"Britt was pretty P.O.'d when I rang you last night," Grog said. "He all right?"

"He'll get over it," I said. "I can't stick around for the main event tomorrow. I've got a house that needs some serious attention, so you're his ride back."

Across the room, a chant went up among Jackie's group: "Go! Go! Go! Go! Go!" Four guys arching their backs like limbo dancers as four young ladies shoveled pitchers of beer down their throats.

"Won't be long before those lightweights start returning some groceries," Grog said. "By the way, I heard Mister Surf Legend trashed your pad recently. That why it needs some attention?"

I nodded but didn't explain, not wanting to relive the night of the party again. The waitress appeared with two more Carta Blancas. I wasn't through with the last one yet, but I raised my new bottle. Grog knew how to put it away. "Cheers," I said.

Suddenly Grog's smile drained from his face. He sank into the deep bucket seat as a man whom I didn't recognize wove his way through several empty tables and headed toward us. "Ah, shit, this is not good. That's David Rausch, guy who runs the amateur circuit."

"Mr. Baker?" Rausch unsmilingly extended a hand. He loomed over the table, with wide but slouching shoulders under a royal-blue windbreaker and a face chapped and rosy from a full day on the beach. I couldn't take my eyes off the flat, shiny tuft of hair resting above his forehead—I'd seen indoor putting surfaces that looked more natural than that rug.

"You got him," Grog said. "A pleasure."

"Hi, I'm J. Shepard," I said to the man.

"Yes, hello," Rausch said, his eyes on Grog. "Mr. Baker, I hear you haven't been returning my accountant's calls. Your check for your son's yearly membership dues was returned due to—"

"Insufficient funds, yeah, I know," Grog said. "I told the guy I'd send him another check, but he won't even take one now."

Rausch looked agitated. "It's our policy to—"

"Listen, partner," Grog said, already losing his cool, "you'll have your precious dues money."

"When?" Rausch said. "The season is already underway. It isn't fair to the other competitors who've paid their fair share."

"Soon," Grog said. "Next month at the latest."

"I'm sorry, but that's not good enough," Rausch said. "I'm pulling your son from the main event tomorrow."

Jackie stepped up to the table and stood between Grog and David Rausch. "Evening, ladies and Doberman. What's the haps?" He eyed their standoff postures. "Trouble in paradise?"

"Stay out of this," Grog said to Jackie without looking away from Rausch.

"Britt's not surfing tomorrow unless we come up with his yearly dues, Jackie," I said. Rausch's face changed when he heard Jackie's name. He briefly studied Jackie's features in the dining room's flat, anemic light. "You mean . . . you're Jackie Pace," he said in a pale voice.

Jackie clapped a hand on Rausch's shoulder. "Damn glad to make your acquaintance, uh . . ."

"David, D-David Rausch. I'm the president of the . . . but David's, um, okay."

Jackie grinned. "David-O, The Prez, I can dig it. So tell me, are we talking *mondo problemo* here? You're looking a mite stressed-out, David-O."

Rausch's mouth hung open. "Jackie Pace. You don't know this, but I saw you surf second-reef Pipeline in 'seventy-two, the day they called Huge Monday. I was there." His voice had swelled as if he was recounting one of the seminal rites of passage in his life. "My first . . . well, my *only* winter on the North Shore. The things you did that day . . . incredible. I, I'll never forget that big one you rode all the way through. Fifteen feet and hollow, top-to-bottom when it hit the inside reef, and you, you were *stalling* to get in the tube. I couldn't believe you even paddled out that day. Incredible."

"I was itching to get wet," Jackie said. "As I recall, the whole week before was flat."

"Yeah, flat," Rausch said, still semi-dazed.

"Anyway, Mr. Rausch," I said, "what if we paid you half next week and the other half the following week? I can get a cashier's check, and—"

"J.," Jackie said, "let me handle this." He put his arm around Rausch's shoulder. "Now David-O, you love the kids, I can tell this about you, am I right?"

"Of course," Rausch agreed. "It's why I do it. I've got a Junior and a Menehune of my own. They're both still alive in their brackets. I can't wait 'til tomorrow."

"Fantastic, David-O," Jackie said. "We do this for the kids. But business is business, am I right? The organization needs its dues."

"That's right," Rausch said, nodding.

Grog's eyes briefly met mine from across the table. He's keeping awfully quiet, I thought, considering that Britt was the subject of conversation. But Rausch was obviously awestruck, and I remembered that Grog Baker was familiar with the scheming side of Jackie.

Grog just isn't much of a wheeler-dealer. He's an earnest but socially clumsy man, and I can understand his resentment of Jackie's vast persuasive talents. But there's something more, a wall between them, a history neither will confirm nor deny when I ask them why they so dislike each other.

Bad blood.

"Dues are critical to our operations, Mr. Pace," David Rausch said, nodding like a windup doll.

"Call me Jackie, my friend."

Rausch looked positively spellbound as Jackie drew him into his web. I cracked a tiny smile at Grog, to which he responded with a surreptitious thumbs-up with the hand that held his beer. For now, at least, he was letting any hard feelings ride and standing aside to give Jackie room to work.

"Now David-O," Jackie said, "I love the kids too. But I'm a businessman when I have to be—that is, when the situation calls for it. And David-O, now's one of those times when I've gotta be all business."

"How do you mean?" Rausch asked.

"The Oceanside Pro-Am contest poster you guys are selling on the beach this weekend? Ho, man! Quite a beauty! Very nice the way the artist overlaid those two scenes, the one with a contemporary guy going off the top of the wave and the other one, the retrospective image of the guy on a longer board carving a cutback. You know, I still remember whipping that carve like it was yesterday. Beautiful day, fall swell at Rincon. That photo made the cover of *Surfer* magazine."

"Come to think of it, you're right," Rausch said. "It does look like you."

"The artist must have used the photo when he painted the cutback scene," I added.

"Tell me, David-O, what would it take to settle Britt's account right now?" Jackie said, leaning closer to him.

Rausch was ready with a total. "Three hundred eighty-six dollars, Jackie."

"Now J. here, he's my lawyer," Jackie said, motioning at me, "and he watches pretty closely for situations where people use my likeness and profit from it without old Jack's ten-four."

Rausch gave me a panicked glance. "Hey, wait, you don't mean . . . you're not going to—"

"Hold steady, David-O," Jackie said. "J. and I are a tandem act, brother. We want to work this out with you. We want to do what's right for the kids."

"I would like that," Rausch said.

Jackie nodded. "Good man. My proposal is simple: you forget about Britt's fee, I'll forget about the poster."

"That's terrific," Rausch said. "Well, alrighty! I was a little concerned there. I got two hundred more posters in the trunk that we were gonna try to sell tomorrow."

Jackie grinned. "Well, alrighty! Bring 'em on in and I'll sign 'em all for you." He winked at me. "Oh, and meet me at the bar, David-O. We'll be putting the next few rounds of debauchery on the presidential expense account."

Rausch smiled at Grog and me. "Pleasure meeting both of you," he said.

"And you," I said, tipping my beer bottle, but Rausch was already scuttling toward the exit.

Jackie winked at me. "We can sue the fucker later, right man?" he said. Then he turned and retreated to the bar area.

"Kinda wish Jackie wouldn't have done that," Grog said. "I don't need his help." He gave me a hard stare. "I wasn't gonna let you pay Britt's way either. Hope you know that."

"I know," I said. "We both just want Britt to surf tomorrow."

When it comes to borrowing money, Grog had his pride. He

hates to accept funds when the prospects for repayment are slim, which is just about always. When my mother departed, he put me up in his home for months, so I don't mind helping him out. No disrespect intended, but I just don't plan on seeing the money again. Grog is like a salesman who has gone so long without a sale he's forgotten how to close the deal. But he wasn't always this way.

Grog was one of the few men my father truly respected. They'd both fought in Korea, but though my father saw little combat, Grog survived some heavy action, saving the lives of four soldiers he freed from the wreckage of a burning schoolhouse. Awarded a Silver Star and a Purple Heart, he came home to Christianitos with no plans beyond surfing and drinking and surfing some more, waiting for the mosquitoes that loitered behind his eyes at night to cease their incessant buzzing.

My father needed a sander, so he hired Grog. They surfed together daily, swapped design ideas with other builders, and somehow sold just enough boards to keep things going. Grog lacked my father's fluid grace in the water, but he, too, was relatively fearless in big surf, especially in the Islands. An old magazine photo, framed on the wall in my garage, captures Grog's staunch figure barreling down the face of a solid twenty-footer at Sunset, driving hard off his inside edge as a mammoth section looms ahead like a cliff wall. The caption reads "Greg Baker, going for broke." No wave he'd ever faced had broken him.

But something took him off his course. Maybe it was just a long succession of letdowns that drained away his confidence and stole his swagger. Perhaps his long-standing money troubles had slowly eaten away the best part of him. I didn't know, and wasn't about to ask.

Grog shoveled a few more tortilla chips dripping with salsa into his mouth. "You know, you and Jackie have a way of just taking care of business," he said. "Thing is, that can rub people the wrong way sometimes."

"Easy, Grog," I said. "Jackie's in quite another league. He's up there with the hippo-riding used car salesmen and personal injury lawyers who use quadriplegics for testimonials."

"Point taken," he said, chugging from his bottle.

I drank with Grog, polishing my first bottle and switching to the second. I read the label—Carta Blanca—and thought of Carmen Manriquez shaming me about my Spanish.

"Besides," I said, "you know he's unstoppable when he catches someone doing the idol-worship thing."

"Also true," Grog said. "Rausch was lucky to leave the table with his wallet intact."

I glanced at the still-jammed bar area. A leggy girl in a purple tube top had mounted a small wooden table and begun a spirited flamenco dance as Jackie and the others hooted and hand-clapped the beat. A stressed-out older guy who had to be the restaurant manager was there, too, jockeying about beneath the girl, hands out, trying to break her fall if it came to that.

"The night's still young," I said. "I've got a feeling Rausch is gonna pay for every one of those signatures."

We sat a while longer without speaking. Grog set his bottle down, straightened the rumpled tablecloth with his forearm and peered into the crimson recesses of the restaurant. "How's Britt's mother?" he said.

"Pam's fine," I answered. "We talked early this morning when I picked him up."

"She say anything about me? About the business?"

I shook my head. "She doesn't talk to me about what you're doing."

"She doesn't know about the products show. If she knew about the show—"

"She knows," I said. "You told Britt all about it. Don't worry, she's sufficiently enthused, Grog."

His eyes welled up. "I'm having a hell of a time making that support payment every month. She's been great about it, too. I know if she wanted to she could haul my butt into court and get an order."

"You know that's not her style," I said. "She's doing all right, for now. The Bardo Gallery's still a tough gig. They just finished a worthless show with that Japanese artist whose sculptures all look like tortoise shells."

"Customers weren't biting?" he asked.

I shook my head. "Nothing sold."

Grog sighed heavily. "It's sink or swim when you're on commish," he said.

I crushed a chip between my fingers. "They're opening a show by that Outer Islands surfer, Lamont Dunne, next week. Pam's luck may be about to change."

"Know I've heard of him," Grog said, his brow knotted.

"He's that guy from Kauai. You've seen his stuff, these surreal airbrushed scenes of sea creatures and perfection surf."

Grog snorted. "Let's hope he goes over a little better than the turtle man did. Wonder how her gallery got him. That owner, Bardo, he's quite a little work of art in his own right."

"Bardo didn't have anything to do with this," I said. "Lamont had a show in Laguna last June. I took Pam by, the weekend Britt had a contest at Brooks Street."

"I remember," Grog said. "Missed that one. Britt got third. Didn't speak to me for a week."

More bad vibes. Grog looked adrift, full of regret. He fumbled for a smoke but couldn't find one. I decided to just power through.

"Anyway, Lamont was there that day in Laguna. We got into a rap about surfing. A few years ago he bought a gun my father shaped for big Sunset at an auction. Restored it himself. He keeps it on his living room wall, over the fireplace."

"Small world," Grog said, his voice trailing away. He flexed the fingers in his right hand, watching them expand and contract as if comforted by the fact that they were under his exclusive control. "I've always said your old man never really left you, even after he died. Pam must be stoked."

I nodded my assent as Grog took a deep swig from his bottle.

"Britt says you've got a new lady on the line," he said.

Precious Phoebe, somewhere in the Orient by now, shooting her next ad. Knowing we were an ocean apart made me miss her even more. "She's probably already history," I told him.

"Heard she was there when the house got trashed."

I nodded. "First time she'd ever been to my place, too," I said. "Jackie was talking orgy as soon as he laid eyes on her."

"Subtle bastard, isn't he? Too bad. Heard she was quite a betty."

Grog searched my face for a reaction, but I gave him nothing. Talking about Phoebe just heightened the pain.

"She was."

Grog stopped eating chips and looked ready to make his point. "You know," he said, "taking care of people who are more goofed up than you is never gonna square what happened."

"Square what happened?" I asked. I wanted to make him say it.

"You know," he said. "What happened with Marielena. It wasn't your fault."

I felt lightheaded from the alcohol, and the rush of bad vibes that came with that name. "I appreciate your concern, but I'm fine."

He leaned forward on his elbows. "Listen man, you were born with a generous spirit, Moondoggie. That's okay, but, just try to take care of *yourself*, too."

I considered telling him about my find in the attic, and my plan to discover what I could about my mother's disappearance. Grog had known Marielena back then. Perhaps he'd have a perspective or two to share, to help point me in the right direction.

"So tell me, what did happen?" I asked.

Grog looked away. "I wish I knew."

So much for that.

"How do you propose that I take care of myself?" I said.

He concentrated. "The broken dishwasher. Make the clown pay."

I doubted that Stone Me Stevie was holding down a steady job at fifteen. "He was just a kid, Grog."

Grog sighed as if his patience was running thin. "I'm talking about Jackie."

"Oh, I plan to make Golden Boy pay. No more free rides. I'm putting him to work."

Across the room, Jackie was busy officiating a swordfight between two young men wielding miniature scabbards they'd plucked from a wall display.

"Jackie, working?" Grog scoffed. "The words sound funny just saying them together."

"I don't know, I've got this interesting court case, and I was thinking—"

"The one with the lady who sold her kid, I know," he said. "Saw it on the news, twice."

"The county's case against this woman is pretty one-sided. I know there's more to it. Maybe Jackie can help me find the handle by doing a little investigative work."

Grog stared at me long and hard. "You lost your fucking mind?"

"So what if I turn him loose?" I said. "What harm could it do?"

"You gotta be joking, kid. You know what he's about, you of all people, J. You're a lawyer, a professional. He's a half-baked demigod to a bunch of surfers who don't even know him. A has-been. Since when did you give a shit about what that bozo thinks?"

"He thinks I don't know how to win," I said. "Thinks I don't have the heart. And listen to you, you're a real confidence booster. You think I can't even take care of myself."

Grog held up his hand as if to stop the flow. "J., I didn't mean—"

"Maybe I'm gonna show you both a few things," I said. "Keep your TV on Channel Six, because that lady's going to get her kid back."

Grog folded his arms on the table. "Fair enough, my friend. Of course, you'll have to beat the Wizard of Oz to do it. You know, that old lawyer with the slicked white hair and fancy clothes. Real bullshit artist."

I gazed at the dusty, black-felt painting that hung on the wall above our booth. An Aztec warrior of Greek proportions knelt at the base of a stone pyramid, a beautiful maiden draped across his outstretched arms in offering.

"I can beat Nelson Gilbride," I said.

Grog tipped his beer bottle. "Course you can. But listen to me, Tubesteak, don't get Jackie mixed up in it. These are things about him even you don't know."

"How's that?"

He looked around as if to make sure Jackie was out of earshot. "That other lawyer, Gilbride? He might try to sell you snake oil. But Jackie . . ."—he hesitated—"Jackie's bad medicine."

Ten

I awoke Sunday morning to a chill south wind that rattled my window blinds, and to the whisper of scattered shore-dump scuffling the inside bar down at the end of Porpoise Way. A south like this, whistling off a haggard sea at first light, will hack the surf to pieces, foiling even the earliest dawn patrol. It is a rare, unpredictable wind. A heady south wind means desperation time.

The inside of my mouth was dry, and my lips felt painted shut. Blades of shadow swayed on the ceiling. I lay on my back in bed, staring up, my sleepy calm fast retreating, making way for a singular thought: one day closer to the Randall trial.

Jackie was downstairs rumbling in the kitchen. He'd barely spoken to me on the drive home from Oceanside last night when I changed my mind and told him I didn't need his help as an investigator after all.

A slender young woman was standing in front of the stove when I came in, perusing my collection of frying pans. She was near-naked but for a tiny pair of black panties, a white tank-top with low-cut sides that exposed most of her breasts, and a Harley-Davidson ball cap she'd pulled down low over her dyed pink hair. Jackie sat at the kitchen table in boxer shorts, chewing on an unlit cigar while he picked his way through the Sunday paper. He was reading and didn't bother to look up at me.

I returned to my bedroom and found a white terry-cloth robe, which I brought downstairs again and handed to the girl in my kitchen. She took the robe without comment and put it on. She seemed not the least bit ashamed of her body—a sexual athlete, I guessed, the kind who always find their way to Jackie. Aside from a distracting pair of silver studs in her left nostril, her skin was flawless and her face was quite striking.

"You wouldn't happen to be Fiona?" I said to her. She must have come in very late last night.

Fiona introduced herself with a nod. "Nice pans," she said, laying a frying pan on the burner. She had another stud embedded in her tongue. "They're French."

"Help yourself," I said, competing with Jackie for various sections of the Sunday *Times* that lay strewn about the dining table.

"I adore all things French," Fiona said. "Jackie and I met in Paris."

"Really?" I said, feigning interest. "Then how about some French toast?"

She nodded, went to the refrigerator and fished out milk, a carton of eggs, and a loaf of bread. I took out a mixing bowl and spoon and put them on the counter. "Powdered sugar or syrup?" I said.

The girl smiled coyly. "Both." A natural flirt.

We dipped the bread and cooked in silence.

"Come on, Jack," I said twenty minutes later, pushing a plate in front of him. "You can't stay mad at me forever."

He put down the Business page and began devouring his food. "I'm not mad. Confused is the word. First I'm gonna be your chief investigator, then two words from Grog Baker and like that"—he snapped his fingers violently—"I'm fuckin' history."

"I didn't know you cared so much about working. This is a side of you I've never seen."

He bore down on his food again. "Eat me, J."

He seemed truly upset, having been fired from a job he'd not yet begun. I ate my French toast, puzzling through the logic he may have been following. He would be against my search for my mother. If he didn't help on the Randall case, I would have to work harder than ever and, as a result, have less time to resume my search for Marielena Shepard on the side. But if he helped, wouldn't I have more time to look for her? I was getting nowhere. I stirred the maple syrup on my plate in circles with a forkful of cold breakfast. Perhaps I'd been wrong about Jackie knowing something.

"Look, man," Jackie said as I cleared the dishes from the table, "let me be blunt. You're obviously in a time of need. Now, I may not have much of a work history, but—"

"You don't have *any* work history."

"Whatever. But come on, J., you know I know how to get things done. You need me on this."

I dumped the dishes in the sink and turned around to face him. "You still want to help?"

"You know I can. Is that so hard to believe, my friend?"

It was. The last time he had truly bailed me out of a difficult situation was the first time, that cold morning out on the reef at Holys. Since then, I'd always been the one to open my checkbook to cover the damages, to reason calmly with agitated authorities, to throttle back whenever the Jackie Pace Good-Time Machine ran a little too rich.

"Okay," I said, "but it's my ass. You've got to take direction from me. You're not a free wheel. You work with me, we work together."

Jackie went to the refrigerator and found a bottle of Heineken I'd stashed way in back. "So what did that tapped out tallywhacker Baker say that made you change your mind?" he said.

I hadn't understood Grog's warning, but I trusted him enough to not repeat it to Jackie. "Nothing," I said, concocting a lie. "It's just, you and I are friends. If you were to make a mistake that would cost me, it might cause a problem between us."

"That was it?" he said as if disappointed. Jackie lifted the bottle and drank, then smiled at Fiona and me. "No worries, brother."

Fiona finished her breakfast and drifted off to the living room couch to sleep. I brought the case file to the dining room table and spread out the various documents and notes. Slowly, a list of work to be done emerged. I told Jackie I would interview the adoption broker, Lois Nettleson, and Arturo, Sue Ellen's former Silverlake neighbor. I would be plenty busy in the meantime doing prep work once I found out who Gilbride's expert would be. The rules of discovery required Belinda McWhirter to provide me with a copy of the expert's report in time enough to prepare for trial; I'd wait until then to worry about the bonding issue.

Jackie would check out the situation with the Randalls' former landlord, the one who claimed they'd ditched the Pontrellis without leaving a forwarding address. I doubted that would lead to much—at best, the landlord's testimony would be circumstantial as to fraud. More important, I instructed Jackie to have a look around at

Woodside Community Hospital, the place where Sue Ellen supposedly had been straight-armed into giving birth prematurely, and in staggering pain.

"What am I supposed to be looking for, boss?" he said.

"I don't know," I admitted. I wasn't sure if Sue Ellen's story was even the truth, so my directions were few. "Just do what you always do," I told him. "Figure something out."

He broke into a manic grin, cupped his hand into a horn shape and raised it to his lips. "Doctor Pace," he said, imitating a public address announcement, "please come to the O.R. immediately." He dropped his hand, still beaming. "Gotta say I like the sound of that. This is gonna be a gas."

His humor had its usual wearying effect on me. "Nothing illegal. And don't cut any patients open while you're there—or at least scrub before you do." I began packing up the file.

"Hey, J., you think she did it?" he said. "You know, scammed those people out of their money."

He needed to have a context for the proceedings, to know what we were fighting for. I could see that much. "Maybe," I said. "I doubt it. But the lawyer for those rich people, he took advantage of her. That much I know."

That was all I could manage in support of Sue Ellen Randall for now.

Jackie was skeptical about Sue Ellen when I told him about Ronny Randall's quiet exodus to Kentucky, and he seemed unimpressed with my meek endorsement. "Is she gonna be cool from here on out?" he asked.

"Probably. She doesn't have any more kids to take out of state, if that's what you mean. All she's gotta do is hang in there and wait for trial."

"The woman who sold her baby?" Fiona said behind us. She'd removed her Harley cap and wrapped a blanket over her shoulders. Her eyes were heavy with sleep. "I saw you on TV," she said to me as if to explain.

"I just hope she and her husband resist the impulse to do anything stupid between now and next week," I said.

"Has she ever seen the kid?" Jackie said. "I mean, since the hospital?"

"Just once," I said. "That's where I went Friday night. Her first scheduled visit is tomorrow at the county's offices."

"Ooh, I hope they show that on TV!" Fiona said.

Jackie frowned at the notion of a televised visit, as did I. "She's gonna get hassled," Jackie said, "isn't she, J.?"

I hadn't really considered attending the first visit, which was set for Monday at four at the department's East L.A. office. I'd never done it before, in any of the hundreds of other cases I'd handled. But none of those cases was anything like this one. Christ, even Fiona and Jackie were dialed in to the situation. What was I thinking? Sue Ellen's first visit with a child she'd given away was an emotional jackpot for interested bystanders. The scene could get crazy.

"You all right, man?" Jackie asked me. "You're looking a little flushed around the gills."

I had that sinking feeling that I was getting too close, too involved. This has never been my way. The key to stomaching dependency was keeping a healthy distance to maintain perspective—and sanity. But the Matter of Nathan Randall was swallowing me.

"I think it is *so* cool," Fiona said. "I don't care what they say about her."

"What do you mean?" I asked.

Fiona looked at me as if I was remarkably hardheaded. "She's the boy's *mother*. It's so dramatic. I love it! She's gonna fight for him!" The girl was rooting for Sue Ellen, which I took as a refreshing change.

"That is, if they don't scare her into bailing," Jackie said. I nodded in agreement.

Fiona shook her head no. "They won't, *mon ami*. You two don't know all there is to know about a woman, do you? She'll be there. *Celui qui veut, peut*—where there's a will, there's a way." She slid onto Jackie's lap and let him enfold her in his arms, the blanket dropping to the floor.

"Teach me more about women, baby," he said, flicking his tongue into her ear.

I left court after three on Monday and took surface streets through the barrio south of Cybil Brand women's prison. Dark-haired kids in school uniforms scurried like ants down the wide, sun-scorched sidewalks. I flipped on the radio to Bad Company's signature tune. *Bad company, I can't deny; bad, bad company, 'til the day I die.*

Sue Ellen's visit with Nathan was scheduled to commence in half an hour, but the lot outside the department's East L.A. office was already teeming with kooks and picketers. A girl in pigtails and braces stalked the sidewalk, hoisting a sign that read HELL NO! NATHAN WON'T GO! Another sign I saw said YOUR STORY'S SMELLIN', SUE ELLEN! I strode forward as if I had life-and-death business and couldn't be bothered by distractions of any kind. An old man in a straw hat waved a huge American flag in front of me, then turned his back, quoting Scripture through an electric bullhorn as his helper, a Latino who looked like a reformed gang-banger, passed out tiny pamphlets heralding the End Time. Holly Dupree's orange hairdo floated above the crowd; she was deep in their midst, interviewing some suitably enraged man-on-the-street whose spit was flying as he ranted.

"Fuckin'-A—It's her lawyer!" Someone shouted as if grieved at the sight of me. Quite a different reception from the one I got that first morning outside Foley's court. "What's he want here?" the same voice shouted.

"Let's send him packing!" yelled another.

Fuckin'-A indeed, I thought. I'm not going to hang around out here. I barreled toward the glass double doors, but a huge man with a bad haircut stepped in front of me. "You're scum," he said, angrily poking a finger into my chest. The others crowded in like hungry dogs.

"Back off," I said into a group of faces I'd never seen. They stared back at me, indignant and mean.

Sue Ellen wasn't even here and the situation was already well out of hand. Someone pushed me from behind.

"Look at him! Fancy pants lawyer!"

The crowd was beginning to scare me, so I turned loose a little temper on the man standing before me, grabbing the top of the hand that was in my chest and pushing his middle finger up and backward. He winced, his eyes popping.

"Move it, fatty, or I'll break your finger," I said, giving him the benefit of full eye contact. He backpedaled, creating a small opening in the crowd. I shot through without looking back, and turned the dead bolt in the glass door as soon as I got inside the department office.

"What happened?" I could hear Holly say to a TV crewman through the glass just outside. "What'd I miss?"

Inside, a woman sat behind a high desk, watching a dormant switchboard panel and doing her best to act as if she didn't see me come in. The reception room was small and shabby, four greasy walls with tilted portraits of county supervisors hanging in a row along one side and a single security door that led to the workplace.

"Who's the head of this office?" I said.

She shook her head as if to prohibit my entry. "Sir, that door must remain unlocked during normal business hours. Those are the rules."

I withered the woman with a look of pure contempt. "Yeah, right," I said. "And which rules apply to parking lot riots?"

She didn't push the point, and after some minor hassling I got her to call someone in charge. The man who emerged from the inner office to meet me five minutes later was not the slick bureaucrat I expected but a tiny guy named Harold something-or-other with glasses, a pencil moustache and a soggy handshake, a regular Walter Mitty. "What can I do for you?" he mumbled.

I glanced through the pane glass behind us at the mob. "I'm Sue Ellen Randall's attorney. She has a visit scheduled with her son Nathan in a few minutes."

Harold concurred. "Yes, I know." His lack of further acknowledgment told me he was not prepared to do a damn thing to address the situation outside.

I blinked with disbelief. "These people outside are here to cause trouble. Get them out of here."

"I can't," he said. "It's a public place." He shrugged as if innocent.

"Listen, friend," I said, straining to maintain my cool, "these visits are court-ordered, and if you've ever met Judge Duane Foley, you know he takes it very seriously when someone defies him."

"Oh?" he said, still playing the game. "Who's defying him? Certainly not me."

I regarded the mob through the front-door glass. This was ridiculous, and the department and this little worm named Harold knew it. I could feel my anger taking over.

"You got a card?" I said. "What's your last name again, Harold? I need it for the subpoena I'm going to send you. You see, in this case, these visits are a bit of a sticking point. You'll get to tell the judge in person why you decided to take a shit on his visitation order."

He raised his hands to calm me. "All right, all right," he said, "there's no need for that. What do you want?" The man was a true civil servant: he may have agreed to comply, but he was certainly not going to innovate.

"You can start by getting me a security guard," I said.

He looked at the receptionist. "Dottie, call Joe Phipps. Tell him to come up front, now."

Joe Phipps turned out to be even more insubstantial a presence than Harold. White-haired and hunched over, he was downright elderly—way past retirement age—and terribly thin. He shook my hand with the grip of a sickly child. Harold stood by, enjoying my predicament.

"How can I help you, young fella?" Phipps said.

"Use your authority to disperse this mob," I said, pointing through the glass. "I'm afraid they might harm my client when she arrives."

"Oh, my," he said, studying the confusion outside. "They look upset, don't they? My goodness."

"Just make the announcement," I said. "Wait here. I'll get you what you need."

I went out again, but no one was looking my way, as they were all focused on Sue Ellen's imminent arrival at the other end of the facility. I found the flag-waving Christian man with the bullhorn.

"Unto every one that hath shall be given," he squawked, "and he shall have abundance! But from he that hath not, shall be taken away even that which he hath!"

I opened my wallet and took out two tens. "Brother," I beseeched the man, "the Lord is wise and wonderful."

"Say amen!"

I handed him a ten-spot. "Amen!"

He pocketed the money. "Amen, halleluiah, brother!"

I grabbed the bullhorn. "I need to borrow this, just for a minute." But he wouldn't let go. "Come on, brother," I said, "give, and it shall be given unto you!" I handed him another ten and he let go.

"Praise Jesus," he said as he folded the second bill into his shirt pocket. "But I want it back."

Joe Phipps was sucking on a throat lozenge when I gave him the bullhorn and asked him to clear everyone out. He spit the half-dissolved disc back into its foil wrapper and coughed hard. "Ready to go," he said, his eyes watering. I thought he must be joking.

We geared up and rushed outside, but the throng was suddenly racing to the parking lot. "Ladies and gentlemen, boys and girls," I heard Phipps announce as I ran toward Sue Ellen. "Say, Harold, is this thing on?"

Sue Ellen was alone in Ty's old pickup truck; she'd pulled halfway into an empty spot but had seen the rush of faces and had tried to back up. The truck was now stalled in the middle of two rows of cars. Holly Dupree was there already, camped outside the driver's window, trying to talk Sue Ellen into rolling it down for a friendly chat. People were thumping the truck's fenders and hood with their hands, making a thundering racket. I came around the passenger side and rapped on the glass until Sue Ellen saw me and let me in.

"Oh my God! Oh my God!" she cried. "Get me out of here!"

"Move over," I yelled. I slid past her and got behind the wheel. She'd flooded the engine—her specialty. People were shaking the truck from side to side now. Holly pleaded with me through the glass with muffled words I didn't care to hear anyway. In the rear-view mirror, I saw the fat man who'd called me scum mount the rear bumper and begin bouncing with all his considerable ballast, jeering at us as he gripped the tailgate.

"Bunch o' lunatics!" Sue Ellen shouted.

"This is nuts!" I shouted back. "Move it!"

Sue Ellen had calmed down a little since I'd jumped into the cab. "What about my visit? What are you gonna do?"

"Don't worry about the visit," I said. "I'm gonna pop it into gear, so hold on." I laid on the horn, but no one backed away from the truck.

"Careful, it's a V-8. You could run somebody over."

My head was getting dizzy from the constant rocking. "Well, fuck 'em if they can't take a joke," I said.

I let off the emergency brake, honked one last time and found second gear just as the engine clicked over. The truck lurched ahead, clearing an instant path before us and launching the fat man off the bumper and into space. I gunned up into the lot until it ran out near the building, then jumped the tires over a curb and cut across the brown lawn that fronted the office until I was at the entrance. We were a mere few seconds ahead of the closing throng.

"Hang on," I said. We slid out the driver's side and I locked the truck and threw my arm around Sue Ellen. Joe Phipps was still fooling with the volume control on the bullhorn when we reached the door. It was locked. The mob encircled us. "Get back!" I shouted, trying to sound fearless. But I was scared.

"Baby seller!" they shouted at Sue Ellen. "Trailer trash!"

Harold unlocked the door and got us inside with a look of feigned relief. Sue Ellen was gripping herself. "Well," Harold said to her after we had caught our breaths, "ready for your visit?" Sue Ellen nodded. "Dottie, have the Danforths checked in?"

Sue Ellen stared at them. "You mean they're not even here?"

"They left a message for you, sir, twenty minutes ago," Dottie said, a tiny smile crossing her lips. "Corwin junior has a cold. They wanted to know if the visit could be rescheduled until tomorrow."

"Oh, that's too bad," Harold the supervisor said.

We'd been suckered. Harold just stood there, enjoying the day. Sue Ellen began to sob. For what felt like the ten-thousandth time, I was reminded how it felt for a client to be overmatched by an uncaring institution that held every advantage. It felt like losing.

I stepped up into Harold until my breath was on his face. "I want your card right now. You can expect a subpoena in the morning. Judge Foley's going to hear about this directly from you. I'll walk the case onto his calendar myself. See you in court."

Harold's face was white. "You, you can't do that. I'm a supervisor."

"I think I can," I said. "You're within L.A. County, which is the court's jurisdiction, so you're gonna get tapped." I took a pen out of my jacket pocket. "Who's your boss, Harold? He'll get a special invite, too."

He looked ready to cave. "Okay, okay, what do you want?"

"This was supposed to be a neutral site," I said. "The visits were to be confidential. Obviously someone in your office doesn't care about that. Call the Danforths. Tell them we've got a new arrangement. From now on, we'll call you on the morning of the visit and set the time with you." I glanced at the mob through the glass door. "If we get the welcome wagon, I'll know you're to blame. So will the judge."

Harold thought about my demands. "But the Danforths will know," he said. "What if they tell the press?"

"You'd be wise to persuade them not to," I said. "You're the one supervising the neutral site. From here on out, it's your call." I shook my head. "Man, this is really going to put a crimp in Judge Foley's jockey shorts. His calendar's already maxed out."

"Now calm down," Harold said. "We can work this out." He was not about to face an angry judge over someone else's crummy visits. "Dottie, get the Danforths for me, please," he told the receptionist.

Harold made arrangements for me to take Sue Ellen to the Danforth home for another visit. The nanny would be there to meet us. No Nelson Gilbride. Sue Ellen was still crying, but she reached out and squeezed my hand so firmly I nearly lost my balance. "Thank you," she said, "thank you so very much." She looked deeply into my eyes.

"It's all right," I said, wishing she'd release my hand. "It's my job." A little gratitude was one thing, but this kind of display was far from all right with me.

Old Joe Phipps was inside, now; he'd used a key to let himself in while I was confronting Harold. "Everything's under control," he told us. The crowd was still outside, and in force. Less than intimidated by Joe's authority. "I'm afraid you're going to have to move that truck," he told me.

"You got it," I said. Sue Ellen was still holding my hand tightly. "How about an escort, Joe?"

Joe nodded and stood before the glass, preparing to unlock the door again. He studied the bullhorn before tucking it under his arm. "Nice noisemaker you've got here," he said.

"Hey Joe," I said, "could you give it back to the guy waving the American flag once you get us out of here? It's his."

"But I saw you pay for it," he said. "I was watching you from right here."

"Things aren't always the way they look," I told him.

I could feel Sue Ellen's gaze on the side of my face. "You believe me," she said. "I knew it."

"Fuckin'-A," I said to no one in particular. I kept my eyes straight ahead until Joe rattled the door open.

Eleven

Carmen Manriquez was in significant demand when I dropped by the Las Palomas office with my mother's old letters from Miluca. A pair of dolled-up girls in white ruffles danced up and down the corridor outside the door, just out of reach of a battered young Mexican couple who strained to hear Carmen's directions above the laughter and play. A black man in a disjointed cream polyester suit paced the tiles opposite the doorway, opening his court order to read it aloud one more time, then folding it up as if he'd confronted an evil curse. My business in Foley's court done, I decided to wait.

The black man peeked at the order and looked up and saw me checking him. "Parenting skills!" he shouted at me. "They think I need skills at bein' a parent! Now ain't that a mu-tha-fuck-a fo' ya! I raised them kids since theys knee high to a grasshopper! No one gonna tell me how to be a parent!"

The family cleared out of Carmen's office and the hyperventilating black man pushed in fast. "Child, you the one gonna teach me how to be a parent?" he said to Carmen. I couldn't see her face from where I waited, but I heard her fluid tone roll out. Within a minute the man was agreeing, then apologizing, explaining himself as he related his frustrations. "That's right. Like, I'm damned if ah do and damned if ah don't!" His sweating face relaxed, then he stood up to go. "Well all right, then, honey, you take care ya-self. And ah thank ye kindly." A new man.

"What did you do," I said to Carmen, "rip up the guy's order?"

Carmen wore a pale pink ribbed cotton dress with her hair loosely pulled into a casual bun. "A new technique I've been using," she said, "and it really works. It's called listening." She folded her arms and smiled as if my visit was a small surprise.

I was glad to see her. "I'll have to try it."

"Did you come for a Spanish lesson?"

"Actually, no." I sat down and hefted my briefcase onto my lap, opened it and put the brittle stack of letters on the desk.

"Quite a collection," she said. "What are they?"

My dilemma was obvious. She had to have some context for dealing with the text of the letters, but if I told her too much and my delivery got shaky, I'd impress her as damaged goods. Better to let my past unfold slowly, and in pieces.

"The first time we met, when I came up for an interpreter, what you said made sense. I thought about it a lot. Then I found these in my attic." I removed the rubber band and fanned the letters like a hand of cards across the edge of her desk blotter.

"Who's Marielena Shepard?"

"My mother. She left home when I was almost seventeen, back in nineteen seventy-nine. I've never known why. I thought these might tell me."

Carmen inspected the envelopes. "May I?" I nodded. She removed a letter and ran her eyes over a few lines. "Small handwriting, but pretty clean. Good Spanish. The writer was educated."

"Can you translate them for me?" I said too eagerly. Easy does it, I told myself. Carmen Manriquez had a way about her, a radiance and poise I'd not before glimpsed in these miserable hallways. My heartbeat quickened. "I can pay you," I said.

"This is important to you," she said. I silently assented.

An enormously pregnant woman pushing an infant in a stroller edged inside the door. Her expression was hurried but aimless— headed nowhere fast. Her heavy breasts showed right through a white tee that advertised a popular American brand of oil filters. A twisted, unhooked bra underlined her tits; she'd forgotten to hook up after baby's last feeding. The stroller's frame was mildly tweaked, and I noticed one of the front wheels didn't quite reach the floor.

"Hell-oh-oh," she said like one might before entering a pitch-black cave. As if we were holding our breaths for her arrival. "I'm hee-ere." I was instantly annoyed by her self-centeredness.

"This Las Palomas? The judge says Scotty—he's my soul mate— ought to take parenting, even though he's not Bianca's real dad." She turned to look behind her. "Goddam it, what is with him?

Scotty, come on in!" she shouted as if Scotty were a terrier who'd slipped free from his leash, but Scotty didn't show his face. *Good boy, Scotty*, I said to myself.

"I'll be just a moment," Carmen told her. "Why don't you just relax outside. I'll come and get you."

"I'm kinda in a hurry," the woman said. I stood up and smiled thinly, glad that for once, this one was not my client. The twice-cursed baby Bianca eyed me disdainfully. I clipped the door shut just inches from the useless wheel of her secondhand ride.

"This place really gets to you," Carmen said.

"Just sometimes. I'm sorry. I don't want to be interrupted right now."

She gathered the letters. "I'll take them home and start tonight. You don't have to pay me."

I swallowed hard and summoned a lick of courage. "Maybe I can do something for you. Are you doing anything Friday evening?"

"I have to watch my brother. I live with him and my mother. She's going out Friday."

"What about Saturday?"

"I'm taking him out Saturday."

"Oh."

"Are you asking me on a date?" she said, so calmly I was instantly worried that I might be making an ass of myself.

"I guess I am. But I want to thank you, too, for translating the letters." Shit. I was about as smooth as the ride on that kid's piece-of-shit baby carriage.

"Saturday would've been good," she said. "But Albert doesn't get out often enough. *Mami's* getting old. She doesn't have the energy to keep up with him anymore. He's usually bored with the things I plan. Wants to do "guy" things."

"What do you two like to do together?"

"We go to movies, but he usually falls asleep before the story gets going. It's hard finding anything suitable anyway."

"There aren't many good movies for kids any more."

"He's not a kid," she said, "but you're right. Albert's twenty-four. He's mentally slow."

"What are you two doing Saturday?"

"Probably bowling. He likes to bowl." She wrinkled her nose at the thought. "We bowl too much. I'm tired of sitting in that dank, smelly alley when outside the sky's blue and the sun's shining. He needs to be outdoors more."

I had an idea that seemed perfectly natural.

"Can Albert swim?"

"He's a good swimmer," she said. "Four summers of lessons at the Y."

"Does he like the beach?"

"He does, but he's a handful."

"How much does he weigh?"

"About one-fifty, I think. I don't know for sure. Why?"

I glanced briefly over her well-proportioned frame. "And you're somewhere between one-ten and one-twenty."

"Aah, an estimate," she said, "very diplomatic." Our eyes had begun a flirtation. "Why do you ask?"

"Your boards would need enough flotation. You catch more waves that way."

"You want to take us surfing?"

"That's the concept. What do you think?"

"I've never done it," she said. "I don't know . . . I mean, about Albert."

"You said he's a good swimmer. Don't worry, he'll be safe, and it'll spring you both from the lanes. He'll have a gas."

Her brown eyes fixed on mine. "He will?"

"I promise."

The woman in the air filter shirt pulled open the door without knocking. "Scotty's back," she said, as if that alone was reason enough for me to clear the hell out.

I sighed. "Marvelous."

Carmen invited me to hang a few minutes until she closed for the day, and I did. We set a time for Saturday morning and exchanged phone numbers, and I promised to call her Friday evening with directions to my place. I walked her from the courthouse out into the four-level, which, by this hour, was all but empty. We found her car, a well-maintained, midnight blue '72 Chevy Malibu, parked in the space next to my dusty Jeep wagon. We both had a laugh about this little coincidence, but I knew Marielena Shepard would have disagreed with our assessment.

A sign, she would have said.

The County Recorders Office in Norwalk is full of map books bearing the legal descriptions of every square foot of property in the region, but if you don't know the basic coordinates of the parcel you're looking for, you're in trouble. My problem was that the Sea Pointe brochures had been vague as to the exact location of the homesites. I knew the lots were somewhere north of Pacific Coast Highway and west of Christianitos Boulevard, amongst the muddy sea grass and eroded bluffs of the Back Bay. But I had no real map, and the brochures themselves were gone.

"Try your town's City Hall," the desk clerk said as they dimmed the lights to give warning that they were closing up. "Most smaller towns like Christianitos have historians. Yours might."

Why hadn't I thought of that? I'd floated down here on a cloud of good karma after saying good-bye to Carmen. My mind was addled with a new sense of possibility, but my hopes swam upcurrent against an instinct to flee to the familiar safety of loneliness.

I found a pay phone and called City Hall. They closed at five, but yes, they had a historian, Charles Baumann, and yes, he was in. When Baumann came on the line I begged him to stay a little late and made up a fairly elaborate lie to seal his agreement. I told him I was a lawyer representing an elderly client—"Confidential" I said when he asked for a name—who needed specific information about certain properties so that they could be properly accounted for in a will.

"Don't you have the deeds?" he asked.

"Well, yes," I said, "but the land is undeveloped. My client is getting on in years and can't recall which parcels are which. His wishes are that certain land go to some heirs as opposed to others."

"I get it," Baumann said. "Stickin' it to 'em, eh?"

"My client is very ill," I said. "Dying. Can you wait for me?" Christ, where did I come up with this garbage?

"Just get here as soon as you can," he said. "I have some work to finish up anyway."

I sailed south down the 605 freeway in twenty minutes, a remarkable feat considering the commuter push this time of day.

Thankfully, the Christianitos City Hall building stood only half-hidden behind the public library, for it offered the clumsiest of paeans to the boxy Bauhaus school of architecture. The parking lot was tiny and looked full, so I parked on the street and walked up. I knocked at the entrance until Charles Baumann rattled some keys and let me in. He was probably in his late sixties with a tanned, jowly face and thin gray hair. We shook hands and I followed him back behind a long counter to a small wooden desk, where he pulled up an extra chair for me. He wore a short-sleeved green plaid shirt, olive slacks and clean, white leather tennis shoes. Definitely retired. I imagined he acted as the town historian on an unpaid basis.

I told him about the Sea Pointe brochures.

"Sounds like one of those Back Bay projects that never got off the ground," he said.

"Do you recall anything about Sea Pointe?"

"Not off the top of my head." He wordlessly invited me to explain.

I tried to piece together another blithe lie to add to the line I'd already fed him. "There may be an issue—a dispute, that is—over ownership within the family." Damn, that sounded weak.

"I see. What about this Provencal Limited you mentioned?" he said. I'd remembered the name on the back flap of the brochures. "Somebody owned that. Why don't you ask your client about that?"

"His memory's failing him. That's why I've got to work fast." I was sounding a little too shady, now. "You know, to protect his interests."

"Uh-huh." Charles Baumann cocked one eye at me.

I was tired of trying to keep pace with this rapidly escalating line of bullshit. "Look," I said, leveling with him, "I'm sorry I made you wait for me, but I'm not into anything illegal here, I swear. I just need to find out what I can about Sea Pointe. Can you help me? Anything you might know, any idea you might have about how I could learn more about it."

Baumann thought about it for a minute. "I suppose we could start by searching the business licenses. This Provencal outfit had to have one to sell land here in town."

"Good," I said. "What can I do?"

"Tell me, how old were the brochures?"

"Nineteen seventy-nine, I think."

"I'll have to do the search myself. All the records from the seventies are in archives. Don't have 'em on microfiche yet. I'm workin' on it," he said, chuckling, "but they don't pay me to work fast."

"How long will it take?"

"A few days, at least. But not this week. I don't come in Fridays," he said. "Golf day. I'll know something by midweek. I'm in all afternoon. Food bank. Try me, oh, say around Tuesday or Wednesday. I'll see what I can hunt up."

"Much appreciated," I said. I gave him a card. "You find out anything sooner, you can call me collect, if you like."

He took the card. "Fair enough."

Charles Baumann walked me to the glass double doors. We shook hands and I thanked him again. "Sea Pointe," he said in reflection. "You know, I think a neighborhood called Sea Pointe went in around 'seventy-nine or 'eighty, but it wasn't Sea Pointe when they finished it. Something else."

"They changed the name?"

"Think so. How 'bout the one just east of the power plant channel, you know, up First on the far side of PCH."

"That's 'The Bluffs'."

"Not the one I was thinking of." He clicked his tongue. "Sorry."

"Thanks. I'll catch you next week."

"Sure thing. So tell me," he said, hobbling toward an electric cart which, come to think of it, I'd probably seen parked in this lot a thousand times before. "There isn't any will, is there?"

"No," I conceded. "There's no client, either. I'm looking for someone who's missing, and . . ." My voice skipped. "She may have deserted me a long time ago."

He stopped walking. "Sure you really want to find her?"

"Yeah," I said, "I'm sure."

"Say Mr. Shepard," he called to me before I was across the black-top, "what kind of law do you practice?"

Had Baumann been tuning into Channel Six lately? Was he mocking me? The prospect of losing such a highly publicized battle rattled through me again. I thought of my father, the commitment he'd applied to his shaping and big-wave riding. No holding back. Or so I'd been told.

"I'm a kiddie lawyer," I said, "the best in town."

The sidewalk leading back to my car was adorned with chalked-in hopscotch squares and assorted arrow-pierced hearts bearing decla-rations of adolescent longing: R. L. + K. H.; T. T. + M. P. 4ever. But the yards and sidewalks on both sides of the street were aban-doned. Five or six houses down, at the corner of Fifth and Edison, a cascade of sprinklers fanned a carpet of lawn. Through the mist I caught sight of a guy on a red beach cruiser turning tail as if he didn't want me to spot him. The spray obscured my view, but the bicycle's color was the same candy-apple red of the cruiser I kept in the garage. I ran to my car.

It could have been a neighbor kid—or Jackie. If it was him, he couldn't have known what I was doing with Baumann. My secret was still safe. But then, Jackie would be back to sweet talk Baumann about the purpose of my visit. He would know soon enough.

But I didn't see the man on the bike as I drove, and every light I hit through town seemed to turn red as I approached. I stared up at the signal at Edison and Main, waiting on green with a purpose of mind that bordered on the paranoid.

When I unlocked the garage door and pulled in, my bike was there in back, just where it had been when I backed out of the garage this morning. A shaft of late-afternoon sun shot through the window above the workbench and sparkled on the spokes and handlebars. Max barked from the other side of the back door until I opened it and let him rush me. Across the small yard, the house appeared closed up and quiet.

The handlebars were warm to the touch, as were the front tire and the seat, but they were also standing in direct sunlight. The back tire was fully shaded by the workbench's table edge. The knobby tread felt equally warm—or so I thought. Perhaps the bike had just been used to follow me. But then, how could Jackie beat me back here without me spying him, then disappear? It wasn't possible.

But I'd seen him! Or had I?

An inner voice gave me counsel. You're losing your grip, J., just maintain. Derangement is a slippery slope. Trust no one, if you must, but don't waver.

I squatted before the cruiser and patted Max on the head, one hand still caressing the knobby bike tire. Considering the possibilities. Hoping against hope that some sort of answer would find its way to me.

Twelve

I dialed the adoption broker Lois Nettleson's office from one of the pay phones down the hall from Foley's courtroom. A young female took the call. "Nettleson Family Consulting," she said.

The girl paused briefly after I identified myself. I imagined she was checking a list that said "Calls to dump" and quickly found my name at the top.

"I'm sorry, sir," she said, "but Ms. Nettleson isn't available to take your call."

"Will she be in today? I really need to speak to her."

"I'm sorry, sir. She's not available to see you either." She exuded the same glib pleasantness you get from kids at fast food windows everywhere.

Unsure about a plan B, I hung up.

This day, Wednesday, was the day to see Lois Nettleson. My calendar was mercifully light. I'd started with two review hearings, both of them no-brainers. For once, the other lawyers and I agreed with the social workers' reports; "submitted" we took turns saying when Foley asked each of us for argument. In keeping with his standard lickety-split morning routine, Foley offered no eye contact from the bench. But I could tell he was pleased.

By 9:15 I had only one task remaining, a 10 A.M. mediation on a molest in which I represented Minor One, the victim, and Ken Jorgensen, the rotund panel lawyer, had daddy diddler. Watching Ken work in the morning is typically about as fast paced as charting the early spring melting patterns of Arctic glaciers. He unfolds his paper. He reads his paper. He goes downstairs for coffee. He buys a fruit pie. He comes back upstairs. He eats his fruit pie. The filling drips onto the sleeve of his jacket. He waits until he thinks no one's looking, then licks it off. A client approaches him seeking clarification about one of Foley's orders, but Ken has no time—he forgot to buy coffee. He heads downstairs again.

But Ken was hustling today. His diddling client was claiming he wasn't the kid's natural father and screaming for a paternity test, and Ken was buying it. It was a sublimely ridiculous ploy. Father had a common-law marriage to Mother, had lived with her for a dozen years, and both he and the sorry lad sported the same weak chin and close-set brown eyes. Foley gave Ken the major stink-eye when Ken asked for the test and a continuance to wait for the results, but he could do little else than grumble and cancel the mediation, putting the matter over until October. To Foley's chagrin I voiced no opposition. But how could I? Ken's absurd contention had sprung me from court hours early, freeing me to concentrate on working the Randall case. Ken nearly fell off his chair when, as I packed up my briefcase to go, I rather spontaneously patted him on the back and thanked him for continuing the case. His round face hardened into a stare and his double neck inflated like a pink balloon as he craned over his shoulder and clawed at his back.

"You stick something on my jacket?" he said.

"Come on, buddy." I smiled, recalling an afternoon in late July when Ken majestically rose from the chair next to mine to argue his case, a "Preferred Service" sticker from Christianitos Mobil plastered to his outsized fanny. "I would never."

I dialed Lois Nettleson's office again. This time I lowered my voice and tried to affect a nervous stammer. This time I told the perky young girl I was a would-be dad who wanted to check out his options on relinquishing a white baby for adoption. She put me on hold to check Lois's schedule while a string section played a soaring version of "We've Only Just Begun." A few bars later I was warmly invited to stop by the office in two hours for a free consultation with Lois.

The drive north from L.A. to Santa Barbara on the 101 is mostly a bore. A long string of generic, newish suburbs hacked into the sides of rolling brown hills, fast-food chains and gleaming car dealerships eating away at gentle ranchlands. An alley of garish billboards pitching you between every turnoff. You don't catch an ocean breeze or glimpse any blue for a long, long while. Then the road slides down out of the hills into the Oxnard valley, running through a hodgepodge of strawberry patches, equipment rental yards and outlet malls. More new developments, more of the same mindless blight.

I passed the California Street offramp in downtown Ventura, and Fairgrounds, a popular all-around surf spot that can handle a lot of kids and longboarders. The parking lot lining the break looked quiet—a rare flat day.

The freeway traffic slowed. The right lane was clogged by laboring big-rigs and, behind them, a procession of hulking motor homes driven by retirees. I passed carefully on the left, watching the Fairgrounds recede in my rearview mirror. A silver Lincoln Continental hovered a dozen car-lengths behind me.

The highway hugged the ocean at last. The late-morning sun had peeled away the gray gloom and the sea looked invitingly deep and vast, as it always does to me. I checked the waves at sixty miles per hour, but the surf was nothing more than gutless local windswell roughed up by a building onshore. I moved over into the slow lane as I passed the Ventura Overhead, a big-wave reef which, like Holy Rollers, lies dormant most of the year. Nothing doing. Behind me, the Lincoln merged into my lane and slid behind a pickup truck full of produce. A car like that, with a big V-8, in the slow lane? I sped up again and changed lanes. The Lincoln followed me over. I could see half the face of the driver beneath the guy's sun visor. Some tourist with a crew cut. He was following me.

Lois Nettleson's office was situated in the middle of a tony block of adobe-style two-story facades just north of the freeway. The building housed an art gallery upstairs, a few clothing boutiques down the sidewalk, an upscale florist's shop, and the offices of a lawyer and a psychiatrist. I parked next door to Lois's place, directly in front of a busy little cafe with a dozen tables shielded by royal blue Cinzano umbrellas. Well-heeled women in white linen dresses ordered lunch, nibbling on focaccia from small wicker baskets. I locked the Jeep and peered over the roof, searching for the Lincoln, but it had dropped out of sight.

The reception area in Lois's office was a compact space, but beautifully furnished and carpeted in a cool shade of aquamarine. Lois had money. Several back issues of *Architectural Digest* and *The New Yorker* had been fanned out around the tissue box. I had a hard time picturing Ty and Sue Ellen Randall catching up on the Talk of the Town while waiting on an appointment here.

A nervous man of about forty was seated on the sofa, wringing his hands as he carried on some sort of private dialogue in his head. He paid me no mind as I went by him and looked around. The back corner of the room opened to a small hallway and the closed door of Lois Nettleson's office. Outside her office was an antique desk with a phone, an answer pad and pen, and an unfinished crossword puzzle spread across the blotter. I could hear voices behind the door, the muted sound of a woman's sobs.

"She's out to lunch," the man on the couch said to me.

"Miss Nettleson?"

"No," he said, "Kari. Girl who makes her appointments."

"Oh, thanks," I said, settling into the leather chair. He gazed expectantly at me. "I'm J." I offered my hand.

"Martin."

"I'm early," I said. "Must be slotted after you."

He wore a blue serge suit, wingtips and the kind of bold red foulard tie that's a standard for accountants and finance types. His red hair was balding and cut conservatively short. On one hand he wore a gold wedding band, on the other the same kind of U.S.C. garnet Judge Foley was so proud to own.

"I've already seen her," he said. "My wife's in there alone." He appeared ready to cry.

"Beautiful day outside," I said. I walked to the window and peered out past a tangle of red bougainvillea, searching the street for the Lincoln. The happy clink of glasses and silverware drifted over from the cafe.

"I want to try again. Miss Nettleson's doing her best to persuade Janet—my wife."

"Your second time around?" I asked.

"Third—if you can believe it." He kneaded his palms. "Even took the baby home this time. Had her room all ready for her, toys picked out. A crib . . ."

"What happened?"

"Wish I knew." The anger was welling in his voice. He sat forward to make his point with me. "The mother . . . came over after the baptism, saw Janet holding little Sarah, saw the home we'd created, how happy we were. My God. Just changed her mind. Like that"—he snapped his fingers in front of my face—"Sarah was gone." He resumed staring at nothing.

"Why'd the mother come see you after the baptism?"

"Open adoption," he said. "Only way she was ever gonna give up Sarah in the first place. I told Lois I thought it was a bad idea, but she said the mother seemed okay with it. Huh." He gulped.

I picked up a magazine and pretended to read, unsettled by what Martin had to say. With all the analysis I'd given to Sue Ellen Randall's position, I'd ruled out any consideration of what losing Nathan meant to the Danforths. Perhaps this was why my understanding about what had played out between them felt so incomplete.

"You trying to adopt?" he finally asked me.

"No, somebody I know had problems, too. I'm just here to see if I can help."

"Hope you brought your checkbook," Martin said.

"Lois expensive?"

"Yeah. But not half as expensive as it is to support an ignorant girl who thinks she just hit the lottery."

"You think you got taken?"

"Jesus, I don't know. We never cared about the money. Maybe that was the problem. We just wanted Sarah." His eyes were wet and he lowered his face in shame.

I began to doubt my mission. Perhaps the social worker's report was true. What if the Danforths were just like Martin, willing to give anything to have a child, and Sue Ellen was just what the department and Nelson Gilbride said she was, a game player, a fraud? It could have been Martin, not the Danforths, writing those checks and painting the new room for Nathan. Perhaps I was here on behalf of another misguided lottery winner.

"How much money are you talking about?" I said.

Martin thought about it first. "Twelve grand the first time," he said. "With Sarah, we paid a lot more. The mother was depressed. I paid the rent, food bills, got her cable, prenatal, even paid for her shrink. Fifteen thousand, I'd say. She was very comfortable." He stared out the window. "Ironic."

"What's that?"

"I'm the one who paid for the shrink, wanted her to be on solid ground. That's supposedly how she decided she wanted to keep the child. A 'breakthrough' in therapy." He exhaled a weary gallows laugh.

"Maybe this time."

"Know what's the worst thing?" he said. "We're so set on this, we'd do anything. And they know it. They can see us coming a mile away."

The door to the inner office opened and a sharp-looking middle-aged brunette in black slacks and a bone-colored blouse stepped into the room, leading a red-eyed Janet over to Martin. We stood and Martin held out a hand to Janet, who smiled gamely.

"Let's do it," Janet said.

Martin folded his arms around Janet and kissed her head. "You know where to reach us," he said to Lois Nettleson, who nodded. "Let's go," he told Janet. "So long, J.—best of luck."

"J.?" Lois Nettleson said, sizing me up with probing eyes. She was twenty years my senior but still slim and very attractive. A plastic surgeon had erased the wrinkles from her face, and her high forehead was perfectly smooth.

"Where have I heard that name before?" she said as if she were the only one in the room. She walked over to the desk and flipped through the message pad. "Here we are." Her nails were painted with clear enamel and beautifully manicured. "I don't remember making an appointment to see you."

"You did, but you didn't," I said, smiling. "I'm Tony, your expectant young dad." I shook her hand. "The noon consultation."

"How deceitful. Nelson told me I should expect to hear from you before the trial."

"Man thinks of everything."

"You know I'm testifying next week."

"Yes, I know."

"Why can't this wait until then?"

"I'm not fond of surprises."

"You don't look like a lawyer." Her tone was observant, but I felt like she was leering at me. "Too tan. Too . . . alive. Not pasty enough," she said. "My ex is a lawyer. Very pasty."

"I don't mean to take up much of your time. Just a few questions is all."

"Why should I talk to you?"

"Why not?" I said. "You're not a party in this, just a witness. I trust you'll go in there and tell the truth."

"Of course."

"I'm just trying to find out all I can, so I won't make an ass of myself next week."

"You represent the lovely Sue Ellen Randall."

I nodded.

"You're helping her get the baby back."

"I'm trying to keep the court from controlling the baby's destiny. Come on," I said, "there's no need for a standoff. You'd really be helping clarify the situation for everyone on the case."

"Nelson won't be pleased."

"Listen," I said, "Mr. Gilbride represents the Danforths only. But you're different. You worked for both couples. You don't owe Gilbride a damned thing."

"I don't owe you a damned thing, either."

"I think you do," I said. "You're part of this case, like it or not. I'm only after a few straight answers. Please. That's all I ask."

We sat down together on the sofa. "I've got a hair appointment at twelve-thirty," she said.

"You're kidding," I said. She wore her hair short, with thick bangs and a forward curl just off her shoulders—a very cosmopolitan look. "It's perfect already."

She blushed. "You're just saying that."

I held up a hand in pledge. "No, I mean it."

Lois liked my gesture. "Ask your questions, Counselor."

"How does your business work?"

She started with a brief history of the privatization of adoptions in California, then described the counseling and parent-matching process in which she specialized. I leaned forward in my chair when she touched on the concept of open adoptions.

"Open adoption can be wonderful, really," she said, brightening.

"Wonderful?" I said. Was she serious? "Sorry, but that's not the first word that comes to mind."

"How do you mean?"

"Look at the Danforths and Randalls. How did you expect them to ever get along watching that kid grow up?"

"Hard to say what works," she said. "I've had couples from more disparate backgrounds than theirs hit it off very nicely."

"I see." I didn't believe her.

"It can be awkward." She walked over to the desk and returned with an opened pack of Benson & Hedges. "My only remaining vice," she said, snapping open a chrome lighter.

"So why do it if it's not likely to work?" I asked, still thinking about the trembling Martin. "Seems like people on both sides can get shredded."

"We're dealing with a very high demand for white babies these days."

"Desperation is a big factor."

She regarded me as one would an equal. "Off the record? Of course the parents I bring together have little in common." She took a luxuriant drag from her smoke. "How could they? One pair wants to give up the child, and the other wants a baby more than life itself. It's a dynamic that doesn't breed a lot of trust for each other."

"Strange bedfellows," I said.

Lois straightened up and glided to the window. I found myself attracted to the way she moved.

"Open adoptions are just another option," she said, "not the ultimate solution. They can make certain arrangements work when they're not otherwise viable. And for people who live on the hope of having a new baby, another option is a good thing."

Lois's last remark sounded vaguely like a sales pitch, the kind I'd heard from Nelson Gilbride in the hallway the day I'd taken the Randall case. I reckoned that, like Gilbride, she was highly adept at her trade.

"Were you surprised Sue Ellen changed her mind and backed out of it?" I asked.

She paused and blew out a tiny jet of smoke. "At first I wasn't.

She was never behind the idea of giving up that baby. Her husband was a lot more sure about it. Unemployed, dead broke, no education, lousy prospects. A real no-account fella."

"Then the open adoption must have been a critical aspect to her."

"Oh, it was. Sue Ellen was very concerned about the terms and conditions. We spent a lot of time on that. Did you know she wouldn't agree to place the baby unless she could hand Nathan over to Kitty herself, right there at the hospital?"

"I hadn't heard that."

"She was apparently quite adamant about it."

"You weren't at the hospital when Nathan was born."

She shook her head no. "Can you imagine, after all Kip and Kitty had done for her?" she said.

"She was giving away her own child. So she wanted to hand him over to his new mother. What's so unreasonable about that?"

"Kitty has a full-time nanny who's very capable. I don't see why—"

"She was guilt-ridden about abandoning her child," I said. "So they did some nice things for her. So what? You make it sound as if the Danforths were specially entitled."

This woman saw the Danforths' perspective as if it was all she was capable of seeing. She was going to hurt my case, that much was clear. But there could be no advantage gained by alienating her.

"You knew Sue Ellen wasn't behind the adoption, Ms. Nettleson, am I right?"

"Call me Lois," she said. "I wouldn't argue with what you said."

"So tell me, Lois, why shouldn't Sue Ellen have wanted to reclaim Nathan? Why is everyone crying fraud now? She never wanted to give Nathan up in the first place."

Lois Nettleson appeared troubled. "It makes more sense when you hear Nelson explain it."

"I'll tell you where you're getting lost here, if I might," I said. "Gilbride says Sue Ellen defrauded the Danforths because she accepted their financial support, yet all the while she had no intention of ever giving up the boy."

"That's right." She looked at me seriously.

"Sounds like fraud, doesn't it? Problem is, he's only partly right.

Unconsciously, Sue Ellen never did fully intend to go through with the adoption, that's true. But did she plan it that way, as a scheme? Of course not. She was goaded into giving up that boy by the promise of a wonderful compromise, an open adoption. She could still see him occasionally, watch him grow up, know how he was doing. She believed more in the concept of open adoptions than you or Gilbride probably do. You just told me how important the open adoption terms were to her."

"So was the money."

"What money?" I said. "They supported her until she had the baby." My central arguments for trial next week were beginning to emerge and take shape, and I sensed I was using the moment as a practice session. But I had to be careful not to go too far with Lois before she even took the stand.

I took a slow breath and flashed my best reasonable guy smile on her. "I think everyone pushed her into this. Gilbride, the Danforths, even Ty. And you."

"You don't know what you're talking about," Lois said. "You don't know adoptions."

"All right, but it wasn't fraud. I do know that."

Lois stared out the window, the cigarette smoke trailing over her shoulder like a breezy scarf. "I see your point."

I walked over and shared with Lois the view out to the street. No sign of the silver Lincoln. "Will they go to jail?" she said.

Did Lois actually care about her poor clients as well as the wealthy ones who paid her fees?

"I don't think so," I said. "Fraud is a specific intent crime. You can imagine how tough it would be to prove intent in a case like this."

"I see."

Gilbride must have been counseling Lois lately, trying to color her perceptions of what had gone down between the Randalls and the Danforths. He'd be unable to help her next week, though, when she took the stand.

"When are adoptions final?" I asked.

She told me about the necessity of an adoption report from the state approving the adoption and the law in California giving natural mothers six months after the baby's birth to ultimately decide. This I knew, but she surprised me with something more.

"Of course," she said, "if you get the mother's signed consent before six months is up, it's final."

I hadn't known that.

"Sue Ellen had never signed over consent?" I said.

"You catch on fast."

Had Sue Ellen signed off, the adoption would've been a done deal. But how did she know to withhold consent? And how did she hold off Gilbride and Lois? They must have relentlessly squeezed her. I sensed a major weakness in one of the county's arguments: Sue Ellen had acted within the law.

"I guess you see Sue Ellen's refusal to sign a consent form as further proof that she set out to cheat the Danforths," I said.

"And you don't? She had plenty of chances to execute the documents but always had a quick excuse as to why she hadn't yet signed."

But it was Sue Ellen's right not to sign. I saved this thought for my cross-examination.

"Oh! I've got to dash," Lois said, checking her thin gold watch. "I'm late. Marco hates it when I'm late."

"Thank you for your time," I said. "One last thing. May I get a copy of the adoption agreement, the contract between the Randalls and the Danforths? My client seems to have lost the copy."

Lois did a playful double take. "She did, did she? Poor, confused child."

"Pardon me?"

"There is no contract. It's illegal in California to have a contract for a baby."

"So the consent requirement . . ."

"Two different things. I'm sorry, but I'm just fresh out of time." She smiled, charming me again.

"It's been a pleasure," I said, shaking her hand. "I'll try to be nice to you next week."

"You'd better." Her eyes openly surveyed the breadth of my shoulders. "You're a bright young man, J. Good luck."

She went back to the receptionist's desk and brought me a beige business card with gold lettering in fancy scroll. A Santa Barbara phone number was handwritten in pink marker across the front. "Here," she said, handing it to me. "My direct line. Call me if you need to talk again."

I walked back toward my car, reflecting on Lois Nettleson's ambivalence toward the Randall adoption and feeling at least some faith in Sue Ellen again. And the card—was this Lois's home number? She didn't seem to be coming on to me, or was she? On one level she'd certainly welcomed the attention. I'd have to confer with Jackie about this matter.

The breeze smelled faintly of eucalyptus and ocean kelp beds. The noon street scene was still in motion, but I could see no sign of the man in the Lincoln. The scent of baked bread, white wine and ladies' perfume carried upwind with the rising sea breeze, and I was struck by the depth of my love of California. I tossed Lois Nettleson's card onto the dash and jerked the gearshift lever into reverse.

Thirteen

The last turnoff out of Santa Barbara on 101 South is for Bates Road in Carpenteria, and Rincon Point. The silver Lincoln had found me again and assumed its previous position three cars back, so I eased down the off-ramp and turned into the long, narrow public lot above the beach. I'd never been followed before, but I knew it didn't agree with me. I was determined to either lose this tourist now or at least convince him to stay off my ass.

The last time I'd surfed Rincon was three or four years ago on a throbbing west swell that lasted close to a week. That day a hundred cars clogged the lot and at least as many riders trolled the point between Third Point and the inside Cove. Too much crowd, really, but God, if you hooked into a good wall you'd go forever. On that day I pumped a ruler-edged, overhead wailer all the way from Inside Third through Second and the body jam at First, then on through the Cove until the swell slapped the boulders piled beneath the freeway. I'd been out only two hours, but that wave was so flat-out fine that I had little choice but to paddle in, for I knew there was no way I could top the feeling.

But Rincon is a winter break and today, a flat day in September, the only cars parked at the head of the beach trail were a VW Thing, a dented mini-truck piled with driftwood and an old school bus hand-painted in faded out psychedelic colors. I slid into a spot behind the bus and cut the motor, wondering if the man in the Lincoln carried a gun.

The trail to the beach at Rincon is a narrow strip of hard dirt just off the freeway embankment. On the shoreward side of the path, a chain-link fence lies behind wild grass and scrub brush, separating surfers and beachgoers from the block of multi-million-dollar homes along the sand. I hustled down the head of the dirt path without looking back until the trail sharpened in its descent to the beach below. No one was ahead or behind me when I jumped behind a weedy patch of brush and hid.

He didn't come down the path for twenty more minutes, and by the time he did, my knee joints were cramped from crouching and I needed to take a piss. The man wore navy slacks with a white knit shirt and navy loafers, a heavy gold chain around his neck. No gun. I was relieved to see that he wasn't an oversized brute, but he appeared plenty thick in the upper body and his head looked as hard as a bowling ball. Seeing nothing below, he scowled as if I were climbing ever higher on his private shit list.

I crouched to take him and had an awful thought: this was a public beach—what if he wasn't the guy? And what if someone saw me jump him and tried to intervene? An arrest in Santa Barbara, a hundred miles from home, would pose an assortment of problems I didn't care to fathom at the moment. My bladder ached for some relief as I peeked down the beach path. Nothing stirred below.

He stopped not five feet from me and eyed the base of the trail. "Goddam," he said, checking his watch and rubbing his buzz-cut hair. Deeply annoyed, perhaps, that the jack-off he was tailing had stopped off for an afternoon stroll on a lonely strip of shoreline. He reached into his breast pocket and flipped on a pair of sunglasses. I still wasn't sure he was the man in the Lincoln. Then he reached into his front pocket, pulled out a card with some numbers written in pink, and studied it. Lois Nettleson's business card.

I leapt from the bushes and clamped him hard from behind, driving him up to take his feet off balance. We went down with a thud in a cloud of soft dirt, my left arm pinned beneath his chest, and I lost my grip for a second. He felt my hand letting go and freed himself enough to drive an elbow into my chin, popping me back and stunning me. I clung to his shoulder blades, trying to shake off the blow as I wrapped my arms under his armpits and worked my hands up to the base of his neck.

"Bastard!" he said, panting. "Leggo me!"

Struggling in the dirt, I was thinking about movies and TV, the way fights are generally choreographed in the same cliched manner every time. The combatants always squaring off in variations of the classic boxing stance and letting fly, duking it out with a succession of big-time, jarring blows. What a fantasy.

"You're gonna be sorry, fucker!" he said. My arms and shoulders were aflame, my head knotted, but I dug in harder.

In a street fight, you don't punch it out toe-to-toe unless you've grown tired of your facial features and want to try out a new look. You don't expose yourself to risk. You get your opponent on the ground and go for position, then wait until you can knock him out.

The wooziness inflicted by the hard elbow to my chin was passing with each second. I worked my left hand firmly behind his neck and pushed his head down into the weeds. He craned over his right shoulder and punched me with a backhanded fist, but he had no leverage and the blows rolled off my head. When he tired and stopped flailing, I freed my right hand and tagged his dome three or four times from the side.

"Aah!" he yelled, writhing. "I'll kick your ass!" But he was weakening. I popped him again and he spit a small glob of blood into the dirt, then raised his head in one last effort to shake free. My arms and shoulders could only hold him another twenty seconds, if that. Though the trail was still deserted, I was tired of this fight and wanted to end it before someone saw us. I loosened my hold enough to make him believe he could escape. Predictably, his head shot up, but my cocked right arm was ready.

I sat him up along the fence and emptied his pockets. Car keys, a greasy comb, nicotine gum, several coins, a wallet with four crisp twenties. A driver's license that said Donald Brill, 4313 Fremont, Los Angeles. A few business cards: Brill Investigations. Thankfully, no gun. I pocketed the keys and scooped up Lois's card from the path.

"Aah, Christ," he moaned, rubbing the side of his face. He fixed on me but couldn't sit up yet on his own and clutched at the chainlink. "Fucking punk! Is this a robbery? I'll call a cop!"

I flipped the wallet at him. "Cut the bullshit, Don."

"You ambushed me. That's assault and battery."

"No witnesses," I said, observing the empty trail, "and you were following me." A flock of birds sang out from a nearby grove of towering eucalyptus trees. I held up Lois's card. "Besides, you must've broken into my wagon to get this. You don't look like the careful type. I'll bet you left some prints inside. Go ahead, Don, make the call."

He worked his jaw and tried to spit. "Knocked a tooth loose, you prick."

"Who hired you? The Danforths? Gilbride?"

"Fuck you. My clients are confidential. You're nobody to me, fuck."

"Hey guy," I said, standing over him, "You can curse all you want, but I'm not impressed. I don't like being followed. From now on, you tell whomever you work for you lost me. I see you again, you'll have an instant headache."

He didn't respond. Donald Brill was through talking. I took his car keys from my pocket and flung them down the trail and into some bushes.

I got back to my Jeep and looked around. My briefcase was resting on the back seat, exactly where I'd left it, and unlocked. Christ. Why didn't I ever bother to use the combination lock that came with the case? The answer was pure laziness. I opened it and looked inside. A few legal pads were there, stacked neatly on top of the case files I'd handled this morning in court. My leather-bound organizer was buttoned shut. I flipped it open to the daily calendar. I'd written the address of Sue Ellen's Silverlake neighbor, Arturo, right on to-day's square. If Brill read it, he'd know where I'd be headed next.

I drove back under the freeway on the turnoff road until I spotted the Lincoln parked along the shoulder of the northbound on-ramp. Not a soul was around. My choices were limited. Trial was next week, and today was probably the only day I'd have time to go to Sue Ellen's old neighborhood to determine whether Gilbride had found anything damaging. Donald Brill needed to be detained.

A big truck roared by on the highway overhead. I jogged over to Brill's car and, circling it slowly, squatted to let the air out of his tires. My bladder was burning full. The fucker creeped my car, I thought.

Quite by impulse, I unzipped my fly and took a long, relieving whiz on Donald Brill's front grill and bumper. Then I hit it back under the freeway and tore down the L.A. on-ramp into traffic, an eye on the rearview mirror. Behind me, the rocks in the cove at Rincon baked hot in the low-tide sun.

Traffic slowed to a standstill when I hit the San Fernando Valley, so I got off on Ventura Boulevard and negotiated the eastbound signals until I came to Solley's Deli. It was almost three and the lunch crowd was long gone. I took a big booth near the front and had a club sandwich and an iced tea. Before I left, I stopped at the pay phone outside the restrooms to call my voicemail at the office.

"You have three new messages," the robotic female voice intoned. The first one was from a drug mom who wouldn't test because she knew she was dirty. Our next hearing was weeks away, but she was already warming up, raving on about the constitutional rights she had coming. Excoriating me for failing, thus far, to reunite her with her baby girl—a poisoned little five-pound shell of a baby so unlucky in life it pained me to think about her. Oh sure. The woman sounded semi-stoned and forgot to leave a number, but she did remember to call me a white-ass, racist chump before she hung up. I deleted the message.

The second call was from Jackie. "J.-man," he said in a half-whisper, "Dr. Pace checking in. Borrowed Fiona's wheels. I'm over at the Woodside medical facility, on duty and strictly incognito. Poised to penetrate the inner sanctum."

Vintage Jackie. Always the clown.

"Trying to get to know some of the nurses," Jackie went on, "ones that were around when the kid was born. It's all under control, boz, but one thing, I may need to borrow your wheels tomorrow for a repeat mission. No, two things! Need some coin, a little expense account action, you know? Lunchroom's the place to get to know people, but I'm flat busted, mate. Looked like a barney suckin' down an ice water in there a little while ago. Oh yeah, talked to the Pontrellis' landlord. Real smart guy. No help. Give you the lowdown tonight. Gonna check out the good doctor's records after they close up. Later."

Breaking and entering: Jackie's forte. I should've known it would likely come to this with him. My temples ached. What if he was caught? I'd surely be implicated. Jackie was my responsibility, taking orders from me. But then, I hadn't told him to burglarize any offices—truth was, he was on his own. Unfortunately, this little piece of reasoning brought me no relief. My lunch bubbled deep in the pit of my stomach. I knew that by not setting any real boundaries for him, I was complicit in Jackie's lawlessness.

The last message was from Sue Ellen Randall. Her husband Ty was out on bail now, but he was depressed and fighting with her. She felt helpless "sittin' around not doin' a darned thing," so she was going back to the Silverlake neighborhood, where she and Ty had lived before she reclaimed Nathan. She thought it made sense to start with Arturo, the old man down the block, talk to him, see if she could learn more about the man who'd been out there asking questions for the Danforths. Find out whether any of the neighbors had said anything damaging.

Great. Just what I'd told Sue Ellen I would do. The message was time-stamped 3:13 P.M.—five minutes ago. I ran back to the Jeep.

The 101 freeway was still buggered, so I stuck it out in the Ventura Boulevard congestion a while longer. What the hell was Sue Ellen doing? I'd told her I'd interview Arturo, check out the neighbors. But she didn't trust me enough to leave it to me. A kiddie lawyer, as Ty had put it, lower than even a harried public defender. It didn't matter what she thought, I told myself. I was her lawyer, and she should have listened to me.

I slid back onto the 101 East at the place where Ventura metamorphoses into Cahuenga and bends up into the Hollywood Hills. People were leaning on their horns, veering around something in the right lane—my lane—a hundred yards up. Damn. Sue Ellen was probably at Arturo's by now. And maybe Donald Brill, had he bothered to look in my organizer. Brill could have got his tires re-inflated by now, and if he were any good at taking alternate routes back to town, he'd be right behind me. Or up ahead.

Sue Ellen's old street was just north of a dumpy stretch of Sunset Boulevard littered with mini-marts, auto repair shops and Mexican *pescado* restaurants. Weeds shot up everywhere through cracks in the sidewalks and curbs. A vagrant guarded a hijacked shopping cart brimming with recyclable cans and other junk. Half a block down the street a full-figured hooker in a busty black halter and matching tight silver shorts and knee boots strutted in circles like a Raiderette cheerleader on the Coliseum sidelines.

I parked and dug into my briefcase for the address. On the opposite corner, Sue Ellen's former bungalow looked like Renters Hell, but the houses on the street were nicer and rather utilitarian in their neatness, most of them painted plain white with no trim, wood framed. Metal bars covered the small windows and hanging pots of bright seasonals creaked in the warm wind. Strips of yellow crabgrass stretched down to the street curbs. They were the kind of houses that, seventy-five years ago, might have cost five grand new. The kind that realtors today winkingly label as "craftsmans" or "traditionals," "starter homes" that will start you at a mind-numbing two-hundred-thousand-plus.

A large dog came to life behind a weathered picket fence when I got out and crossed the street. Arturo had a German shepherd, Sue Ellen had told me. The dog barked louder as I reached the front gate, spinning as if to catch its tail in its teeth.

"Rocky!" an Hispanic man shouted. He had coppery, dried-out skin and wore an orange "Cat Powered" ball cap. The dog growled at me and lunged at the fence. I didn't move as the man hobbled down the front walk, leaning on a cane made of manzanita. "Stay!" The dog sat up obediently. "Stay, Rocky."

"Afternoon," I said. "I'm J. You must be Arturo."

He had a rumpled face and a thick mustache dusted with gray. His V-neck tee was wet with sweat, and his denim work pants were dirt-chalked at the knees as if he'd been tending a flowerbed.

"Who wants to know?" he said.

"I'm a lawyer. I represent Sue Ellen Randall, your neighbor. You may not have seen her the last few days. She moved."

"Few days?" he said, chuckling. "Try ten minutes ago. She was just here."

I looked up and down the block but saw no signs of life. "Where did she go?"

He shrugged his shoulders. "To talk to some of the neighbors, I think. I tried telling her not to bother, 'cause nobody saw nothing."

The man had just committed himself without knowing it. "What

do you mean, nobody saw nothing?" I said. "What were they supposed to see?" He regarded me as if I'd tricked him into something.
"Please," I said.

Arturo was still deciding whether he would talk to me. "The boy,
you know."

"You mean Ronny?"

"Yeah, Ronny," he said. "Some man, he come around here after
she moved, asking about the boy."

I described Donald Brill to Arturo, checking the street for signs
of Brill's Lincoln. An orange Chevy van was parked across from us.
Halfway down the block toward Sunset, a lowered black LTD was
marooned on cinder blocks in front of a weedy little yard. Across
from the LTD was an old red pickup truck; it had to be Sue Ellen's.
I looked back up the street. No Lincoln. Brill was probably still
stuck on the 101 South.

"Sounds like the guy," Arturo said. "He went around to see if
people say she hit the boy. Said she used a coat hanger." He laughed.

"What's so funny?" I said. In this case, there had never been even
a suggestion of physical abuse. Manufacturing evidence was a dirty
business. "I don't get the joke."

"No, no, he showed the hanger to me," Arturo said. "Know
where it's from? It's one of those fancy wood ones, the kind they
give you in a fancy store. That's what's funny. I didn't know the
lady and her husband too good," he said, grinning, "but I bet you
they don't shop at no stores with wood hangers."

The man had rather casually made a damned good point.
"Thanks," I said. "You also mentioned—"

The big dog started going nuts again. Arturo pointed down the
street. "There she is!"

I saw Sue Ellen standing on a porch about eight houses away. It
sounded like she was yelling at someone in the doorway. I ran down
the sidewalk and up the front walk. She wore shapeless gray sweats
and a yellow T-shirt—looking more like Ty today. Her elbows were
locked, her fists balled at her sides.

"I don't care what you got to say!" a woman shouted at Sue Ellen
from inside the house, her features muted by the screen door's mesh.

"You're trash, baby-selling trailer trash! Get the hell offa my property!"

"How dare you talk to me that way!" Sue Ellen screamed.

I'd initially planned to scold Sue Ellen when I saw her, to talk about trust and respect, to make all the points I'd worked on earlier in the car. But the screech in her voice gave me pause. Her entire body was shaking. A rambling, didactic speech would be a vain mistake. I let go of some of my kiddie lawyer's indignation. She was my client. She needed protecting.

"Do you even . . . know what it's like . . ." Sue Ellen said.

I mounted the triple porch steps in one bound. "Excuse us," I said through the screen. Carefully I guided Sue Ellen away from the screen door. "We'll be going now."

"Wait a minute, Mr. Shepard!" Sue Ellen protested. "I wasn't finished."

I put my arm around Sue Ellen's shoulder and gripped her. She felt surprisingly frail to me, as if she might break apart if handled too roughly. "Come on, let's go talk about this somewhere else," I said.

"Ya better go before I call the cops!" the woman yelled as she slammed the door. I turned Sue Ellen toward the street and slowly walked her off the porch. She wept onto my shoulder, hiding her face.

"Time to go home," I said. "Is that your truck?"

She nodded at the beaten red pickup down the street.

A young, dark-skinned man in a paisley long-sleeve and dirty white jeans pushed an ice cream cart up the street from Sunset, ringing a little chrome bell on the handlebar as he went. Sue Ellen continued to cry. I walked her over to the truck and gently leaned her against the door. "Go home," I told her. "Take it easy. Thank you for helping, but I want you to forget about all this for now."

Without warning she threw both her arms around my shoulders and clung to me as if she were drowning. More tears. I softly patted her back, uncomfortable to be held this tightly for this long. Sue Ellen squeezed me harder, her cries muffled against my chest.

I rocked her slightly. "It's all right. Just go home."

Finally she let go, turned, and climbed into the cab. She looked at me once more with those sad eyes. "You're so kind," she said. "You know, you're my only real friend."

"Go home," I said. She didn't argue now or even answer, but I knew she'd wanted me to keep holding her a minute ago when we were in the street. "Call me if you need to talk." I stepped clear of the vehicle. She turned away, the engine starting with a shudder and a cloud of smoke, and drove off.

I sat in my car for a good long while waiting to make a simple left turn onto Sunset. The Raiderette was gone, replaced by a blond, mini-skirted Latina with brown roots and a harsh glare. A diminutive old woman in a black dress held hands with a toddler as they crept past the hood of my Jeep. A uniformed man unloaded cases from a beer truck double-parked in front of a liquor store. High, bent palms drifted in a steady late afternoon westerly, a breeze that was too far inland now to carry with it even a hint of the cool Pacific. When the traffic finally broke, I swung out into the eastbound lanes on Sunset. Out of habit I checked my rearview mirror. I couldn't be sure, but I thought I saw a big American sedan—maybe silver—pull onto Sunset heading the other way, toward Hollywood.

Jackie hadn't gotten very far at Woodside Hospital—a receptionist who'd stayed late kept him from accessing Dr. Weinstein's employee records. But he was sufficiently optimistic about what he'd find the next day, enough so that when he filled me in on his day, I felt compelled to spring for dinner.

We dined on shrimp cocktails and fresh mahi mahi at the Captain's Galley. I told Jackie about Carmen and Albert and asked him to help with the surf lesson. Sure, he said, but he seemed distracted— probably too excited about the prospect of more serious surf on the way to pay much mind to anything else. He'd heard a rumor from a "mega-reliable" source that an intense Antarctic storm with an enormous fetch was kicking up a huge swell for next week. The action was about to heat up. With luck the swell would hit after— not during—the trial.

We talked about Lois Nettleson. Jackie was certain she'd given me her home phone number when I left her office. "Sophisticated lady," he said. "Wants to see how you hold your fork at dinner before you get any dessert. You'll probably have to take her out, show her a good time. She'll make you wait 'til she thinks it's the right time. Then she'll make her move. The most important thing with a woman like her, making good money and divorced from a hot-shit lawyer, is to let her think she's in the driver's seat." He looked around, then at me. "Ever let a woman handcuff you? It's a trip and a half."

I related the details of my scrap with Don Brill, the private investigator. Jackie was enthralled. "He was shading you, boss?"

I rolled my eyes. "That's what I said."

"Was he packing heat?"

"Packing heat? I don't know if anybody 'packs heat' anymore. You watch too much bad TV, Jack."

He shrugged. "What other kind is there?"

I poured the last of a bottle of Chardonnay.

"Well, was he?" he said.

"No, he didn't have a gun. I wouldn't be here if he did."

Jackie looked stoked. "But you tapped him," he said. "Unreal."

I described the finishing touch I'd put to Donald Brill's car.

Jackie slapped the tabletop. "No way! You gave his hood ornament a golden shower? That's classic!"

"What about the Pontrellis' landlord?" I said.

"Forget him. Everything the social worker said he said was pretty much word for word. He hates your client, buddy. Said she's a lyin' hillbilly. An inbreeder." Jackie took an extended swill from his glass of wine. "You seen Sue Ellen's husband?"

"Yeah."

Jackie rubbed his knuckles in contemplation. "Well, you think she and the happy hubby kinda look alike?"

"Knock it off," I said. "You're gonna have to focus more on what happened at Woodside. Talk to the nurses who were there. They made her have that baby prematurely, and in pain. There's got to be a reason."

He thought for a moment. "Maybe I could tail the rich folk around town a bit. Hubby probably goes to work all day, but I'll bet she doesn't work." His blue eyes narrowed. "Leaves a lot of idle time. Never know what she might be up to."

"Just keep your distance," I said. "I don't want you hassling the Danforths. If they find out you're following them, I'll never hear the end of it. And remember, do *not* break the law. You do anything that compromises me and—"

"Uh, J.?" Jackie said, gazing across several tables toward the bar. "I think you've got more immediate problems. Check it out."

I turned my head just in time to see a shaky videotape image alighting on the big-screen TV above the bar. The first thing I recognized was the tailgate of the old red pickup, then Sue Ellen's yellow T-shirt. "Christ," I said.

We tossed our napkins on our chairs and rushed across the room. "Turn up the volume!" I yelled to the bartender.

The bartender began to greet us, but we both stared up at the screen without another word. "You got it," he said, pointing the remote over his shoulder.

"Quiet!" Jackie roared. The dozen or so patrons at the bar fell silent.

". . . a case in which emotions have run high from the start," came Holly Dupree's voice-over. "But is J. Shepard, the court appointed lawyer for the suspected baby-seller Sue Ellen Randall, crossing the line by . . ." The whole room watched as Sue Ellen pressed herself into my chest, her head nestling under my chin.

"Hmm," Jackie said, "the lady definitely digs on you, man."

". . . right and wrong, between zealous advocacy and personal involvement . . ." Holly's peppy narrative went on. She must get off on making people look bad, I thought. Then she was questioning a law professor—a bespectacled guy seated before a phalanx of golden case reporters—about the rules of professional conduct concerning sex with clients.

"What does this intimate embrace tell you?" Holly asked the professor.

"Well, Holly," the professor said, "from what you tell me, this young woman is quite vulnerable. Her attorney is in a position of trust with her, one of authority. Now if he is in fact having intimate relations with her . . ."

"Where'd she get the video?" Jackie asked.

"Donald Brill, Brill Investigations," I said under my breath. Had to be. He'd seen my organizer, copped the address. The payback for my punching him out had been far swifter than I'd imagined.

"What's all this shit about, J.?" Jackie said, still staring at the big screen.

Nelson Gilbride's delighted face was now on camera from another live remote set up by Channel Six. "Oh yes, I think it's highly unethical, Holly," Gilbride puffed. "But then, Sue Ellen Randall is a very crafty woman. She could well be manipulating this young man much as she manipulated my clients. . . ."

I briefly turned away from the unfolding spectacle. "They're going to try to get me thrown off the case," I said to Jackie.

"Can they?"

"Maybe. I don't know." I closed my eyes. How had I missed Brill? And what had made me think for even a second that he—or Gilbride, for that matter—would back off just because I'd pushed back a little? These people were bent on winning any way they could. They didn't care if my job and reputation were sacrificed in the process.

"I haven't done anything wrong," I said. We watched another replay of the embrace. By now I was beyond shame or self-loathing. I was truly scared. "They're just trying to muddy the waters."

"You ask me, they're doing a damn fine job," Jackie said.

I glared at him. I knew I'd fucked up again, but this thing was far from over. "You get somewhere out at Woodside, it might help matters a bit."

"Yeah, right."

No one spoke for a while. The crowd at the bar had regained its normal noise level. Thankfully, the TV had been switched to a football game.

"You shag her, boss?" Jackie said at last.

I stared at him queerly. "You're quite the sensitive guy, aren't you?"

He shrugged innocently. "Hey, you broke up with the goddess recently, or vice versa."

"Meaning what?"

"We all have our needs."

"Nice insight. Listen, Phoebe's history," I told him, "but this has nothing to do with getting laid. I would never sleep with a client. I'm surprised that even you would ask me that."

Above us, football disappeared from the big TV and, like a recurring nightmare, the Channel Six News was showing a rerun of my embrace with Sue Ellen, this time in slow motion.

"Christ, somebody change the channel," I said.

Jackie's eyes were on the TV. "Ho, we're back. Oh, my. That why they call it attorney-client privilege? Mmm-mm." He grinned at me. "You sure you're not—"

"I'm sure!" I said. "Knock it off."

"Well hey, sorry I asked." Jackie gestured at the TV as if vindicated by the on-screen evidence. "It seemed like a logical question."

Fourteen

Carmen Manriquez and her brother Albert were right on time Saturday morning. Jackie jumped when the doorbell rang.

"I'll get it," he said, bouncing out of his chair. He'd been dying to lay his eyes on Carmen ever since last night, when I'd enlisted him in some last minute house cleaning in anticipation of her visit. Any woman who caused me to clean sinks and toilets on a Friday night had to be super-fine, he'd reasoned.

"No, I got it," I said, cutting in front of him in the dining room, but he squirted by me and we both raced for the door.

"Listen," I said before he turned the knob, "you get X-rated and you're dead."

"Trust me," he said, opening the door. "Well, hello!" He grinned at our guests. "Everybody's stoked."

Carmen was looking super-fine indeed, in a loose khaki army shirt and cuffed shorts made from a pair of old fatigues, *huaraches* on her feet. Around her neck was the same small gold cross she'd worn in the Las Palomas office the day I'd met her.

"Cowabunga," she said.

Albert was half a head shorter than his sister, but stocky and thick-shouldered. He wore a Dodgers baseball cap tilted up on his forehead and a blue warmup suit with vertical white stripes on the pantlegs and sleeves. The suit was probably a half-size too big, the fabric bunching around his ankles and sleeves. He had the slow eyes and listless expression of a young man with Down syndrome, but his features were otherwise average. I thought he looked more like fifteen than twenty-four.

I pushed open the screen door. "Cowabunga!" Albert said, mimicking Carmen.

I invited them into the living room. "Hot sauce," Jackie whispered to me, ogling Carmen from behind.

Albert had brought a black vinyl carry bag, which he lugged over to the coffee table and set down. Jackie was watching Albert with a strange puzzlement. Afraid he might bail on me, I'd purposely not told Jackie that his pupil for today was mentally handicapped.

"Hey J.," he said, "you thought about what might happen if he gets hurt? I mean, this dude doesn't look quite normal. What if he can't swim? Is he a re—"

"Don't even say it," Carmen said, stepping in front of Jackie. "My brother can swim fine. And he's not ignorant. He knows how to use his head. Know how to use yours?"

Jackie retreated, stunned. Carmen stood her ground, arms folded, while Albert fiddled with his bag, oblivious to the confrontation not five feet away.

"J., you didn't tell me this guy was such a stud," Jackie said, instantly changing course. "Hey, my man," he said to Albert, extending his hand. "Put her there." They shook hands. "Like granite!" Jackie reacted as if his hand had been squeezed in a vise. Albert laughed wildly.

His sister looked on, totally unruffled. Here was a woman who could back off Jackie Pace without hesitation. I felt something for Carmen that I'd never felt for Phoebe.

"By the way, Carmen, this is Jackie," I said.

"Pleasure meeting you, Carmen." Jackie flashed a brilliant smile, which seemed to have little effect on her.

"You too," she said.

Jackie looked to me, chastened. "This is going to be an interesting session," I said.

"My brother Albert," said Carmen. "Albert, this is J., and Jackie."

"Hola, compadre," I said.

"I'll arm wrestle you," Albert said to Jackie with a pronounced slur in his speech. "I'm strong . . . like Mighty Mouse." He flexed his biceps, his arms wrenched up into tightly curled fists.

"Well all reet!" Jackie said, backing up to make room for Albert's pose. "You're on, iron man!"

Jackie and Albert proceeded to arm wrestle on the coffee table,

Albert winning every bout over his almost comically larger opponent.

"How are the waves today?" Carmen asked me.

"Haven't looked, but last night it was three feet or so. Windy, but a few nice peaks. Good beginner size. How'd Albert like the idea of surfing?"

"You kidding?" she said. "He could hardly sleep last night, he was so excited." Across the room, Albert was in ecstasy after pinning Jackie's forearm to the table yet again. Jackie had turned Albert's Dodgers cap backward and was now describing surfing to him in what sounded like the broadest terms possible.

"J., you're sure Albert will be safe?" Carmen asked.

"You watch. Like the man said, he's gonna be stoked."

"Stoked?"

I smiled as she fixed her lovely eyes back on me. "Stoked is the operative word around here."

"I brought your letters. They're all translated."

"Thanks," I said. "We'll have lunch here after we surf. Let's talk about it then."

Jackie and I fitted Albert into an old wetsuit Britt had outgrown in recent years, and I handed Carmen the women's suit I'd rented at the Bay Surf Shop the night before. "Hope it's your size," I told her. "I had to guess."

She held up the wetsuit, which looked like a decent fit. "Good guess."

After suiting up, Jackie and I grabbed our sticks and the boards we'd chosen for them, a couple of used seven-two speed shapes (mini-longboards). I stuffed a bar of wax under my wetsuit sleeve and we walked the four blocks to the pier.

The morning was calm and cloudless, the tide medium-low and slowly ascending to a three-foot high at noon. A chest-high southwest swell was pushing in, crossed up by a touch of local windswell, and the peak just north of the pier pilings was already jammed with die-hard weekend longboarders and kids on boogies.

We walked the length of the Northside beach until we reached the warm water jetty at the far end of town. The surf was as big as at the pier, but less shapely and without the crowd. Albert was thrilled just to be carrying a board by himself. Jackie watched surfers taking off on waves and pointed out to Albert the difference between a left and a right, a goofy-foot and a regular-footer.

"I saw you on TV," Carmen said to me.

I grimaced. "I'll be glad when this case is over," I said. "My client hugs me and all hell breaks loose."

"I know something about local news," she said. "They did a slam piece on us a few years ago when that woman buried her twins in cement."

"I remember that case," I said.

"She'd been in the system, had a Las Palomas parenting certificate from us. People were just looking for someone to blame. Believe me, I know what you're dealing with."

Jackie halted us. "Okay, groms," he said, "this is where we hit it." We were just south of the jetty, at the place where I'd ridden my first wave with my father twenty-three years ago. "Let's go over a few basics, eh?"

We studied the surf, much in the way my day taught me on my first day of surfing. Three to five foot faces on the sets; four waves in a set; long lefts and a few short rights; medium tide causing the midsized waves to back off quickly; the biggest waves rolling nicely all the way inside; no apparent rip currents. Then Jackie laid Albert and Carmen's boards face up in the sand and had them practice grabbing their rails and swinging up to their feet in one fluid motion. Carmen was lithe and agile, while Albert struggled mightily but with great determination, popping too far upright to keep his balance even in the soft sand.

"Lower, Alby," Jackie counseled him. "Lemme explain. You learn to ride a wave, it can take you anywhere you want to go. High off the top"—he swept his hand in a tight arc in front of his face—"or hard off the bottom"—he banked his left hand in a low, scooping motion. "But the best place you can ride is in the tube, man. That's where you get your stance." He dropped into a crouch. "Try it. Like this."

Albert sprang up too high again but observed Jackie and slowly lowered himself like a loaded spring. "What's it like—the tube?" he said.

"You tuck into the face and the lip pitches over you, not touching you," Jackie told him. "It's the purest rush. When you're in the green room, time stands still. It's the sweetest part of the wave; you're one with it. Spending time in the green room is like going back to the womb. It's the essence, man."

"Yeah . . ." Albert said, still in his crouch.

"Ready bro?" Jackie said.

"Ready!" Albert shouted.

Carmen's eyes were full of concern for her brother. "J.?" she implored me.

"He'll be fine," I said. "I promise."

We strapped on our ankle leashes and waded out past the shore-pound. A set broke in front of us, dunking Albert, but Jackie quickly righted him and they paddled off into deeper water.

"Don't worry," I told Carmen. "Jackie's one of the best surfers that ever—"

"J., I may not live at the beach," she said, stopping me, "but I didn't grow up under a rock. I know who Jackie Pace is."

"My mistake," I said. "Let's go."

Carmen slid onto her board but centered herself too far back, the nose kicking up as she floundered. A tiny line of whitewash rolled through and toppled her. I flipped her board over and held it steady with one hand. "Try it again," I said. "Move up a little farther, 'til the board's planing as flat as possible."

Standing in chest-deep water, I unfastened my ankle leash and let my surfboard wash in. Carmen whipped back her wet black hair and slid onto her board again, adjusting her weight forward. I put my arm around her so I could grab both rails, my forearm grazing the small of her back. Then I pivoted the board toward shore. When she looked back to watch for an incoming wave our faces were no more than a foot apart. Her lips were wet and her eyelashes and brows glistened in the warming sun. She was so beautiful I had to look away.

A set wave dumped and a solid line of whitewash rumbled in. "Paddle hard!" I shouted, shoving the board's tail as the soup bashed into me.

I stayed with Carmen the first half hour, helping her line up set waves and providing encouragement. She belly-rode several lines of soup, paddling back out on her own each time before deciding to wave me off. "Think I've got it," she called out.

I went in and collected my board, then paddled farther out and rode a few waves by myself, thinking about how I'd misjudged her. That first time we'd met she'd seemed so strident with her talk about my not speaking Spanish. But she knew firsthand about the kind of shit that people like Holly Dupree sling, knew who Jackie Pace was—and how to put him in his place. She was good to her brother, if a bit overprotective. I wondered how she ever planned to make a break from him.

Jackie and Albert were lining up farther down the beach, Albert belly-riding line after line of whitewash, laughing the whole time. Another set came through and Carmen caught the largest wave, racing along prone, just ahead of the soup, steadying herself as the whitewater pushed for shore, then springing into a textbook stance while Jackie and I hooted. She rode five or six more re-forming waves in that fashion before hauling her board up the beach and collapsing.

Albert continued to hop up and flop badly. Jackie took off his leash and ditched his board, which I retrieved in the shorepound as I went in to sit with Carmen. Then he went back to pushing Albert into waves. A solid hour had passed since we'd first hit the surf. Albert's arms must have been jelly.

"He looks tired," Carmen said. She got up and walked closer to the surf as I followed. "Albert? You all right?" she called out. She turned to me. "J.? What do you think?"

I reached out and took her hand. "He's all right. He's with Jackie."

A clean, medium-sized peak popped up just outside of Albert and Jackie. "We're goin'!" I heard Jackie cry as he lay on top of Albert's legs, paddling furiously. The peak folded behind them as they slid down the hooking face, the whitewash partially engulfing Jackie until they broke ahead of the soup. Albert snapped to his feet with his hands still gripping his rails, wavering like a drunk.

"You got it!" Jackie shouted as he slipped off the tail. Albert committed his weight too far forward, and I shut my eyes at the instant I thought he would pearl, but he hung on and slowly straightened into an ugly crouch that was so low he could've rested both his palms on the board's deck.

"He's doing it!" Carmen cried.

Quaking awkwardly, Albert spread his arms like a big bird's wings and somehow found his balance. He rode the soup a good forty feet until it died.

"Yeah, Albert!" I shouted, distinctly relieved.

Albert straggled up the beach a few minutes later. "I did it!"

Jackie slapped him on the back. "You shredded it, Alby!"

"In the gr . . . green room," Albert stammered, a huge smile lighting his face.

"That was great," Carmen said to Jackie.

"Thank-ya-ma'am." Jackie was into his rapid-fire, early Elvis impression, and he bowed his head humbly. "Thank-ya-very-much." Carmen rolled her eyes and laughed.

The four of us strolled back down toward the pier and home. The rising tide had improved the shape of the surf and a local crew was swarming the fat Northside peaks.

"Yo, Jackie! Whas up?" a small contingent of grommets called out from up on the pier.

"Hey, you little hoodlums," Jackie called back, squinting into the mid-morning sun. "Go buy me some chili fries and a Coke. Pay you back."

Two boys broke from the group and raced off the pier, vying for the dubious honor of fetching an aging surf-hero's food.

Bob McClanahan, an old high school friend who now works as a financial planner, walked dripping from the shorebreak. "J.," he said, shaking my hand, "what's the haps?"

I introduced him to Carmen and Albert, describing the waves we'd encountered up the beach. We watched a set pour through while Bob ran down the conditions at the main peak. Two of Britt's buddies emerged from the lineup and joined us. One of them had been testing a brand new four-fin. We examined the board's outline, its fin placement, the crescent-shaped channels grooved into the planing area of the tail. Carmen described the first wave she'd ever ridden standing up, the pure buzz she'd experienced. Her story was met with characteristic fervor.

"Unreal."

"You're stoked."

Then Albert took his turn, and we hung on every slurred but passionately spoken word.

"Insane."

"He's hooked for life."

By the time the two grommets returned with Jackie's chili fries, several more people had stopped just to hang and talk. Bear and Lindy, a young married couple who'd been surfing the pier together every weekend since they met a dozen years ago riding Northside. Rachel, a sunbaked, longboard-toting waitress from the Captain's Galley, enraptured by Jackie's tale of a chance surf discovery he'd made on a lost island in the Atlantic. And Magic Man, an old-time character from my father's era who used to do card and coin tricks for the tourists on the pier to help finance his wave-chasing winters.

Carmen removed her necklace and handed it to Magic Man, who promptly made it disappear, then reappear from behind her ear. Albert clapped and laughed with pure joy. A set of sparkling lefts peeled away from the pilings. Magic Man reminisced about the failed surf shop he'd once owned, then waxed rhapsodic about his charmed youth and the early days of surfing in Christianitos. "Best days of our lives, they were," he lamented.

Jackie stiffed the grommets for the tab on the chili fries, explaining that groms were the lowest life forms on the beach and needed to pay their dues. "Like barnacles under the pier," he said with a dismissive wave.

Hearing Jackie, I remembered the time when I was twelve when some older boys lashed me to a pier piling with surf leashes, sprayed whipped cream all over me and stuffed a pack of hot dogs down my trunks, then sat back and howled laughing as a pair of hungry, stray mongrels went to town on me. Fortunately my trunks fit loosely enough to shake out the bait before those mutts clamped their teeth on the wrong wiener.

"Come by later and I'll pay you," I told one of the boys who'd gotten Jackie's food.

"It's cool," he said. "Jackie's always short on coin."

The afternoon onshores came, ruffling the wave-faces and dispersing the crowd in the water. We said our good-byes and continued south, toward home, but Jackie broke off to go have a few clandestine beers in the parking lot with one of his admirers.

"Later," he said almost as an afterthought over his shoulder, the willing buddy carting his board for him.

When Albert realized Jackie was not coming straight home with us his face grew desperate. "Wait. Can I go with him?" he implored Carmen.

"He'll be home soon," I said. "Jack," I yelled, "we're eating in half an hour." Jackie waved a hand but didn't turn around. Two cute girls in bikinis had stopped him dead in his tracks and he crouched in the sand next to their towels, spinning off a fresh line of dazzle. The girls smiled and turned to accompany him to the parking lot. Neither looked of age to drink beer, a minor detail that I was certain troubled no one.

We cut under the pier and continued along the sand. "So how did you and Jackie meet?" Carmen said.

I pointed to the dormant patch of dark water at Holy Rollers. "Out there."

"In the ocean?"

"There's a reef offshore, a surf spot where big waves break a couple times each winter. That's where we met. It's called Holy Rollers."

We trudged along in the wet sand, moving slowly so Albert could keep up. "How did it get its name?" Carmen asked.

"There's a story to it. I suspect it's a pack of lies."

"Those are the best kind."

I told her the tale as I'd heard it from Robert Shepard.

My father had had a fondness for names and the stories that went with them, and he particularly loved the outlandish piece of surf lore that surrounded the reef at Holy Rollers. As he'd heard it, Christianitos was once occupied by local Indians who'd farmed what they could from the marshy flats, clammed a bit, and fished by tossing nets from handcrafted canoes they launched from the beach every morning.

"The farming was lousy, though," I said to Carmen.

"How come?"

"Unfavorable combination of sandy topsoil and salt water intrusion.

"As the tribe grew, it became increasingly dependent upon the sea for its harvests, sending a small fleet forth through the wave-tossed inshore waters on all but the stormiest days. Somewhere around this time, the Spanish missionaries began passing through on northern treks from the mission at San Juan Capistrano. The Europeans would merely stop to rest and water their horses, as they had no formal business with the tribe, but during their brief stopovers they were both mystified and appalled to observe dozens of sick, hungry children milling about, begging for food. The children, the missionaries learned, were castoffs, left alone when their fathers drowned on ill-fated fishing expeditions."

"God, that's awful," Carmen said.

"I guess tribal customs were pretty harsh when it came to survival," I said. "Once a father died, the mother was forced to fend for herself. A single mother could no longer provide for her children, so the children were as good as orphaned."

"Didn't they do anything to help?"

"When the missionaries wrote the Church describing the situation and requesting instruction, an order of nuns was dispatched to establish an orphanage. They called the orphanage Los Christianitos, after the little Christians orphaned by the sea.

"Apparently the nuns were not content with indoctrinating only the young ones under their care. They were troubled that the tribesmen engaged in a form of pagan ritual whenever the surf grew too large to launch the fishing boats. The fishermen, it seemed, believed that big surf was a sign that the great spirit of the sea was angry. So they'd load a canoe with flowers, beads and assorted other trinkets, then ceremonially launch it into the maelstrom in a gesture of appeasement. During one unusually large swell, the nuns mustered the courage to step in and intervene, but the fishermen were as unmoved as they were unbelieving. They promptly rewarded the good sisters' bold advance by crowding them into a large dory abandoned years earlier by Spanish explorers and shoving the poor soldiers of God into waterborne oblivion.

"The entire village watched as the boat drifted out through the surf-line, teetering on huge swells but refusing to capsize, miraculously liberated by a strong seagoing current. The nuns were beyond the surf now, in deep water, and a few of the fishermen began to talk of rescuing them. Perhaps this Jesus the sisters spoke of, a god who had protected them well this day, was worth knowing. But before anyone could make a move to go after the nuns, a huge, black wall of water rose way offshore, directly in the oarless dory's path. With one horrible surge, the mammoth wall folded straight over the boat."

"Did they all drown?" Carmen asked.

"No one survived. And no remnants of the dory were ever found. But in the years that followed, on days when large swells rose deep and long-lined far out on the horizon, the fishermen swore they could hear the nuns wailing in the hiss of spray and whitewash on the reef."

Carmen shivered. "Creepy story."

"Another good reason for haired-out surfers to stay away on big days."

I stopped walking when we reached the foot of Twelfth Street, the perpendicular lineup marker for Holys.

"They say the spot where the nuns went down was the big wave reef out there," I said.

Carmen blinked into the sun, squinting at the reef beyond. "Who named it Holy Rollers?"

"An early crew of local surfers. Sardonic bunch of wags."

Carmen stared out to sea. "How sad. Those women gave their lives trying to save the children."

"And they died and got a fickle surf spot named after them for their trouble," I said. "They tried to do too much."

Carmen regarded me silently for a time. "You really feel that way? You think those children weren't worth saving?"

"That's not what I said. It just seems to me there's an order to things, a pre-set measure of cruelty and stupidity we're stuck with. Seems to me it's the state of humanity. You do too much, try to upset the balance, you get zapped."

"What a bleak picture you paint." She watched the surf lap around our ankles, foaming and white. "You're talking about your case, aren't you?"

I didn't answer. We walked on slowly, Albert happily lugging his board as he mumbled something about the green room over and over.

"You haven't lost, J.," Carmen said.

"You're right. Trial isn't until next week," I said. "That is, if I don't get the boot first."

The Randall case had been nothing but an extended bummer. I wished I could just walk away somehow, take a night flight to another life, find some lonely beach with waves that needed riding. Disappear.

Standing here at Twelfth, the place where my father passed away, I thought of Marielena Shepard, dropping her flower petals in the break every afternoon for ten years after.

"You read my mother's old letters," I said to Carmen.

"I did."

"Excellent." I stopped walking, propping my tail block against the wet sand. "So, what do you think?"

She stood not two feet from my side, surfboard slung low, her black hair trembling in the breeze. Like my mother, I wanted some kind of sign, but Carmen gave me none. "I'm cold," she said. "Can we go?"

Fifteen

There is a certain poise that comes with understanding the ocean's moods, tapping a pulse borne of a distinct, untamed, unfathomable energy source. An equilibrium, located on a singular track between the sucking trough and the pitching crest. A sense of perfect balance on a rolling, temporary stage, not a single movement wasted. A spray-blinded late takeoff in roaring Santa Ana winds. A confidence, knowing your instincts won't let you down.

Two sunny blocks from home, and I was purely, bitterly lost. Carmen's reaction down on the sand had sent a shock through me. She didn't say it, but she didn't have to say it. The letters were bad news.

We were a silent trio, shuffling back over the berm, the morning's waves behind us now. Confronted with an untidy past, my street-smart posturing deserted me. My act was a tongue-tied sham, all lone-wolf bravado, petty sarcasm and restless activity. Could I manage to stand still and cope with what had been—and what was to come?

I lit some coals in the barbecue and hosed off the wetsuits while Carmen and Albert showered and changed. She came out in her khaki shorts and shirt with a white tank top beneath the half-buttoned shirt. Her bangs were dry and she'd woven her hair into a lovely, thickly braided ponytail. The sight of her kick-started something in my brain, and I found myself over at the wood-barrel planter in the corner of the yard. A wild mess of daisies overflowed the barrel and spilled down the sides. I picked a perfect white flower and brought it back.

"For you," I said.

Carmen wordlessly placed the daisy in her hair above her ear. *Thank you, God*, I thought.

"Carmen," Albert called from the porch, shattering the moment. "TV won't work."

"He brought some videos," Carmen said. "He takes them just about everywhere."

"I'll go set him up," I said, handing her the spatula and a plate of hamburger patties. Max, who was sleeping in his favorite spot under the pepper tree, lifted his head and eyed the plate. "Be good, Max," I called across the yard. "If he bothers you, just give him a patty," I told Carmen. "Three of them are for him anyway."

I showed Albert how to operate the VCR's remote. "Ready to go, partner," I said, loading the tape, "but let's eat first."

"Wh . . . where's Jackie?" Albert said.

"He'll be back soon."

We ate our hamburgers outside at the picnic table with chips and a green salad I'd made while Carmen was turning the patties. Albert sat and stared at the burger on his plate. "Eat your food, *m'ijo*," Carmen said, but he continued to sulk.

"Don't worry about Jackie," I told him. "He always turns up where there's food." Albert didn't crack a smile.

We ate in relative silence until Albert asked Carmen to be excused. "You haven't eaten three bites," she protested.

"I'll cover it," I said, taking his plate. "We'll heat it up later."

Albert went inside, leaving me alone again with Carmen. "He really likes Jackie," I said.

She sipped her ice tea, eyeing the house. "I wish he wouldn't get his hopes up. Albert forms attachments too easily."

"Jackie's not the kind of guy who'll let anyone get too attached to him," I said. "He craves an audience, but he's basically a loner."

She put down her drink. "What about you, J.?"

I'd never thought of myself as a loner. Twenty-nine, no family, only a few close friends, a best friend I didn't trust. Wisecracking my way through a burnout job, surrounded by lawyers I often don't respect and clients I can't relate to. I was closer to being a loner than I wanted Carmen Manriquez to know.

"I'm not like Jackie," I told her.

Albert came to the kitchen door. "Is he back yet?" His eyes searched the yard for a sign of any kind.

I shrugged. "Not yet, buddy. He'll be along." Albert hung his head and went inside again. "Wow," I said to Carmen, "what are you going to do when he discovers girls?"

Carmen watched him waddle back to the living room. *"Pobrecito,"* she said.

"You and Albert are really close," I said. "It's like you're his guardian angel."

"He needs one."

"What are you protecting him from?"

"I don't know. People—sometimes the world." She stared back at me. "What kind of question is that?"

I'd overstepped an invisible line. "Sorry, none of my business."

Carmen rubbed her forehead. "No, it's not you."

"I shouldn't have asked."

Carmen was silent, as if deciding whether I was to be trusted. "My father—our father—he left us, when Albert was very young."

"I'm sorry."

"It's not like that. He was very macho, like many Latinos are. When I was born he was so disappointed."

"How come?"

She closed her eyes as if weighed down by the memory. "I was a girl. I couldn't carry on the family name. You probably know, this is a very typical, stupid problem in our culture." She sipped her tea. "And the day Albert was born was the happiest day of his life. But Albert was always . . . different. You've seen him. He didn't walk until he was two, couldn't talk like a normal baby. My father took it as a slap in the face from God. His only son, and he was ashamed of him. *Pendejo.*"

"Why did your father leave?"

"One day when Albert had just turned four, my father was drunk again, feeling sorry for himself. He told Albert to speak up and flicked a burning cigarette butt at his head. It caught Albert under the eye and he cried, hard. *Papi* went into a rage and yelled at him to shut up. Albert just kept screaming."

"There was a fight?"

"A terrible one."

"Your parents?"

She shook her head no. "My mom was at work. She was the only one with a job back then, so it was just Albert and me. But she knew how *Papi* could get. I was supposed to watch out for Albert until she got home."

"What did you do?"

"His cheek was burned and he wouldn't stop crying. I got between them but *Papi* hit him, kept hitting him. Albert fell, hit his head on the coffee table. We both went to the hospital that night." All the life had gone out of her face. "I didn't protect him."

"You were a little girl," I said.

"Pobrecito," she said, shaking her head. "I'll never let him be hurt again."

Max had walked over and snuggled his head onto Carmen's lap. She stroked his big, black nose, rubbing the short hair between his eyes.

"You think your father might still hurt Albert?" I asked.

"I just know my brother needs to be safe."

I reached for Max and rubbed the area behind his ears. "Is that why you live at home?"

"Yes." She sighed, reconsidering. "I don't know." She looked away.

I wanted to take her in my arms and hold her, to say something pithy about everything being all right, but I couldn't summon the nerve. "You're a good sister," I managed. "But you can't stay with him forever."

"I know, but *Mami* can't protect him. She's too old now."

"I could talk to your father," I said. "Feel him out."

"No. Thank you, but no. I can handle it."

The bundle of letters from Aunt Miluca to my mother sat there between us like a purple elephant neither of us was ready to acknowledge. In my work, I had long ago become expert at avoiding eye contact, at looking away from certain harsh realities in order to focus on the motions, the evidence, the objections that lay in my path. Hell, this was my primary game plan for getting through the calendar each day. I'd pushed Marielena Shepard out onto the shadowy margins as well, and left her there permanently. That was a mistake, I knew now. But it was easier to talk about Carmen's father.

"Maybe if I see him, just talk to him," I said, "I can get an indication of some kind. At least you would know. That's a good thing."

Carmen regarded me seriously. "Is it?"

The letters stared up at me from the picnic table. In the fewest words possible, I took something of a stand on the issue. "It is."

"Thank you for offering to help," she said. "I'll think about it."

I was fresh out of diversions. Before she started in, Carmen asked me about my family, "for purposes of context." I told her it was all right for her to ask. I told her about my father meeting my mother, his shaping skills and big wave exploits; her singing with the church choir, her initial solo journey from Chile, the accounting work. My father's bad heart, his early death. September of '79, my mother's disappearance. My surreal senior year at Christianitos High, an early introduction to Gilbride's manual. The filing cabinet in the attic, these letters and the Sea Pointe brochures. I tried to go slowly, but my tone seemed reaching and overanxious, like when I'd spoken to Baumann, the town historian. Carmen rolled with me with her sublime, social worker's patience.

"Let me read you the letters now," she said when I'd stopped.

The first ten letters revealed nothing unusual: anecdotal asides about child rearing and the high cost of living, recipes, gardening tips, a cold snap in Chile. The last two, written in the summer of '79, were more serious and philosophical. Aunt Miluca was instructing Marielena on love, loyalty, the church and its teachings, and sin.

"Sin?" I said, sitting up straighter.

"Your mother was facing a personal dilemma," Carmen said. "Let me translate this passage to you from the very last letter. 'Marielena, the Lord bestows the gift of life upon us, a gift so profound and holy, one has only to accept it. It is not wise for you to question this gift, this mystery of life. Pray. Open your heart to God and let his gifts flow over you and make you whole. No mother can deny her own child's place in her life.' "

A child's rightful place in his mother's life. I had my answer to the central question of my mother's disappearance. "She left me."

"J., no, wait," Carmen said, placing her hand on mine. "I don't think this is about you." She shifted the pile of pages in front of her.

"Here, listen to what Miluca says in the second-to-last letter: 'Only a witch would give holy counsel outside the church, *m'ija*. The *comadrona* is a witch.' "

My mother's superstitions again. "You think she was talking to a witch?" I asked.

"Not exactly. A *comadrona* is a midwife."

"I don't follow. Holy counsel from a midwife who Aunt Miluca thought was a witch?"

Carmen put down the final letter. "I think your mother was pregnant."

"Pregnant? No, she . . . how? She never had anyone . . . a boyfriend . . . or lover, not a lover, not . . . since my father died. I lived here with her, right across the hall." I picked up the last letter from which Carmen had read and inspected it. "No. That can't be right."

Carmen said nothing. She'd read the letters, though. She was simply too diplomatic to push her point with me. I was acting like a fool.

"Sorry," I said. "I don't know what to make of this yet."

She nodded in support. I thought of the leather portfolio I'd found in the attic, the one embossed with my mother's initials. The gold pen and pencil set. Gifts from an admirer—or perhaps, a suitor.

"I guess anything's possible," I said. "But why would she want to see a midwife?"

"In Mexico, midwives deliver babies. Some of them perform abortions."

"My mother was Catholic. She wouldn't have had an abortion."

It sounded all wrong. Marielena Shepard had lived a life too quiet, too studied for all this mess. "We don't even have midwives here," I added, but Carmen was hardly in need of convincing. She'd never known the woman. I was arguing with myself.

Cool it, boy, just cool it. "What else do the letters tell you?" I asked more evenly.

She put the last two down without reading from them. "That's really all there is."

I buried my face in my palms.

"I'm sorry, J.," Carmen said. "I wrote the translations out in light pencil above the words. Maybe later you'll want to re-read them."

I thanked her and folded the letters in their creases again. For the second time today, I was at a near total loss for words. Carmen instinctively reached for Max and cajoled him to stem the silence.

"You have fun surfing today?" I said. It was the best I could do.

"I did." Her teeth were a flawless white. "You're a good teacher."

I returned Carmen's smile, then looked away.

"You know what I liked even more than riding my first wave?" Carmen said a moment later. "Standing on the beach later. Talking with your friends."

"That was good, wasn't it?"

"I think you're lucky, J."

My insides warmed. Just then, I think I would have sold my pitiful soul to find the words to say something upbeat and witty, to make her hopeful about her prospects with me. A feather-light endearment or two, a brief rhapsody on the beach life—anything halfway intelligent would have done. But my mind was as dull as tar. The moment died.

Saturday at five I went to mass at Saint Ann's, still mulling over the letters from Aunt Miluca. The services were sparsely attended, a westerly sea breeze flickering through the open panels of stained glass. The church's interior was calming, the lengthy nave cast in serene, blue shadows and diffused light among the rows of pillars and stones. I sat on the right near an alcove that held a small shrine to the Virgin Mary.

The old pastor, Father Ashton, was sermonizing in a familiar vein. Whatsoever you do to the least of my brothers, that you do unto me. I gazed at the statue of the Virgin and tried to say a prayer for guidance. Hail Mary, full of grace, the Lord is with Thee, blessed art Thou . . . blessed . . . I lost my place and had to start again.

I'd always thought my father was the love of my mother's life, which was probably just my own, kid's fantasy. But Marielena didn't have any real boyfriends that I could recall. She was a lovely, graceful woman who turned heads simply by walking into a room, so the phone rang for her often enough, yet her standards were probably pretty high because few men came calling over the years, and even fewer had a lasting impact. A kindly grocer who wrote his own pop songs for her—not exactly Beatlesque stuff. A well-to-do hotel owner who got the brush when he booked a trip for two to Paris for them without her knowledge. A local grade school principal who fell so hard he proposed on the fifth—and last—date. Nice guys, but not much in the romance department, and none to compare favorably with my old man. But how could I be sure? She could have loved someone and kept it from me, not knowing how I might react. It would have been like her to wait for just the right time to tell me. She was careful like that, respectful.

But what was careful about Marielena being pregnant, with no man on the horizon? Nothing. And, though we'd never openly discussed the topic, she would not have aborted. I felt reasonably certain of that much.

Thirteen years ago, in '79, midwives may still have been popular in Chile for all I knew. But in America women had their babies—and their abortions—in hospitals, under the care of doctors. My mother took care of herself. She knew what she was doing.

Then again, she had her nutball superstitions. An absolute prohibition against leaving a hat on a bed. The garlic beneath the mattress to ward off spirits while she slept. The crazy way she'd suddenly ask me to pick a number at random. "Seven," I'd say. She'd count up the alphabet until she stopped on the letter of the person who was currently speaking ill of her. "Seven. A, b, c, d, e, f, g. G . . ." she'd say, her eyes narrowing as she strained to decipher a secret message. "I had a trim from a girl named Greta this afternoon. Hmm—did I forget to tip her?"

She'd also kept to her daily ritual of visiting the Twelfth Street shorebreak, the place where my father had drowned, and casting a few rose petals. Every day for ten years.

I tried to pray again, mouthing words drilled into me as a child by the Saint Ann's nuns. Bargain-seeking, solicitous words they were, spoken from the lips of the unbelieving. I called off the exercise in shame.

After mass, I walked to the side altar and pondered lighting a candle. The church seemed to have shrunk a little with each year I'd been away.

"You take communion?" Father Ashton was at my shoulder, which gave me a start. His wrinkles were much more apparent up close. He seemed to have shrunk with age.

We hadn't spoken in a dozen years, since the night he came to the house to talk about doing some kind of memorial service for my mother. I was instantly pissed, pointing out that she might be just gone, not dead; and if so, why honor her memory? Besides, my father died and didn't even get a Catholic burial because he was cremated, I said—and what was with that bullshit? The conversation rapidly overheated, Father Ashton defending the Church, adamant that it was my father's choice to do that, and that he was here to talk about my mother, anyway. I remember suggesting that Father go ask God what happened to her, and not to come back with any hot ideas about any special services until he had an answer.

I tried to smile. He knew I hadn't received communion, so I ignored his question. "Nice sermon, Father. You've still got the gift."

"Devil always gets their attention," he said. "I think Catholics prefer a touch of fear in the proceedings."

He'd grown thinner and his dark hair gave way to more scalp than ever. His face had lost its handsome dash and his hands were deeply blotched with purple age spots. I noticed a small bandage beneath his left ear and failed to look away in time.

"Oh, this?" he said. "A reminder of my own mortality, you could say."

Someone in back cut the overhead lights up on the altar. Father turned to regard the crucifix that now hung in darkness.

"Is it serious?" I asked.

He nodded. "Cancerous. It comes off Thursday. They think they caught it in time."

"Thank God," I said without irony.

He crossed himself. "Done."

An old lady with a massive purse and a black veil on her head emerged from the front pew, bowed and said good day to the Father. We surveyed the rows of flickering red candles before us.

"I should go," I said. "Good luck on Thursday."

Across the blacktop near my car, some teenaged kids were playing half-court basketball. I drifted over, stopping briefly to watch. There was something liberating about the way they moved, darting and reaching and leaping at once for a rebound, seemingly oblivious to their surroundings.

Father Ashton walked over and stood next to me, his eyes following the movement of the ball. "So, what brings you here? Is that reporter, Holly Dupree, giving you fits?"

"You know about Holly Dupree?"

"I keep tabs on all my former altar boys."

"It's nothing," I said. "I comforted a client. Holly turned it into a love affair."

"I figured as much." He looked back at the church as if he didn't quite know why he'd walked out here to meet me.

He was right to wonder why. I'd come to mass seeking counsel from a God with whom I was seriously out of step, my feeble prayers coming up short. But Holly Dupree? No, the Randall case was not the thing. I was here because of those letters.

I didn't trust Father, not since that day at my house. Still, I needed answers.

"You know how my mother . . . disappeared a long time ago."

"Marielena was a beloved member of the parish. Very sad."

"I'm trying to figure out what actually happened, what became of her, but I'm not getting anywhere. Maybe I shouldn't press it, but, these letters I found . . . she may have seen a witch—I mean, a midwife." I was babbling. "Sorry. I'm not making any sense."

He put his hands behind his back, trying his best to act casual. "Take your time."

We watched a pair of gulls float over the playground and turn into the wind. "You knew her, Father."

"I did."

I hesitated. When it comes to big issues, you never know when a priest will resort to spouting the party line and clap the mighty hand of the Church down on you like the weight of the world. It was the way I'd been indoctrinated. Every kid who attended Catholic school in the sixties was dealt the Official Word, and it made a lasting impression. I was a fatalist by the second grade, shitting bricks that I'd committed a mortal sin and was already damned. Of course, I didn't actually know what a mortal sin was, as Sister Clementissima hadn't bothered to give examples—too salacious. We weren't ready to comprehend such wickedness, she explained. Yet I was all too ready to suffer for it.

Father Ashton waited. I swallowed, the faint taste of incense left over from mass sliding down the back of my throat. My school days were harmless, history. I had to tell him. "Do you think she would have had an abortion?" I said. "I mean, she was a practicing Catholic. It's a pretty big sin."

Father regarded the silver crucifix around his neck as if he were pondering the death of his savior. The doubt in his eyes struck instant fear in me. If he knew the truth about her, he also understood that speaking it could damage me. But then, perhaps I was misreading the situation. His eyes were merely haggard. The man was slowed by his years, more deliberate with his speech, merely taking his time to answer. Not wanting to touch off another argument.

Shit. I was losing my grip again.

"There's no answer to that, J.," he finally said. "People don't always sin for simple reasons. Sometimes you have a chain of events. Sometimes it gets complicated." He paused. "Life today is very complicated. That's why original sin is such a central concept to belief. It traces humanity back to the Garden, back to man's essential failing. Which is sin."

"She left me—isn't that a sin?" I said.

"I knew Marielena," he said. "She came here twice a week, for twenty years, sang in the choir. She never said good-bye. That wasn't like her."

"What are you saying?"

He seemed mildly surprised by the question. "Keep looking."

I frowned. "Last time I saw you, you acted like you knew she was dead."

"My mistake," he conceded.

The basketball game wore on, the church casting a shadow over the backboard now. I was worn out, fried from the inside out. All control of my life had dissolved. My resolve was for shit. I doubted Jackie in spite of his eagerness to help me work the Randall matter. In my zeal to reach out to Sue Ellen, I'd only further confused her feelings and now faced being kicked off the case in disgrace. I wouldn't accept Carmen's translations, couldn't accept what was plainly spelled out in those old letters. I closed my eyes, unable to speak.

The old priest studied me. "You don't look so well."

I looked around to make sure we were alone. "What's the use?" I said. "Certain people—like you—they're meant to help others. I'm not. When I do, it just comes out wrong."

"I don't understand."

"I'm a hypocrite. I don't want to be bothered with someone else's mess. I only help others to help myself."

He waited before speaking. "Let me tell you a little something about your father," he said. "I knew him, too."

"I don't know," I said. "Last time we talked about him, you said some things—"

"Just let that go for a moment," he said. "Please." Shaking his head. "Anyway, we talked about a few things over the years, your father and I."

I was skeptical. "What about?"

He paused as if waiting for his memory to take shape more fully. "Faith. Prayer."

"My dad used to pray for surf a lot," I said. "Or so I've heard."

Father Ashton smiled. "He had a zest for life, he did. But he prayed for more than surf. He was very hard on himself—like you, J. he had . . ." A thought seemed to dim the light inside him. "Tell me, have you ever heard of a young man named Roger Nelly?"

"Sure. Jelly-Belly." Grog Baker had told me stories about the original crew from Christianitos, and about that particular, unlucky soul. "He's the guy who drowned."

Father Ashton nodded. "You know how?"

"I heard he went surfing with my dad at some spot down south, a gnarly, cliffy break in La Jolla. No one else was out. A giant day."

"Your father told me all about it," he said. "The sun was going down. Nelly had a bad wipeout, got pushed in without his surfboard, pinned against the rocks in surging, shallow water. He panicked. Your father came in after him, tried to rescue him, but Nelly had hit his head and gone under. Your father was very seriously injured."

"I never heard that part."

"He dislocated his shoulder, badly cut his leg. He might have bled to death in the water had he not crawled up that cliff so quickly to get his friend into the ambulance."

"I . . . didn't know."

"I don't think your father was the type to broadcast his injuries, even among friends. But that wasn't it. He was hurting on the inside, too."

The image I'd built of Robert Shepard was cut from granite, sanded smooth with time, as flawless as the vintage surfboards hanging in my garage at home. "How?" I asked.

"He experienced a personal crisis. That is, when he went after his friend. Surfers have a term for it, as I recall. When you're stuck there, in shallow, rocky water, caught between the land and the ocean, the waves pounding you, trying to knock you off your feet. Forcing you to go forward or back, but you can't do either one."

"The reef dance," I said.

He nodded.

"Funny," I said. "I've always heard he was pretty comfortable in the surf."

"Right you are. Very capable. But that day when Nelly got in trouble, your father came to his side, never thinking of his own safety. That day, he nearly lost his own life trying to save a friend who was probably already dead. And it troubled him, deeply. He found himself wishing, praying even, to never be put in such a situation again."

"He told you this?"

"Eventually. Some years after Nelly's death. He felt ashamed of his misgivings. He wanted me to give back Nelly's medal." The priest shook his head. "I wouldn't take it."

He'd lost me. "What medal?"

"Before Nelly went to fight in Korea, his parents gave him a medal, a simple Christopher."

I knew the kind, silver medals the size of a quarter with a profile of Saint Christoper and the prayer for his protection inscribed around the edges. The nuns sold them with the rosary beads and holy cards from a small counter in the back of the church.

"At Nelly's funeral," he went on, "his parents gave your father his Saint Christopher, in gratitude for being their son's protector."

"He wanted to give it back," I said.

"He didn't feel worthy."

I couldn't remember whether my father wore a Saint Christopher—it was too long ago. But my mother had one. "You wouldn't take it?" He shook his head. "What did you tell him?"

Father Ashton's eyes met mine. "That God loved him."

"That's it?" I said a little too forcefully.

He paused the way he did during his sermons when he was about to make a weighty point. "You know about your father's heart, J."

I did. "The growth in his arteries. Coarctation of the aorta."

"He knew he could die young."

I felt the memories pressing in, that nagging sense of missed opportunities. "And he was right."

"Know why he was cremated after he died?"

Not this shit again, I thought. "No, I just know it wasn't cool with the Church."

"Never mind that," he said. "You're a Catholic all right. We've done a fine job teaching you rules. No wonder you don't come here anymore."

"I have my own reasons."

He looked at his shiny black shoes, then at me. "The rules have changed since the sixties, for your information. But I suppose . . . no. Anyway, that day I came to your house . . ."

"The cremation," I said, "just tell me."

He waved me off. "I'm trying to." I'd apparently rubbed him a bit raw, but he took a deep breath and forced a little smile my way. The man was really making an effort.

"Sorry, Father."

"You had every right to be upset with me that day. See, I'm the big boss around here, pretty used to having my way. You really struck a nerve with me."

"Likewise. You couldn't have picked a worse time to criticize my dad."

"I left your house angry, just burning mad, and for weeks I wondered why. But I realized later . . . I'd got what was coming to me."

Not from me, he hadn't. "I don't see how. All I did was rant and rave."

"I thought I knew your father better, assumed we'd bury him. The instructions . . . the cremation was a surprise. I suppose I took it personally."

"It doesn't matter anymore," I said.

"No," he said, "I was wrong. A few months later, I looked into it, talked to some of his old friends around town. Found out he was cremated because his vital organs had already been earmarked for transplants. Course, I should've known it, because of his heart condition. You see, it was an act of responsibility. My anger that day . . . was vanity."

All this talk of my old man made him less of an abstraction to me at the moment, and my mood continued to darken.

"I appreciate the explanation. Why didn't you tell me sooner?" I asked.

Father Ashton's shoulders twitched as if he was chilled. "I figured I'd see you around here sometime. Sometime never came."

I didn't know what to say—my confusion over my mother, the bad memories about my father, it was too much to process right now. I just stood there and watched a procession of kids shoot free throws to decide new teams.

"That was your father, J.," the old priest said. "He was just a man. I think he learned to live with his doubts, his human imperfections. Maybe he didn't always follow the rules. But he did what he thought was right. He was worthy of Nelly's medal."

The bells in the high tower clanged to six. Another game of hoop got underway amid long shadows and stripes of late-summer gold, the two of us wordlessly observing along the sidelines. I found myself formulating another prayer. Reflexively I prayed for surf, but I promised the Lord there was more to follow.

Sixteen

Lamont Dunne's art showing was well attended. Eugene Bardo, the gallery owner and Pam Baker's boss, had promoted the show for weeks by running print ads in the local papers and further hedging his bets with a slew of strategic invites. When I arrived just after eight, Bardo was a peppy blur, plying would-be buyers with white wine and *hors d'oeuvres* as he chatted about ocean art with childlike awe. Patrons fell in love with Eugene faster than they could absorb an easy seaside composition. Having seen Lamont Dunne's work before, I instead took note of the tiny white, deadly serious price stickers staring up from the bottom corner of each piece like a detached evil eye. No matter, for I'd come not to buy, but to watch Pam sell, and the buzz was encouraging. The waterfront section of downtown Long Beach is often a sleepy scene even on weekends, but tonight the sidewalk fronting the gallery hummed with motion. I was panhandled twice before reaching the door.

The people inside were casual but moneyed. Older men in sportcoats and club ties, studying their price sheets and calling out friendly greetings to country club acquaintances. Crisply tailored wives issuing forth opinions as to who had the best interior designer or Mercedes mechanic. Young professional men sipping wine in pleated slacks and black turtlenecks, their sideburns razor sharp. Model-thin young women milling about like bored gazelles. Everyone talking at once, some on sleek, handheld phones, others jabbering straight at the canvases as if expecting the breaching whales and winking dolphins to hold up the other end of the conversation. I'd forgotten how many wealthy people chose to live near the ocean.

I'd dressed in the same university-stripe shirt, tan slacks, rep tie and navy blazer I'd worn to court many times on laid-back Friday mornings. Presently I considered the choice a mistake, a personal reminder of the tonnage of files that lurked in my drawers thirty miles due north, waiting to be worked up sooner or later.

Jackie arrived alone. He was decked out for the occasion in a tan, gabardine thrift-store number, an ecru silk shirt and a bizarre, hand-painted tie depicting a red sun setting behind a bending palm that was anchored amid creeping marijuana growth. By some minor miracle of fashion, the ensemble worked perfectly, his slicked hair and wraparound shades boosting his air of big-city *élan*. More than a few females took note of his entrance.

"No offense, J.-man," he said as he drank in the energy in the gallery, "but a *connoisseur* needs room to fully appreciate fine art and—oh, yes"—he ogled a beauty as she drifted past my elbow, smiling at Jackie—"there is some very fine viewing to be done."

"Suit yourself," I said, "but you break or steal anything, I don't know you."

"Tut tut," he said, grinning. "Say, Lamont," he called out across the room to the artist, who was chatting with a group in front of a flaming tropical sunrise. "*Great* show! A veritable *tour de force*."

Lamont Dunne looked up from his conversation and eyed us stolidly, as if we'd come to collect on an old debt. I turned to pluck a stuffed mushroom from a passing tray.

Jackie stroked back his hair and massaged the back of his neck, contemplating his next action. He seemed to be rolling over a complex problem in his mind, and at one point, I thought certain he'd determined to shine me on and venture out among the paintings. But he stayed.

"You're not getting anywhere, are you?" he said finally.

We both knew he was talking about Marielena Shepard. I didn't really care how he'd found out. I just didn't want to hear the rap that was coming.

"I don't know how many times I've tried to tell you," he said. "Better to be in forward than reverse. It's easier to see the turns in the road."

"That's the least of my problems," I said. "My mother's been gone a long time, Jack. That may be that. But I could be kicked off the biggest case I've ever been on, and even if I'm not, at this rate we're gonna lose anyway."

"Not so fast. Couple of bets I placed earlier in the week just paid off big time."

It was the first good news I'd heard since the case began. "Why didn't you let me know?"

"I went by the pad twice after your new girlie friend and her brother split. You weren't around."

"What have you got?"

"Found Weinstein's nurse, the one who was there when Nathan was born. Name's Rosemary Egan."

"What did she say? Will she testify?"

He grinned, self-satisfied. "Dig this, she's a two-for-one witness, man. Not only was she there for Nathan, she was there back when the rich bitch had her baby, too."

"Kitty Danforth had a baby? When?"

"I dunno, couple years ago, I think. Didn't work out, though." Jackie stopped to reflect on something. "Miscarriage, I think it was. Guess it explains why she's such a sketch. You know she had her tarot cards read yesterday? 'Madame DeBalzac,' this high-class gypsy broad in Pasadena who specializes in conning the rich and powerful."

He'd been getting nowhere tailing Kitty Danforth. "Weinstein was Kitty's doctor," I said, trying to keep him on course. "He was her choice to handle Nathan's birth." I remembered Sue Ellen's charge that she'd been pushed into having her baby early. "Did you ask Egan about the induced labor, why Sue Ellen had to give birth by May sixth?"

"Oh yeah, yeah! You won't believe this, man. They went to a party."

"A party?"

"Not your typical, everyday rage. They attended a *ball*. In Washington, at the White House."

"Wait a minute. May sixth was a Monday, I looked it up. They went to a ball on a Tuesday night?"

Jackie sighed as if waiting for me to catch up. "Saturday, the eleventh. I told you old Kitty was a sketch," he said. "According to Egan, Kitty had Tuesday and Wednesday carved up just for gettin' ready. They left Thursday. Wanted to see the town a little before they did the ball."

"But their week would've been shot if they were on standby, waiting for Sue Ellen to give birth."

"They have a housekeeper," he said.

"I know."

"Why didn't they just have her cover for 'em while they were in D.C.?"

It was beginning to make sense to me. "Sue Ellen wouldn't have it," I said. "She demanded they be there when Nathan was born. She was screwing up their trip, so they told her she had the due date wrong and induced her labor."

"That is the definition of cold," Jackie said.

I'd underestimated the Danforths' social status. "What kind of ball did Egan say it was? They tell her?"

"I think they're heavy campaign spenders. Kip's company has something to do with hardware for jet fighters."

"Defense," I said. "They're Republicans."

We stood in silence, mulling over the news. "This mean you got 'em sussed?" Jackie asked.

"It's significant, but I don't think it's enough," I said.

"Why not? You thought they were using her, now you got your proof. That was beyond harsh."

"They'll deny everything," I said. "And we can't prove otherwise."

"What about Egan? If she testifies, she'll tell the judge. She'll set 'em straight."

My hopes sank. "What do you mean *if*?" I said. "This is all total hearsay without her. You did tell her she'd have to testify."

He held up his hand. "Take a chill-pill, brother. You just dialed into her sore spot. She's retired. That's why I couldn't find her until now. She's seen the whole shit-storm coming on the TV. Face it, you're looking like the captain of the Titanic and she's not too stoked about going down with the ship."

I wasn't worried about disturbing Rosemary Egan's golden years. I just wanted to win. "I'll type a subpoena tonight. Can you get her to testify?"

He nodded in the affirmative. "Just loan me your ride Monday. She's got a little transport problem, but I'll get her there."

I sighed, partially relieved. "We'll carpool."

He took off his shades and winked as he slipped them into his breast pocket. A server offered him a white wine, which he took. "Cheers," he said to me. "You got the whole sitch wired."

But I was too beset with a new series of problems. "The Danforths will lie on the stand to keep Nathan," I said. "We need corroboration."

Jackie kept smiling. "No worries. A White House bash? Man, you know it was a grand affair."

"There had to be a news story," I said. "If I can find it."

Which was doubtful. Tomorrow was Sunday; the public libraries would be closed.

"And pictures," he said. "Rich folks love to have their picture taken, especially in fancy threads."

I thought of the immense living room in the Davenport home, the pictures on the Steinway that never got played. There was a handsome outdoor shot of Phoebe and both her parents at sail on a gleaming yacht, the spinnaker spooled out full in a billowing white backdrop above a slash of tropical water. But no photos of people in tuxedos or evening gowns. I pictured Bill Davenport's study, that time I talked Phoebe into lifting a few cigars from his private stash. A row of photographs on the deep-paneled wall above his desk. Bill Davenport shaking hands with the mayor, the governor. More pasty faces, as Lois Nettleson would say, than you could shake a meaty stick at. A framed invitation with the Seal of the President of the United States on it, the '88 inauguration.

"J., you still with me?" Jackie said, snapping his fingers in front of my nose.

"I need the photos. I only know one rich conservative with political connections. He might have been there, too."

"Excellent."

I frowned. "One minor problem, he hates my guts."

"Don't sweat it, man," he said. "Probably nothing personal. Conservatives hate everybody."

Jackie spotted an unattached young female and left my side to pursue her. I took stock of the Bardo milieu. The gallery was divided into three rooms—two small, square spaces in the front and rear, and a larger, rectangular room in the center that displayed the bulk of the collection. Pam Baker was in the main room, standing before an enormous, mural-like painting filled with frolicsome undersea creatures awash in an ocean aquarium of deep, fluid blue. A dapper white-haired man stood next to her, scribbling dimensions on the back of one of Pam's business cards. She thanked him, then waited for him to walk away before leaning over to place a "sold" sticker on the identifying placard.

"J., thanks for coming," she said when she saw me. "This is *so* amazing . . . that's my fourth," she whispered.

Pam looked radiant in a black skirt and silk blouse, a houndstooth blazer and black stockings. Her skin was brown and sun-creased, the wrinkles tracking out from the corners of her eyes like tiny spokes. Her autumn blond hair was short in back and perfectly tousled on top.

We exchanged kisses on the cheek. "I just wanted to check in," I said. "Looks like things are flowing."

"Pamela," Eugene Bardo discreetly called to her. "The Single-tons."

"Thank you, Eugene. Gotta run," she said to me. "Have a look, J. Talk to Lamont. I'll catch up with you later." She briefly surveyed the congestion. "They'll probably all be gone in another half hour."

I spent the next twenty minutes drifting from one painting to the next. Lamont Dunne had talent, no doubt, a sure sense of perspective and tremendous control of his ethereal, airbrushed palette, yet his subject matter seemed limited. You could almost see the progression from schoolboy doodlings of perfect waves on Pee-Chee folders to cosmic surf scenes airbrushed onto virgin surfboard blanks before they were glassed, then onward and upward to the lush renderings of roiling undersea mammals and fiery sunsets that dominated the walls tonight. Viewing a gallery full of Lamont Dunne's work was like perusing a *Playboy* calendar: the calculated perfection was pleasing enough for a time, yet ultimately a hustle.

Jackie and I had apparently seen the same pictures. "Quite a *coup,* brother," he said to Lamont. "Surf art . . . I see. Kinda like the pet rock. It's like, man, why didn't I think of this and seriously cash in?"

Lamont Dunne looked rather stunned as Jackie threw an arm around his shoulder. I imagined this was the first pointed criticism Lamont had heard all evening, and he did not seem prepared to handle it.

A waiter appeared, offering drinks, and Lamont grabbed a white wine and took a long drink. He was a small, compactly built man in his mid-forties, younger than Pam by a few years. His black suit was double-breasted. He'd slicked his dark hair wet and pulled it back in a short ponytail. As I stepped closer, he touched his tie—a saffron, Italian-silk beauty—and checked the time on his Rolex, as if to reassure himself that even if he wasn't an artist in the truest sense of the word, he was still, in some circles, an unqualified success.

"Evening, Lamont," I said, shaking his hand.

"Hello J.," he said, still wary of Jackie's presence. "Didn't know you two were friends."

"Don't let him rile you," I told Lamont. I was tired of hearing Jackie's counterfeit protestations against commercialization. "He's just jealous."

A lanky brunette in black denim and a low-cut white blouse brushed my shoulder, backing up as she took in a large painting across the room. She didn't stop retreating until she landed atop Jackie's cordovan loafer.

"Oops!" She jumped, half losing her balance. Jackie reached out and gently steadied her. "I'm so sorry. Clumsy of me," she said. Her lips and fingernails glistened in a rich vermilion sheen. "I just got so lost in the . . . the motion of the waves." She gazed at the painting, then at Jackie again. "I know it sounds silly, but these paintings, it's like, they speak to me."

She struck me as a bit of a phony.

"Oh no, no, my dear, that isn't silly!" Jackie said. "I know what you mean. Tell you a secret. They speak to me, too, to my inner child."

"What's the matter with the outer child?" I said. "He hard of hearing?"

Jackie bore down on the girl. "Allow me, Miss . . ."

"Nikki," she said, blushing.

"Aah, Miss Nikki." Jackie bowed before her. "Allow me to introduce you to the *maestro* himself, the incomparable Lamont Dunne," he said with a grand sweep of his hand.

I'd had enough of Jackie for the time being, so I gave Lamont my regards and moved on.

"Hi kiddo," Pam said, sliding in beside me. "Glad you could stay."

"Good opening night?" I said.

"Best ever, I sold eleven. They went so quickly, Lamont's heading back to Kauai for more pieces. And J., thank you." She squeezed my hand. "You made this happen that day in Laguna."

"But not tonight," I said. "You did this."

"J., I need a favor," she said. "Lamont wants me to fly back with him to Kauai. We'll be back in four, five days. The weekend."

I briefly mulled over her revelation. "You and Lamont."

"I know, it seems sudden. But we've been talking on the phone a lot ever since La Jolla, nearly every day. We saw each other again when he flew out to meet Eugene." She smiled. "He's a good man. Long time since I've been with a man who had his own life, no demands on me."

We gazed upon a bleached-white South Pacific seashore.

"What's the favor?" I said. "You know I can't afford one of these things, even with the Baker discount—if there is one."

"Just keep Britt. Can you?"

"Of course. He's no trouble. We'll see you next weekend."

Our eyes met briefly again. "You all right?" she said.

"Fine."

Pam stood closer, as if to create more privacy between us. "You look exhausted, like you're somewhere else."

"I wanted to talk to you about something. I went up in the attic a few days ago."

"This is about Marielena."

I nodded. "I found some of her old things."

She sighed. "Oh boy. J., honey, I wish you wouldn't do this to yourself."

Pam and I never spoke of my mother anymore. By the time I'd turned eighteen and moved out of the Bakers' house, I was too tired of the whole damn topic of What Ever Happened to Marielena Shepard to even talk about it. It was like staying home sick from work one day each year, setting up on the living room couch and turning on the tube to find the same old episode of *Gilligan's Island* playing for the ten-thousandth time. Not this again. The castaways are never rescued. Marielena Shepard never returns. Shit happens. Gilligan's time would have been better spent romancing Ginger or Mary Ann instead of sweating an unlikely escape.

But Pam was not swayed by my lack of vision. Expecting me to continue the search unabated, she'd packed up a milk crate full of the lists and cross-references—the net result of ten months of prodigious effort—and trundled the stuff right up my walk on Porpoise Way. Pam felt a good spot to set up might be the kitchen table, but I'd pointed to the garbage cans out back. An epic screaming match followed. Of course, it was all my fault, but I never apologized. The subject was dropped for all time.

Until now.

"That private eye you hired to lift her prints," I said, "didn't he do some checking around town, see who she'd been doing accounting work for before she split?"

"Disappeared," Pam said. Still loyal to my mother.

"Disappeared. Right."

"He didn't find out much," she added.

"You remember if she ever worked for a company named Provencal Limited?"

"No," Pam said plainly, fiddling with a gold bracelet on her wrist. "No, I don't."

We stood in awkward silence again. "What was that detective's name again?" I asked her.

Pam hesitated before answering. "Hugh Gilman."

"Maybe I could look him up, see if—"

"He's been dead for ten years." She took my hand. "J., listen to me. We tried everything. I remember what this did to you. Let it go."

A sudden commotion arose in the front room of the gallery, several raised voices yammering at once.

"Just one more thing," I said.

"I've never been to Kauai," Pam said, trying to shift gears. "Have you?"

The noise in the front room grew louder. I could hear two men shouting over each other now. One of them was Eugene Bardo. The other guy was furious, growling like he was ready to fight.

I still had one more question for Pam. "Hey Pam. Have you ever heard of a development around town called Sea Pointe?"

"What?" Pam blinked at me as if stunned. "What . . . what do you mean?"

"Sea Pointe," I said again.

"Why do you want to know about Sea Pointe?" she said, her voice trembling.

"It's a public place and I'll go when I want to go!" Grog Baker shouted as he pushed past a furiously backpedaling Eugene Bardo and spotted Pam. Lamont Dunne swept in behind them but kept a safe distance from Grog.

"I'll call the police, Mr. Baker!" Bardo shouted.

Grog planted himself face-to-face with Pam. Jackie and the brunette crowded up close like school kids eager to see a playground tussle. The shouting died and for a few seconds, there was calm.

"What the hell are you doing?" Pam demanded of Grog.

The slender gallery owner stood wedged between his best saleswoman and her soon-to-be ex-husband. His freckled forehead had turned salmon pink in all the excitement.

Grog was in a black tee and a denim jacket, his massive shoulders straining against the seams. "Step aside, little man," he said, flicking Bardo away with a beefy forearm. "I just want to have a word with my wife."

"Are you all right?" Lamont asked Pam. Grog turned and glared murderously at Lamont, who swallowed hard and retreated a few steps.

Bardo wasn't backing down. "This is my establishment! I'll not stand for this kind of gate crashing!"

"It's okay," I said to Bardo. "Mr. Baker will be heading home with me in a minute. No trouble, I promise. Just leave us for now. One minute, I promise."

Bardo mulled my proposition. "All right," he said, tapping the face of his gold watch. "One minute, and he goes out. That's it." He shot a final look at Grog, whose eyes were on Pam, then turned and stalked away.

"Kauai, huh?" Grog said. "Britt told me everything. You hardly know the guy. Might I remind you, we're still a . . ."—his voice broke—"a family."

"That's it?" Pam said. "I can't go to Kauai because we're a family? Dear God, Greg Baker, is that the best you can do?"

"What about Britt?" Grog said. "You can't just leave him alone. You're his mother. Good mothers don't leave their children alone."

Grog looked at me dumbly, realizing what he'd just said.

"I *am* a good mother," Pam said.

"You're breaking up the family!" Grog shouted, stamping his work boot. "Not even divorced and you're already with another man." He scowled at Lamont. "Goddam it, Pam. You probably planned it this way."

"Ha!" Pam shrieked. "I've heard enough of this." Her eyes brimmed with tears. "You think this is about me hurting you?" She shook her head. "Well why not? That's my whole life. It's always about someone else." A tear started down her cheek.

"You're his mother," Grog said, "and you're still my wife."

"Stop it!" Pam cried. Her mascara began to puddle a muddy black beneath her eyes. "You have to do this on opening night, humiliate me this way?" She sniffled inelegantly. "I'm tired of financing your hare-brained schemes. I'm through"—she paused—"taking care of you."

"Come on, Pam," Grog said, softening, "don't say that. Vic and I got a good thing goin'. " He pulled out his wallet and unfolded what looked like a payroll check. "Forty-two-hundred in commissions." Still in love with his wife quite beyond reason.

Pam hung her head. "It's always the same. I'm not going to review our marriage in the middle of this gallery, in front of—"

"This crap?" Grog said, waving a hand at the gallery walls. "This somehow better?" He sized up Lamont. "What's it take now to sell a painting, Pam, a trip to Kauai?"

"Bastard," Pam said, quaking. She turned to me. "You want to know about Sea Pointe?"

"It's okay," I said, confused by her switch in topics. "We'll talk later."

"Tell J. about Sea Pointe on your way out," she said to Grog.

I was dumbfounded. "What about it?" I asked Grog. "Tell me, man."

Grog faced me but said nothing. He turned and looked at Lamont, then at an emotionless Jackie. I focused again on Grog's blank face, but from the edge of my peripheral vision I saw something astonishing: Jackie ever-so-slightly shook his head as if to tell Grog no.

Grog turned and blew out of the room.

"Grog, wait!" I called after him as Lamont moved in to console Pam.

"Not now!" Grog shouted over his shoulder.

I rushed up front. Bardo was standing at the door, still recovering from his earlier confrontation, when Grog approached. A handsome young man in thick biker boots, leather chaps and a neatly creased white tee—Bardo's companion, I guessed—stepped into the doorway, blocking Grog's path. "I'd like a word with you, mister," he said. "Now."

"Fuck off, fairy," Grog said, thumping the guy's chest hard with the butt of his palm and knocking him back onto a barstool next to the door.

"Grog," I called out to him as he climbed into his double-parked VW bus. But he gunned the engine, popped it into gear and roared off into the somnolent evening gray.

I fumbled for my car keys, watching the VW's exhaust fade like a ghost at first light. My mind leaped uncontrollably. What did the Bakers know about Sea Pointe, and why would Pam be hurt by its mere mention? What did Jackie have on Grog?

"Bad scene," Jackie said from the sidewalk behind me. "Gonna go chase him down?"

"I don't think he wants any company right now. Where's Pam?"

I peered in through the gallery's big window. The exodus Pam had predicted earlier had come to pass, as the front room was near empty. A cleanup man stooped to scrub a spill from a square of polished wood while two food servers scooped empty plastic cups and trash from a tall metal ashtray. More patrons scurried off into the night. Bardo righted the barstool near the door and peered into the street, not recognizing me.

"Lamont squired her out the back," Jackie said. "The Big Man looked pretty bent, eh? Back door was the way to go, for sure." He grinned. "I think self-preservation was at the top of old Lamont's list."

"And why should Lamont get his ass kicked?" I said. "He didn't create that situation. He's like me, Jack, totally in the dark." I glared at him. "Unlike some people I know."

"What's your problem?" he said as if calling me out.

"I saw how you looked at Grog," I said, still unsure of what I'd seen inside. I'd already asked Jackie once about Sea Pointe, the night I climbed up into the attic. He said he'd never heard of it. But Grog warned me that night in Oceanside not to trust Jackie.

For an instant, a hint of regret registered in the grip of his blue eyes. Then they went stone cold. "You don't know what you saw in there," he answered.

I stepped closer, as if to cut off his escape. "You're in it with him. Tell me."

"What is it with you, man?" It sounded like the beginning of a standard deception, and I didn't bite. "Well, I guess it comes with that job of yours."

"What's that?" I said, unable to resist his taunt.

He shook his head. "You just can't stay out of people's problems, let 'em work them out on their own, can you? Grog Baker's a joke. Not your worry. Why sweat it, bubba?"

"That's not it at all," I said, "and you haven't answered my question. What about you and Grog?"

The tall brunette named Nikki spilled onto the sidewalk behind us. "Right with you, doll," Jackie said to her. "What can you say about the man, J.?" he said. "He's a fucking loser. I got nothing to do with him."

I folded my arms. "I don't believe you."

"I'm gonna say this once, my friend," Jackie said. "Don't look back, it'll only fuck you up. You want to lose this case, go ahead."

"What's my mother got to do with the case?"

"Leave it alone. You want me to bring in Egan, you leave this shit about your mom alone."

I was enraged. "You're straight-arming me?" I said, poking a finger into his shirt. "You jive-ass piece of—"

"Back off! I'm not straight-arming you, I'm saving you from fucking up the whole thing. I'm trying to spare you the distraction. Look at you, man! You want to lose, go ahead, fall knee-deep into the Baker's shit with them, roll around in it for all I care. You want to win this case? Do you?"

I nodded.

"Then I'll help you. But stick with the plan, man!" He shook his head tiredly. "Let your poor mother's memory alone."

I stood back and regarded him with extreme caution, unable to tell whether he was acting in my best interest or manipulating me to suit his own designs. This was probably how my dependency clients saw me every day of the week. Great—another pin thrust deep into the side of my inflated self-image.

"You want your witness or don't you?" Jackie said, his swagger coming back.

"I'll back off," I said, "but you'd better deliver. Call it winning if you like, but this is coercion."

"Suit yourself," he said, sliding an arm around Nikki. "Think what you want, it's a free country."

"Gee, thanks for the permission."

He stopped, but didn't turn around. "Don't wait up for me tonight," Jackie called out. "And don't get any bright ideas. You do and I won't be around to bail you out."

"I don't need your kind of help," I said.

He stopped and turned, smiling joylessly. "Maybe not, but you owe me. On your word, pal. Don't forget it."

I drove slowly home along the coast road, my radio off, the front windows down so that I could listen to the surf. But the tide was high and the swell was nil, and I heard nothing but the efficient drone of the Jeep's engine. Flatness had descended like a biblical curse on the black, nocturnal sea.

Jackie had called my longest standing debt. I remembered the day we'd met, the day he'd found me in a maelstrom of raging water on the reef at Holy Rollers. All these years, the deal we'd struck that day on the beach had seemed like such a bargain to me. But I'd been mistaken. Headlights flashed in my rearview mirror and I saw my own wary eyes, framed in dark rings and leaden with the weight of my troubles.

The price had been heavy.

Seventeen

I spent Sunday morning in the Legal Project's offices, studying the psychologist's report submitted by the Danforths' hired gun. Jackie and the art-loving Nikki had stayed out all night, which, I suppose, spared us another confrontation. My disbelief at his audacious gambit still lingered, but there was too little time to do anything but prepare for trial. I pushed Marielena Shepard out of my mind completely.

My file was in decent order for trial by 2 P.M., my witness notes written out longhand on legal pads, the key passages in the social worker's and shrink's reports all but memorized. My stomach was empty, but it ached as if a phantom breakfast had gone undigested. Lunch seemed out of the question.

Bad nerves. All morning I'd felt sick and slightly disoriented. I popped two more non-aspirin painkillers, stuffed the Evidence Code into my briefcase and shut off the lights.

I needed corroboration that the Danforths made the trip to Washington in May, just after Sue Ellen gave birth. Bill Davenport was my only shot.

I drove up Fremont Avenue through an offensive stretch of cheap, boxy little houses that I suppose were somewhere in Alhambra, maybe South Pasadena. The blight receded as the highway slowly rose toward the foothills beneath Mount Wilson. I found Huntington Drive and headed east.

The afternoon was hot, but an ardent breeze had shaken off the smoggy funk. High clouds perched plump and yellow above the vast reaches of the inland valley. The neighborhood grew increasingly grand. I took my time driving, gazing at the deep lawns and stately trees, the classic stone figures blazing in the heat, the fountains and fluttering white butterflies over rows of tended roses. The street names I passed were self-consciously classy: Chelsea, Windsor, Shenandoah.

The Davenport's doorbell was a gorgeous waterfall of sound. A uniformed maid met me at the door. She was slight and very dark, probably Indian. I told her I was Phoebe's boyfriend, which, by now, qualified as a lie. I needed to speak to her father, to plan a surprise for her. Another fat one, but it got me in the door.

The maid led me down the marbled hall past an enormous vase filled with cut flowers. Bill Davenport was alone in his study, putting golf balls into a black plastic receptacle across the floor. He'd just stroked a ball that rolled straight into the cup and was promptly spit back at him. "Bingo!" he said.

I wanted to start off with a friendly handshake, but he kept a firm grip on the handle of his putter and looked at me as if he was contemplating smashing my skull with it.

"Hello, Mr. Davenport," I said amiably. "How's Phoebe?"

He was dressed in white golf slacks and a crimson polo shirt. The side of his craggy face was pink from the sun. He'd been out on the links this morning. On a color TV across the room, the Rams were losing to the Forty-Niners. A French window across from his desk afforded a pleasant view of flowerbeds, a flagstone patio and a kidney-shaped, black-bottom pool.

"What do you want?" he said without smiling. "She's not here."

"Actually, I came to see you." I saw no point in bothering with pleasantries that wouldn't work. "I wanted to ask you if you'd been back to Washington this year, for a political function in May. A formal ball, at the White House."

"Get out," he said.

"Pardon me?"

"Get out!" he shouted. His deceased wife's dog Muffins barked from another room, then appeared in the doorway—a little Maltese that Max would've eaten as an appetizer. I stood there dumbly, doubting my next move. The dog looked me over. Unimpressed, she turned and padded down the hallway and out of view.

Bill shook the putter's club head at me. "You come around here for my daughter, so smart and self-assured. Always letting me know you're in charge."

"Where are you getting this?" I said. "You never say boo to me."

"Well, look at you now, not so much in charge anymore, are you?"

"Look, I didn't come here to argue with you," I said.

"Wheels falling off the cart, eh?"

"Come again?" How could he know so quickly why I'd come?

"You shouldn't sleep with your clients, son. Better learn that before they disbar you."

Bill Davenport was far too sophisticated to take a hopped-up local news piece as gospel truth. He was out of line, but I was in his home, at his mercy. I sucked up my pride.

"Did you go to Washington last May?" I said.

Bill Davenport began to laugh. "This how you prepare your cases for trial, Counsel? Harassing an old lawyer whose daughter finally came to her senses and dropped you flat?"

"Dropped me flat? Did Phoebe . . ." No, I thought, struggling to stay loose. Don't rise to his bait. "That wasn't necessary," I said. "Whatever was said that night at the Biltmore, was said. I meant no harm to you. Phoebe's a good girl."

"What if I was in Washington in May?"

"A White House ball? I'm sure there were pictures taken."

He went behind his desk to a paper shredder and flipped the switch. "Would you like to send me a subpoena?"

"No thanks," I said. This felt like a waste of time.

"I happen to know that those are fine people you're tormenting, mister," he said. "That little tramp you call a client isn't fit to tie their shoes."

"Daddy!" Phoebe shouted from the hall door. "How can you do this to him?"

She wore a candy-striped leotard, white tights and leather high-tops. A red headband arrested the great flow of her blond curls, and her skin glistened as she caught her breath. I could hear a pounding dance beat echoing down the hallway now.

I was not sure how long she'd been standing in the door.

"It's all right, Pheebs," I said. "This was a bad idea. My fault."

She and her father glowered, silently at odds.

"Show it to him," she ordered her father. "Now."

He put down his putter and folded his arms across his chest. "What are you talking about?"

"You know. I was in the hall. I heard. Give it to him!"

"I will not!"

"Then I will," she said, moving behind his desk to the recessed, built-in bookshelves that covered the wall from floor to ceiling. She searched the contents until she located a thin black hardbound album the size and shape of a high school yearbook.

"Thank you," I said when Phoebe handed me the album, a handsome memento with embossed golden border and scrolled lettering on the cover that stated simply *"An Evening With the First Family."* Inside the first few pages was a write-up of the event, but the rest was photos and cutlines. It was a picture book.

I did not glimpse William Davenport's photo as I flipped through the pages, but I quickly located a picture of Kip and Kitty Danforth walking through a portico lined with military brass and government functionaries.

"I'll get this back to you, I promise," I said to Bill Davenport. He and Phoebe were still locked in a standoff.

"Silly girl," he said. "Just like your mother."

"Phoebe," I said, "I really appreciate—"

"Good-bye, J.," Phoebe said, firm but without anger. She did not look away from her father. "You can see yourself out."

"Looks like a little jam-boogie right up the middle might do the trick, mate," Jackie said, peering through the windshield at the milling crowd outside the courthouse. "I don't see any cameras anywhere."

"Me neither," I said.

Monday morning. I'd let Jackie drive me to court, a relief, I'd thought, not to have to negotiate the crush of cars pushing into the city myself.

"You know what you've gotta do, man, right?" I asked him.

He nodded, running the palms of his hands along the arc of the steering wheel like he was at the helm of a large paddlewheeler. "Aye-aye, Cap." His bronzed face was so calm it unsettled me.

We'd said very little about the trial on the commute to L.A., both knowing what had to be done, but choosing to plot our final courses in private. I couldn't rely on Sue Ellen Randall to sparkle as a witness, or hope that Boris Kousnetsov, Ty's lawyer, might shake off his cough-syrup stupor and become Clarence Darrow for a day. I had to tear great holes in the county's case, present a responsible, reasoned defense without exposing my client to too much damage, and supply Judge Foley with a factual and moral basis upon which he could base a decision to send Nathan home with his true parents.

Jackie's objective was simpler: he'd bring in Rosemary Egan.

Neither of us had really spoken since the night at Bardo's gallery. The bargain had been struck, and would be adhered to for practical reasons.

I looked up the wide cement steps leading up to the building, a gentle incline of maybe ten feet at the most—kid-friendly courthouse steps. I felt tired just the same.

"You sure you'll need her today?" he said. "Like, what if the trial goes until tomorrow?"

"Get Egan," I implored Jackie, leaning in through the open passenger window. "If we can't use her today, Foley will order her back. Just get her here."

"No worries," he said. "She's mine." The back tires chirped as he peeled out, alarming a small boy and his mother. Jerking the boy's arm like a leash, the woman wheeled and shot me a major stink-eye.

"Good morning," I said.

The woman scowled as if she knew I was to blame for letting Jackie loose on the highway. Madam, I thought, you don't know the half of it.

I stared up at the green tinted windows facing out from the courthouse waiting areas, each floor buzzing with the new day, hundreds of squirming silhouettes promising a thousand of the same old problems. The morning air was muggy and rank with ozone, the sunlight dulled by a sheet of scalloped clouds. Just down the hill the big trucks wailed like nose-diving planes along the Long Beach freeway. Beyond East L.A., the faint outline of the San Gabriel Mountains floated in a dusty haze.

The time had come to slide by Holly Dupree. I buttoned my jacket and started up the steps with my head down, intentionally tagging behind a large Asian family in hopes of going unnoticed. An old man with no front teeth glared at me for standing so close to his granddaughter. I heard someone call out my name and looked up just in time to see Holly Dupree and her camera crew rushing me.

"Mr. Shepard, a word?"

Her outfit was bold red, her massive hairdo as shiny and hard as a conquistador's battle helmet. "Do you intend to withdraw from the case," she paused, "due to your involvement with Ms. Randall?"

"Gee, Holly, I don't think a hug from a client is news, but thank you for asking and have a nice day." I slipped through the double doors before she could pose her next question.

Last night I'd reread the rules of professional conduct on permissive and mandatory withdrawal, and even the new one on sex with clients. No violations, not even close. No way was I pulling out of this case without a fight.

When I came into the courtroom, people looked at me as if I'd just returned from a stay in prison. Respectful, keeping their distance, a little voyeuristic. I saw perhaps a dozen faces of court personnel who normally didn't belong in here. Ken Jorgensen I recognized.

"Nice day, J.," he said with an evil grin.

"You got something to say, say it," I told him.

He hitched up his massive trousers and squared off with me. "You're going down today, big guy."

"You're calling me a big guy?" I set down my briefcase and surveyed his corpulence. "What does that make you, Godzilla?"

"Always the wiseass, Shepard."

"Sorry, Ken. I can see you're irritable. Those first dozen donuts giving you gas?"

He just stood there like a punching dummy. "You're going to crash and burn, and I'm going to enjoy the show."

I smiled icily until he walked away.

Foley barreled through his calendar by 10:15 without a break. "Miss McWhirter," he said to Belinda, "be ready to call your first witness ASAP. People," he said, surveying the room, "we're going to do as much of the Randall trial as we can today. We'll stop for lunch at around one-thirty, half an hour. Then we'll go as late as we can this afternoon. With luck, we might even finish. If we don't, we'll wrap up tomorrow after calendar call."

All this was highly unusual. I supposed the case, with its attendant high media profile, had been a cause of dread for Foley these last few weeks. He wanted the matter decided now.

"Oh, God," Belinda McWhirter said to herself. "Shelly?" She turned to Chilcott. "Did the worker check in yet?"

I felt a rolling sensation in my belly, so I gingerly got up, walked out of the courtroom and down the hall to the men's room. I found an empty toilet stall, flipped the door latch, knelt and tossed my breakfast. This I still do before every significant trial.

I was splashing my face with cold water when a man tapped me on the back. "I'm not done yet," I said without turning around. I reached for the paper towel dispenser and saw Ty Randall's reflection in the wide mirrors just as he swung to hit me.

"Mister lover boy!" he shouted. His fist landed just above my right eye, and I felt that familiar, cold numbness pass down my spine as I fell over the sink. Ty Randall stepped up and cocked his fist to hit me again. "You're gonna pay for what you did!"

His fist came down hard but wild, grazing my chin and collarbone. The faucet handle stabbed at my kidney. My feet were off the floor, but I grabbed his hand before he could recoil and twisted it until his elbow was vulnerable. He thrashed to break loose but I straightened up, twisting his arm harder and raising my free arm to strike behind his elbow. I had a good fifty pounds on him and easily pinned him against the dispenser.

"Cool it, Ty!"

"Go to hell!" he shouted. His left hand was free, and he made a fist again.

"Hit me again, I'll break your arm," I said, panting. My head felt tingly and hot now where he'd punched me. He stopped struggling and wiped the loose hair off his forehead. He was crying. I let go of his arm and checked my eyebrow. No blood, but a nice bump was already rising.

An elderly black man holding a toddler by the hand came in. Both of them eyed the two of us suspiciously. Ty's shirttail spilled over his belt, and his navy tie hung crookedly. He looked like a gas-station attendant who'd just been jumped by a customer. My jacket was water-spotted down the lapels. I wiped the hair from my eyes.

"C'mon," the man told the child as he turned to go, frowning at Ty and me.

"Nothing happened between your wife and me," I said to Ty, wiping my face with a paper towel. His eyes were hidden beneath his bangs. "One of your old neighbors screamed at her, called her a name. Did a nice job making her cry. I comforted her."

"I seen what you did!"

"Oh, get a clue," I said. "Those news people want to see the Danforths keep your baby. You start buying into their bullshit, you'll really be in trouble." I straightened my tie in the mirror and went past him to the door.

"I believe you," he said, "oh, yes indeedy." Smiling at me now. "All my wife talks about the last two weeks is Mister Shepard this, Mister Shepard that, gets up at five-thirty this morning to start gettin' ready, makin' herself look nice for court. Christ almighty!" His face narrowed into a scowl. "Bullshit, huh? Well I'll just buy into who-ever's bullshit I choose to! Yours ain't no better than theirs."

I had heard enough. "Suit yourself." I pushed through the door as if I resented it being there.

Sue Ellen Randall was just rounding the corner near the phones when she spotted me. She wore a blue skirt down past her knees and a ruffled white blouse under a white sweater. Looped under one of her arms was a puffy carry bag made out of blue material adorned with tic-tac-toe patterns.

"Mr. Shepard," she said running to me. She saw the lump above my eye. "Did Ty do that?"

"We had a talk," I said. I took her arm and turned her back toward Foley's court. "Trial is about to begin. What's in the bag?"

"Diapers, a bottle, a few new toys I got for Nathan. Pacifier." I said nothing. We reached the courtroom door and stopped. "Thought I'd need his things," she said, patting the bag.

"Right." My stomach gurgled. I pictured a cadre of tiny gremlins doing laps in there, banking hard along the walls like cyclists locked in a velodrome.

"I believe in you," she said.

The gallery was filled to capacity. Ken Jorgensen, Gerry Humbert and several of the usual attorneys took up the back row. A few people I didn't recognize sat in front of them. The Danforths were there, Kitty talking on her cell phone and Kip nervously adjusting his cuff links. Nelson Gilbride was up at counsel table, chatting with Belinda and Lily Elmore, Nathan's court-appointed lawyer. Their backs were turned to Sue Ellen and me. Shelly Chilcott was on her phone with a call blinking on her other line. The bailiff leaned back in his chair at his small desk, reading *The Sporting News*. Boris Kousnetsov sat at counsel table, poring over the social worker's report, as if one more pass might yield a new insight. Poor Boris. He looked like death this morning in his brown worsted suit. Foley had not yet resumed the bench.

"Hello J.," Boris said. He nodded to Sue Ellen. "Where is the father? Is he out of jail?"

"In the hallway," I said.

Boris hurried off to locate Ty Randall. I opened my briefcase and began setting out my notes and legal pads.

"Well, Mr. Shepard, good day to you," Gilbride said with his usual transparent charm. He was attired in a black three-piece suit with a muted burgundy tie. The gold pocket-watch chain dangled gracefully from his vest pocket.

Gilbride handed me a blue-backed motion to disqualify me as Sue Ellen's counsel, then looked over the still-visible water spots on my jacket. "Just come in from the beach?" he quipped.

I inspected his somber duds the way one might eye the smoldering aftermath of a head-on collision. "Who died?" I said. "You help carry the casket?" Sue Ellen fought to suppress a smile.

"Very good," he said. "You're quite the humorist."

"You've got to be kidding with this thing," I told him, flipping through his motion. "Since when do you give a damn about what kind of representation my client is getting? My duty to provide competent representation is owed to Sue Ellen Randall. You have no standing to even assert such a motion."

Gilbride didn't answer, but I knew why he'd made the motion to disqualify me. He was thinking a step ahead, as usual. Of course he didn't care about Sue Ellen receiving adequate counsel. He'd seen some of the talent hanging around this place. Lonely Boris, confusing one child with another. Ken, back there in the gallery, presently applying spit to what looked like a breakfast burrito stain on his tie. Lily Elmore, the small-fry specialist who sometimes didn't even bother to interview her clients. Not that I was the best lawyer in the building, but Sue Ellen could have done a lot worse for herself.

What if I was disqualified? The trial would have to be continued to give the lawyer who replaced me time to get up to speed. The Danforths would hang on to Nathan several more weeks, which, with bonding an issue, would heighten their advantage.

Judge Foley came out and listened to argument on the subject of Gilbride's motion. "This young man's conduct has shown that his judgment is impaired," Gilbride lectured the courtroom, "and his lack of ethics is a matter of professional concern. He's taken advantage of his position as trusted counselor, taken . . ."

The words pounded hammerlike at the back of my skull. I'd never be able to show my face in this courtroom again if I got the hook in this case.

Gilbride's salvo was followed by a few obligatory words of support from Belinda. I stood up when Foley nodded at me, but Lily Elmore had begun to speak. "Your Honor?" she said tentatively.

Foley shut his eyes. "Yes, Miss Elmore."

Lily looked around at the silent courtroom. The court reporter's fingers floated just above her black keys, poised at the ready. "I'd just like to say that I think . . ."—suddenly, Lily seemed to forget what she was saying—"well, it's just . . . disgusting."

Foley drummed his fingers on the open court file. "Thank you, Miss Elmore," he said. "Let's hear from Mr. Shepard. You understand, Mr. Shepard, that technically it's unfair for me to decide on this motion without you having had a chance to respond in writing. Of course, I'd have to put over the trial." Gilbride and Belinda exchanged glances to my left. "But I'll rule on it today if you'll waive time and respond orally now. I can tell you," he said, holding up his copy of the motion, "it doesn't look like a motion you'd need to file a written response on."

He was saying he'd shoot down Gilbride's latest motion now if I could give him the ammunition.

"I'll argue it now," I said.

I kept it brief, starting first with an explanation of what had actually happened that day in front of Arturo's house, then with a discussion of the rules of professional conduct regarding withdrawal as counsel. I made the point that the question of bonding made it important to settle the case by trial now, not later.

"You've heard a lot of bad things about my client these past few weeks," I told Foley. "I'm ready to defend her. It's only fair that you let me fight for her now."

"Ms. Randall," Foley said, "are you comfortable with your representation?"

"I am," she said. "Mr. Shepard's worked real hard. He's been my only friend through all this." She glanced at Ty. "And he's been a perfect gentleman."

Ty had stopped picking dirt from under his fingernails and looked up at me, trying to stare me down.

"Motion denied," Foley said to Gilbride, who was still standing beside Belinda at counsel table. "Mr. Shepard stays."

What a relief. Now I could get after Gilbride.

"Uh, Your Honor?" I said. "Thank you, but shouldn't Mr. Gilbride be going?"

"Your Honor," Gilbride said, "my client, Kitty Danforth, will be testifying soon, and I just feel—"

"Feel your way to the back of the courtroom, Mr. Gilbride," Foley said.

I smirked at Gilbride as he passed by me and through the partitions. When I faced the bench again, Foley was glaring. "Listen, gentlemen," he said, "we have a lot of ground to cover in a short time. I will not tolerate any petty bickering from either of you."

"Yes, Your Honor," Gilbride and I said in chorus like a pair of obedient schoolboys.

"I've heard your positions on this case twice by now," Foley said, looking at the lawyers at counsel table, "so I assume you won't be making opening arguments." No one objected. "Good. Ten minutes, people. I need to do something for this headache. Miss McWhirter, you may begin with your case when we come back."

Ken Jorgensen slapped his fat hands like a trained seal behind us after Foley departed from the bench. "Get ready for the main event!"

"Oh my," Sue Ellen said breathlessly. "I feel . . . funny."

I knew the feeling. "You're committed," I told her. "Get used to it."

Eighteen

Belinda called Doreen Williams, the county caseworker, as her first witness. Williams was a stoutly built woman in her mid-forties, with a large, square jaw, a short, brown boy's haircut and a single curl on her forehead. Her navy, knee-length dress was as formless as a shower curtain and her leather boots squeaked as she walked. Were she a man, I'd have typecast her as an ass-kicking bully. The sound of those boots coming down the front walk had surely struck terror in the hearts of more than a few parents.

Her testimony was highly predictable and almost entirely scripted from her report. But she was an important witness for the county because she set the scene for Foley, taking him through the history of the adoption of Nathan Randall, first with the Pontrellis and later with the Danforths. She was also quite fond of numbers and did a nice job tallying all the moneys that both hopeful couples had lost doing business with Ty and Sue Ellen Randall. Close to twenty grand. By focusing Foley on the big dollar figures, Doreen Williams was purposely diverting his attention from the routine nature of the actual transactions, trying to make him see Sue Ellen and Ty as heartless thieves.

I wasted no time going back over the money issues on cross, starting by having Doreen Williams restate the big totals.

"My," I said, "that's a lot of money."

"You're darn right it is," Doreen said. "Least you admit it." Her wisecrack drew a flurry of muffled laughs from the gallery.

I smiled. "Now, let's go over these numbers in terms of expenses, nice and slowly."

For twenty minutes I broke down the impressive totals she'd quoted into essentials such as rent, grocery bills, prenatal care. "All of these expenses were agreed to by the parties, weren't they?" I asked.

"I don't know," the social worker said.

"And yet, your report makes it sound like we're dealing with stolen money. But you don't know."

"Objection!" Belinda shouted. "Argumentative!"

"Move on, Mr. Shepard," Foley said.

When I was done tallying, only a hundred and forty-seven dollars were left unaccounted for. "And did you find out what happened to that hundred and forty-seven dollars, Miss Williams?"

She shook her head slightly. "No."

"Did Ty Randall blow it at the track? Did Sue Ellen spend it on a fancy haircut? Have you tracked down her stylist yet to question her about the kind of tipper Sue Ellen was—that is, back then when she was flush all that extra cash?"

"Objection! He's badgering," Belinda said.

"Withdrawn," I said. "A hundred and forty-seven bucks, Miss Williams. I agree with you. This case does involve fraud. We just disagree on who committed it." I thanked her as if I never wanted to see her again.

We broke early for our half-hour lunch. I was too keyed up to think about eating and stayed in the waiting area just outside. When the bailiff unlocked the door again, twenty of us crowded in at the same time, dead silent.

"Well hello," I heard a sultry voice say from behind. Lois Nettleson, the adoption broker, smiled as if she were glad to see me.

Belinda McWhirter turned just in time to see me nod affably toward Lois. "You're insane, J.," she muttered.

Foley resumed and Lois Nettleson stepped forth from the anteroom like royalty arriving at the palace steps. She took her oath to tell the truth with perfect posture, her right hand raised like a delicate fan. Ken Jorgensen and Gerry Humbert murmured their approval from the gallery, and the bailiff's chair squeaked as he strained for a clandestine perve. Her outfit was gorgeous: a teal dress-suit with thin black trim that expertly set off her carefully coifed raven hair. Her earlobes sparkled with round diamonds the size of my shirt buttons. As she settled into her seat, she and I exchanged fleeting glances of acknowledgment.

I imagined what Jackie might have whispered in my ear had he been here now to observe that furtive exchange. Bone patrol, mate. You can dig it, she can dig it. Dial in quick.

Lois's testimony was slow and thorough, Belinda asking short, pointed questions to establish a clear chronology of events. Lois seemed perfectly at ease explaining why she believed the Randalls had never intended to go through with the adoption. "The Danforths were so giving. Anything Sue Ellen and Ty needed was theirs—whatever they asked for." She paused to consider Sue Ellen, whose face had been calm and rather stoic since trial began. "Then the money stopped when the baby went home with the Danforths. Suddenly, the Randalls wanted out. They wanted more of the good life that—"

"Objection, this is speculation," I said.

"Sustained," Foley said, but he shot me a hard look, as if I'd been rude to interrupt his personal guest.

So far, the county was scoring a direct hit with Lois Nettleson. I knew her words were far more damaging than those of Doreen Williams. Because Lois was an adoption broker by trade and had presided over many previous baby transactions, she could render her opinion and impressions based on her previous experience. Foley was transfixed—either with Lois's take on the case, or simply with her refined femininity, I could not tell. During testimony, his usual practice was to hunker down and scribble quick notes as the witness prattled on, stealing only the briefest glance now and again to gauge demeanor. But with Lois on the stand, his pen was idle and his eyes stayed locked on her. Near the end of her direct, while she was describing Sue Ellen's reluctance to sign the consent papers as another sure sign of her intent to commit fraud, Lois briefly coughed. Foley abruptly stopped the proceedings, inquiring into her health and dispatching his clerks to fetch her water with the conviction of a general sending men into battle.

Lois daintily sipped her water from a clear plastic cup. Foley then gave Lily Elmore the floor. I was hoping Lily would take up a little time with Lois—Jackie was still not back with Egan—but she had only a handful of inane questions that Belinda had already asked in slightly different forms. Foley was not pleased.

"Cumulative, Miss Elmore," he objected on his own initiative. Five minutes later, it was my turn.

Lois Nettleson sat calmly in the witness chair. Unshakeable.

I had to try to discredit her motives and expose her bias. She'd long ago made up her mind which of the two couples she sided with in this case.

I started by getting Lois to admit that there was nothing illegal about Sue Ellen's refusal to consent in writing to the adoption before the child was six months old. She quickly neutralized my point. "Still an indication to me, Mr. Shepard," Lois said coolly. "Birth parents who truly want to go through with adoptions ordinarily consent early."

"Did you make sure Sue Ellen knew what her options were? Did you answer all her questions?"

"I took great care to see that your client was happy and well taken care of." She acknowledged Sue Ellen. "I wanted to see everyone succeed in this adoption."

"Who paid your fees in this adoption, Ms. Nettleson?" I said, pacing behind counsel table.

"Corwin and Kitty Danforth." She knew exactly where I was going and seemed not the least bit perturbed.

"And who represented both couples legally in the adoption?"

"Nelson Gilbride." She exchanged nods with Gilbride.

"But aren't the couple giving up a baby your clients too?" I said. "Even if, like the Randalls, they aren't the ones paying your bills?"

"I know what you're getting at." She sat up straighter, mildly offended now. "I treated both couples with the same high level of commitment and professionalism. I'm in the people business. If I can't get both sides, both families working together, then my services are not of much use." As her voice trailed off, Lois expertly made eye contact with Foley to add a dash of sincerity. The gallery murmured.

"You didn't give your fee back to the Danforths, did you?" I said.

"Objection," Belinda said. "This is totally irrelevant."

"What's the relevance, Counsel?" Foley asked.

"Bias, Your Honor," I said.

"Overruled." Belinda crumpled back into her chair. "But get to the point soon, Mr. Shepard," Foley implored me. Then he apologetically instructed Lois to answer the question.

I thought of Foley's red Porsche, imagined him and Lois scrunched into the Recaro seats, blazing down some freeway at a less-than-rebellious fifty-five miles an hour.

"No, I did not refund my fee," Lois said.

"Of course not," I said as if an important point had just dawned on me. "They still have Nathan. Why should you have to give them their money back? I see how this works. If the Danforths keep the baby, you keep your fee."

"Objection!" Lily Elmore shouted, but both Foley and Lois ignored her.

"It doesn't work that way," Lois said. "I'm a professional, not a black marketeer. These aren't used cars. They're human lives."

"Come on, Ms. Nettleson. You come here and testify just the way the Danforths and Mr. Gilbride would want you to, do everything you can to help them keep Nathan, and you're telling me you're a people person, that this has nothing to do with you keeping your fee?"

"That's exactly what I'm saying." Lois glared at me as if I'd insulted her deeply. Then she made a giant mistake: she kept talking.

One thing I tell every witness of mine before they testify is to never, ever offer free information. Listen to the question. Answer the question. Then shut the hell up. But Lois Nettleson wanted to show me—and everyone else—that I was wrong about her.

"I'm not here to protect a fee," she said. "I'm sorry for your client, but this is how things happened. Sue Ellen and Ty never intended to give up Nathan. They cheated the Danforths out of thousands of dollars. I'm not just saying this now. We, we all saw the signs way before."

"You *all* saw signs?" I folded my arms and turned toward the gallery. "Who saw the signs? You? The Danforths? Mr. Gilbride?"

She had not yet realized her mistake. "All of us," she said.

"You said you saw signs way before. You mean, before Nathan was born?"

"Your Honor, might I say a word?" Gilbride said. He was standing now, his hands held out like a pauper.

"I'm cross-examining a witness!" I said.

"Mr. Gilbride, be seated," Foley said. "Don't interrupt again." Gilbride shook his head in disgust, which drew a glare from Foley. "No more warnings," Foley added. "Monetary sanctions come next."

"These signs of bad things to come, Ms. Nettleson," I said, "was this before Nathan was born?"

"Yes."

"How did you know that you and the Danforths and Mr. Gilbride all felt the same way, saw signs of fraud?"

"We discussed it," she said.

"When was the first time you discussed it?"

"The first day we all met in Nelson's office. The day we decided on the open adoption."

"What concerns were raised about the Randalls that day?"

Lois paused to think. "Corwin and Kitty thought they were greedy, asking a lot of questions about how much allowance for food and rent, whether Corwin would pay for cable TV in their new place. Ty even hinted to Corwin that he wanted him to try to get Ty a job with his company, as if, if Corwin didn't, there might be a problem."

I imagined Ty Randall making just such a clumsy come-on. But was it an indication of fraudulent intent?

"I didn't really buy all the questions Sue Ellen kept asking about the terms of the open adoption," Lois said. "It was like she was trying to prove to us how interested she was in holding up her end of the deal."

"When in fact she really wasn't going to give up Nathan," I said. Sue Ellen closed her eyes, quietly fuming.

"That's right."

"What about Mr. Gilbride?"

Lois looked searchingly at Gilbride.

"Ms. Nettleson," I said, "please answer."

"He didn't like the looks of them," she said. "Thought they looked . . . too desperate to be trusted."

"He told you the Randalls couldn't be trusted?"

"Objection, calls for hearsay," Belinda said.

Foley leaned forward. "Overruled, I want to hear this."

"He predicted they'd do something like this," Lois said. "He also reminded us how hard it is to find suitable birth mothers."

"Suitable—hah!" I cried. "What Mr. Gilbride meant by a 'suitable' mother was a mother who had a *white* baby to give up, didn't he?"

"That's just the reality today," she conceded.

I bent over and whispered to Sue Ellen. "Did you know they were meeting behind your back?"

"No idea."

I paced the floor again. "Now here you are, Ms. Nettleson, the first day this adoption gets off the ground, and you, Mr. Gilbride and the Danforths have all got serious misgivings about the Randalls. And yet, no one says anything to them. They weren't invited to this little meeting, were they?"

"They'd already left," Lois answered.

"But they were your clients, just like the Danforths. And they were Nelson Gilbride's clients"—I leveled a disdainful stare at Gilbride—"just like the Danforths. True?"

"True."

"Your clients, Gilbride's clients. You'd think they'd deserve the same treatment, the same level of input and support the Danforths got. And yet all of you met privately and talked behind their backs, without their knowledge."

"We were concerned."

"Concerned?" I said. "Look at these two people, Ms. Nettleson." I stood between Sue Ellen and Ty and placed my hands on each of their shoulders. "Look at their faces. Do they look concerned enough for you?"

"Objection, argumentative," Belinda said.

"Withdrawn," I said. But I was rolling. "Let me put it differently, Ms. Nettleson. We've heard a lot about the dishonest way Ty and

Sue Ellen supposedly behaved. But don't you think it was dishonest for you, Mr. Gilbride and the Danforths to secretly confide in each other that you didn't trust them?"

"It's . . . not that simple," she said slowly.

"No, it isn't. If you told them how you really felt, they might have backed out. They might have said 'these people have got us all wrong, they think we're criminals, we better rethink our dealings with them.' They might, Ms. Nettleson, have given their white baby up to someone else, isn't that right?"

Lois Nettleson was deflated by the poor turn her testimony had taken. "It's possible."

"Oh, I think it's darned likely," I said. "Then again, if you had the courage to tell them the truth, they might have been surprised, probably a little hurt. They might have assured all of you that they were on the level. They might have been more outwardly appreciative of the Danforths, more realistic about how tough it would be to eventually give up Nathan."

"Objection," Belinda said. "No question pending."

I ignored the objection, and Foley let me. "Had you told the truth, this adoption might have had a fighting chance. But you didn't tell them the whole truth, did you?"

Lois Nettleson looked ready to stand up and walk out. "Not in so many words."

"Nelson Gilbride didn't tell them the truth."

"Objection!" Belinda and Lily shouted.

"The Danforths didn't tell them the truth."

"Objection, Your Honor!" Belinda said again, but Foley dismissed her with a shake of his head and kept watching me.

I went back to my chair at counsel table. "Don't feel bad, Ms. Nettleson," I said. "You told the truth today, and I appreciate it. I only wish you could have done it sooner."

Belinda got up after Lois left and went outside to find her expert witness. Two thirty-five. Where the hell was Jackie? Dr. James was next up, so I laid out a legal pad of questions I'd written out for his testimony. Kitty Danforth would be last to take the stand for the county; she'd be their star witness and this case's emotional favorite. I'd fared well with my cross on Lois, but I knew I'd been lucky. Kitty Danforth would be better prepared by Gilbride and more careful. I needed Rosemary Egan.

Foley called a five minute recess, but I stayed in my chair, rereading the expert's report Belinda had supplied me with a mere three days ago. It's sadly typical to receive critical information this way, at the very last minute. The Welfare and Institutions Code says that in dependency, the rules of discovery are relaxed. The ever-popular best interest of the child mantra dictates this area of practice as well. But in reality a parent's right to due process is often squashed. Lawyers who come into these courts from the outside are unfailingly dumbfounded by the Mickey Mouse way that evidence is handled.

Last night, sitting up late in bed, I'd highlighted certain portions of the report; but now, I was having difficulty remembering why I'd done so.

I stared at the top of the page. Wilfred Scott James. What a name, I thought, like a character from Jane Austen, perhaps a well-meaning yet sniveling bachelor from a neighboring hamlet. But Dr. James's *curriculum vitae* was impressive. Yale undergrad. Doctorate in child psychology from Stanford. Adjunct professor there. Author of *Ties that Bind—Bonding and the Psychological Health of the Adolescent—* which, of course, I hadn't had a chance to locate, let alone read— and a wealth of articles in professional journals. That's the problem with doing a no-time-waiver trial; at times you can't help but operate by the seat of your pants.

Dr. James was a slight man of about sixty-five. He had Gilbride's sparse, snow-white hair, but his face was hollow and curiously lacking in color and his lidded eyes were narrow and set deep in their sockets. He had the look of a man who'd spent the balance of his years reading and doing research in closed-off rooms, breathing stale air. When he pushed through the partitions and ambled forth, he prodded the carpet with an ebony cane, his dull black wingtips squeaking. The gallery grew very quiet, as if the headmaster had returned to the classroom.

Normally I might have waived the necessity for Belinda to spend time establishing Wilfred James as an expert, but Kitty Danforth was testifying next and Jackie was still nowhere to be found. Belinda lurched page by page through the esteemed doctor's lengthy *vitae*, finding time to cast an occasional sideways dirty look my way as she went. Come on, Jackie, I silently prayed.

Dr. James said just what we'd all expected him to say. He aptly described the concept of bonding, starting first with the characteristics of mammals and their young, then narrowing the scope to humankind. He described the misguided perception and belief infants hold, that is, that they are at the center of the universe. He talked about the natural growth of a child's personal boundaries, the infant's expanding sense of self, the important role that interdependence between parent and child plays in the healthy development of the young adult. At one point Boris rocked slowly forward, eyes closed. Sue Ellen had to reach over beneath the table and goose his knee or he'd have probably fallen asleep. Judge Foley sat very still as he listened, gazing down at his blotter, pen in hand. He didn't seem to be taking many notes.

Belinda finished strongly with the doctor, extracting from him an opinion I'd known had been coming now for fifty minutes. It was like watching a slow train snake into the station from way down the tracks.

"And what effect would his removal from the Danforths have on little Nathan?" Belinda asked at last.

"A quite serious adverse effect, I'm afraid," Dr. James said gravely. "He has spent every formative moment of his young life with Corwin and Kitty Danforth . . ."

"Yeah, and their nanny," I whispered to Sue Ellen.

". . . bonded to them," he continued. "To the child, they are his true parents, the only family he knows. To lose them now, the upset," he said, "would be immeasurable."

Lily Elmore expended twenty more minutes, extracting not a thing that was new, with her cross on Dr. James until Foley grew agitated and pressured her to stop. "Ten minute recess, people," he said, gazing at the metal clock on the far wall. Inching up on four o'clock. "We're making good time. Mr. Shepard, your witness in ten minutes."

"Where's you're friend?" Sue Ellen asked me. Her nerves looked shot.

"He's on his way," I said with utterly false conviction.

The gallery was still full when we resumed. Jimmy Nicholsen, Belinda's boss, had come in during the break with a few gray-suited men who looked like county honchos. They'd slipped behind Shelly Chilcott's work area and pulled up three chairs to watch. The Danforths and Gilbride must have made their share of calls to County Counsel's higher-ups this past couple of weeks. Shelly looked nervous as hell, sorting files for the next day's calendar and smiling politely as Nicholsen and his guests whispered amongst themselves.

Dr. James's weakness was in the hypothetical nature of his testimony. Nathan was pre-verbal; he could not be interviewed as to his wishes, nor could he attest to any discomfort or difficulty in assimilation that a move from one family to another would cause him. The concept of bonding, with infants at least, was built entirely upon theory and conjecture. And one thing I knew about theories from my college days was that professors loved to compare and contrast them. It was what they did to fill their hours-long lectures.

"Doctor," I said to the expert, "do you know how dependency court cases are ultimately resolved for the parents of children who are taken from their custody?"

"No, I don't, Counselor," he said amiably.

"Well, the death penalty for parents who lose their kid is termination of their parental rights. But that doesn't happen very often. You see, the system is designed to repair families, not to tear them apart, so parents get a long time—eighteen months—to fix their problems, go to counseling, visit the child, or live with the child again under a social worker's and the court's supervision. It's called reunification."

"Objection, relevance," Belinda said.

"Overruled, but keep it moving, Mr. Shepard," Foley warned me.

"I know something about reunification rules, Counselor," the witness said to me.

"The reason I'm telling you about this, about reunification, is because I firmly believe that Nathan Randall is going to be reunified with his natural parents, the Randalls. Now I can't say when that will happen—today, a month from now, six months from now, but it will happen."

"Is there a question, or is Mr. Shepard going straight to his closing argument?" Belinda said. Jimmy Nicholsen's presence had increased her nasty quotient.

"I'll ask my question," I assured the judge. "Doctor, I want you to assume for a moment that this judge"—I motioned to Foley—"is going to one day send Nathan home to Sue Ellen and Ty Randall."

"All right," he said.

"Now, that being the case, Nathan inevitably going home to the Randalls, what would be best for Nathan? With all you know about bonding, would it be better for Nathan if he were to be reunited with the Randalls sooner, so he can immediately start bonding with them, or would it be better to wait six months, a year, a year and a half?"

Dr. James looked stymied. He knew he was stuck, at least on the facts I'd given him. How could he say it would be better to wait?

"Wouldn't Nathan's bond to the Danforths only grow stronger over time?" I said, circling in. "Wouldn't a breakup down the road be that much more shattering for him?"

"Well," he said, "at this age, if the child's going to go one day to new parents, hmm . . ." He was hedging.

"Objection, overbroad, and calls for speculation," Belinda offered.

"Overruled."

"Sooner or later, Doctor? If Nathan is one day going home to the Randalls, should it be sooner or later?"

Dr. James sighed. "I would have to say sooner."

A big murmur went up from the gallery. Gilbride was red-faced, his eyes bugging. "You quack!" Kitty Danforth cried. "Nelson, what the hell is going on?"

"That's enough, Mrs. Danforth," Foley said.

Kitty Danforth momentarily glared at Foley then thought better of challenging him and nodded in compliance. Gilbride whispered something to her in an attempt to calm her down, with little visible effect.

"Mr. Shepard, continue," Foley told me.

I checked my watch: 4:25. Kitty Danforth was fuming, Gilbride tittering into her ear. Jackie was still out there somewhere—had he made his connection? Even without him, I thought this was the perfect time to have Kitty Danforth take the stand. Upset witnesses tend to testify more impulsively, and truthfully.

"Thank you, Your Honor," I said. "Nothing further."

Belinda's redirect was brief. "Doctor, let's try another hypothetical," she said. "Let's say that the judge orders Nathan to be with the Randalls. But then let's say the Randalls screw up, try to sell him again and get caught."

"Objection," I said. "This is more pointed innuendo than a hypothetical question."

Foley frowned. "Get to the point, Miss McWhirter."

"Yes, Your Honor." She smirked at me. "Okay, Doctor, Mr. Shepard wants us to stick closer to reality. We can do that. Doctor, let's say Nathan goes back to the Randalls today, but they wind up going to jail on the criminal charges that are currently pending against them."

"Ouch," I whispered to Sue Ellen. Belinda was as sharp as she'd ever been today.

"So Nathan gets handed back to the Danforths again," Belinda said. "Wouldn't the back-and-forth handoffs of this poor child be disorienting?"

Dr. James perked up at the chance to redeem himself. "Oh, absolutely!"

"Damaging?"

"Clearly. The child would have to reestablish his bond with the Danforths, but having had it broken once before with them and once with the Randalls, he might lack the requisite sense of confidence in himself, that is, in his inherent lovability. He believes he's been rejected and may find it difficult to reach out all over again. He could develop into an emotionally isolated young boy, insecure with his place in the world and incapable of trusting those closest to him." The doctor looked right at me. "One cannot underestimate the deleterious effect that rejection from a parent, even if it's only a perceived rejection, can have on a child."

I closed my eyes and saw my house on Porpoise Way, the door that I always kept closed at the end of the hallway. Outside the master bedroom, an empty, windburned sundeck. A rusted planer in the garage. A pile of junk in the attic, blanketed in dust.

"Mr. Shepard?" I heard Foley's voice say.

"Yes, Your Honor?"

"I asked if you had any re-cross."

I'd apparently blanked. The doctor tugged at his lapels and sat up, readjusting his posture. "No, thank you, Your Honor," I said. I'd heard enough.

Belinda thanked the doctor, as did Foley, and called her final witness. Kitty Danforth regarded none of us as she strode determinedly between the bailiff's desk and counsel table to take her oath. She wore a tight, tailored coatdress, notch-collared with three buttons, the jacket and skirt a soft lavender hue that somehow struck me as motherly. Matching low-heeled pumps. Impeccable. Gilbride had probably supervised the choices himself.

For the next half hour, Belinda and Kitty pounded home the image of Sue Ellen and Ty, the greedy, cruelly fertile young couple, exploiting the emotions and pocketbooks of the childless Danforths.

"We gave them everything they asked for," Kitty said, "but they kept wanting more."

She stopped to dab away the tears, but had no handkerchief. Where was that box of tissues, the one that was always stationed on the witness stand? Gilbride grinned behind me when Foley offered his own handkerchief to Kitty. Son of a bitch Gilbride—he'd probably stolen the Kleenex during the last recess.

I felt a tap on my shoulder. It was Shelly Chilcott. "You have a visitor," she whispered.

Behind her work station, in the back of the courtroom next to Jimmy Nicholsen and the county suits, stood Jackie. When we saw each other, he smiled slyly, put his hand over his breastbone, and coolly but emphatically shot me a thumbs-up sign.

Jimmy Nicholsen sat a few feet to Jackie's left, arms folded, studying Jackie's tight jeans, snakeskin cowboy boots and permanent tan as if he were viewing a freak. Jackie took notice and stared back menacingly until Nicholsen turned away.

"All right," I whispered to Sue Ellen, who had also seen Jackie. "Time to rock 'n' roll."

Lily Elmore took a deeply sympathetic turn in her questioning of Kitty Danforth, emphasizing the love that had developed between the Danforths and Nathan. "Whatever happens here," Kitty said, tearful again, "Corwin and I know in our hearts that we are Nathan's true parents, his real parents." She stared hard at Sue Ellen. "I'll always be his mother."

Sue Ellen sat rigid in the chair next to mine, her fists balled tightly in her lap. "Don't let her get to you," I said. "We know the truth."

I looked over my shoulder at Jackie. He was slumped casually along the back, his right knee bent, a boot heel riding up the wall. Like saving my ass at trial was a routine part of his day. Would Rosemary Egan give me enough to convince Foley?

It was time to find out.

Nineteen

We pushed into the interview room without speaking and closed the door. "You brought Egan?" I asked Jackie. He nodded. "She's here?"

He buffed his fingernails on his shirt. "You need me, I won't let you down," he said. "Don't forget that. I delivered for you, man."

"Good. Bring her here. I've only got five minutes to talk to her before Foley reconvenes."

Jackie hustled back out to the waiting area, leaving me alone. I sat back and closed my eyes, angling for a moment of relaxation. I pictured a cool green wave spilling over a lonely sandbar, its cresting hook blown back in a rooster-tail plume by a warm desert offshore. An old trick, but it failed to work this time, for all my imagination could muster was Belinda jumping to her feet to object, a grumbling Foley, Ty Randall swinging on me. I thought about the county's witnesses so far, wondered if I was winning this case. I closed my eyes, tired of thinking.

Someone rapped on the door; it was Nelson Gilbride, alone.

"Sorry, this room's occupied," I said.

"A moment of your time is all I ask," he said.

"Can't spare it now, Mr. Gilbride." I started to close the door.

"Hold it!" he said, wedging himself into the doorjamb. "You remember our conversation the first day we met, don't you?" I didn't respond. "We can still work this out, Mr. Shepard."

"Not on your life. My client wants her son back."

"Talk to her."

"Already have. Tell your clients they can keep their money. It's not going to happen."

"You're losing this trial. Sue Ellen Randall is a thief. The judge saw what she did to spirit away the other child right out from under our noses. She'll turn around and peddle Nathan to another unsuspecting couple and wind up in jail."

"I don't agree with your assessment," I said. "Excuse me, but I'm busy."

Gilbride stamped and half-started to speak a few times, apparently flabbergasted at the quick death his proposal had met. "What are you saying?" he demanded. "Have you even thought—"

"About the best interest of the child?" I said. Gilbride said nothing. "Yes, I have. Know what? It gave me a headache, not unlike the one you're giving me now."

"You're a foolish young man!" he said.

I started to close the door on him. "Better than being a foolish old man."

"You've got a lot of nerve! Huh-ho." His laugh sounded false. "I'll take care of you! Tomorrow morning I'm going to pay a visit to the presiding judge down here."

"You aren't going to do a damn thing, Mr. Gilbride," I said. I was in no mood to hear his hollow threats. He'd burned Sue Ellen in the adoption, savaged me on TV with Holly Dupree. "The Randalls were also your clients in the adoption. You never told them you were against them, never let them know you were working behind their backs. You deceived them. The State Bar would call that an act of moral turpitude."

"Oh would they?"

"I checked," I said, bluffing. "You had one hell of a conflict of interest going there, too."

"Both couples waived any conflicts of interest when they signed on with me. It's in the retainer agreement."

"Oh, I forgot," I said. "You studied for the bar exam sometime around the turn of the century." His face reddened. "The rules of ethics have changed a bit over the years, Mr. Gilbride. You have to disclose any actual conflict that arises when it arises, in writing. Gotta get your client's consent to keep working for them, in writing."

"Fine, so there's no problem," he said, his eyes darting.

"You never told Ty and Sue Ellen that you were working against them because you didn't trust them. Problem is, how could they waive that conflict when they didn't even know it existed?" He stared back, temporarily mute. "The Randalls go to the Bar with a transcript of Lois Nettleson's testimony, I don't know . . ." I said. "I think they have a legitimate complaint. Have you got an associate who can fill in on your cases while you're suspended?"

"Ho, you think you can . . ." He jabbed a finger at me, off stride.

"You're spanked," I said. "Tell you what, though. You stop trying to give me the official hose job every time I'm not looking, I'll gladly leave well enough alone."

Jackie pushed in behind Gilbride. "Howzit, chief?" he said to me.

"Otherwise we'll both go down swinging," I said to Gilbride, "guaranteed. What do you say?"

"You've got one hell of a nerve," Gilbride said.

"Say, what I miss?" Jackie said, his face lighting up.

"Nothing, Jack," I said. "He was just leaving. Give it some thought, sir," I told Gilbride, opening the door.

"Don't put yourself ahead of this case," Gilbride said with some finality. "I came to you with that little boy in mind. He's all I'm thinking of."

Jackie studied Gilbride's face closely. "Hey, man," he said, as if deeply disturbed, "wait just a minute!"

"Who, who is this?" Gilbride said, backing away from Jackie's eye-popping scrutiny.

"Thinking of little boys? Aw, Christ!" Jackie shouted. "Knew it!" He turned to me. "He's one of those molesters you represent, J., isn't he?"

I shrugged. Jackie had seen Gilbride on TV with Holly. I was pretty sure he recognized him now, but the panic on Gilbride's face was a sweet sight to behold.

"Whaa? Leave me alone!" Gilbride said.

People were filing by the door to head back into court, and several slowed to peer in at the scene we were making. "Molester, really? Which one, the old guy?" someone commented from the hallway. Gilbride looked positively stricken.

"Chester the Molester, eh?" Jackie said, bearing down.

"You'd better go," I told Gilbride.

"Gladly!" Gilbride said. "Let me out."

I told Jackie to step aside, and Gilbride slithered out the door, his face drained of color. "I'm fuckin' watching you, Chess," Jackie told him as he passed.

"Leave him alone," I said. Gilbride was a little old for Jackie's scabrous brand of humor. I didn't need a heart attack victim on my conscience.

He turned back to me when Gilbride was gone. "Hey man, how come the guy in the cop uniform kept giving me the stink-eye in the courtroom?"

"Don't be offended. The proceedings are confidential."

"You mean I can't watch you? Can't we say I'm your assistant?"

"You're not a lawyer. I could try to get you in, I guess, but there's no room and I've got no time."

"Well, that sucks."

It was true, but I had no spare time to squabble over admitting him as a spectator. "Sorry. Nothing personal, just the rules. So where's the nurse?"

"Ladies room. She'll be right here. Said it couldn't wait." He shrugged.

The bailiff poked his head into the room. "Mr. Shepard, judge is ready," he said.

I closed the door again. Damn. My key rebuttal witness and I'd have to take a run at her cold on the witness stand. "Tell me, man," I said, "is she ready?"

Jackie smiled like a jungle cat. I was lucky to have him here, by my side, bringing in a key witness at the end of a trial. My best friend, he was. I felt a renewed sense of self-confidence, one I knew I entirely owed to his presence, his aura. His sense of stoke.

"Hang on to your hat," he said, "cause she's going to blow them away."

I eased back into my chair at counsel table, Foley regarding me with a slight nod. Kitty Danforth had retaken the witness stand. None of the gallery watchers had left, nor had Jimmy Nicholsen and his cronies budged from their corner behind Shelly.

"Try to be more prompt, Mr. Shepard," Foley said. The clock read ten-of-five.

"Thank you, Your Honor."

"You may cross-examine the witness."

I stood up. "It's late, Mrs. Danforth," I said. "I don't have many questions for you."

"Good," she said with a nonplussed smile, setting off a ripple of laughter from the gallery.

"But the questions I do have may be rather upsetting to you, so try to bear with me. I just want to get at the reason this adoption fell apart. Let's talk about what happened at Woodside Hospital when Nathan was born. Let's talk about what you did before he was born."

She shifted in her chair, checking on Foley. Instead of taking notes, he was staring right at her.

"You remember the day Nathan was born?" I said.

"Of course."

"May sixth of this year, correct?"

"That's right."

"That was an important date for my client," I said, standing behind Sue Ellen. "One I'm sure she'll not soon forget. You know why that is, Mrs. Danforth?"

"Well, she did give birth," she offered. "Though to her it was just a business transaction." Kitty waited for the titter to rise from the gallery, but it never came.

"The childbirth didn't go so well, did it?" I asked her.

She studied the oversized diamond on her left ring finger. "No."

"She had to have her labor induced."

"Yes, she did."

"Right," I said. "And she was in a lot of pain."

She tilted her head as if to show me she was unimpressed by my queries. "I wouldn't know about that."

"Oh, I think you would," I said. "Isn't it true that you were the one who insisted that Doctor Weinstein induce Sue Ellen's labor on the sixth?"

"No, that is not true."

"Isn't it also true that you were the one who denied Sue Ellen an anesthetic, even though she was half out of her mind with pain?"

"Absolutely not." She paused and regarded Sue Ellen. "She was . . . exaggerating. The girl's always had a flair for the dramatic."

"Oh, I see." I nodded slowly. "So, you knew what she was feeling?"

"I didn't say that."

"You're right," I conceded, "you didn't say that. You didn't know the pain she was having giving birth to that child, even though she was screaming most of the time. You were guessing that she was exaggerating, maybe even faking it."

"Wouldn't be the first time she's faked something," she said. This time she got a few chuckles from the gallery.

"Or were you guessing at what she was feeling based on your own personal experience?" I asked.

"What . . . do you mean by that?" Kitty said, instantly wounded.

"You had a painful experience giving birth once yourself, didn't you? A few years ago." Kitty Danforth blinked and looked away. When she turned back to face me, her eyes were full of tears.

"Objection!" Belinda said. "What's the relevance of this?"

"Bias, Your Honor," I said.

"Overruled."

"Your Honor!" Gilbride had jumped up from the gallery. "I must object to this line of questioning! It's highly unfair for—"

"Life is unfair, Mr. Gilbride," Foley said. "I've made my ruling. Sanctions come next if you wish to interrupt any further." He turned to the witness. "Please answer the question."

She pursed her lips and composed herself. "I'd been in labor before, yes."

"His name was Andrew," I said. "He was stillborn." A murmur rippled through the courtroom. "You had complications giving birth, a lot of pain, but you couldn't have an epidural for some reason. They thought it might make matters worse. Isn't that how it happened?"

She regarded me with a quizzical expression. "I don't know why you're asking about this."

"You've never gotten over it, have you? The loss of Andrew."

"You don't know the first thing about me," she said, wiping away a tear.

"Objection!" Belinda shouted. She could see Kitty Danforth was in trouble. "How is this relevant to anything, Your Honor?" Foley paused to think.

"I'll show the relevance," I told the judge. "I promise."

Foley overruled the objection. "Just keep it moving," he directed me.

"You forced Sue Ellen to have the baby on the sixth of May, didn't you?" I said.

Kitty Danforth sat up straighter. "I did not!"

"She wanted you there, Nathan's new mommy, to take him from her arms and hold him. You had to be at the hospital as part of the open adoption agreement, didn't you?"

"It was no real trouble."

"Oh yes it was," I said. "You had somewhere to be that weekend, a formal party at the White House, to be exact. You spent the whole week getting ready."

"That's not true."

"You told Doctor Weinstein to induce Sue Ellen's labor on Monday because you had things to do. Your dress, shoes, hair, a tuxedo for your husband. Tell us what you wore to the ball, Mrs. Danforth. Did the president take special notice that night?"

"I don't need to listen to this!" she snapped. She eyed Gilbride in the gallery. "Do something, Nelson."

"Your Honor," Gilbride said, "on behalf of my client I must object to this spurious line of questioning! It's demeaning! Unnecessary! Totally irrelevant!" Corwin Danforth stood up next to Gilbride as if to show support.

I started to talk, but Foley waved me off. "Five hundred dollars, Counselor," he told Gilbride. "See my clerk before you leave today. And one more word," he warned, "and I will have the bailiff remove you."

Gilbride swallowed and sat down. Foley gazed on Kitty Danforth, then nodded at me. "Next question."

"That ball was more important to you than the welfare of Sue Ellen Randall, wasn't it?" I said.

Kitty folded her arms. "I don't know what you're talking about."

"Saturday, May eleven," I said. "You and your husband dined with the First Lady in the State Dining Room. The president dined in the Blue Room. Seemed like they both mingled a lot, though. What manners." I took Bill Davenport's picture album out of my briefcase. "You were there, weren't you?"

She eyed the book in my hand and began to shake, but recovered and composed herself. "Yes, we were there," she said proudly. "What of it? I've done nothing wrong." Her eyes searched for her husband's approval. The onlookers rumbled behind me. Corwin Danforth sighed and stared at the carpet beneath his feet.

Judge Foley rubbed his temples as if to signal the arrival of an even sharper migraine as Kitty left the stand. The courtroom went still. Foley surveyed the jam of onlookers with a look of contempt, as if they were buzzards to be shooed away.

Belinda rested the county's case. Foley asked me how many defense witnesses I planned on calling. Two, I told him.

"I wanted to finish this trial today, people," Foley said in a gravelly voice, "but it's late, and the county won't pay my clerk and the court reporter overtime. Tomorrow, eight-thirty, we will proceed directly after I call the calendar." He ordered everyone back and fled the bench.

Sue Ellen and Ty left together, which I found to be encouraging. Perhaps he could protect her now that he was out on bail. I needed a break from my client.

I sat in the back seat of my Jeep wagon and interviewed Rosemary Egan as Jackie drove her home. Everything Jackie promised she would say, she said. The White House ball, Kitty's miscarriage, Sue Ellen's hurried due date and excruciating labor pains. We dropped her off with a promise to pick her up at 7:30 the next morning, and made the long trek home with few words beyond a comment or two about what tape to play next in the stereo.

Jane's Addiction. Tom Petty. Nirvana. The miles rolled on, the music cranking twice as fast as the river of red lights before us.

Things were still not right between Jackie and me. I no longer cared about my years-old promise to him, and he knew it. When this thing was over, I would find my mother.

I let him borrow the car for the night. He had a hot one lined up with Nikki, the art student he'd hooked up with at Bardo's gallery. She was cooking for two at her place. Jackie dropped me at the curb. I gave him a ten spot for a bottle of wine.

"We bail at six-thirty tomorrow," I told him through the car window.

"Dawn patrol," he said without looking. His wraparound shades were still parked on his head. "I'm on it."

I watched Jackie blow down Porpoise Way, the taillights flashing as he hung a right on Ocean and cut out of view. I must have walked right past the white BMW parked in front of my walk without even registering its presence, for when I saw Phoebe's silhouette on my porch, I turned and inspected the street again.

"Surprise," she said.

It was dark in front of my house. I never bother with the porch light on weeknights because I always enter through the alley and backyard. Perhaps the cover of night was a good thing, though, because when I looked at her, I could hardly see. I could only feel, and when she touched my face, my whole world felt warm.

We came inside. The living room was nearest, and I thought about taking her over to the couch, but before I could even flip on a light, she kissed me. Then I kissed her back. Eventually, we made our way into the room.

I brushed a row of soft gold behind her ear. "I don't even know why I'm here," she said. "When I saw you in my father's study, saw you stand up to him like that . . ." She nuzzled against my shoulder. "Knew I had to see you again."

I remembered the night of Jackie's impromptu bash. Had he stayed in Africa an extra couple of weeks, this was how my evening with Phoebe might have ended. But then, nothing else would have been the same. Without Jackie, I would not have found Dr. Weinstein's nurse in time. I would never have taken the stand against Bill Davenport that had delivered his daughter to me now.

Yet so much more had happened in these early days of fall. Something fundamental about me had changed. This was our moment, yet it felt like the past.

Phoebe pulled back. "What's wrong? You're holding me like you're somewhere else. What did . . ." She studied my face. "Have you met someone else?"

"Hey, wait, you broke up with me," I said. "Remember?"

She let go of me. "That was unfair. I'm sorry. God, I'm such an idiot."

"That's not it anyway." I let go of her and walked to the front window. Phoebe followed me. I stared through the glass at nothing. "I . . . don't know."

"I'm sorry about what I said that night at the party," Phoebe said.

"No, you were right," I said. "You had me pegged."

She took my hand. "I want to be with you, J. I . . . need you."

"Pheebs," I said. "I don't know. It's just . . . I'm sorry."

Phoebe started to cry, and I held her for a time, so tightly I almost wasn't breathing. I knew that I loved her, but it was different somehow, not what I'd expected.

"I'll miss you," she said. "I know I will."

"Then call me. I'm still your friend."

Outside, Max let out a bark that let me know he didn't appreciate going without his dinner tonight. "Oh Christ," I said, "what time is it?"

Phoebe brightened. "You got a dog?" she said. "Can I meet him?"

I smiled and kissed her forehead. "Are you insured?"

When I called Rosemary Egan as my first witness the next morning, Gilbride had only to observe the looks of astonishment on Corwin and Kitty Danforth's faces to know he had to do something, even risk being thrown out of Foley's courtroom, to block her testimony.

"Uh, Your Honor," he said, "I don't mean to interrupt, but would it be possible to put this matter over until another day?"

Sure, I thought, to give him enough time to approach the witness and either buy her silence or scare her off.

"You see," Gilbride said, "my clients have a commitment later this morning, a medical appointment for the baby, and—"

"The witness is ready to testify, Your Honor," I said. "Mr. Gilbride has no business—"

"Calm down, Mr. Shepard." Foley was looking at Gilbride. "No sir, you heard me yesterday, we will finish this trial now. And you will remain silent during the proceedings or you will really need to have your checkbook handy." Gilbride shrank back onto his bench, shaking his head.

Rosemary Egan moved with the low center of gravity of a weightlifter. Her features were coarse, but her skin was fair and her blue eyes were inviting and kind. She wore a pea-green sweater over a yellow, high-necked blouse and a matching knee-length pleated skirt. Her shoes were flat-soled, the orthopedic kind that nurses wear, the patent leather polished white many times over, but dull just the same. She sported no makeup, her graying hair pulled back and braided into a bun. I guessed her to be around sixty. She could have passed for an off-duty Irish Catholic nun, I thought—very plain, but serious. When she stood to take her oath, her back was slightly stooped as if the years of hoisting invalids from their beds had taken a toll on her lower vertebrae.

I took a final glance at my notes from Kitty Danforth's testimony. Sue Ellen smiled benignly. "God bless her," she whispered.

"Let's see what she can tell us," I said. My stomach churned on cue. I pulled out my chair and stood again.

Foley sat up and nodded to me. "Proceed."

I began with some simple questions to get my witness talking comfortably, which she did without hesitation. "How long have you been a nurse, Ms. Egan?" I asked at the end of the background questioning.

"Oh, let's see, forty, forty-one years."

"A long time," I said. "And how long have you been with Dr. Weinstein?"

"Ten years, give or take a month."

"So you were in his full-time employ the last several years?" She agreed. I turned and faced the gallery. "Do you recognize the woman in the front row of the spectator gallery, Ms. Egan?"

"Yes, yes I do," she said slowly. "Kitty Danforth. That's her husband, next to her." She studied Gilbride momentarily. "And that man, next to Mr. Danforth, I've seen him too. Can't quite place him, though." Gilbride must have looked insulted, because Egan visibly tried harder to place him. "I know!" she said. "No . . . hmm," she muttered, doubtful again. "Are you the man who came to the children's ward last Christmas dressed as Santa?" she said to Gilbride.

Those in the gallery laughed. "Oh, I'm so sorry," Rosemary Egan said, realizing she'd goofed.

Gilbride stared at the floor, arms crossed. "Go on, Mr. Shepard," Foley said.

"Were you the nurse who attended the birth of Kitty Danforth's child, Andrew, about two years ago?"

"Objection, relevance," Lily Elmore said.

Foley raised his eyebrows as if impressed that Lily could posit a viable legal objection. "Overruled."

"Yes, yes I was," nurse Egan said. "So sad. Poor baby Andy."

"What do you remember?"

"I'll never forget that day. We were equally concerned about mother and child. Poor Andy was stillborn. So sad." She shook her head.

Behind me, Kitty Danforth blew her nose into a hankie.

"Did Mrs. Danforth suffer certain complications?" I asked.

"Objec—" Gilbride started to say, then caught himself.

"Mr. Gilbride, I'm warning you!" Foley said.

"I'll object, Your Honor," Belinda said. "This is doctor-patient privileged information." She was right, and Foley sustained the objection.

"Let's talk about the birth of Sue Ellen Randall's child, Nathan," I said. "You attended that childbirth too, May sixth, correct?" Rosemary Egan agreed. "Tell me, were there any complications attendant to that childbirth?"

"Same objection," Belinda said. "This is privileged information. It's unethical for this witness to come in here and divulge personal, medical secrets in this way. It's wrong."

"Your Honor," I said, "the doctor-patient privilege in the birth of Nathan Randall is between my client and the doctor. It has nothing to do with Mrs. Danforth. The Evidence Code says the holder of the doctor-patient privilege is the patient. That's my client." I looked at Sue Ellen. "On my client's behalf, I waive that privilege."

This time I was right.

"Overruled," Foley said. "You may answer the question, Ms. Egan."

"There were complications."

"What, in your estimation, brought on those complications?"

"Objection!" Belinda was up again. "The question calls for an expert opinion and this witness is not an expert."

"Forty-one years as a nurse, Your Honor." I held out my palms. "I'm only asking her what she observed."

"Then ask it that way!" Foley said. He turned to the witness. "What did you observe when you attended Nathan's birth, madam?"

"Well," she said, "Mrs. Randall had her labor induced on the sixth of May. It seemed to cause a reaction in her."

"What kind of reaction?" I asked.

"She didn't dilate right away. When the contractions started, she screamed. I don't remember her exact words, just that it hurt, it hurt terribly. She was beside herself."

"Did you have any idea what was wrong?"

"No." Egan looked to be deep in reflection. "Sue Ellen was so upset the whole day. She was certain her due date was a week later, around the middle of May. Mrs. Danforth and Dr. Weinstein worked on her a lot that morning, insisting she was wrong. I could tell she wasn't convinced."

"Why was Mrs. Danforth so adamant about Sue Ellen giving birth on the sixth of May?"

"She told me—"

"Objection, hearsay," Belinda cried.

"No," Foley said, "this is proper rebuttal of Mrs. Danforth's testimony. And I want to hear it. Overruled."

Rosemary Egan nodded to acknowledge Foley's wishes. "She told me they'd been invited to the White House, to a big party of some kind. No, a ball, she said it was a ball. They were invited by the president of the United States. 'Of the United States,' she told me, as if I didn't know what 'president' she was talking about." Egan tried for a little eye contact with Foley, but he resisted.

"She went out of her way to make a point with you about that?" I asked.

"Oh yes." Egan looked at the gallery and the Danforths. "She said it like it was nothing, just another lovely evening for people who were used to lovely evenings. But I could tell she was very proud."

"Was Sue Ellen present when Kitty Danforth said these things about the White House ball?"

She shook her head adamantly. "Oh, no. Mrs. Danforth even told me not to say a word to the girl."

"Why not?"

"Well, she didn't want to upset her, of course."

"Of course," I said. "Did she say why they were invited?"

"Her husband"—she nodded at Kip Danforth. "He was some kind of mucky-muck with the Republicans. Gave a lot of money to the right people during the last election." She paused and eyed the Danforths.

"Did she say anything else?"

Rosemary Egan's face was wrought with concentration. "She said they'd earned their spot on the dance floor, and no stupid country girl was going to stop the music."

I picked up her cue. "So she got Sue Ellen to believe the baby was late and should be delivered on the sixth."

"Yes," Egan said.

"Even though the party wasn't until Saturday, the eleventh?"

"She said her dress cost eight thousand dollars, but it needed fitting and tailoring. That was going to take at least a day, maybe two." She blinked back her disbelief. "Eight thousand dollars for a dress that didn't even fit."

"What else?" I said.

"Her shoes weren't the right ones. Husband's tuxedo had problems of some kind, I don't know what. And she wanted to go a few days early to see the sights. I'm originally from Baltimore. We talked about the cherry blossoms in spring, the time of year."

I waited a few seconds to let the testimony register with Foley. "So," I said, "she couldn't be tied up at the hospital if she was going to make this wonderful party?"

Egan smiled. "You can't be two places at once."

"Regarding the terrible pain Sue Ellen experienced the day she gave birth, how did Mrs. Danforth respond?"

"I told you Sue Ellen was upset," she said, "and she was very upset about the pain, too. She wanted medication. Begged for it. In my experience, an epidural would've done the trick."

"Why didn't she get one?"

Egan looked at the gallery. "Mrs. Danforth wouldn't allow it."

"You mean she wouldn't pay for it?"

"She said the girl was being 'dramatic.' Said Sue Ellen had spent enough of their money already. Talked to Dr. Weinstein about it, too. He directed us to discuss the advantages of natural childbirth without medication if Sue Ellen asked again. Which she did, about every ten minutes, she was in such agony. I finally called the anesthesiologist myself and gave the order." Choking back the emotion. "Didn't care if they fired me."

"Did it help?" I asked.

She rolled her eyes. "She never got it in time. Had Nathan while we were waiting. Screamed for twenty minutes solid. I still get the chills thinking about it."

I let those last words sink in slowly on Foley before I spoke. "Kitty Danforth didn't like Sue Ellen Randall, did she?" I said.

"Objection," Belinda said. "Irrelevant. Calls for speculation."

"I'm just asking for Ms. Egan's impressions based on her perceptions," I told the judge.

"Overruled. You may answer," Foley instructed the witness.

"It was like this," Egan said, "she liked her, but she didn't like her. She liked Sue Ellen fine to her face, but behind her back she could hardly stand the girl."

"Are you saying she deliberately created false impressions in Sue Ellen to get her to give up her baby?"

Egan folded her hands in front of her as if she was tired of stating the obvious. "How would you feel if the new mother of the child you were bringing into the world—your child—cared more about a party than she did about you?"

"Thank you. No further questions."

Belinda stood and straightened the hem of her tailored suit. "Ms. Egan, you weren't privy to the terms of the adoption agreement between the Danforths and the Randalls, were you?"

"No, no I wasn't," Egan admitted.

"So, you have no idea of how much financial support the Danforths had already given to Sue Ellen Randall before Nathan was born, do you?"

"No."

"You don't know whether Sue Ellen had taken unfair advantage of the Danforth's generosity, before then?"

Rosemary Egan lowered her gaze. "No, I don't."

"Now let's say for argument's sake that Sue Ellen did take advantage of the Danforths, money-wise. Let's say the Danforths and their lawyer were worried that Sue Ellen was using them for their money, with no intention of actually consenting to the adoption. Under these circumstances, do you think it would be fair for Mrs. Danforth to be suspicious when Sue Ellen began demanding an expensive pain medication?"

"The girl was truly suffering, Miss. I was there."

"But if Kitty Danforth had reason to believe Sue Ellen was a fraud . . ."

"I follow your meaning," Egan said. "If that were the case, I could see why they'd look at the need for one. But that doesn't mean the girl didn't need—"

"Thank you, Ms. Egan, you've answered my question," Belinda said. "Now, you testified about what happened May the sixth, about Mrs. Danforth and the doctor's insistence on inducing Sue Ellen Randall's labor. Ms. Egan, if Dr. Weinstein was wrong about Sue Ellen's due date, wouldn't there be some risk to the child's health, if labor was induced early?"

"Most certainly. Any number of—"

"Thank you, Ms. Egan. Now, you were there, a trained nurse who'd seen thousands of childbirths. Tell us, Ms. Egan, wasn't Nathan born perfectly healthy and happy?"

"Well, yes, but his mother—"

"He wasn't underweight?" Rosemary Egan shook her head no. "Had no breathing problems? Vital signs were good?"

"That's right," Egan said, "but I don't think the doctor was right to induce labor and risk—"

"You're not a doctor are you, Ms. Egan?" Belinda said.

"Objection, argumentative," I said.

"Overruled."

"No, I'm not a doctor," Egan said slowly.

"And yet, here you are, contradicting the opinion of the doctor you worked for, even though the child was born in perfect health." Belinda frowned. "Does Dr. Weinstein even know you're here?"

"Objection, what's the relevance?" I asked Foley.

"Sustained."

Belinda paused to look at some notes on the table. "How long did you say you'd worked for Dr. Weinstein?"

"Ten years. No, ten and a half. Until this July."

"What happened in July?"

"I retired," Egan said, looking straight at Foley.

"Retired, huh?" Belinda paced behind counsel table. "You're sure the doctor didn't fire you?" Rosemary Egan blushed.

"Objection!" I shouted.

"Withdrawn," Belinda said, gliding back to her seat. "I have nothing more for this witness."

The witness was excused. The bailiff stretched and arched his back in his swivel chair, clawing at the ceiling. Shelly Chilcott propped her chin on a foot-high stack of tomorrow's files on her desk. I saw Jimmy Nicholsen grin secretively among his cohorts as if he were pleased with Belinda's expedient work on cross. Foley's jaded countenance seemed set in stone.

"What's next?" Sue Ellen whispered to me.

I nodded in the direction of the empty witness stand.

Twenty

Sue Ellen Randall told her story well on direct, having obsessed for months, by now, over the many mishandled details of the adoption. What the Danforths, Lois Nettleson and the social worker had seen as a cold calculation on Sue Ellen's part began, instead, to present as a deep reluctance to give up Nathan in the very first place. Following the county's case, her words brought the adoption breakdown their witnesses described into much sharper focus. As I listened, a shift occurred inside me. I began to believe in her.

"So why did you even enter into the adoption, if you didn't want to give up Nathan?" I asked.

Sue Ellen brushed her hair behind her ear. "We were so poor, Mr. Shepard. Still are. Ty was out of work. His prospects weren't lookin' so great. I knew the adoption would help us at least make ends meet."

"Who's idea was it to give up the baby?"

"It was ours." She regarded Ty with forgiving eyes. "My husband mighta brought it up first, but the truth is, we both made the decision."

"When you agreed to give your child to the Danforths, did you at the same time privately plan to take your baby back?"

"Oh no, I did not," she said. She surveyed the faces staring at her from around the courtroom. "You think I'd want to go through all this for money? I'd have to be insane, and no sir, I am not insane."

"I still don't know for sure why you went through with it," I said as if puzzled. I thought back on the first hearing we'd had in this case, when Sue Ellen talked of having continuous contact with Nathan even after the adoption, how strange the notion had sounded to me then. "There had to be something more," I said.

"There was." Her voice trembled. "It was supposed to be an open adoption. We were gonna be part of the family. Exchange pictures. Visit him. Aunt Sue Ellen and Uncle Ty."

"But it didn't happen that way?"

Tears shot down her cheeks. "No," she said.

"Was that your fault?"

She started to answer, but held up. "Yeah, I think it was, Mr. Shepard." She bit her lip to keep from crying.

I wasn't sure where she was going. "How was it your fault?"

"Because of who I am," she said. She looked at Ty, whose face and eyes were red like hers, then studied the faces of those in the gallery, Jimmy Nicholsen and his cronies, the attorneys at counsel table. Shelly Chilcott, Foley's clerk, the bailiff. No one moved. "You all look at me like you can see right through me. You think you know me. White trash. Welfare bums. Think that, because we got no money, we must be no good, lazy, dishonest people. White trash. Well, I can't help that." She looked up at Foley. "It's like you said before, Your Honor, life's not fair. And I can't help it if you believe them instead of me because they're rich and I'm poor. All I can do is tell the truth."

"Tell the truth about the adoption," I said. "Did you ever really give it a chance?"

Her wide eyes found the Danforths in the gallery. "I shoulda known an open adoption with them and us would never work out. We were fooling ourselves." She sat up straighter. "But we never intended any of this to happen this way."

"But what about the money they spent?" I asked.

"I'm going to pay it back, every last penny. It'll take a long time, but I will, I swear." She sighed audibly and regarded Foley. "I know it's no good sayin' this now."

Kitty Danforth's face was tear streaked but taut.

"Why is that?"

"Because I want my baby," she said, "and I know he's the only thing they want, not their money back. It's an impossible situation for both of us." She stopped to wipe her eyes. "I know it'll break their hearts, losin' Nathan, but I know I made a mistake givin' him up. I want my baby back," she said resolutely, as Kitty Danforth's lip trembled. "I want him back."

"No more questions," I said with a nod to Sue Ellen.

Belinda paced the length of counsel table until she was directly in front of the witness stand. "Five months you were with the Danforths," she said. "Five months of having them support you, pay your bills, buy you things."

"Yes."

"Sixteen thousand dollars worth of support, perks and goodies during that time." Belinda paced. "That's pretty good."

"They were very generous."

"Now tell me, how much money did you and your husband make the year before you met the Danforths, ten thousand, twenty thousand, thirty thousand dollars?"

"Ty was outta work a lot last year," Sue Ellen said. "I guess if you count AFDC and the money he picked up doin' odd jobs, a few pies I sold, wheat harvest in Kansas . . . twelve, maybe thirteen thousand dollars."

"Gee," Belinda said, "that's not much compared to fifteen thousand in five months. And you didn't even have to work."

"Objection, argumentative," I said.

Foley stared at Belinda. "Sustained."

"And now you get your baby back," Belinda said.

"Miss McWhirter . . ." Foley said.

"Quite a sweet deal, Miss Randall."

"That's enough!" Foley yelled, Belinda smugly gliding to her chair as if the judge wasn't even in the building.

Foley took another recess. When he came back, he limited our closing arguments to ten minutes each. Lily Elmore deferred her comments to Belinda and Boris Kousnetsov concurred with mine. Belinda spoke first, assailing the Randalls much as she had on the first day we'd argued detention two weeks earlier. Fraud, deceit, baby selling, emotional risk to Nathan if he was returned to Sue Ellen and palmed off on another unsuspecting couple. Foley's face was tired and drawn, but he scribbled onto his pad as she spoke, which troubled me. The courtroom was still full when she sat down.

I reviewed for the judge the weaknesses in the county's case, the fact that there was no baby sale, that only bills for essentials were paid. I reminded Foley that the Danforths' own expert had agreed that if Nathan was eventually headed home with Sue Ellen and Ty, the best time was now. I decried the manner in which Gilbride, Lois Nettleson and the Danforths had secretly conspired against the Randalls, the rank manipulation of Sue Ellen's due date, the painful inducement of her labor for the sake of a grand evening at the White House. And still, through all her travails, Sue Ellen had delivered Nathan up to the Danforths. Decency in the face of gross mistreatment, a willingness to hold to an agreement until it was painfully clear that the open adoption was nothing more than a convenient fiction. I paused before making my final point, and the sight of Foley jotting notes again bolstered my resolve.

I spoke, at last, about the bond between mother and child. "The love a mother feels for her baby, this wonderful gift of life, is profound," I said. "It is a far-reaching love, a sustaining love that ensures the survival of our race. A powerful thing."

I rested a hand on my client's shoulder. "Sue Ellen Randall has acted upon that love. How? Belatedly, no doubt, and as such, at the risk of great peril. Your Honor, I ask you to see her for who she really is, a woman who needs to be with her child. A woman who wants the chance to love her son."

Foley paused to read from the mess of notes on his desk, then re-read the petition, jotting more notes. The rest of us remained seated.

Sue Ellen leaned over to me. "Whatever happens," she said, "thank you."

Ty leaned forward in his chair to establish eye contact with me and shrugged with a wait-and-see rise to his eyebrows. The lump above my eye was still red and painful to the touch, but I answered Ty's gesture with a nod of assent.

Foley recessed to look at his notes but told us all to remain seated. The few conversations that started up in the gallery were muted. The court reporter wrung her hands and replenished her paper supply. Belinda whispered with Gilbride and Mr. Danforth behind the partitions, Kitty pursing her lips as she watched the big clock keep time. I made no effort to confer with Sue Ellen, for there was nothing more to be said.

"All right, people," Foley said, "we're back on the record. I'm ready to make my ruling."

Sue Ellen stopped breathing. The bailiff put down his magazine and the mutterings in the gallery stopped cold.

"I'm taking jurisdiction over this Minor," the judge said.

"Oh God, we lost, didn't we?" Sue Ellen whispered. To my left, Belinda and Lily Elmore were beaming. Behind us, Gilbride was clasping hands with the Danforths.

"Hold on, people, I want quiet!" Foley said. "Now I'm taking jurisdiction, but only as to one count, that the child is at risk of emotional harm, and I'm rewriting the facts of that count. The county did not prove that the Randalls placed Nathan at risk by defrauding Nathan's current caretakers—"

"But Your Honor!" Gilbride said.

"Not another word, Counselor!" Foley said. "By God, let me make my ruling!"

I turned and saw that Gilbride wore the very face of confusion, which gave me instant hope. In custody matters, the man's instincts were otherworldly. The air in my lungs seemed to evaporate. Jesus, I thought, I'm not wired for this kind of action.

"Sorry, Your Honor," Gilbride said.

Pained again, Foley rubbed the sides of his head. "Mr. Shepard, I still don't like the way your client and Mr. Kouznetsov's client spirited the eldest child back to Kentucky. It was wrong. That's why I want to retain jurisdiction. I want to monitor Nathan's progress in their home for awhile."

He was releasing Nathan to the Randalls. We had won.

"Here's my disposition: I'm ordering the minor released H.O.P.," Foley went on. "Mother and Father are to attend parenting counseling beginning . . ."

"What's H.O.P. mean?" Sue Ellen whispered.

"Home of parent," I said. "That means he's coming home to you." Sue Ellen began to cry. Boris was already shaking Ty's hand.

Foley read the rest of his orders and thanked the Danforths for their cooperation in caring for Nathan. Kitty was too angry and broken up to speak, but Corwin Danforth raised his hand to ask a question. "Go ahead," Foley said.

"We'd like to spend one last evening with Nathan, if we could," he said, "to get his things together. To say good-bye." His anguish was evident, and I felt my mouth going dry.

"Mr. Shepard?" Foley inquired.

I looked at Sue Ellen, who was already gripping the straps of her baby bag. She turned to look at the Danforths. "What do you think?" she asked me.

"You've won," I said. "I think it'll be all right."

"Tomorrow morning's fine, I guess," she told Foley.

"Eight o'clock tomorrow morning, right here, before calendar call," Foley said. He folded his court file shut a final time and adjourned, the gallery draining out behind us.

"We're locking up for lunch in one minute," the bailiff called out to those of us who milled behind, "so pack your briefcases and head on out, everyone."

Belinda flashed by me, obviously distressed. She didn't lose very often in here. Lily Elmore shook her head at me as she hoisted her bag lady's monster purse to leave.

"Hope you're proud of yourself, J.," Lily said.

I was tempted to tell her to kindly go fuck herself, but I was too pleased with Foley's ruling to let her bother me. "You look like you could use a cigarette, Lily," I said.

"We gotta go," Sue Ellen said, hugging me ever so gently. I could tell she regretted having caused me so much grief with her previous untimely displays.

An older man in a cheap gray suit and a western string tie ducked his head in and waved at Sue Ellen. "Comin', R. G.," Sue Ellen called out to him. "Truck broke down again," she told me. "Our friend who drove us this morning has to get back. R. G. works the night shift, security at a mall in the Valley."

"The Valley, huh?" I said. "You're starting to sound like you know your way around L.A. You're practically a local."

She laughed. "Get out." She compared the back of her white hand against mine. "Not until I start sportin' a tan like that."

I found Jackie outside, at the far rim of the deserted waiting room. Every other court in the building had adjourned for lunch already. He was gazing at the slice of East L.A. that lay across the freeway junction. Rosemary Egan was seated twenty feet away, dozing upright.

"How's it hanging, *kemosabe*?" he said. I saw my reflection in his wraparound shades when he turned to me.

We stared out the big windows together. "Quite nicely," I said. "Sue Ellen got her kid back."

He briefly looked over his shoulder at the slumbering nurse. "Egan do her thing?"

"She did."

"You owe her a lift home, brother."

"I've had enough of this place," I said. "Let's bail."

We woke Rosemary Egan and went downstairs and out the front, where Holly Dupree was waiting.

"Ah, shit," I muttered as Holly and her crew jangled toward us, "let's run for it."

"No dice," Jackie said, sizing up an opportunity. "Let's give the viewers at home something to chew on tonight."

"Mr. Shepard, a word?" Holly said. "Tell us what happened today."

"Pardon me, ma'am," Jackie said in a phony Texas lawman's drawl as he stepped squarely in front of me, "but I have orders to escort all civilians from the premises. Please remain calm and exit in an orderly fashion."

"Who are you?" Holly said. "Cut the camera . . . Who is this guy?" she said to one of her equipment jockeys, who shrugged in response.

"Security personnel, highest level," Jackie said. Nurse Egan and I slowly backed away from the confrontation.

"Let's see some identification," Holly said.

"Can't do that, ma'am." His eyes surreptitiously darted to and fro. "Under cover."

Holly groaned. "Get off it, you're not for real."

"I'm afraid the bomb threat we just received is very real, ma'am," he said.

That got Holly's attention. "Let's get it on tape," she said to a clipboard-wielding assistant, who agreed. The camera began to whir again. "What can you tell us? What kind of threat is there?"

334 ≋ John DeCure

"Well, ma'am, it's really quite diabolical . . ."

I silently prodded Egan to keep heading for the parking structure as Jackie blathered on. How did his brain manufacture this crap with such chilling efficiency?

Turning back, I saw Jackie put his index finger into his ear as if he were receiving a report on a tiny radio transmitter. He glared at Holly, aghast. "Good Lord," he shouted, pointing at her big hair, "I believe we've located the bomb!"

"What? Where?" Holly spun on her heels, scanning the empty courthouse grounds.

We had a good laugh when we got back to the car. "I dare her to use any of that footage," Jackie said.

Rosemary Egan blushed. "You sure gave her a start," she told Jackie.

"She had it coming," I said.

Egan craned and smiled at Jackie, who'd piled into the back seat. "You're a bit of a wild one, aren't you?"

I didn't know the full story about what Jackie said and did to persuade her to testify, and I wasn't about to ask either of them. It really didn't matter.

He'd saved my life again.

Twenty-One

Midday traffic was thick, so we drove surface streets up into South Pasadena, where Rosemary Egan lived with her husband, a retired X-ray technician. I'd started with some polite conversation about the apparent rewards of a nursing career, but Jackie hijacked the topic and veered the discussion into a gore-fest, featuring the most bizarre and unusual medical conditions both he and Egan had ever seen.

Eyeballs hanging by a thread from their sockets—"No way!" Surfboard skegs severing testicles—"Heavens!" A mammoth boil on a small man's ass, an inflammation so formidable that the entire buttock withered and collapsed when the lance was performed— "Please, that is just *too* rank!" A thumb bitten off by a shark, but recovered posthaste from the reef and sewn back on with fishing line—"Goodness! Where did you learn how to stitch like that?"

And on and on. I attempted to stem the flow of gruesome details with a quick stop-off at a burger stand that sold soft-serve ice cream, but the two let up only long enough to inhale their cones. At least the ice cream helped settle my stomach somewhat. I felt glad I chose to pursue law instead of medicine.

We stopped at the curb outside Egan's modest home, a red stucco job with white trim slashed diagonally across the fake shutters and a garage with a roof sloped like the sides of a barn. Jackie and I both got out to help her from the Jeep. We thanked her for testifying, but she shrugged us off. I reflected on the unbiased affability Rosemary Egan displayed today. In my experience, such a combination is rare in a witness. I'd been lucky to be able to rely on her.

Crooked elms lined both sides of the street. A mailman scooted up the narrow brick walkway of the house next door. Rosemary Egan buttoned a few notches of her sweater.

"Thank you again," I said, shaking her hand.

"Just think," she said, "the Randalls are probably home with their little one by now, starting a new life together."

"Homey homey," Jackie said.

"Actually, the baby's still with the Danforths," I said. "They're keeping him one more night."

Jackie put his hand to his chest. "What?" He looked stunned.

"Yeah, they're getting his stuff together, saying good-bye," I explained. "We worked it out that they would bring the baby in to court tomorrow."

Jackie's eyes flashed. "Holy fuck, you're joking, right?" Egan looked taken aback. "Sorry," he told her, "but J., why? I thought the judge gave . . . Oh, man. Not good!"

"What?" I said.

"The kid," he said. "They're not gonna give him up."

"What do you mean? The judge made the order."

"You don't get it, do you?" he said. "They're gonna give him to someone who will hide him so your clients never get him back." He looked at Egan. "You better call the cops, get 'em over there. The D's live in Old Pasadena." I stared at him when he recited the address from memory. "You said investigate, man," he said. "I investigated."

"Call the department, too," I told her.

I jumped in the wagon and revved the motor. Rosemary Egan turned to wave from her doorstep, but thought better of it. As we pulled away from the curb I saw her drop the uneaten stub of her ice cream cone into a row of ivy near the porch.

Jackie held the road atlas in his lap and gave shortcut directions as we drove. Once I was confident we were making time I hit him hard for more information.

"What difference does it make how I know, I just know!" he said.

I looked both ways and jammed through a red light at a vacant intersection. "Don't give me that shit," I said. "Just tell me how you knew."

"Promise you won't blow a gasket first."

But I was through making promises to him. "Out with it, man."

He sat back, resting a boot up on the dashboard. "Remember how I was tailing the old lady? Well, she made a stop at a hair salon and I just knew she was gonna be a while. So I kind of went back to their place and checked out their mailbox."

"What do you mean, you *checked out* their mailbox? You tamper with mail and get caught, that's a felony, Einstein."

"Knew you'd fuckin' wig," he said.

I passed a small U-Haul van on the wrong side of the double-yellow. The driver took exception to being blown off the highway and leaned on his horn. "Give me the rest," I said to Jackie.

"I'm on the porch, my hand in the damn box, if you can picture that, and this van pulls up. But I don't see 'em and next thing I know, this nerdy dude and a long-haired chick—they look like Mormons on a lost mission or something—they're standing right there behind me! I'm thinking 'Fuck me, I'm dead.' Thought for sure I was caught in the act. But they start feelin' me out, so I figure hey, I'll just go with the flow and see where it takes me. You wouldn't believe the wild-ass story I came up with."

"Try me."

"I tell 'em I'm a concerned relative of the D's, trying to help out with the baby any way I can. I tell 'em I'm building a new nursery for the kid and I was looking for a check the D's were supposed to leave out front, so I could buy more building materials."

"Very creative."

"And they went for it. But here's where it gets crazy."

I was tired of being the last to know what the hell was going on. I began to think of my mother again and the deal I'd made to get Egan. The trial was over. I was free to keep looking for Marielena Shepard, and Jackie couldn't stop me.

"You mean we're not to the crazy part yet?" I said.

"Ha-ha," he said. "Anyway, the dumb turds start confiding in me. Chick said they were going to see to it that the Randalls never got the baby, even if they had to take drastic measures. I asked what she meant, but she wouldn't say. Her man was just standing there with his thumb up his ass, lettin' the chick do all the talking, but when she went back to the van to get her shades, I leaned in to him, asked him 'What kind of drastic measures you got in mind?' He tells me they were part of a network of like-minded individuals who would see that the child got lost and never found. A 'network of like-minded individuals,' can you believe that? Like he was part of an international spy ring." He laughed. "Fucking pantywaist."

"They steal babies," I said. "In my book, that takes some serious sack."

Jackie grew pensive. "Stealing babies . . . Jesus."

The Danforths lived in a gorgeous Pasadena neighborhood off Fair Oaks, just north of the Norton Simon Museum. Driving there in daylight, the homes looked older and smaller than those in Phoebe's part of town, but they were equally splendid. We found the street and Jackie pointed out the house, the lovely Country English I remembered from the night they'd almost done the adoption without me.

A white van was at the top of the driveway, facing the three-car garage. It looked like the one that was blocking my garage that day I'd come home from work two weeks ago. I could see the tailpipe vibrating—the engine was running. A guy was in the cab, behind the wheel, waiting for something. The Danforths were standing on their huge front porch a few feet from the van, looking forlorn. Through the van's side windows I could see little Nathan in the arms of someone on the passenger side. A long-haired girl. The girl looked up and saw us, paused, then jumped in the van.

I cut the Jeep across the base of the driveway just as the van started jamming down backwards. They were headed straight for us, and if they didn't stop, we'd have to bail. But about halfway down the long drive, the van braked to a halt, the driver reconsidering.

"He's gonna fly over the curb!" Jackie shouted. "Just keep it here!"

He leapt from the car and ran up the driveway as the van redirected its front wheels and cut hard in reverse onto the lawn. Jackie reached the cab and leaned in to grab the wheel. I was out of the

Jeep and headed up the drive behind him when I heard a woman inside the van yell "Go! Go! Go!"

"Jackie!" I yelled. "Look out!"

The van lurched again in reverse, with Jackie hanging on, his head and arms inside the cab. "Go! Just Go!" I heard the woman inside the van shouting.

The van wobbled drunkenly in reverse, found some purchase on the grass and shot backward, Jackie hanging on and screaming at the driver, the full warrior cry. A brick-lined flowerbed, anchored by a white-lantern lamppost and two large, smooth boulders, lay directly in the van's path at the foot of the driveway.

The van's back bumper cracked like a rifle shot against the lamppost, buckling the rear doors and thumping the post into the soft dirt with a tremendous slap. The tires spun as soil and bright flowers exploded into the air. Jackie moaned from the far side of the van. "I said stop, dickwad!" I heard him shout.

I ran to the passenger door and pulled out a mousy young woman whose long black hair fell down to the small of her back. Nathan was wailing his head off, and I pried him from the girl's arms. She tried to dart past me but I reached out with my free hand and caught her hard by the arm.

"Get back in the van!" I ordered her. The Danforths stood frozen on the porch.

The woman wriggled against me, and it took all my strength to hold her. I squeezed her biceps so hard she let out a crazed yelp. "Get in the van," I said again. The girl stopped struggling, slid back onto the passenger seat, and spit in my face.

A man grunted in pain on the other side of the cab.

"Stay put," I heard Jackie tell the driver. "Or your ass is grass." He jerked the keys from the ignition.

A police cruiser pulled in behind us a few minutes later and quickly secured the scene. The van was pretty much dusted, the kidnapping couple hooked up and stuffed into the back seat of the squad car to cool out. They were the same pair Jackie had run into on the Danforths' porch. Two emergency social workers showed up; one handled Nathan, the other took our statements. The police did the same with the Danforths in their living room. The Danforths looked terribly subdued to me. Deflated. I wondered if they would be arrested.

Jackie had turned his ankle badly, and the paramedics loaded him into an ambulance in front of a dozen curious neighbors as he shot the crowd a Hawaiian *shaka* greeting. The driver told me they'd have X rays taken at Woodside Hospital, and asked if I knew how to get there. I got directions and headed over.

Holly Dupree was already outside Jackie's room when I arrived. She was alone, no microphone, no crew.

"You look naked without your little band of merry men," I said to her. "How did you hear about this so fast?"

"I have friends in the department," she said.

I recalled the fiasco that was Sue Ellen's first scheduled visit at the county offices. "There's a news flash."

She looked offended. "I try to be as evenhanded as possible in my reporting."

I stared at her hard. "You mean backhanded."

Holly's crew was jangling down the hallway now. I cut past her and into Jackie's room.

"Hey, man," Jackie called out from the edge of his bed, "life is beautiful. A nice, firm bed. Convalescing with a little help from my friends." The head of the bed was tilted upright, and a comely young nurse was spoon-feeding cherry Jell-O to him while another one fluffed a pillow behind his head.

"Tough break," I said.

"Well hey, I just might pull through," he said, flashing a brilliant smile on his helpers. "What do you think, ladies, am I gonna make it?" They giggled as he took another spoonful of colored sugar.

Within seconds, Holly was stringing together a live hallway spot in her usual indefatigable way. She'd collared the doctor who'd X-rayed Jackie and was wheedling a prognosis out of him when I shut the door with a hardy pull.

"Unbelievable," I said to Jackie. "You outdid yourself this time."

"What do you mean, this time?" he said. "Like I've ever helped you on a case, man."

"You know what I mean. You saved my life on this case. Just like that day at Holys."

His face grew pensive. "Ladies, a million thanks," he told the nurses. "But would you leave us, please?" He waited until they'd gone out. "Forget what happened at Holys," he said. "I mean it. It's ancient history."

"I misjudged you," I said. "I'm sorry."

He waved me off. "Don't apologize."

His modesty made me blush. I felt truly inadequate in his presence.

The phone on the nightstand rang and Jackie answered it. "Yeah, he is." He held out the receiver to me. "For you."

"Hello, J.? Is this J. Shepard?" A familiar voice I could not yet place. An older man. "It's Charles Baumann, the historian from City Hall?"

"Sure, hi," I said. "What's up?"

"I'm at home. Had the TV on just now, four o'clock news on Channel Six. You know they're doing a live interview, right there at the hospital?"

"I figured as much. They're right outside."

"The reporter said your associate, the fellow who injured his knee—"

"His ankle."

"Right, his ankle. She said his name is Jackie Pace."

"That's right."

"Well, I went in half-day today, this morning. Found a copy of the business license for Provencal Limited, the one you wanted? And the name on it is John Hampton Pace, the Second. Thought maybe that was your friend, there, so I figured I'd call to let you know. Imagine that, I turn on the TV and say to the wife 'Hey, honey, I know this guy, I helped him search an old license just today, just today!' Can you imagine?"

"Thank . . . uh, thank you . . . very much for all your help," I said blankly. I handed the receiver back to Jackie.

"What's up?" he said. "You don't look so hot."

"You're John Hampton Pace, the Third," I said. He nodded. "That makes John Hampton Pace, the Second your father."

His blue eyes didn't blink. "Who was that on the phone?"

"Provencal Limited," I said. "Your father owned it." Jackie said nothing, which confirmed his answer.

"J., I'm telling you, leave it alone," he said. "You don't know—"

"What I'm *talking* about? Damn right I don't know! So help me out here, Goddam it. What's your father got to do with Provencal and Sea Pointe?"

His face was ashen. "She's dead, J. Your mother is dead."

My mother had been gone for thirteen years, and I'd often thought logically, out loud, that she must be dead, but to hear the words spoken like this, with such conviction, confirmed it as fact for the first time ever. My shoulders shook, and my tongue couldn't form any sounds. Then my knees went weak and I crumpled onto the edge of the bed.

Jackie waited to speak and wouldn't look at me directly when he finally did. "You want the full story, you'll have to talk to the old man himself."

"Where can I find him?" I said.

"Go up Christianitos Boulevard a mile or so from PCH and turn left at the police station. Follow that road all the way."

"To what?" I said. "There's nothing but marsh out there, a one-laner full of potholes. That's not a through street."

"It is if you own the land," he said. "There's a metal cable across the road. Looks like it's locked but it isn't. Mailman wouldn't deliver if he had to screw around with a padlock every time."

He was still avoiding my gaze. "How do you figure into it?" I asked. "How did she die?"

"Go see him," he said. "Not now. It'll probably be close to dark by the time you get there. He's been ripped off before, so he watches the road sometimes at night. You don't want to get shot. Wait until morning." He swallowed hard. "Go!" He rolled over and stared at the bare wall opposite the TV. The bowl of red Jell-O lay on its side, spilling across the sheets like synthetic blood.

I made my way along the walls and stumbled past Holly and her crew in a fog of shock and grief. Whatever she might have asked me didn't even register. I had no answers left.

Twenty-Two

The gate at the end of the road past the Christianitos Police Department was just as Jackie had described it, with a rusted heavy cable looping a few feet above the crumbling pavement and a sign that said ABSOLUTELY NO TRESPASSING! dangling in the center of the road. I unhooked the cable and drove over the flattened sign, a fat jackrabbit lighting out into the brown weeds just ahead. The sun was high and rising in the midmorning sky, and wide rays fanned down through the last scattering patches of overcast. The stale scent of dry mud and salt air filled the air. I drove slowly, carefully avoiding the many pockmarks in the narrow lane, which was about as bad as the typical neglected coastal roads I'd bounced down many times before in Mexico. My Jeep wagon was the right vehicle to have at the moment. I was surprised the mailman came out here at all.

I drove another quarter mile, past gentle dunes and high-tide marshes blackening in the September light. In the distance, the waters of the Back Bay crept languidly inland like the outstretched fingers of a dying man.

The road had been steadily rising, and rounding a slow, westward turn, I saw a remarkable ocean vista: the North Jetty, Long Beach Marina, a wisp of Point Fermin; and when the morning haze cleared off completely, I imagined, Catalina and beyond. The place was magically desolate. A large home stood in solitary relief against the bleached sand and sea grass, a grand, two-story redwood ringed by elaborate wooden decking below and an enormous balcony across the second level, facing out to the sea.

The road ended in a circular drive in front of the house. Outside, a long, black Mercedes-Benz was at rest, its chrome sparkling. Beside the three-car garage, a red tractor was partially tucked beneath a tarpaulin. A dented American sedan was parked half in the dirt near the far opposite end of the drive, as if its owner didn't feel worthy to take up a better space near the house.

The front walk was made up of sandstone slabs carefully laid to blend with the delicate dunes and desert shrubs that led to the house. I rang the buzzer, studying the stained-glass window that was built into the top of the wide front door. Through the colored panes I could see the glow of the Back Bay lighting the house's interior.

A thin man with hollow cheeks and a brown pencil mustache answered the door. Probably the guy who'd parked his old car half in the weeds. "Yes?" he said.

"I'm here to see Mr. Pace. Is he home?"

"Mr. Pace doesn't normally take visitors." He was dressed in black slacks and long-sleeved white shirt with a plain black tie. His side panels of hair were greased straight back. "Perhaps you could call and arrange an appointment." He began to close the door.

"Tell him Marielena Shepard's son is here, friend," I said. "Tell him it's important."

"One moment."

He closed the door, and I watched his shadow pass behind the stained glass. I silently rehearsed a few key questions for Jackie's father. The servant returned. "Mr. Pace will see you," he said without passion. "This way."

He led me inside past a large living area with vaulted ceilings and huge windows that beautifully framed the Back Bay's sinuous inlets. The furniture, low-slung enough not to obscure the view, was all Western style—a couch with an Indian weave print over white leather, a manzanita coffee table beneath an oval sheet of glass, end tables in knotty pine. We ascended a staircase carpeted in dark red and went through an opened sliding glass door onto the long balcony.

"Mr. Shepard," the servant announced, then disappeared.

John Hampton Pace II was seated in a padded rocking chair with gracefully rounded runners, a nubby wool blanket across his lap. On a metal table next to him was a hardbound book, a pair of tortoise-shell reading glasses, and a half-empty martini glass. His hair was a sallow gray, as if it was once blond, and when he stood, he had the bearing of a stooped, old man. But his eyes were the clearest blue, like Jackie's, and his face was still strong and handsome beneath the deep folds and wrinkles. He was wearing white pants, a safari shirt with big pockets and brown leather sandals over thick crew socks.

"Well, Marielena Shepard's son," he said with a swagger that instantly reminded me of his son. "What took you so long?"

"Point is, I'm here." My arms were folded tightly. "Tell me what happened to her. Tell me about Sea Pointe."

"I see." He reached in his shirt pocket and pulled out a cigar, biting off the end. "This could take a little while." He pulled a lighter from his pants pocket and slowly lit the cigar.

I shifted my weight. The view was magnificent, but I tried not to look. "I've got plenty of time."

"Sit down," he said, "you're making me nervous." He puffed on his cigar as I sat down in the chair opposite his. The vistas beyond the wooden railings were too striking to ignore. The puddles in a shallow marsh were lit up like a handful of gold coins. I watched a red-tailed hawk cruise the updrafts, waiting patiently. "You want a drink?" he said. "I'll get you a drink."

"No," I said before he could call out to his servant. "No, thanks. Just tell me what happened."

He settled back in his chair again. "Ah, Marielena," he said. "From the minute I laid eyes on her, she stole my heart." He gazed into the wetlands. "The lady had something very special, a certain freshness, a purity of being, a way of making you believe she was the most wonderful creature God had ever designed. She was pure heaven."

"She never told me about you," I said, hoping to back him off. His worshipful reminiscence was creepy. "No offense. You don't seem like her type."

"You're right, I probably wasn't much her type," he said, pointing a hooked finger at me. "Twenty years older. But we had a few things in common."

"Like what?" I didn't believe him.

"We talked a lot. Business. Politics in Rome. The novels of Marquez. He was her favorite."

I looked away. "I know." The fact that he was right galled me.

"I went back and read *One Hundred Years of Solitude* just for her.

And some of Pablo Neruda's poems." His lips looked dry and cracked when he smiled. "But it wasn't all talk. I could make Marielena laugh."

My fists were tight at my sides. "Heartwarming."

"Hadn't felt anything special for a woman in so long I couldn't remember." His tone was somber. "Haven't felt that way about a woman since."

He sniffled, then puffed on his cigar too hard and coughed horribly. The servant appeared and glared at me as he glided in to attend to Mr. Pace. "I'm all right," Jackie's father said hoarsely. "Leave us." The servant vanished again.

"You gave her a leather portfolio," I said. "I found it in the attic with some of her old things. Brochures for Sea Pointe."

"The infamous Sea Pointe." He grinned through teeth cigar-stained a soft yellow. "That idea came and went a long time ago."

"Where was it?" I said. "I've been asking around, and—"

"You're looking at it, son," he said with a laugh, waving his hand in front of the railing. "Not exactly the money-maker I envisioned. I was trying to develop some of this wonderful view you see."

"Provencal Limited."

"Oh." He looked impressed. "You've been doing your homework."

"She did some accounting for you?"

"That's right, at first. But I wanted to see her more, so I made her a salesperson."

"You what? My mother never sold anything in her life. She was the quiet type."

"I know, but you have to understand, I was in love with her. Had to have some pretense to keep seeing her. So I paid her an advance, paid her handsomely just to spread the word about Sea Pointe. Even hired that idiot friend of hers."

"Grog—Greg Baker?"

He nodded. "Shot my mouth off a little too much about needing to get the word out locally, to build interest. She brought him over one day, practically begged me to hire him."

That was my mother, always trying to help a friend in need.

"I don't get it," I said. "Why did you need to build interest, as you said? This place is gorgeous. Why not put some flags in the ground, set up a trailer, and sit back? This land would sell itself."

"You don't understand what was going on back then, how many problems I was having. Soil tests were coming back poor, the city was set to re-zone, but they kept waiting for the okay from the Coastal Commission. The hearings were a nightmare. That little trickle of a creek"—he waved his hand to the north—"got designated a tributary. Goddamned activists with their signs, 'Save the Back Bay.' Save it from what? We were talking about a very small development, twenty-two lots. Damn birds would've still had plenty of room to spread their wings."

"It never got approved."

"Very good," he said.

"Why did you call Greg Baker an idiot?" I asked.

He shook his head. "He talked me into subdividing a smaller parcel and selling it to him. Said he planned to build on it, but I knew he could never afford to. He was going to turn around and sell it, try to make a quick killing." Jackie's father laughed hollowly. "As you can see, he never got the chance."

"How much did he lose?"

"Twenty-five, thirty grand, I don't remember. Whatever it was, it was his life savings."

That explained Pam Baker's bitterness at my mention of Sea Pointe the night at the gallery. She had suffered through quite enough of Grog's quick-buck schemes and could stand it no longer.

His smirk was beginning to annoy me. "You really had it in for Grog, didn't you?"

"No, I didn't. Likeable fellow, but he was in love with your mother, too. You could see it in the way he looked at her."

"Jackie told me she's dead," I said.

His eyes narrowed. "Your mother and I had, how should I say this? We ran into some complications." He stopped, as if that was all he planned to tell me.

I thought of the letters and Carmen's translations.

"She was pregnant," I said. He sipped his martini as I glared at him. "It couldn't have been you."

"It was . . . me."

Something was terribly wrong about the way he said it, as if he'd admitted to having done something ghastly. I had a sudden instinct. "You raped her."

"That's not altogether fair. I never intended—"

"You sick son of a bitch," I said, standing over him, now. "I ought to throw you over this balcony."

"Don't . . . now please," he said. "Please, sit down." His hands were shaking. He tried to set his cigar into a glass ashtray on the table but missed, and the cigar rolled off the far end of the table and onto the decking. "Jesus Christ!" Scrambling to put it out.

I stepped around the table and squashed the cigar with my left foot. "Keep going," I said.

He eased back into his rocking chair and wet his lips. "It was only the one time. She was here one night, delivering some numbers I'd asked her to work up for a new prospectus," he said. "I asked her in. We talked. I showed her the view up here. The Santa Anas were blowing out of the desert that day. The sunset was magnificent."

"Then you raped her."

"It wasn't like that. I . . . wanted her so much. I loved her, I really did. She didn't exactly welcome my advances, but she didn't say no, either."

"What happened after that? How did she die?"

He studied the Back Bay vista. "That's a little more complicated."

"Then explain."

"My second wife, Jackie's stepmother, was a powerful woman, a woman of means."

"Let me guess," I said, "you married her for her money."

"I did," he admitted. "My father's fortune was all but wiped out during the Great Depression. Now, when your mother became pregnant, she stopped seeing me, stopped doing any work for Provencal or Sea Pointe. I had to go to her church to find her. She said she never wanted to see me again."

I frowned. "Good for her."

"Yes, well . . . but that's not the point. She said she didn't love me, but she was probably going to keep the child."

"That doesn't surprise me. She didn't believe in abortion."

"It caused a problem for me," he said.

"A *problem*? You know, you're a pig to even say that."

"Wait, wait, listen," he said. "I told you about my second wife."

"What about her? You were afraid she was going to find out?"

"Not exactly. She was dead. But it didn't matter."

I'd lost him. He noted my expression and started again. "Leonora was the jealous type, always suspected I'd snared her for her bank account."

"Which was true."

He raised a hand in oath. "I admit it. I told her I loved her, and for years, I tried. Tried to be faithful, too. But she knew I only wanted the comfort her wealth could provide."

"What's this got to do with my mother being pregnant?"

"All this and then some was Leonora's before we met," he said. "I was just a sailing bum down at the Long Beach Yacht Club, a single parent with a good name, an old car and not much savings. The bulk of her estate was separate property, all hers. Stayed that way through the entire marriage. I never brought in a dime. She supported me for years."

"Even though you didn't love her."

"That's right. She was bitter about me—and about Jackie—before she died. Jealous." He stared over the railing into the afternoon glare.

"What do you mean about her being bitter about Jackie?"

"He was a handsome, charming kid," he said slowly. "Leonora was spellbound by his guile."

It was an unusual situation, but my dependency experience helped me process it quickly. "She wanted Jackie."

He nodded. "I could never tell if she did it to get back at me."

No wonder Jackie never spoke of his family. "What did Jackie do?"

He looked away, over the dunes. "He didn't reciprocate, not as often as she wanted him to, at least."

"He gave in."

"Never said a word about it." He shivered and took a drink. "But I could tell. Eventually she drove him away. Boy practically lived on the beach, from the time he was fifteen or sixteen. But that was all well before Sea Pointe."

"I'm missing the connection to my mother," I said.

"Leonora's trust. When she died, I got a call from a fellow in town at First Fidelity, her bank. Apparently, she'd created an *inter vivos* trust that was designed to persist after her death. It allowed for a generous monthly payment to me, but with a condition subsequent that if I was to remarry or father a child by another woman, I'd be cut off."

"I'm a lawyer," I said, "and wills and trusts aren't my specialty, but that sounds illegal."

"Oh, I fought it! Took it to court and spent a lot of money to have a judge tell me it was legal. As long as the purpose of the trust wasn't 'void as against public policy,' he said. Can you believe that?"

"So if my mother kept the baby . . ."

"And Leonora's executor found out, both Jackie and I would've been out in the cold. The only asset in my name was this land." He swept his hand across the balcony.

"That's why you were trying to develop Sea Pointe," I said.

"To free myself from Leonora's grasp."

"Why would she want to cut off Jackie?" I said. "He didn't marry her for her money. He didn't cheat. She used him."

"Leonora never quite got over his rejection of her." He shook his head. "He was the one she really loved. So she left him with nothing. I always took care of the boy, so he'd have no interest in the outcome of this, I made sure of it."

"But Jackie was a surf star by the time he was eighteen."

Mr. Pace chuckled. "Sure he was. But I was pretty much paying his way."

"What happened to my mother?"

"I had to persuade Marielena to terminate her pregnancy," he said, "which at the time seemed near impossible. She didn't want to see me in the first place, much less talk about an abortion. Jackie's the one who got through to her."

"No . . ." I said. Not my best friend.

"He dug around, talked to some of the people she knew in town. Heard about some of the unusual things she did."

"Her superstitions."

He nodded. "He knew about your father's death, the heart problem. So I cornered your mother after mass one Sunday, to talk to her about the pregnancy. Lied to her. Said I'd had a vivid dream that the child was born with a heart that wouldn't beat, as punishment for what I'd done. I told her the dream was a sign that she had to abort the fetus."

"So she did."

"No." He held up a finger as if to redirect my thought. "She was torn right down the middle, said it was against her beliefs, but maybe my dream *was* a sign. She was in a quandary that day." He closed his eyes. "It was the last time I ever saw her."

"What happened to her?"

"Jackie gave her the sign she was looking for. Your father was a famous surfer, too, I guess."

"Around here, but nothing like Jackie."

"Right. Jackie knew your mother used to walk on the beach, to the spot where your father died. That day, the last day I saw her, he went out surfing on a board just like one your father used, in trunks like these ones he'd seen in an old magazine photo of your father."

It was as if a trap door had swung open beneath my feet. I held the railing and concentrated on my breathing. "Jesus."

"He waited for her to take her walk. When she got there and saw him, he rode in on a breaker, did it in the style your father used to ride the waves. Jackie knows these things. Then he went down, boom! Fell right where your father did years earlier."

"She didn't recognize Jackie from around?"

"He was pretty sure she wouldn't know him. His appeal was with a younger crowd. Turned out he was right."

"Just like he was right about the draft board."

Jackie's father's teeth flashed. "Kid's got a special genius for knowing who he's playing to."

My earnest, conflicted, unsuspecting mother had gotten the Jackie Pace hustle, right when it mattered most. Probably never had a chance. I stared into the sun without blinking. "Go on."

"There's not much more to say, really, if you—"

"Go on!" I shouted.

He tried to take another drink, but his hand was shaking. Suddenly he was just a withered old fool who'd carried a painful secret too long. He took out a handkerchief and blew his nose, then rubbed his eyes hard.

I looked on him impassively. "You were saying."

"Your mother ran out to help him, asked him if he was all right. She was suitably terrified, I guess. Poor thing. Jackie clutched his chest, told her it was the strangest thing, but when he looked up and saw her walking on the beach, it was as if his heart gave out."

I rubbed my eyes and tried to breathe evenly. "Another sign. That did it. She had the abortion."

"She did," he said. "Damn tragedy. I would have paid for it of course, gotten her the finest medical care. Apparently she had other ideas. Went down to Mexico by herself one morning, met up with some religious woman in Rosarito Beach who claimed to provide some sort of absolution through prayer during the procedure. Ridiculous. They butchered her." His eyes were red again.

"How do you know this?" I said.

"I sent Jackie down there to look after her. He'd asked around at the church, figured out something was wrong."

"A little late," I said.

"She bled to death right on the table." He gazed at me. "You understand, I didn't mean for any of this to happen."

"No, you sorry sack of shit, I don't understand. You killed her, both of you!"

"Go ahead, hate me," he said, "but don't blame Jackie. I'm entirely to blame."

"How's that? He was in on it with you."

"No, not by choice. He'd tried to make it on his surfing, was the best in the world, and is that just the damnedest thing? He still couldn't pay his way."

"Oh, come on. That's no excuse."

"Say what you want, but he needed my money. How do you think he paid for all those trips to other countries? The contest people knew he wasn't making enough to support himself. He had too much pride to hang around with them, so he went off on his own. I could understand his shame, what with his image, and all."

"Jackie knew everyone," I said. "He didn't need you."

"Yes, he did. Had quite a lifestyle going, too. Real taste for the high life. Inherited that from yours truly, I suppose. You were too young to know him then."

This was true. What I knew about Jackie in his early heyday was mostly recycled old stories I'd heard years later on the beach and in the water.

"When the problem with your mother came up, I told him he'd better help me or he could kiss his little endless summer good-bye."

I gazed out into the mud flats, following the low flight path of a solitary white heron. "All he's ever done is lie to me."

"Don't be too hard on him. The whole experience changed his life, it did. He's had a shadow hanging over him ever since."

"What do you mean?"

"He hates his father," he said. "Never visits, won't take a cent of my money."

"What about his real mother, your first wife?"

He stared at the far-off glint of the sea. "Jackie's real mom was a gold-digging little bitch, if you must know. Such a fool. Too dumb to realize I'd already blown what was left of my family inheritance by the time I married her. She never gave a damn about Jackie. You know," he said, dabbing his eyes, "I still don't know how he makes ends meet."

I did. Jackie had become a small-time con artist and moocher to survive.

"He's always felt bad about you losing your mother that way. Feels responsible for you. He's tried to watch over you."

I knew now why Jackie had been there to save me from drowning that day at Holy Rollers, and why he'd always been so visibly uncomfortable with my gratitude.

I felt woozy. The sight of Jackie's broken-down father was more than I could take anymore. "I have to go."

"Wait," he said as I walked to the sliding glass door. He slowly stood up and hobbled along behind me. "Damned arthritis. I should be in the desert."

"I'm picturing a salt pit in Death Valley," I said.

He laughed lightly. "I can see how you two are friends."

His words halted me. "He's no friend of mine."

"Let me show you something before you go," he said. "Please."

He took me downstairs again, and we walked down a long hallway just off the living room to the only door that was closed. It was a bedroom, with a single bed in the far corner and a modest maple dresser and desk in the other. The wall above the desk was lined with bookshelves holding more surfing cups, plaques and trophies than I'd ever seen before in one place. Behind me, on the wall above the door, was hung the surfboard my father had named Honey Child, the board I'd ridden at Holy Rollers the day Jackie pulled me out. I'd always assumed it was lost, washed out to sea in a heavy rip. Jackie had never uttered another word about that day, or Honey Child.

Mr. Pace flipped a light switch and two recessed ceiling lights popped on, illuminating the board, which looked flawless, more perfect than when I'd ridden it on that rainy, gray morning thirteen years ago.

"It's beautiful," I said.

"He had it restored. I'm keeping it for him." He studied the board's sleek outline ruefully. "It's his prized possession. Used to come by just to look at it." He spoke as if he knew he'd never see his son again.

I showed myself out and drove home in a deep internal haze. Max was there, cordoned off in the kitchen, and when I opened the back door he rushed me as if he knew I was in a bad way. I sat on the porch step with him in my lap, hugging him in spite of his crushing weight. The strength to do anything more had simply left me, and I just sat there, talking to Max, for a very long time.

Twenty-Three

The sound of large waves breaking floated down my street in a briny mist, and sometime later that afternoon I determined to paddle out alone on Northside. Though I can't remember how or when I decided to have a go and I didn't even bother to first check the surf, it turned out to be just what I needed. As soon as I began with the ritualistic preparations one must take before riding waves of consequence, my mind stopped racing and my grief was quieted enough to hear myself think again.

I spent time first in the garage, choosing the right board, a seven-four semi-gun with down rails and a drawn-in tail—a board that had worked well last winter on a scary day at Baja Malibu, a hard-breaking spot just south of the Mexican border. I stripped the spoiled, oil-spotted wax from the deck, working a plastic spatula behind the hot air blasts of a handheld blow dryer. Slowly peeling away the old wax until the fiberglass surface was slick and the board's bold, airbrushed colors—an orange sunburst on top, bordered by ice-blue rails—shone brightly again. Then I rubbed in a fresh coat of wax from a brand new bar with a root beer scent, employing a tight, clockwise stroke I'd picked up from a long ago part-time job detailing autos. The water was still warm enough to wear my short-john wetsuit, which I pulled on over a gauzy black rash-guard shirt.

I stopped on the beach and stretched, bending and loosening un-used muscles. As I arched and leaned, small bursts of seawater rushed the beachhead to nip at my toes, then slid back again, the wet brown sand hissing like a hot griddle.

All of this a return, for me, to the rhythms of the sea, and nor-malcy. No jive-talking hype, no posturing hyperbole, no damaging secrets to unearth by way of a careful records search or a pointed cross-examination. Paddling out again was like taking a first step toward reclaiming my sanity.

The ocean was sullen and brittle green, a steady westerly wind ripping wild ribbons of frost across the Pacific. Big swells heaved onto the outer bar as if, after traveling thousands of miles, they were angry at finally having to die. It was a quiet afternoon—no surfers in the water, a few anglers on the pier, a schizoid wanderer slumped under an empty lifeguard tower, railing at the cloudless sky, arguing with some higher power. I counted five waves in each set, five-and-a-half minute intervals between the onslaughts. Then I waited for another set to dump before making my move through the shore-break.

The side current was strong and the smaller, inshore waves were surprisingly powerful, disdainfully tossing me back as I ducked to elude them. By the time the next big set rose up in deep water, I was stuck in the impact zone, bogged down on a slippery sheet of foam and gripping for a serious drubbing. Caught inside.

The walls that came to clean me up loomed thick and nearly double overhead, and each successive pounding I endured seemed more frenetic than the last. My lungs burned deep and hot and my sinuses loaded up as if mortar was being piled behind my eyes. After the third wave bashed me silly, I dove deep and crawled along the bottom, my board thrashing behind on my ankle leash like it wanted no more part of this little adventure. I surfaced, stole a quick breath and slithered back down among the chilly undercurrents.

Some surf session, I thought. Cowabunga. And yet, I began to take a measure of solace from the ocean's sheer indifference to my presence. Alone and rolling in the turbulent shadows, nothing about my life could change my situation—not my profession, my IQ, my powers of reason. No room for regret or sorrow, or anger over an old betrayal, no place for shiftless personal longing. What mattered most was a thin breath of oxygen floating beneath my ribs.

The rolling surf released me from its grip and I chugged toward calmer water. Over the next few hours I picked off only five or six waves, passing on dozens of misshapen walls and patiently waiting for the occasional shorter line that might offer a reasonable chance of success. None of my rides were very good. The wind bump on the surface was a hindrance to down-the-line speed, and every wave finished abruptly in a vicious closeout section inside. But they did afford me a chance to indulge in some self-expression, to dance across a canvas of water in a manner that pleased only me. It felt sublime to do something so objectively pointless, so selfish.

The wind backed off just as the sun simmered into the sea. I slid into a racy left that held up long enough to shoot me through a series of looping sections. I carved and banked all the way to shore, feeling the high deep in my bones and hungering for another wave as soon as I kicked out. But it was dark now, too late to stroke outside and play the complicated waiting game again.

I stood on the beach, feeling cheated by the night, unwilling to forfeit my place among the swells. This was where I belonged. A chill descended and a thin mist hung like an apparition above the sand. Shivering hard, I turned and started for home.

I returned to my job the next day unsure of how I would be received, but that was folly on my part, for nothing had changed. Foley was there, eyeing files in his stark black robe, as were Belinda and Lily Elmore. Shelly Chilcott smiled, jockeying her blinking phone lines. Just before calendar call, Ken Jorgensen licked the sugar from the tips of his fingers and kissed the last greasy bite of a glazed doughnut a fond farewell.

I picked up four new clients. A teenage mom on crystal meth. A hot-blooded father who used his belt buckle like a martial arts weapon on his terrified brood. A drug baby with a decent chance of surviving. And my personal favorite of the day, an exhausted working mother who'd loaded her groceries into the car, driven home and run a bath, leaving her screaming child marooned in a grocery cart in the middle of the supermarket parking lot. It was hard not to laugh at such a lightweight predicament, and I ended up talking more that morning about vitamin supplements and the declining quality of late-night TV than the impact of the Welfare and Institutions Code on parenting.

Later, when my cases were done, I went upstairs to see Carmen Manriquez. She was alone in the Las Palomas office, and I sat down again in one of those hard little chairs opposite her desk and began to tell her about everything that had happened in the past few days—

except Phoebe's visit. She told me about Channel Six's final news installment on the Randall case, which had apparently aired last night while I was stretched out on a lounge chair on my mother's balcony, listening to the surf rumble in the dark. The Danforths had been questioned but not arrested, since Nathan had been recovered and delivered to Sue Ellen. I hadn't really expected the Danforths to run into trouble with the law. Though they'd aided a kidnapping, losing Nathan had made them too sympathetic to be burdened with criminal charges. How would a shot of a handcuffed Kitty Danforth look on the Channel Six News, anyway? Like a public relations disaster, and the police knew it. In spite of all that had gone down, I was privately relieved to know the Danforths were free to find a new baby. Perhaps they would get it right the next time.

A shy Hispanic man in a shiny blue suit a size too small came to Carmen's office, received directions from her in Spanish, and vanished again.

Another urgent call. "I'll mail you a schedule," Carmen said into the phone. "But you'll be enrolled in the meantime, so just start attending. Yes, I'll call the instructor today for you. You're welcome." She smiled and held up one finger for me. *"No es nada."*

As if I were going anywhere.

I sat there, fighting the impulse to take over. I wanted to seek out Carmen's father, to persuade him to back off, to make her safe. Yeah, right. What I really wanted was to help set her free from her brother. Carmen put down the phone and looked at me sadly, as if she was reading my thoughts.

I offered to have a word with the man, feel out his intentions. "It'll be better if you know," I told Carmen. "Trust me."

"No thank you," was all she said.

The air felt heavy and stifling. I remembered the first time I'd stumbled into this dinky office looking for an interpreter. The high-handed way she'd schooled me in matters of heritage and familial pride. She'd taken me for someone who just wouldn't understand. But I'd believed her when she spoke of her menacing old man; I'd seen his shadow in her face that day at my home. I wanted to help, and Carmen wouldn't let me.

"This isn't about my father, is it?" she said.

I went to the door and stared into the waiting area. Two pigtailed girls were fighting over a doll just beyond their mother's reach. Near the big windows, an attorney cradled a manila file, pen in hand, shaking her head as an unshaven father in a wheelchair pleaded his case to her.

I felt tired and out of step, frustrated. It was as if Bill Davenport had just been replaced by Albert Manriquez. "Sorry," I said. "Bad idea, I guess. I should go."

"People have problems, J.," she said. "Problems you can't fix, okay?"

"You're not his mother, you're just his sister."

"That's my problem." She got up and walked over to me. "Maybe you could help me, but right now, I don't want you to. Can you understand that?"

I honestly couldn't. Taking care of other people's business was what I knew. "I'm trying," I said.

I pictured my father caught on a reef in La Jolla a long time ago, his bare feet bloodied, the surge rushing him at the knees, his next move critical. His friend had died that day, and he had lived. But he had acted without thinking, on instinct. It was all he had to go on, and it had been enough.

I put my arm around Carmen's shoulder and pointed her back into the Las Palomas office. "Can we sit down?"

Carmen had to help a few more unhappy parents get counseling before we could talk, but I waited. When we were alone again, I revealed the sad and inglorious end to which my mother had come, the letters Carmen translated making perfect sense now. We decided that it would be a good thing for me to go down to Rosarito Beach and search for Marielena Shepard's grave, that this would be a fine way to say good-bye and move on. This Friday the dependency judges were to attend a conference and the courts would be dark. I asked her to come with me then, to help interpret as we explored the town's cemeteries.

She smiled cautiously. "That all I am to you, your private interpreter?"

I shook off my little chair, kicked the Las Palomas door shut, and held her in a long, sweet kiss.

We decided to take Albert with us and spend the rest of the weekend camping and surfing. I had gone well over a year without a break and felt dead to the world. According to Carmen, the day she and Albert had spent riding waves with Jackie and me had been the highlight of Albert's summer. I hadn't seen Jackie since the hospital, nor had I any desire to see him again. She would have to feed Albert some excuse, for Jackie would not be making the trip. I dearly wished that California's great surf legend would simply fade away, back into his own bloated myth.

We left at 5 A.M. on Friday. Britt wanted to come along, but he had a few classes to contend with first. "I'm bailing right after my second period quiz," he promised. I told him that if we didn't hook up in Rosarito, we could meet that night forty-five miles south in San Miguel, a spot just outside Ensenada. An old friend of my father's owned a trailer there on a bluff overlooking the right-hand reef, and he'd given me the okay to stay there any time I wanted. It was a nice setup, with toilets and public showers nearby and a simple but good restaurant at the front of the trailer park. Not exactly camping, but San Miguel seemed like a good place to rest before we ventured farther south into the vast emptiness of the Baja Peninsula.

Carmen and I talked quietly while Albert slept in the backseat, snoring with his mouth wide open. She'd been on the phone last night with a relative who'd once briefly lived in Rosarito Beach during the sixties. Back then, there was only one cemetery, the relative had said, a slanted place on a windy hillside a quarter mile above the main highway. We decided to try there first.

Oceanside was head high and a little ugly, as devoid of sun as it had been that morning of the contest. We drove on until I found a nice sandbar a few miles south, in Carlsbad. Carmen and Albert sat on the beach, wrapped in a Mexican blanket as I worked over a few dozen peaks. The tide was on the rise and the surf improved. I kept waiting for someone to paddle out, but no one ever showed.

I bought four days worth of Mexican car insurance at an office just north of the border at Tijuana, and a case of Tecate at the first liquor store in town. We drove the new road that skirts the northern edge of the great, dilapidated city. Across the road through a mile or two of rough scrub and muddy, polluted streams, lay America. As we headed toward the coast we saw dozens of dark-skinned men and women, some carrying tiny children, lining up behind a long dividing wall. They milled about, watching the expanse to the north through the cracks, poised to make a dash as soon as the chalk-green Border Patrol trucks motored out of view.

I smiled. "Future clients."

"For you and me both," Carmen said.

Rosarito Beach dozed in a foggy overcast just after one, the garish hotels and motels that lined the main drag showing precious little life. A vendor sat before row after row of plaster birdbaths and piggy banks, waiting. We slowed and Carmen asked him for directions to the old cemetery with the view.

"*Sí, la mirada,*" he said, pointing to the hills.

The road was narrow and worn, with no divider. A mixture of gravel and disintegrating asphalt pinged against the Jeep's undercarriage as we sped along, a huge cloud of dust tailing in our wake. We came over a rise and saw an old stone wall stretching in both directions, parted in the middle by the road we were on. At the juncture, a uniformed *Federale* and a nun sat in folding chairs by a rust-eaten gate. They both stood up to greet us, the nun readying a Red Cross can for our donation. "*Hola.*"

"*Hola, señor,*" I said to the *Federale*. "*¿Como están ustedes?*" I handed the nun a few dollar bills while Carmen asked the guard if there was a map or registry to be found inside the cemetery grounds. The man turned and pointed to a slab of cement foundation jutting up through some weeds not far from the entrance. They talked in Spanish until Carmen thanked him.

"What did he say?" I asked Carmen.

She nodded toward the cement slab. "That was the caretaker's house, I guess. It burned down a long time ago. Nothing was saved. He doesn't know if the records were burned too, but as you can see, they never rebuilt."

We drove slowly forward, surrounded by gravesites ringed by white rocks and small, flat headstones. No trees. It was an ugly place for anyone to be laid to rest.

"This cemetery's been full since about nineteen eighty," she added. "Guess we're on our own." There was nothing to do but go from grave to grave.

"I'll take this side," I said, waving my hand at a weedy expanse the size of a football field. Below us the ocean lay hidden in a thick gray haze.

A half hour later I heard another car bounce up the road. Britt's truck. He fed the nun some change, drove forward to where I'd left the Jeep and cut the engine. Jackie got out from the passenger side and walked to the front of the truck.

I stalked over, my hands clenching into fists. "What's he doing here?"

"Don't lose it, J." Britt said. "He came by last night. I told him what you were doing. He said you'd never find it if he didn't help."

"What happened to your quiz?"

"No worries, I took it. We bailed right after."

Jackie planted a boot on Britt's front bumper and tucked his black T-shirt tighter under his belt. He looked right past me at the hillside before us. Farther up, Carmen and Albert moved slowly down a row of headstones, oblivious to Britt and Jackie's arrival.

"This way," Jackie said as he began to walk. I followed him warily. Thirty yards up the hill he turned right, took a few more steps, and stopped. "This is it."

The headstone was flat and rectangular, larger than those around it and carved from white marble. I knelt down and tugged at the crabgrass that spilled over the edges until I could read the inscription. A simple crucifix had been carved into the stone in relief, and above it, the words "Beatiful Marie Elana, 9–15–76."

"What the fuck?" I said.

Jackie looked over the headstone. "I know. Guy wasn't the hottest speller."

"You did this?"

"The stone? Yeah. Had it done in town." He looked away.

I waited until he faced me again. "You've lied to me so many times," I said.

He stared at the dirt. "I had to."

"No, man, you did not. Don't give me any of your jive-ass bullshit, not now!"

Jackie shot me a quizzical stare. "What would you have done had you known?" he said. He waited for me to consider his question. "That's right, nothing. She's been dead all this time. You couldn't have saved her, man."

The way he said it seemed to trivialize all my most recent efforts to find her. The bastard thought he knew better.

Standing amid the utter desolation of this place, a rage broke loose in me, a hatred for the father and son whose collective self-interests had delivered Marielena Shepard to this miserable patch of dirt. What happened next I cannot recall with much clarity, but at some point I remember being down on the ground with Jackie, flailing at him with blow after savage blow.

My ears rang painfully. Someone was screaming.

"Stop it, J.!" I heard Carmen cry. Behind her, Albert was jumping up and down, shrieking.

I rolled over and lay in the prickly dead grass, panting as I stared up into the blank overcast.

"It's okay, baby," Carmen said to Albert, hugging him close. Albert wiped his eyes and regarded me with great suspicion. Then he pulled free of Carmen and slowly approached Jackie.

Jackie's nose was flowing red from both sides, and his chin and right eyebrow were smeared with blood and dirt. He sat up gingerly on one elbow a few feet from me and spit into the weeds, working his lips and gums.

The fight—and Albert's horror—had dissipated much of the anger in me. In spite of all the hype surrounding the surf star, Jackie was always known to be able to back his act with his fists if it came to that. In a subtle form of apology, he'd let me punch him out.

"At least you helped me find the grave," I said.

"Yeah, at least," he said. He grunted, still in pain, as he dug into the front pocket of his jeans and pulled out a shiny lump of silver. "This was your mom's. I've been holding it since the day she died. Take it."

It was a Saint Christopher medal, badly tarnished and nicked around the edges. I turned it over and read the name still faintly engraved on the back: Roger W. Nelly, U.S.M.C. My father's drowned friend.

"Why?" I said.

"I caught up to your mom in Rosarito, figured out what she was doing. She recognized me from that day on the beach."

"Why didn't you talk her out of it?"

Jackie touched his lip and inspected the gob of red on the tip of his finger. "I tried—hard, man, I did. A Mexican abortion, you kidding?" He looked at Carmen. "No offense." But Carmen didn't move.

I spread the chain through my fingers. "This was my father's," I said.

"I know. Your mom told me. She had it after he died, said she wore it as your protector."

I stared at Jackie. "So how'd you get it?"

He rubbed his jaw. "She gave it to me before she went inside, you know, to have the procedure. Just in case." He looked away toward the sound of the sea. "She wanted you to have it in case anything happened. Obviously I couldn't do that, not without you knowing."

I still resented the years of deception. "Obviously."

"I know I sketched on you, but I did the best I could in the meantime."

With all that had transpired these past few weeks, one thing had never changed. "You were there, at Holys," I said. "You did okay."

My dear, sweet, superstitious mother had passed a sign of her own on down the line to a cynical young surf star, and it had made all the difference. I wished I could thank her properly—and ask her forgiveness for having ever believed she'd just leave me cold.

I handed the Christopher back to Jackie.

"No, man," he said, "it's a family heirloom."

I laughed and shook him off. "It's just a beat-up old medal. Keep it. You never know, I may need you again."

Albert shuffled closer to Jackie. "Hey, Alby," Jackie said, "whas da haps?"

Albert threw his arms around Jackie as if to shield him, and I felt ashamed when he turned and glared at me. "L . . . luh . . . leave him alone," he said. "He's mm . . . my friend."

Jackie sat up straighter and coughed, still shaken from the beating he'd taken. "I'm sorry, J."

I moved toward Jackie to help him up. Albert held his ground even firmer against me. "I ss . . . said, he's . . . my friend," he told me.

The misspelled gravestone of Marielena Shepard stared up at a widening patch of pale blue sky. I extended a hand to Jackie. "I know, buddy," I told Albert. "He's my friend, too."

We spent the afternoon surfing solid beach break peaks at La Fonda, a tiny little bluff stop on the road to Ensenada, then headed down to San Miguel as planned. After a dinner of sea bass in a garlic-butter sauce at the restaurant, we walked over to the bar for a few pops. A small group of surfers near the door took instant notice of Jackie.

"Jackie Pace! Whoa, stoked!" one of them swooned.

"Evening, ladies and germs," Jackie said. "Which one of you radical rippers is buying the first round?" He winked at me, a purple shiner ringing his left eye. Still got it.

The next morning we packed up early and headed south again, through the dusty streets of Ensenada with their *pescado* restaurants and tawdry souvenir shops. And past Hussongs, that absurdly famous bar filled at all hours with drunken Americans leering over each other's shoulders as they wait for something excitingly Mexican to go down. We followed the highway through a series of stooped foothills, then down a grade and into a verdant valley and past fields of lettuce and corn and pastures mottled with grazing livestock. For a half hour or so, the road switched back and forth along the banks of a shallow, silt-laden river littered with shiny boulders the color of rain clouds. Then quite suddenly the river disappeared. The road became straight and unvaried, the greenery fading into an obdurate desert landscape of blowing sand and chattering scrub. We must have passed through a dozen tiny towns along the way, always slowing to put money in the Red Cross cans of the wrinkled nuns who stood by the highway.

Carmen pointed to a series of cone-shaped hills on our right. "What's that?"

"That's where we're going," I said. "To the other side. They're volcanoes."

"I can smell the ocean," she said, sniffing the breeze. We had not seen the sea since we'd left San Miguel four hours ago.

"We're close," I told her.

We stopped in the only sizable town in the region and bought more Tecate and a huge stack of fresh tortillas. The sun was hot and hanging straight overhead and the air was sweet with the scent of dried sage and eucalyptus. Passing the last Pemex gas station on the road out of town, we turned right and followed a thin gravel path through a canopy of craggy oaks planted decades ago as wind brakes for fields no longer tilled. A sign pointed left, and the road trailed off in that direction toward an old hotel on the sand, but we headed right, onto a dirt path, instead, and bounced along slowly north.

Ten minutes later a wide beach backed by gentle dunes came into view on our left. To the right, a low-lying estuary that resembled our own Back Bay in Christianitos stretched inland as far as the eye could follow. Behind the great marsh and the slow streams that fed into it, the brown volcanoes Carmen had seen earlier quivered in the heat that rippled up from the prairie floor.

Albert laughed as we caromed about inside the wagon, the camping gear rattling with each dip and chuckhole. "Ya-ha!"

"Where in God's name are we going, J.?" Carmen finally asked. In the rearview mirror, I could see Britt and Jackie craning hard for a view of the surf.

"Secret spot," I said.

The road ended in a patch of dry grass, and I turned the Jeep at a hard angle to provide a shield from the wind for our camp. Britt pulled in behind, creeping forward until his truck kissed my rear bumper. We rolled out and stretched our creaky limbs.

Wind direction means everything at this spot. The beach is so far south-facing that the prevailing westerly breezes that blow down the coast every afternoon whistle side-offshore into the surf. The only variable you really worry about when you come down here is swell—if it's not strong from the south, the place will be flat.

We were lucky this day. A cool blue peak rose beyond the dunes, its spray whipped back in a translucent blossom. "Oh yeah!" Britt shouted. He and Jackie tossed off their slaps and began to run for the water.

"Wait for me!" Albert cried, following them.

The surf stayed excellent all afternoon, the heady offshores smoothing the sandbar peaks into playful, tunneling tubes. I traded waves with Britt and Jackie for three hours, ducking into my share of caverns but not quite outshining the master and his young protégé. Carmen was tired from the drive and chose to lounge in the sun and pick seashells and sand dollars from the shallows. Albert worked hard at riding the tiny lines of soup near shore, snapping into his awkward stance and keeling over almost as quickly. But he hung on a few times, and when he did, Carmen clapped and cheered for him.

A red tandem surfboard lay in the sand where Jackie had dragged it down and left it. I explained to Carmen the concept of a man and woman riding together on a single board as the man hoisted the woman through a series of classic poses. Carmen looked amused. "Sounds a little retro, J."

"The concept goes back a ways," I said. "But sometimes, that means it's pretty good."

A little before dark, I came in at last from the surf, dried off and changed into some warm clothes. The sky was turning an ecstatic pink when I walked back through the dunes and met Carmen and a dripping-wet Britt at water's edge.

"Where's Albert?" I said. The shorepound was deserted. The big red tandem board was gone, a lengthy gash in the sand where Jackie had dragged it on a rail to the water.

"Out there," she said, pointing toward the surf. "J., you think he'll be all right?"

A gorgeous, glassy wave lifted in the dying breeze. Jackie was perfectly positioned for the right slide and dug hard at the bottom as the trough overtook him. Then he stood, and I saw that he was riding the red tandem with Albert aboard and clutching the rails up front. Britt began to hoot. I wrapped an arm around Carmen's shoulder.

"He'll be fine," I said.

Carmen held me close, resting her head beneath my chin. I could feel her even heartbeat on my breast.

The wave jacked and readied to throw, and at the same time, Jackie crouched lower and pulled a prone Albert to his feet. He leaned right, his hands on Albert's shoulders, and the board shot down and off the bottom, angling away. The peak buckled over with a pop, swallowing their tracks as a long wall formed before them.

Jackie let the board drift up the face as he gathered more speed, tucking in ever tighter over Albert's stooped silhouette. Then, as the wave reared higher, threatening to scuttle them both in a single, explosive burst, he set his edge.

The line Jackie drew was inspired, almost poetic, and the surfboard shot forward as if it were floating on jets. We watched them as they streaked through the feathering sections in the purest, consummate trim, and I suppose that the thrill of this life became simply too much for any one heart to contain, for across the water, the two riders let loose with a soul-shaking, beautiful wail.